A Twist of Murder

A Dickens of a Crime Mystery Series
By Heather Redmond

A Twist of Murder

A Dickens of a Crime

HEATHER REDMOND

KENSINGTON
PUBLISHING CORP.

www.kensingtonbooks.com

KENSINGTON BOOKS are published by

Kensington Publishing Corp.
119 West 40th Street
New York, NY 10018

All Kensington titles, imprints, and distributed lines are available at special quantity discounts for bulk purchases for sales promotion, premiums, fund-raising, educational, or institutional use. Special book excerpts or customized printings can also be created to fit specific needs. For details, write or phone the office of the Kensington Special Sales Manager: Attn. Special Sales Department. Kensington Publishing Corp, 119 West 40th Street, New York, NY 10018. Phone: 1-800-221-2647.

Library of Congress Card Catalogue Number: 2022939753

The K with book logo Reg. US Pat & TM Off.

ISBN: 978-1-4967-3797-7
First Kensington Hardcover Edition: November 2022

ISBN: 978-1-4967-3798-4 (ebook)

10 9 8 7 6 5 4 3 2 1

Printed in the United States of America

For Leander and Andy, who had to survive pandemic virtual schooling with me during the writing of this novel

Cast of Characters

Charles Dickens*	24	Our sleuth
Kate Hogarth*	20	His fiancée
George Hogarth*	53	Kate's father, a music critic, a newspaper editor
Frederick Dickens*	15	Charles's brother and boarder
William Aga	29	Charles's fellow journalist
Mrs. Julie Aga	18	An underemployed actress
Lucy Fair	14	The Agas' maid
Eustace Aga	52	William's father, a headmaster
George Aga	50	William's uncle, a dairy farmer
Monks Aga	15	William's cousin, a student
Agnes Aga	12	William's cousin, a servant
Fagin Sikes	40	An educator and member of the workhouse board
Nancy Price	14	A servant
Noah Claypole	13	A student
Littlejack Dawkins	36	A gardener
Barney Wynd	28	A curate

*Real historical figures

"Although Oliver had been brought up by philosophers, he was not theoretically acquainted with the beautiful axiom that self-preservation is the first law of nature."

—Charles Dickens, *Oliver Twist*

"Now, Hawkins, you do me justice with the cap'n. You're a lad, you are, but you're as smart as paint. I see that when you first come in."

—Robert Louis Stevenson, *Treasure Island*

"She was unlike most other girls of her age, in this— that she had ideas of her own."

—Wilkie Collins, *The Moonstone*

Chapter 1

Harrow on the Hill, England, Tuesday, March 1, 1836

"Drat." Charles Dickens bent to retrieve a letter, fallen from his greatcoat pocket, as he dismounted the stagecoach in front of the Crown and Anchor Inn.

A russet-haired youth in a new suit of clothes jumped down from the stair and swiped up the missive. He had been inside the coach along with Charles, a Unitarian minister, and his wife. "Here you go."

"Thank you." Charles considered the lad. "Do you attend Aga Academy?"

Wind caught at his curls, making the lad look like an Irish setter. When he shook his head, the resemblance grew even more pronounced. "I'm at Harrow. Aga is much smaller."

The coach shifted as a hostler disconnected the horses that had hauled them the thirteen miles from London. A yardman climbed to the top of the coach and untied ropes securing bundles and baggage on the roof. Charles tugged the shivering Harrow lad out of the way just before a large bundle of cloth dropped on him.

"Watch yer 'ead," the yardman shouted a few seconds too late.

Charles shot a disgruntled look at the man, then spoke to his youthful companion. "I'm going into the public house. Would you like a hot drink, too?"

"Yes, but I have to fag for Stafford this afternoon. At least I can black his boots in front of the fire." He gave Charles a mock salute and trotted out of the yard, shoulders hunched against the wind.

The letter held in Charles's glove caught his attention again, so he headed through the yard, dodging puddles.

Low voices made a pleasant hum in the coffee room when he entered. A few men from the top of the coach had already taken the better benches, eager to make up for the midday meal they had missed on the road. Charles called for a hot rum and water, then took a stool at the bar, all that was available. After dropping his bag next to the stool, he glanced at the grimy directive again.

He'd taken the first stage available out of the city, per his friend and fellow *Morning Chronicle* reporter William Aga's letter. William had begged him to come to the school quickly, so Charles had made his apologies to his editor, George Hogarth, and left the office late that morning.

Charles had been here briefly a few times, accompanying charity cases to the school, which was owned and run by William's father, Eustace Aga. Charles and William's scholarship fund supported three of the students, known to them from their former career as mudlarks, scouring the banks of the Thames for coal and any pieces of portable property the ever-shifting river cast up.

The most senior Aga, William's grandfather, had died a few weeks before, and William had made the journey here then for the funeral, but Charles had no idea why William found trouble here now. His fellow reporter had traveled out of London the day before to report on a local disaster and must have stopped in at the school for a quick visit.

A barman appeared at Charles's elbow, holding the steaming drink with calloused fingers. "Wot are you 'ere sellin'?" the man asked in a friendly fashion.

"I'm a reporter from London," Charles explained.

The man shrugged. "What is newsworthy 'ere?"

"I understand a collapse occurred in a local gravel pit," Charles suggested. "A man died?"

"Oh, 'im." The barman lifted the hem of his apron to his nose and rubbed. "Likely 'e caused it 'imself with shoddy work. Drunk all the bloody time."

Charles took the vessel. The hot metal instantly warmed his fingers, which began to tingle, not unpleasantly. "In truth, I've been summoned to Aga Academy. Any news of it?"

The barman's lip curled under his whiskers. They covered his face in a luxurious black fur, while what hair was left on the top of his head stuck out in sparse quills. "'E's an ''Ard Fact' man, that schoolmaster. You never see a boy from there larking about in a 'appy manner. Not like the 'arrow lads."

Charles attempted to translate what the man was saying. "A 'Hard Fact' man? You mean Mr. Aga has become a disciple of utilitarianism?"

The barman sniffed. Two travelers close to the fire called for bowls of stew. "I mean Fagin Sikes, 'is partner. Whatever 'e is, the boys don't like it."

"Mr. Aga has brought in a new partner?" Charles frowned and downed his cooling glass of restorative as the man moved down the bar to his other customers. An application of hard facts might be what was needed for education, but it left little room for whimsy, and what was a boy but a whimsical creature? What would his own, often pain-filled childhood have been without his father's books and his sister Fanny's songs?

Charles had never had a reason to dislike Mr. Aga. He'd seemed pleasant and reasonable, like his son. Why had he chosen such a different sort of partner? Why take on a partner at all?

Charles ought to have made more of an effort to keep in contact with the boys they sponsored. Little Ollie, though maimed by a terrible accident, probably had learned to write by now. Cousin Arthur could still be too young, but Poor John, they had decided, likely had obtained twelve years and might have learned quickly, given the benefits of a regular diet and a bed that didn't consist of a ragged blanket under Blackfriars Bridge. However, as a result of Charles's work for the newspapers, his first book, and his upcoming marriage to Mr. Hogarth's daughter Kate, he hadn't visited the school since the start of the year.

One thing he suspected, though: his young ex-mudlark friends who were at the school on charity wouldn't handle an authoritarian regime well. They were used to following only the tides and the dictates of the mudlark gang's leader.

"Oh, aye," the barman said, returning. "Mr. Sikes 'as 'is finger in a few pies hereabouts. 'E's on the board of the workhouse, for one thing."

"A local man?" Charles sniffed as two bowls of stew passed by his nose, but it didn't smell fresh. Rather, the scent of burnt potato wafted into the air, a top note that did not entice. He'd likely much prefer the contents of the men's Toby jugs, for the rum had been more than passable.

Tea at a school might not be any nicer, but he suspected the masters would eat better than the students. Even bread and butter might be better than the stew. Harrow on the Hill was a rather small enclave, and he didn't know what he might find to eat on the street, but that was another possibility.

He rose from the stool, the muscles of his legs complaining of their hours of crablike bending in the coach, and picked up his bag.

"Yes, grandson of the local squire, a local fixture," the barman said.

"No stew?" asked a friendly maidservant as Charles handed his coins to the barman.

"I'm more in the mood for a pie," Charles explained.

The gap-toothed girl worried at her lip. "Stephen had to close his bakeshop for a couple of weeks to tend his parents at their farm. His father broke his leg."

Charles sighed. No wonder he preferred London. One person would be too insignificant in a large city to damage the workings of everyone's stomachs. "Very well. Off to Aga Academy, then. I shouldn't wait for my friend any longer, if something is wrong. Heard anything about the state of their kitchen?"

The maid shook her head. "You never see their boys here. They are too busy having facts forced into their heads."

Charles walked south past an assortment of businesses on the rather horizontally challenging High Street. For once, he didn't have a young charity student to shepherd along and reassure, so he could assess the town for himself. It had a prosperous air. Two more inns appeared; the area had a great deal of traffic for such a small place, perhaps due to the schools. He admired the yellow-brick front of a chandler shop with living space above. Sweet beeswax wafted from an open window. Many buildings were constructed from red brick in a familiar Tudor style. He passed a chapel, a library, and various houses. Few students were evident at this time of day.

Sadly, he did not pass any pie sellers. He expected the street merchants knew to come out when the students were free to buy their wares. His stomach gurgled, not being on the Harrow schedule.

His mind intent on his stomach, he did not see the branch until he tripped on it. Catching himself on a stone urn that marked the start of the Aga schoolyard, he discovered someone had chosen today to trim the box hedge surrounding the yard behind the low fence. Though the school had fewer buildings and a more commonplace appearance than Harrow, someone took pride in the entrance. Hopefully that meant the school didn't need funds, as he had no money free for raised fees, what with his marital home to furnish.

The front door of the aged timber-framed main school building opened. Charles spotted William in the doorway, his neckerchief askew. He clapped his top hat over his thick tawny locks as he pulled the door shut behind him. His mouth, which usually looked ready to smile, was rounded with frantic energy. Faint lines etched the skin around his eyes, proving that he was closer to thirty than twenty. And horrors, was the seam attaching the right sleeve to his coat ripped?

"Have you been attacked?" Charles called, speeding up.

William's gaze focused into the yard. "Charles! You're here!"

"I came on the next coach after your letter arrived. I didn't even return to Furnival's Inn. Just grabbed my extra shirt from my desk at the *Chronicle*." Charles stopped at the base of the stairs. Yes, he did see a thread dangling from his friend's shoulder. "You need your wife's services."

"What? Why?"

Charles and William met on the last step. Charles reached for the loose thread on the other man's jacket.

"What?" William asked, swatting Charles's hand away.

"You don't look as well turned out as usual," Charles observed. "What is going on? Are the mudlarks in trouble?"

William's breath left his chest in a mighty blast. He might have been a wind god himself, the way his frustration-soaked breath blew Charles's hair. "It has been a matter of multiple calamities."

"Nothing that can't be solved over tea and buns?" Charles asked hopefully.

"Would I have called you here, a month before your wedding and risking Hogarth's ire, if that were the case?" William asked.

"Any minute now you'll be pulling at your hair like a state mourner," Charles observed. "Can we enter at least?"

His friend visibly gritted his teeth and opened the front door. Charles stepped inside, then dropped the valise containing his writing desk and spare shirt under the table with the guest book.

The environs looked much as he remembered them. The main building held the classrooms and dining room. On either side were two smaller houses, which acted as boardinghouses. Mr. Aga's house was directly across the street, the most distinguished of the structures, with ivy winding around trellises along the walls. Two other boardinghouses abutted the master's house. The operation was smaller than Harrow but still managed to employ seven lower masters and a couple of assistant masters as teachers and student managers.

Charles paced forward and looked to one end of the front hall, then the other. A sheen of dust adorned one corner, and a spider had spun a delicate line across the left window. "Someone has missed the morning tidy," he observed.

"And no surprise," William snapped. "Can you cease your perambulations and direct those penetrating eyes to me, please?"

Charles turned, shocked at the outburst. Straightening, he clasped his hands behind his back. "What has happened? Your father?"

"Ollie, John, and Arthur have run off. That was the first difficulty," William reported.

"Together?" Charles remembered what the barman had said and knew he shouldn't be surprised. The ex-mudlarks had scarpered.

"Yes, or at least we assume. It's imagined they ran off with a traveling circus a couple of days before. I stopped here yesterday on my way back to London and learned they had already been gone a day."

"Blazes." Charles exhaled. "If your father had sent a note to three-thirty-two Strand or your home, you wouldn't have been there to receive it."

"He had not, at the time," William said, "being far more used to the management of unruly lads than I am. But as their bene-factor, eventually he would have notified us."

"Hmmm," Charles muttered. Perhaps they might have been notified after quarterly fees were paid, but that was a couple of weeks from now. "You might have sent for me for the sheer ad-venture of chasing a traveling circus. It does sound like a good caper for the mudlarks and myself, but Kate will not be pleased if she does not have a bed to sleep in when we return from our wedding trip."

"I thought the adventure would be brief," William ex-plained. "And both of us chiding the boys would have more ef-fect. You are, after all, the one with many younger brothers."

"True. We shall find the boys and then return to London posthaste," Charles declared.

William shook his head. "The situation has deteriorated since I wrote."

"More boys to the circus? They must have some unusual acts," Charles mused. "Something more than the usual bearded lady and equestrian riders?"

"I have no idea. I have yet to complete the most basic in-quiries. A storm came through last night and then—"

Charles frowned as William's voice caught. "What has hap-pened?"

William cleared his throat. "My young cousin Agnes, who works as a maid at the school, went missing after breakfast this morning."

"Is she tasked with sweeping and dusting here?" Charles asked.

William shrugged. The motion of his broad shoulders split the seam of his coat farther. "No one is doing their duties this morning. They are too busy searching the school grounds and making inquiries in town. She must be the first priority."

"What were you doing after breakfast?"

"I went to the church to notify the vicar, so that word of the boys' disappearance would spread. I stopped in at Harrow and a couple of the shops. Then I returned to eat with Father, intending to ride out to the circus next. Then this troubling matter . . ."

Charles glanced about the spare space. The walls were meant to be white but had the dinginess that meant a coat of paint needed applying in between terms. A staircase led up to the schoolrooms. The lower floor contained a parlor for the parents, Mr. Aga's office, the dining room, and kitchen.

"As a maid, Agnes must be up early. Is she the one to light the fires?"

"No, there is another maid who does that. Since Agnes is family, she was never tasked with the most menial of duties." William nodded to himself. "She does, however, share a room with that person."

"Who is?"

"Nancy Price. She is fourteen. Agnes is only twelve."

Charles straightened his hat. "Not likely to have been an assignation gone wrong, then."

William's lip curled. "And not before breakfast, either."

Charles's gaze went back to William's coat. "When did that rip begin?"

William touched his shoulder. "It caught on an exposed nail in the coach. A very large person pressed me against the wall for the entire trip from Wembley Green."

"I am sorry to hear that. I had a very pleasant minister with me. We discussed his efforts at an institution in Watford."

"Blast it," William muttered. "I suppose I should change."

"No, we should find the girl," Charles sighed. "I just wondered if the rip was tied in to the situation here, as it isn't like you to be untidy. What is the routine? Nancy Price rises early from their chamber somewhere to light the fires."

"They are in the attic in this building," William said. "Just the pair of them and the kitchen staff. The boardinghouses have their own accommodations."

"How many kitchen staff?"

"Three. Two girls share a room, and the cook has her own. She told me the young staff are put directly to work upon rising and dine after the students are fed. Which means Agnes disappeared some six hours ago."

"She ate in the kitchen with her fellow trio of servant girls," Charles clarified.

"Yes."

"Where was she meant to go after that?"

"Cook said Agnes spilled oatmeal down her apron and her attempt to sponge it away made the cloth even more disgraceful, so she was sent to her room to fetch her clean one."

"Laundry day yesterday," Charles observed, for today was Tuesday.

"Yes. After that she'd been meant to collect her broom and get to work on dusting and polishing here on the ground floor."

"Explaining the condition of this room."

"Exactly." William followed Charles's glance toward the spiderweb. "But no one noticed until time came for the students' midday meal. The maids seem to be quite independent."

Charles frowned. "You father has four unsupervised young girls in this building, along with a quantity of boys?"

"It's not so bad as that. The kitchen maids are in the kitchen. Only Agnes and Nancy would ever be said to be unsupervised."

Charles listened while staring at the sparsely decorated

space. He crossed the front hall and peered into the parents' receiving room. No rugs and the fire had gone out. Fluff in the corners and the four oil paintings of the Chiltern Hills were turning yellow with age and poor varnish. He imagined the school was running short of funds. Too many charity students, perhaps. "I expect hiring family saved money. Does your father pay Agnes?"

"I don't know the arrangements," William snapped with an air of impatience. "Come up to her room with me, will you? I haven't checked it."

"How long have you known she was missing?"

"Less than an hour." William gestured to the stairs. "I was with my father at his house, helping him with the accounts. For a schoolmaster, he is not good with sums."

"Running a school is difficult," Charles murmured, remembering his mother's failure to successfully open her own school when he was young. She hadn't managed to attract a single pupil.

He followed William up the steps leading from the front hall. As soon as the staircase curved out of sight, the walls become dingier, displaying the handiwork of boys running sticky substances along the surface. William took him down the hall past a set of four schoolrooms, then opened a door to a smaller staircase leading to the attic. They went up.

"The main area is for storage, extra schoolbooks and the like." He gestured at crates of books. Broken chairs and a deal table carved with a naughty word also waited forlornly.

"The boys' trunks?" Charles asked, pointed at the evidence under the eaves.

"Yes. It makes the process more systematic to have them all here. Cook's room is to the right, and the two maids' chambers are on the left." William walked across the floor, leaving footsteps in a layer of dust.

Charles coughed in his wake, smelling a hint of coal and fish.

William stopped at the end of the room. "I don't know which one is hers."

Charles stepped around him. "Just open one of the doors. I'll take the other. No one is up here at this time of day."

"True." William grasped one doorknob, and Charles turned the other.

He looked in at a rather large space for a pair of maids. The cook's lodging must be positively palatial. One window let light into the space. The windowpane had the appearance of a fresh cleaning, and both beds were made up with faded but warm counterpanes, perhaps ones that had served student rooms until the dye had leached from the fabric. A simple cross made from branches tied together was nailed to the wall between the beds, and an engraving of the king, torn from a magazine, was nailed above four pegs on the walls. Aprons and cloaks were aligned on the pegs. At the foot of each bed were simple wooden boxes. Charles flipped up each lid and saw spare garments of modest nature.

He closed the lids and turned in the space. All and all, highly respectable and homogenous.

Leaning his head into the main room, he called, "Find anything? I can't identify the inhabitants."

"This is Agnes's room," William responded, his voice muffled by the walls.

Charles went into the other room and found chaos. "This is different from the other room."

Nothing hung neatly on the walls here. One glove was stuck onto a peg, pointing accusingly into the room, but otherwise cloaks were draped on the floor. No sign of clean aprons, but Charles saw an oatmeal-stained one lying half in, half out of a chipped enamel basin with the morning's washing-up water still in it. Proof that Agnes lived here. The cross and the king weren't on these walls, so they must have been a sign of individuality in the kitchen maids.

The beds had the same basic coverings, but neither bed had been made. Charles saw the linen looked clean enough.

"Look." William pointed at a red stain on one coverlet.

Charles's pulse leapt as William leaned over it and touched a finger to it.

"Never mind. It's jam," he reported. "I did think the color looked wrong for blood."

"Does your cousin have a sweet tooth?"

William responded after a pause. "More like a savory, I would have said. Her father is a dairy farmer."

Charles went to the boxes at the foot of each bed, both of which were open and jumbled. "The other room is quite a different story. Neat as a pin."

"These girls are younger than the others." William turned in the space, like Charles had in the other room. "I don't like the looks of this."

Charles glanced in the boxes again. "It doesn't appear that anything is missing, compared to the other room. Except maybe an apron belonging to the other girl. Agnes's spare is accounted for."

"We don't know what we'd be looking for, however. Does this mess indicate signs of struggle?"

"Impossible to know without talking to someone with intimate knowledge of the room."

"Nancy Price is cleaning the sickroom in one of the boardinghouses," William said. "We can talk to her when she's done and find out if she knows where her extra apron is."

"For now, we need to retrace Agnes's movements," Charles declared. "We know that story of Agnes spilling oatmeal and coming up here to replace her apron was true. The question is, Did anyone see her after that with her clean apron on?"

"Let's check the cook's room," William suggested. "But then we've cleared the attic."

Charles went to the door. "Agnes can't possibly be on the

main floor. Let's check the classrooms quickly, then search the rest of the property. This isn't an unsubstantial area."

"No. What money my father inherited from my great-grandmother is tied up in the land and buildings. He really needs every penny of tuition for the school."

Charles waved his arm. "We'll have to work on an endowment, rather than this piecemeal fundraising we've been doing. A project for after the wedding."

"I hope we don't have to attend a funeral first," William said soberly.

Chapter 2

Charles and William returned to the ground floor of the school. They went through the empty dining room, full to the walls with long rows of tables and benches. The scent of burned porridge started at the large cauldron at one end of the room and followed them into the kitchen.

"Any news of that dratted child?" demanded a petite woman with bulging eyes. Her bare forearms were dusted with flour, the tiny hairs on her arms waving white like spiky flags.

"We've scarcely progressed since I saw you last, Cook," William said with a friendly smile. "Can you tell me if the girls keep their rooms poorly?"

Cook pulled a face, exposing an empty spot in her lower gum. "Mrs. Bedwin is meant to be supervising them, but she's usually focused on Mr. Grant's building."

"Bedwin is the . . . ?" Charles inquired.

"Housekeeper," William explained. "Mr. Grant is the mathematics master who has charge of boardinghouse Alpha."

"Her rooms are not in this house?"

"They are in the basement. The floor slopes, so she has windows."

Cook sniffed.

"What?" asked Charles.

"The windows open. She's no better than she ought to be," Cook said darkly.

"You don't think she sleeps in her rooms?" William asked.

"She's meant to check on the girls every night to make sure their candle is out, isn't she?" Cook demanded. "Used to come upstairs in her dressing gown and slippers to make sure all four of 'em were where they were supposed to be."

"When did she stop doing that?"

"After Valentine's Day," the cook sputtered, her mouth pursed.

"Thank you," Charles said, not wanting to indulge the woman in her distasteful gossip. "But as to the rooms? Do you check them?"

"Enough to know my girls are toeing the line, unlike that tweeny and your cousin, sir."

"I see," William murmured.

Charles turned to his friend and nodded. "We'll be on the grounds searching, unless you think we should check the basement."

"As you like," Cook said, picking up her dough and settling it into a baking pan.

"A quick look," William told Charles.

They headed down the stairs behind the kitchen into the subterranean regions of the school. The familiar smell of a coal chute greeted them, and William had to light a lantern intended for the purpose to check dark corners. The housekeeper's rooms were imperfectly tidy and empty of humanity.

Charles pointed to the mantelpiece in the sitting room.

"Ah," William said, setting down the lantern, which wasn't needed here, thanks to the promised windows. He picked up a card with a silhouette of a Cupid pasted to it. "The genesis of the Bedwin and Grant romance, I expect."

Charles nodded as he poked his head into the bedchamber.

"Agnes isn't in the house, William. Has anyone been sent to this dairy farm her father owns?"

"Yes, my father directed one of the lower masters to go there."

"Blast," Charles muttered. A drop splattered the window-pane. "It's starting to rain, and it doesn't stay light very late in early March. We had better search outside."

"I don't like this, Charles," William confessed. He blew out the lantern but kept it with him. "I wouldn't say Agnes is a pillar of respectability at twelve years of age, but she knows her duty."

"Was she taken by force?" Charles mused, following William upstairs and out a rear door behind the main staircase.

"The longer she is missing, the more it concerns me. The servants' tea will be on the table in half an hour. If she doesn't appear then, something has gone terribly wrong."

Charles remembered the reason he'd been called here in the first place was the lost charity students, not Agnes. Was there any sort of connection? He stared through the drips falling from the gutters of the old building. "Was this the Aga family home?"

"The Earnshaw family home," William said. "My great-grandmother's family. Died out now, but they were prominent before the fifteenth-century civil wars. Titled."

"At least the family didn't have to sell the property, even if the name was lost." But then Charles thought about the new Fagin Sikes partnership and wondered if the sale had come to pass in this generation.

"There's no reason to check the boardinghouses again." William pointed to the houses to either side of the main school building. "We've done that."

"What lies behind?" Charles gazed across a substantial lawn, perfect for taking walks or playing sports. At the back of each house was a tidy garden plot, ready to be seeded. He watched a trio of boys trail through the one on the far left, then enter the house.

"There are some sheds, that sort of thing. An icehouse that is perhaps as much as two hundred years old. Then the woods."

"I suppose Agnes knows them well?"

"I expect so. She's not a dizzy little thing. She could find north." William gestured, then set off across the lawn.

Charles kept alongside, hunched into his hat and coat. As they reached the end of the path that led to the outbuildings, a man approached them in a clerical collar and a damp hat.

"Barney Wynd," William greeted him. "This is the curate from St. Mary's."

Charles nodded at the slender man, a few years older than he. His hat was jammed down on his forehead, all the way to the eyebrows. "Are you searching for Miss Aga?"

The curate blinked. "I have not seen her."

"Has anyone checked these buildings? Did you?" William asked.

The curate waved vaguely. "I was in the woods. Is there a problem?"

"She vanished after breakfast," William explained.

The curate tutted.

"Surely someone thought to come out here," Charles said. "That is probably what those students who just walked into the boardinghouse were doing. We should confer with them."

"I don't want to trust the boys," William said. "They would get to playing or arguing and forget about hunting a mere servant girl."

"One of them looked to be nearly as old as my brother Fred," Charles pointed out.

William's lips tightened. "Still."

"Very well. We shall look ourselves." Charles nodded as the curate made his apologies and moved past them, probably to his own tea. A couple of lads, likely Agnes's age, came toward them from the woods. A busy crossroad, it seemed.

"Their tea?"

"Served in the boardinghouses," William explained. "Just a slice of bread with milk."

"Good afternoon, lads," Charles said. "Do you know if anyone from your house is looking for Agnes?"

"Mrs. Bedwin came to ask," one of them, spotted and runny nosed, reported. "And Nancy asked the prefects if they'd seen her."

"What about the gardener?" William inquired. "Has anyone spoken to him? I know he's here today. I spotted him out the window."

The light changed suddenly as the waning sun went behind a cloud. "It will be dusk soon," Charles murmured. "We had better check the outbuildings before it's too late."

"I saw Mrs. Bedwin going that way," the younger boy reported, pointing toward a shed, barely visible through the greenery.

"When?" Charles asked.

"Just as we finished Greek. I stare out the window a lot during our Greek lesson," the boy admitted.

"Not so long ago," William said. He rubbed his hand over his eyes. "Let's find her and assist."

Charles dismissed the boys to their errand and followed William toward the back. He saw a garden shed. They peered inside, but no one was there.

"I'm going to have to light the lantern again," William said, setting it on a barrel.

"At least we don't need to search the woods." A drop of rain splattered against Charles's hat. "What about the church? Or a sweetshop? Does she have any particular friends in town?"

William shrugged and huddled over the lantern. Charles saw a flash of yellow flame as it came to life, and opened his mouth to offer another suggestion.

A scream interrupted him before he could speak.

"Good God," William exclaimed. "Who was that?"

"A woman," Charles said. "Not a girl. Come."

They ran past a lean-to filled with seed bags, then into the final part of the clearing before the woods began.

Charles glanced into the woods. "Did the scream come from there?"

"The icehouse is hidden in a stand of trees," William said. "But the old stable is over there."

They heard a moan, then the sounds of running feet. A woman cried out. "Agnes is dead in the icehouse!"

Charles, shoulder to shoulder with his friend, felt him stiffen as the shock ran through his body. "Do you recognize the voice?"

"It's Mrs. Bedwin, the housekeeper," William said in a low voice. He broke into a lope.

Charles paced him as they followed a path between the old stable and the lean-to. When William slowed, Charles saw a low building made of dull stone that blended into the dirt and debris around it. The structure had been formed in the shape of a mantel clock or a half-moon. He'd never been in one before, but he understood most of the structure nested underground to keep the Scandinavian-import ice cool.

The Earnshaws must have owned an even larger property once, to make such an exotic building necessary. Had the Agas still been using it?

The half-height double door had red paint fading and peeling on it. One side hung open, and a woman, in her mid to late thirties, trim and plain, stood in front, wringing her gloved hands.

William spoke to her in a low voice. Her eyes were unfocused, and her face looked bleached. As his friend gently pulled her away from the door, Charles peered into the dark space. The extreme cold kept any smells from escaping, and the building's dark was impenetrable without additional light. Why had the housekeeper been so certain a body lay inside?

Charles took the lantern from William's hand. Sobs carried in the air, as William's comfort made the woman react with a full-throated lamentation.

Charles went to his knees in the open doorway and lifted his lamp over his head. First, the wavering yellow light caught on bricks. He lowered his arm and saw straw piled halfway up the curved wall. The space appeared to be two-thirds or more full of ice. Mr. Aga must rent out the space to some entrepreneur for their business use, for Charles had never heard of an enterprise running from the school. More sign of financial trouble?

He couldn't see a body. Carefully, he set the lantern on the first ice block, keeping it at a distance from the highly flammable straw, and crawled in. He tucked himself into the shape of a praying mantis and balanced himself against an ice block. When he lifted the lantern again, shivering with cold, he saw the floor sloped down to what would have been an open drain.

If it hadn't been blocked by the staring-eyed body of a young girl, blond hair spread out and frozen into icicles. Her skirts were up around her pale, stork-like thighs, and her apron had been wrapped around her neck. She still wore shoes, though her toes were pointed at an angle too uncomfortable for life.

Charles gasped, sickened by the open eyes. He had seen a number of bodies in his twenty-three years, but none had torn so at his heart since his sister Harriet had died as a young child. Light headed, he dropped the lantern to his side, then turned in a mad rush and awkwardly made his way out, shaken to his core by the sight of a dead child.

His normal powers of observation had deserted him. How had she died? Strangled by her own apron? He hadn't looked for anything else. Maybe that was for the best, since he might have frozen to death in there. He shut the door, in a pathetic human attempt to shield himself against the cold and horror, and realized his breath came in pants.

"What did you see?" William asked, his eyes wide.

Charles could only shake his head dumbly. Had Mrs. Bedwin just killed the girl? He had no idea how she would have known about the body otherwise. The icehouse was hidden along here, on the outskirts of the wood. The clergyman had been the only person nearby besides the children, and he hadn't mentioned the housekeeper or the icehouse.

He pressed his icy fingers between his eyebrows and forced himself to think logically. The child had snakelike icicles in her air, like a dead Medusa. She had been dead for some time. Seven or eight hours must have passed since she went to her chamber to change her apron. They had not caught Mrs. Bedwin coming from a fresh kill. But again, how had she found the child in the dark?

He set the lantern on the ground and stared coldly at the sobbing form in William's arms.

"How did she know?" Charles demanded. "She couldn't have without a lantern."

"What?" William asked, his lips rather muddled by the housekeeper's gray-streaked hair, windswept into fluffy wisps around the remnants of a pin-shaped roll.

"How did she know?" he repeated. "I'm sorry, William. Your niece is lost, and she's been deceased for hours."

Chapter 3

William crouched to meet Charles's eyes. His fingers swept restlessly through blades of grass around the icehouse. "She's been dead for hours? But everyone has been searching."

"Not back here, perhaps." Charles stood from his bent position, hearing his knees creak after his time in the cold icehouse. His friend matched his movements. Charles tucked one hand under his waistcoat and lifted the lantern in his other.

William stepped away from Mrs. Bedwin. She turned to Charles, as if seeking comfort from him next. Trees protected them from the steadily dripping rain.

"Why did you check the icehouse?" Charles asked her.

Her eye sockets, hidden from full sight by the growing gloom, caught the light from the lantern and glowed momentarily, like she was some otherworldly creature, and not a very nice one.

"One of the boys has a fever," she said in an unusually slow voice. "I was collecting ice for him."

"You're the housekeeper. Surely that's too menial of a task for you," he suggested.

She touched a ring of keys at her waist. "We don't let anyone in here. Long ago someone slipped inside and broke their leg."

"Where is your light source, madam? Did you intend to do this in the dark? No one could see in there."

She sighed and reached into a hidden pocket in her skirt to pull out a small box. "Matches."

"Where is your ice pick?" William asked, his voice sounding rusty.

She pointed to a stone vase that was half hidden by a fern to the left of the icehouse. Charles reached in and pulled out an ice pick. The wooden handle was stained and blackened, and the long piece of metal came to a point at the end. Charles examined it carefully in front of the lantern. It appeared to be clean and not connected to Agnes's death. He set it back in the receptacle.

"Why weren't you holding it when you walked in?" he asked.

She shivered. "Not thinking clearly, I suppose. It's been a long day between Agnes's disappearance and the ill student. Mr. Aga has not been much in evidence."

"Do not complain about your employer," William said in a low voice. "It is a mark of disloyalty, and I ask you not to forget I am his son."

"I mean no disrespect. He has his own concerns." She shivered again, making Charles wonder how long she had been in the icehouse with the body. "Besides, there is Mr. Sikes now."

"He is focused on bringing in new pupils, not running the school."

Mrs. Bedwin looked dubious at William's words.

"I see one of us needs to notify the authorities," Charles said. "The other should take Mrs. Bedwin to her quarters before she takes ill."

"I know the town better than you," William said.

Charles nodded. "Take the lantern. Mrs. Bedwin can lead us back to the main house."

* * *

Charles woke from an uneasy sleep the next morning when the house began to stir. He'd been given a guest chamber in Mr. Aga's house, nicely appointed since he used it for potential students' family visits. As he pulled on his clean shirt and the rest of his clothing, a brown-skinned, black-haired maid came to the door with hot water, then set his cleaned boots inside the door.

"Did you work with Agnes?" Charles sat in the provided armchair and put his shoes on, since the maid hadn't moved to light the fire.

"No, sir." She blinked thickly lashed eyes. "I only work here at Mr. Aga's. Me and Mrs. Elm take care of the house."

"Did you know her at all?"

"She spent Sunday afternoons here after church if she didn't return to her father."

"Her mother is deceased?"

The maid nodded. "Both Mrs. Agas died in childbirth, and while Mr. George Aga remarried, the second wife didn't live long."

He noted she didn't have an accent, despite her obvious Indian heritage. Her family must have come to England long ago. "Are William Aga and Agnes Aga both the only children?"

"No, sir. Agnes has an older brother. He's at the school."

"Oh, I see." The boy was a student, and the girl worked. It had been the opposite in his family. His sister Fanny had stayed in school while he was sent to work when the family had financial troubles. He wondered if the dairy farm had been in similar straits.

The maid bent her head. "Breakfast is served in the morning room, sir. I was told to tell you that you are wanted at the school immediately after."

"Thank you." Charles stood and went to wash his face after the girl left. The hot water was a treat in the unheated room.

Downstairs, he dined on porridge and toast. Presumably, the

household had not pulled together the more substantial meal they would offer to prospective families. He would have liked some bacon or cold meat, though.

William arrived as he was pouring a second cup of tea. Charles poured for his friend, too.

William opened the lid of the dish containing the porridge and spooned out a large portion, then dumped the rest of the toast rack's contents onto his plate.

Charles watched from his seated position, then pulled out the chair next to him. "Hungry?"

William's nostrils flared as he sat. His plate thumped onto the table. "I'm not sure I can even eat, given that the inquest has been pulled together in the school parlor this morning."

That was quick. No wonder he was wanted at the school. Someone in Harrow on the Hill was efficient. "Did they leave the body in the icehouse?"

"Of course. Best place for it until the inquest. Plus, the jurors can see the situation exactly as we did." William kept his eyes on his porridge and shoveled a bite in his mouth.

"I'm sorry your cousin died," Charles said gently. "You don't have much family."

"I will have my own child soon enough," William said. "But it does seem that our happy expectations continue to be broken by these tragedies."

"She was young to die, your poor cousin," Charles said. "Have you spared a moment to think who might have done it?"

"I'm having difficulty thinking in a professional matter about this. I know I should do my duty to the *Morning Chronicle* and start an article, but I could not bring myself to it."

"Then do not," Charles suggested. "I can dash off the particulars after the inquest. Spare yourself the pain."

William nodded. "You are a good friend to me."

"Not better than you are to me." Charles forced a smile. "Try a few more bites. I hate to bring it up, especially with the inquest before us, but we must look for the boys today."

"I agree. We have a lot of walking to do."

"Also, I do want a look at this Mr. Sikes. Does he reside at the school?"

"No, he's something of a silent partner. As you heard me say, he isn't very involved in the day-to-day operations."

"I see." Charles took a slip of paper from his pocket and made notes in pencil while William ate.

Somehow the coroner and his cronies had managed to find twelve men available on a Wednesday morning, though the body had been found only some seventeen hours before. The coroner must live locally, despite the miles he had to cover for his duties in this part of the county. Perhaps they had picked off every man of reputation who'd come to drink in one of the local inns or taverns the night before. However the bailiffs had accomplished it, Charles and William sat to one side of the parlor room of the school some half hour later, witnesses for the proceedings. Charles had his desk ready for note-taking. The jury had been seated in chairs brought in from the dining room.

Harrow, being in the western part of Middlesex County, had a different coroner than those parts of London where Charles had discovered dead bodies before. Therefore, instead of the welcome sight of Sir Silas Laurie, a well-wisher if not exactly a friend, he was faced with a different man.

Charles took an immediate dislike to Mr. Bumbleton when the coroner took his seat. The man had the broken-veined face and bulbous nose of a chronic heavy drinker. The coroner huddled with a factotum in front of the fire, his red plaid–bedecked bulk blocking the heat from the rest of the rectangular room. A deal table in front of them held nothing but a register and writing materials.

After his consultation finished, Mr. Bumbleton gestured to the bailiff, who had been waiting in the corner. The man stepped in front of the table and said, "Oyez! Oyez! Oyez! You good men of this county, summoned to appear here on this day to inquire of our sovereign lord the king when, how, and by what means Agnes Aga came to her death, answer to your names as you shall be called, every man at the first call, upon the pain and peril that shall fall thereon."

The bailiff turned to Mr. Bumbleton, who made a circular motion with his finger. The bailiff continued. "This is the court of Tobias Bumbleton, the coroner. Gentlemen of the jury, you need to choose your foreman. He will be sworn in first, and then the rest of you will be in turn. Then the witnesses will be seen to."

Bumbleton pointed at one of the assembled men, with a similar heavy drinker's nose. He possessed stained yellowish whiskers but snowy-white linen. Charles watched as the other eleven men nodded. So much for the jury choosing the foreman.

The coroner sped through the oaths. Then he gestured again to the bailiff, who stepped forward and announced, "Gentlemen, you are sworn to inquire on behalf of the king how and by what means young Agnes came to her death. Your first duty is to take a view of the body of the deceased, wherein you will be careful to observe if there be any marks of violence thereon, from which, and on the examination of the witnesses intended to be produced before you, you will endeavor to discover the cause of her death, so as to be able to return to me a true verdict upon this occasion."

The coroner stayed in the room as the jury departed, shepherded by the bailiff and the coroner's assistant. Charles assumed Bumbleton had visited the icehouse earlier in the morning. Perhaps he was an early riser.

Charles and William trailed behind the men as they walked across the rear yard to the woods.

"Why aren't we doing this in the tavern?" one of them grumbled. He didn't look as sozzled as the coroner, but his substantial belly was matched by a thick watch chain that stretched across his waistcoat. The chain clinked softly as he waddled down the path between the lawns. "At least we'd get free ale."

"Longer walk to the body," said another. Diminutive, he kept his top hat down around his ears and took a couple of inches off his minimal height by sinking his shoulders into his body.

"How can they ask us to look at a girl?" demanded another, who was too young to have been called a grown man for long. He had mud on his boots.

"George Aga's girl," said the first. "I knew her mother. We called her 'Lou' when she was young. I'm glad she passed before the likes of this."

William winced at that. Charles knew his friend couldn't be having an easy morning, fighting the internal war between reporter and grieving cousin. Any passing thought down the normal pathways of his keen intellect would be countered by grief.

"Died young, eh?" said the young juror.

"Birthing her second son," said a local blacksmith named Wells. His coat strained at the shoulders, and his face had a ruddy complexion, which gave him the look of being on fire internally. "Her first son was about five years old."

"Four," William corrected quietly. "Just four. Agnes was one."

The foreman stared at William hard. "I'm sorry for your loss, Aga. I had forgotten she was your kin."

"Thank you. It's O'Dell, right?"

"That's right. I still own the Harrow bookshop."

William put out his hand to shake. "I'm here often enough that everyone looks familiar."

The bailiff stopped them when they reached the icehouse. In the daylight, Charles realized how small it looked, huddled in the clearing. He had already forgotten that he'd had to go to his knees to enter.

The jurors glanced around the clearing, most of them looking everywhere but at the icehouse.

"Any sign of violence?" the foreman asked the bailiff. "Any signs of dragging or blood out here?"

The bailiff shook his head. "Just the body."

"We were here last night," Charles said.

"Did you see the body?" O'Dell asked.

Charles nodded. "But only for a moment, in lantern light. I could not see how she died, other than she was well frozen and the ice pick that is kept outside had not been used."

The foreman grunted and gestured to the bailiff to unlock the heavy chain that someone had been smart to secure over the door.

In respectful silence, each of the men took a turn looking inside, huffing as they knelt and rose again as if in a religious ritual. While this transpired, more men came though the clearing with a one-horse cart. A simple coffin rested inside.

Charles winced as he wondered how they were going to get Agnes's body off the ice. But how would they be able to discern how she died without a more thorough examination?

He turned and saw William shaking the hand of an elderly man wearing thick glasses and a massive comforter around his neck that hung down his coat in loops.

"We'll take her to my surgery for an examination. Then my nurse will ready her for burial," said the doctor in a high-pitched voice. "This is a most peculiar and tragic situation."

"Indeed," Charles said. "Have you been the doctor in town long?"

"Forty-seven years, or my name isn't H. W. Goose," he said.

"Then you knew Miss Aga. You must have formed some sort of opinion of her character."

"I don't recall ever seeing her. I don't, you know, the healthy ones. It would be better if I had been called before the body was placed in the icehouse," the doctor complained.

Charles blinked. "The murderer put her there," he explained.

"Then how do you know how she died?" Dr. Goose quavered. "It may have been natural causes."

"A healthy twelve-year-old girl?" Charles inquired.

The doctor shrugged. "Could have locked herself in or become trapped by the ice somehow. I cannot say without an examination."

"Then you'd better bring her out," Mr. Wells said. "We can't bring the inquest to any kind of conclusion without it."

"Mr. Bumbleton won't want me to spend the time now," Dr. Goose said. "You know how he is."

"Bumbleton be dashed," Mr. Wells exclaimed, setting his hands on his hips. "We will return to the parlor and wait for your report."

Mr. O'Dell sniffed loudly. "Will Aga send to the Royal Lion for us? I'm perishingly thirsty."

Charles glanced at William, who seemed numbed by his pain. He honestly didn't know if Mr. Aga could afford to water and victual all these people, and if he spent the money himself, it would be taken out of the furnishings budget for the home he was making for Kate.

"Chip her out of the ice," the doctor said to his two attendants. "It's going to be a busy day, and these fine fellows do not want to wait until Jesus blesses us with his Second Coming."

The two men left the side of their cart, where they had been minding their own business. One of them went to his knees in front of the icehouse door, holding a sack of tools at his side, while the other lit a lantern.

"Thank you, Doctor," William said. He seemed unable to offer more.

"Can you do a cursory exam here, after you bring her out?" Charles asked, worried about the expense of a meal on top of beer.

"I'll do my best," Dr. Goose said. "But I can't promise results."

"Of course not. Let us hope an obvious answer appears with a visual inspection." Charles inclined his head and took William's arm, then waved his hand in the air to usher the other men back to the main building.

Charles heard a lock turn as the back door of the school opened upon their return from the icehouse. Mr. Eustace Aga greeted them, a spare gray man with his son's vitality leeched out of him by cares and encroaching age. Over fifty, he seemed to think of nothing but his school.

"I've canceled classes for this morning so the children do not have to hear any of this," he said. "But do you know how long this will take, Mr. O'Dell?"

The foreman shook his head. "The doctor hasn't even seen your niece yet. If he doesn't observe a cause of death as soon as his attendants can have her decently removed from the icehouse, we'll have to reconvene at another time."

"That is up to the coroner," Mr. Aga said. "Please go inside. I've sent for refreshments."

Charles gave the man a sympathetic smile as he passed by.

As the jurors returned to their seats, the bailiff whispered in the assistant's ear, then the assistant whispered in Mr. Bumbleton's ear. The coroner looked annoyed and took a minute to polish off the contents of a flask before throwing his arms wide and giving his next formal speech.

"I shall proceed to hear and take down the evidence respecting the fact to which I must crave your particular attention. We wish to understand what caused the death and who. If anyone can give evidence on behalf of our sovereign lord the king when, how, and by what means Agnes Aga came to her death, then let them come forth, and they shall be heard."

Foreman O'Dell's expression matched the degree of peevishness exhibited by the coroner before the bailiff spoke, calling Mrs. Bedwin to testify about her discovery of the body. He had her stand in the center of the room.

The housekeeper wore black, as she had the day before, but appeared considerably paler. Charles thought her young to be a housekeeper, perhaps a decade older than himself. She twisted to look at the coroner, then the jury. "I was fetching ice, sir."

"Had you sent Miss Aga for ice previously?"

"No, it was no safe place for a child."

"Have children played there in the past?"

"No, we've kept it firmly locked up."

"Who has the key?"

"Myself and Mr. Aga, sir."

Bumbleton cleared his throat. "Any opinion on the manner of death?"

Mrs. Bedwin clutched her neck. "Her apron was tangled around her neck."

The foreman spoke up. "Could that have happened when she, err, fell?"

Mrs. Bedwin's head drooped. "I don't know."

"Is this the whole of the evidence you can give?" the coroner asked, very prematurely to Charles's ears.

The housekeeper glanced at Mr. Aga, then returned her gaze to the coroner. "Yes."

"You the jury, do you have any questions before this witness signs her examination?" Mr. Bumbleton asked.

The foreman said he didn't. Charles wondered if the entire examination had been foreshortened to get the men their libations quicker.

The coroner conferred with his assistant again, then called William, then Charles in turn, to put them under oath and interview them. Though witnesses to Mrs. Bedwin's actions if nothing else, he allowed them to stay for the rest of the testimony since they were "down from the London papers." Charles kept notes in shorthand so he could write his article later. William sat motionless, his hands hanging between his legs, his head bent.

Mr. Bumbleton called Mr. Aga next and asked him questions about the employment of his niece. He inquired about Agnes's associates, and Mr. Aga mentioned the name of her fellow maid, Nancy Price, and Agnes's brother, Monks Aga.

Miss Price was called first. A scraggly-haired, slim creature of scant years, she had rather protuberant, piercing eyes for a girl that young. Charles thought the most important question she needed to answer was if the state of her bedroom was normal, but she wasn't asked that, much less if she had an apron missing.

"Did you find Miss Aga to be a girl of good character, my dear?" Mr. Bumbleton said in a kindly matter.

"She liked to tease, sir," Nancy said, standing very tall, not at all cowed by the powerful man.

"Tease? About what?"

"She told the students she had a treasure map, but she wouldn't let them see it," the girl explained. "It made for a lot of upset and her in the middle of it."

Bumbleton frowned. "She liked to cause trouble?"

"Yes, sir," Nancy piped. "She had airs, what with being the sister of one of the students. Thought she was better than the rest of us."

"Did she have any particular friends among the students or the servants?"

"Just me, sir."

Charles doubted this girl was capable of true friendship.

"Who was most interested in this treasure map?"

Nancy Price showed a bit of unease for the first time. Worrying at her lip, she said, "Master Claypole?"

"One of the students?"

"Yes, sir."

"Did you ever see this map?"

Nancy Price shook her head derisively. "I never saw such a thing. I don't believe it exists. She just liked to cause excitement."

The coroner put his hands behind his back and bowed his head for a moment, then turned to his secretary. "Call Master Aga next."

Charles was desperate for the man to ask where this supposed treasure map was. It might be the key to the entire matter, if someone killed the girl to steal it. But Bumbleton asked nothing. Once again, he queried about character.

"Did you like your sister, young Aga?" Mr. Bumbleton asked.

Charles could see a future resemblance to William in the boy's growing body. His shoulders had broadened with coming manhood, but his body resembled a slender reed more than a full-grown man at this time. He had very dark hair and eyes that separated narrowly over his nose, though he had a fine set of lips, which Nancy Price had stared very hard at when she was dismissed.

The boy shrugged, not seeming intimidated by the situation, either. "She was my sister."

"I'm sorry for your loss."

Monks nodded. "Thank you, sir."

"You are now your father's only living child."

"Yes, sir."

"What do you know about this treasure map?" Bumbleton's voice went up to a high pitch, as if he found humor in the question, indicating it wasn't to be taken seriously.

"She was a bit silly, my sister."

"Were you interested in it?" Bumbleton asked sternly.

"Not at all, sir."

"Who was?"

"Claypole. He even offered her three shillings for it." He kicked at the floor. "Maybe if she'd taken it, she'd still be alive."

O'Dell, the foreman, sat up straighter. One of the other men whispered in his ear.

Mr. Bumbleton's hands reclasped in front of his watch chain. "Then you believe the map exists?"

"She was a dramatic girl, but not very imaginative," her brother declared. "She must have had something."

"Very well, you are dismissed." The coroner turned to his assistant. "Call Master Claypole."

Noah Claypole, a lad of thirteen, two years younger than fellow student Monks Aga, boarded in the house to the left of the school. He had met Agnes cleaning at boardinghouse Alpha when the household was between maids.

"Were you aware of the treasure map?"

Noah rubbed at his nose, which seemed perpetually reddened by his ministrations. "She liked to natter on about it while she did things."

"When did you have the opportunity to talk to a servant?" Bumbleton asked.

"She didn't know the house, sir. She was very slow and would have to finish her work while the students were moving about."

"Did you offer her money for the map?"

Noah shrugged. "I had pocket money for my birthday. Why not? It was a bit of a howl."

"But she didn't sell it to you?"

"No, she laughed it off and said maybe for three pound, not three shilling." He swiped his nose again. "Silly girl."

The coroner turned to the jury, pulling a face. "As you know, as coroner, I have the duty to search out a treasure trove." He turned back to the lad. "Can you tell me where this treasure is to be found?"

"I don't know if there is a real treasure," he said. His nose wiggled, as if he tried to keep in a sneeze.

"You saw the map and found it worthy of your pocket money. What was upon it?"

The boy blinked. "I don't know. She had a way of fluttering it. I never really saw the page."

"How did you, a boy at Aga Academy, think you were going to obtain this treasure?"

"It was local, sir. She said the treasure was near the school."

The coroner turned to Mr. Aga. He shook his head, wide eyed. In Charles's estimation, this story of the map had never reached the headmaster's ears.

The coroner returned to his assistant and had him make some notes. While this went on, two girls in their late teens entered the room carrying trays of cups and saucers holding a steaming beverage. Tea, probably not what would satisfy the jurors. They passed them out, then departed silently. They must be the orderly kitchen girls.

The coroner dismissed the boy from his interview and consulted with his assistant again while the jury sipped, expressions of distaste on most of the dozen faces. Before Bumbleton could make other decisions, the doctor appeared in the doorway.

Chapter 4

"Ah, Dr. Goose." The coroner gestured the doctor into the parlor.

Charles didn't like the obvious air of relief in the coroner's eyes as the doctor walked in. He much preferred the cool competence of Sir Silas. The other coroner would have recalled Monks Aga and Nancy Price to discuss the matter of the treasure map more fully.

"I have some initial conclusions," Dr. Goose said, unraveling his green wool comforter from around his neck.

"Very good." The coroner clapped his hands together. "Let us take care of the formalities, shall we?"

After the bailiff swore him in, the doctor spoke, facing the jury, as if giving a speech instead of being interviewed. "I was able to disentangle the apron around Miss Aga's neck. A difficult chore due to it being frozen."

"Were you able to ascertain how she died?" the coroner asked.

Dr. Goose's faded face was suffused with satisfaction. "Indeed, the apron was the weapon. My examination showed that some of it had been stuffed into her mouth, blocking her airway, and the rest wrapped around her throat. Between those two factors, she could not breathe."

"It wasn't in her mouth when we saw her. Who moved it?" asked the coroner.

"The killer, most likely, because it had been frozen like the rest. He probably pulled it out to make sure she had ceased breathing."

"Can you be sure?"

"I found threads from it in her mouth."

Charles's gaze slipped from the quick shorthand notes he was taking to William's eyes, fluttering shut. He was listening like a bereaved cousin, not a reporter.

"Did she die in the icehouse?" the coroner asked.

"I didn't see any sign of a struggle inside the wee building, and it would be hard to take someone by surprise in such a space," the doctor said. "But from my cursory examination, I will say she was on her back at death, due to the way her blood has settled, and was placed in the icehouse immediately after death."

Charles exchanged a glance with William. Where did she die? Had they missed the site of a struggle in the growing dark? Now much potential evidence would be destroyed, because the jury and others had visited the area.

"Very good, very good," the coroner muttered. He conferred with his assistant again before turning back to the jury. "You are permitted to ask questions of this witness. Do you have any?"

Mr. Wells lifted his chin. "It is common to bind over the person who found the body to jail, correct? Is there any reason to believe Mrs. Bedwin, the housekeeper, killed the girl?"

The doctor pinched his lower lip between his thumb and forefinger. "While the apron is a tool of females, the girl's skirts were disarranged, which leads me to believe the crime was committed by a male. Besides, would female hands be strong enough to strangle someone?"

Charles wanted to shout an emphatic yes. Any cook had very strong hands. Any farmwife, as well. Just because Agnes's skirts were disarranged didn't mean she'd been violated. That would take further examination, which he doubted had been done on a cart outside of the icehouse. Surely the doctor had more delicacy than that. Agnes had been such a young girl. Did she not deserve some privacy, even in death?

His ruminating was so loud to his inner ear, and apparently took so long, that he didn't mentally return to the inquest until William grasped his sleeve. He was horrified to hear what the coroner said next.

"The witnesses are examined, and the evidence has been gone through. Here is the evidence. That the body of Agnes Aga was found in the icehouse on the property where she resides and is employed, that she went missing after breakfast and was found after tea on March second, eighteen thirty-six, after boasting of a treasure map in her possession. She met her death by strangulation, and there are indications of other wrongdoing. I direct you to consider your verdict."

The foreman nodded, looking very keen.

Mr. Bumbleton continued. "Now, I can bind you into some other room on this property and leave you there without food or drink, as is in my power." He stared very hard at the cup in the foreman's hands, prepared by that very housekeeper they had the power to put into jail. "Or you can make the quick and obvious decision right here."

"We will confer amongst ourselves," Mr. O'Dell said, then stood and turned to the other men.

Charles froze in shock as the dozen men formed a circle and conferred in low voices. They had scarcely begun to hear the relevant evidence. Not that this bothered any of them. A mere five minutes had passed when they reseated themselves.

Mr. Bumbleton set down his own cup, and burping gently, he rose from his chair. "How do you find Agnes Aga came to her death, and by what means?"

The foreman spoke the expected words. Charles shook his head. What other verdict could have been offered? At least the incompetent, lazy coroner hadn't attempted to blame the housekeeper.

The coroner erected himself into a magisterial posture after directing his assistant to a bit of writing. "I call this *ex dicto majoris partis juratorum* taken and considered as the verdict of all. Gentlemen, hearken to your verdict, as delivered by you, and as I have recorded it. You find 'sudden wrongful death by the hand of another where the offender is not known.'"

He nodded to Dr. Goose. "I shall grant my warrant to bury the deceased, to prevent infection. My thanks to you all."

Wasn't Agnes to receive further examination? Charles hoped the deeds did not entirely follow the words.

The doctor departed, having received a sheet of paper.

The bailiff said, "You good men of this county, who have been impaneled and sworn of the jury to inquire for our sovereign lord the king touching the death of Agnes Aga and who have returned your verdict, may depart and take your ease. God save the king."

Charles watched, still dumbfounded, as the assistant packed up the signed examinations. The doctor left, hopefully to examine the dead girl's body and see what had actually happened, rather than just bury her. The jurors agreed to meet at their favorite public house to talk about the case and departed en masse.

"Not promising," William said, leading Charles into the dining room across the front hall.

"They didn't even call the curate we saw near the icehouse during our search," Charles said.

"Whoever killed her had done it hours before," William offered in a tone of reason.

"He still should have been at the inquest."

"No one but us may know he was back there. It's not as if we'd communicated with anyone on the subject."

"The inquest happened with great haste," Charles agreed.

"That's really what you want, before the corpse spoils," William countered.

Charles watched William's face blanch as he realized he was speaking about his own cousin in this way. He patted his friend's arm. "Can you speak to your uncle to ensure the doctor takes a real look at Agnes?"

William's eyes had gone dull. "What do you want to know?"

Charles gentled his tone. "We need to know if she was violated. If she was, a man or older boy did this."

"Excuse me." William raced out of the room.

Charles suspected he'd gone to be sick, and no wonder. He'd have done the same if the body had been one of his sisters, Fanny or Letitia. Though he rather suspected Letitia would have fought back more fiercely than Agnes.

He thought about that. Had Agnes fought back? He cursed himself for not finding a way to get a better look at her himself. The conditions had been so very far from ideal. He didn't want to upset William further by going to Dr. Goose's office and asking to witness the examination. In this small-minded set, it might make him a suspect, no matter how improbable it would be, since he must have still been in London when she died. These people might not be intelligent enough to discern that, however. They would want someone, possibly anyone, to bind over to jail and the next court sessions. Just not, it seemed, the housekeeper, Mrs. Bedwin.

Mr. Eustace Aga came into the dining room. "We are meeting in the chapel, Charles. Where is William?"

"He went in the direction of the kitchen. I think the emotion of the day became too much."

Mr. Aga frowned. "I need him to set a good example for the boys. There is no place for emotion now."

Charles flashed to the initial reason he'd been called here. His three young mudlark charges were missing—still missing—and problems abounded at the school. Now a murder had intensified the situation, but he couldn't focus only on that.

Mrs. Bedwin appeared, rather breathless in black. "Mr. Aga, the vicar is calling for you."

Mr. Aga touched Charles's arm. Charles, considering the woman's abilities to effectively continue her duties when she could easily be in prison, followed him to a separate building, one he hadn't noticed before. A small chapel, tucked in on the street next to the school building and in front of one of the boardinghouses.

William had already arrived, looking rather pale. Charles sat next to him, behind the rows of students. He tugged William's sleeve when he recognized the curate from the afternoon before.

His friend nodded. "Let's grab him after prayers. We can't confront him now."

Before Charles could reply, he saw the doctor's assistants coming by the chapel windows, leading their horse. Behind rolled the cart containing the small plain coffin. He whispered a prayer as it passed.

In front of the pews, Mr. Aga stood next to the vicar as the elderly man mouthed platitudes. Not a single boy looked more than indifferent. They had glazed expressions in their eyes, in that way a poor diet and limited stimulation and exercise damaged a child. How were they supposed to glory in God when they were being educated in a rigid manner free of imagination? Charles didn't understand how one could believe in God and facts and nothing more. He had brought the mudlark children here in good faith. William had never expressed any concerns about their education. Where was Fagin Sikes? Was he responsible for the situation, or had Charles merely ignored the truth on his brief visits to the school?

He rubbed his face. He'd never had the time to visit properly, between his duties to the newspaper, his writing projects, and his upcoming marriage. It hadn't occurred to him to correspond with the boys. They had not known how to read or write upon entering the school, anyway. When they were retrieved, he'd have to find them a new school. He'd worry about how to pay for it later.

He couldn't leave them to the circus, if they even found places there. His understanding was that circus folk were mostly a tightly intertwined group of related people, often from foreign climes, and outsiders needn't apply. His fear that Ollie, John, and Arthur would fall into pickpocketing or other crimes seemed a fair one.

The service ended, and the students were lined up in perfect rows to be marched to the main building for a noon meal. At least they were fed three times a day.

Charles waited with William as the students filed past. A man came in the chapel's side door while they progressed, and stood next to Mr. Aga. He took off his top hat, exposing a head of thinning russet hair. Patchy whiskers dotted his chin and cheeks. Funereal black protected him from the elements, including a well-shined pair of top boots. His linen appeared clean but yellowed. A decade younger than Mr. Aga, he gave a sense of looking down his nose at others.

When the students were gone, Charles took William's elbow and propelled them off their bench and toward the two men. "I'll bet that's Mr. Sikes."

"Of course," William said. "I've seen him around town many times over the years."

"Father, Mr. Sikes," William said, inclining his head to the two men when they reached them.

Mr. Aga finished a quick thank-you to the vicar so the elderly man could depart. Mr. Wynd, the curate, passed by them holding a vestment in a solemn religious attitude, as if they had never spoken the day before. Charles knew he'd have to keep an eye on that one. But for now, he resolved to spend a few moments on the issue of the mudlarks.

The headmaster greeted them. "I've started the process of taking on a partner, Mr. Sikes here, since we saw you last."

The other man twitched his thin lips at Charles. "How are you today, my dear? I hope it was a pleasant excursion up from London."

"I didn't have to sit on top of the coach, all the better," Charles said. "But listen here, I want to speak to you about the curriculum changes I heard about in town. And the money, of course. We've been paying the tuition for our three boys through our charity. Surely your funds aren't so low as to feed the children a starvation diet. They all look thin and hollow eyed."

"They were receiving too much meat in their diet," Mr. Sikes pronounced. "The games between the students were painfully rambunctious, and young Toby Grimwig broke his arm falling from a tree."

"Too much meat," Mr. Aga echoed. "And too much imagination."

"You've removed imagination?" Charles asked, incredulous.

"Art," Mr. Aga said. "Chaucer."

Mr. Sikes nodded. "The treasure map nonsense proves the soundness of our new utilitarian policies."

"Why does it prove that?" Charles asked.

"The situation was out of control." Mr. Sikes spoke each word after a long pause and sprayed spittle with the last. "The boys need more discipline, more rules, less excess."

"And if they then run away in protest?" William's voice was terse.

Mr. Aga's eyelids half closed. "I am sure the missing children are earning a few coins sweeping the grounds of the circus, which is still outside of town, and there is no reason to worry about them."

"Why are you so certain?" Charles asked.

"They had talked of nothing but the circus when it came to town, and had scraped up coins to visit it every day."

"They will return when the circus moves on?" William asked.

"I am sure of it," Mr. Aga said, clasping his upper arm.

"But I am also sure of this," Mr. Sikes interrupted as Mr. Aga attempted to proceed. "This school won't survive the drama of Mr. Aga's own niece being murdered on the grounds."

"Please, I beg you," Mr. Aga added when his partner had run out of breath, "if you are to stay a day or two, focus on poor Agnes's demise. I have no idea what might have happened to her."

"Can you think of anyone who might have had a special interest in her?" William asked.

Mr. Sikes shook his head. "Just another servant girl." As Mr. Aga's face paled, he added, "Though a treasured member of the family, of course. But truly, she made no waves in our little community."

"Despite the treasure map?" Charles asked.

Mr. Sikes lifted his hand to shoulder level and spread his fingers. "My dear, the young must have their amusements."

"Yet you say your desire is to remove them," Charles said.

"I think it is clear they endlessly invent their own dramatics," Mr. Sikes said, lifting his gaze to the heavens. "It is our job to steer their young minds and, indeed, souls as much as is possible."

"Please, Charles." Mr. Aga's gaze met his directly. "I know

you have a knack for solving mysteries. And my son has the keenest eye imaginable. Please, find my niece's killer."

Charles couldn't be convinced that Mr. Aga's thoughts were entirely sound on any of these matters, but this was William's father, whom he had known to be good, kind, and honest for the year and more that they'd been acquainted, so he acquiesced for now. "I will do my best for a day or two."

"Very good." Mr. Sikes rubbed his leather glove–clad hands together. "Now, if you will excuse us, we have a meeting regarding the tea budget." He inclined his head to Mr. Aga, and the headmaster followed behind him, sheeplike, out the side chapel door.

It was only a moment before Charles and William were alone in the chapel. Charles collapsed into one of the heavy ebony chairs belonging to the teachers, and William followed suit.

"I think we can both agree the inquest was thoroughly bungled," Charles opined.

"Agreed," William admitted. "Though I do not think imprisoning Mrs. Bedwin would have done much good."

"She must know something, even if she's not the killer."

"It had to have been a man." William ignored Charles's point. "Skirts up?" He shuddered.

Charles pulled a pencil and a scrap of paper from his pocket. "It is scarcely bearable to contemplate, so let us go about this in a more journalistic manner."

"Please," William said.

"A timeline?" Charles suggested, wetting the tip of his pencil on his tongue.

"Of the murder, yes. Let us do our own inquest, since the official one was incomplete."

"It starts, really, with Agnes spilling oatmeal and going to her chamber to change her apron."

William nodded. "Item the first. In kitchen with Cook and

others. Oatmeal spilled. Did it herself, right? Item the second. Agnes goes to her room and changes her apron."

"Where did she go next?"

William shrugged. "That's the end of the trail as far as we know. No one seems to have seen her after that."

"We know she was meant to dust the ground floor next."

"She didn't do it," William said. "Ergo, she must have been abducted from her room."

"After changing her apron. Perhaps she was followed and surprised," Charles suggested.

"And then some eight hours later is discovered across the property, in the icehouse."

"No one might have noticed two people walking across the lawn," Charles said. "Not an unusual sight."

"But they might have noticed a girl being carried."

"A wheelbarrow?" Charles suggested.

"I don't think she was killed in her room," William countered. "The mess seemed normal enough."

"No blood," Charles agreed. "A note? Enticing her to the woods? An offer of quite a lot of chink?"

William scratched the edge of his jaw. "Could be. But no note in the room or on her body."

"Easiest thing in the world for the killer to take it with him. Literate?"

William frowned. "I would imagine so, or near enough. I think she had some schooling."

"No mother to teach her."

"No, but there is a dame school run by a woman in good standing at St. Mary's. I know the average working-class sort of girl gets completely left behind in education, but Agnes had a schoolmaster for an uncle. I can't imagine Agnes being left out of learning her numbers and letters."

Charles subsided. "Then there might have been a note, rather than a situation where someone physically removed her from the room."

"But we can't rule it out."

Charles tucked away his paper and pencil. "Let's take a look at the room again and the grounds. When we have a view of things, we will know who to ask who might have seen her."

"Agreed." William rose from the chair, moving without his usual grace.

They left the chapel and went back to the main building, then went upstairs.

"We need a school and servant schedule," Charles said, glancing around the artifacts of Agnes's life again. Nothing much had changed in the room, despite a night having passed. Had Nancy Price slept here? "To know who should have been where, when."

"We worked on that a bit yesterday. Cook said she'd never seen Agnes again."

Charles passed his hands over his eyes. "I see the stained apron is gone." It had been in the basin.

"Nancy probably changed the water so she could wash up this morning," William said, then pointed.

Charles couldn't see what he was pointing to, so he walked around the bed and saw a balled-up scrap of cloth in the corner. "Very disrespectful," he said as he picked up the stained apron.

"I agree," William said dolefully. "Nancy may not have liked my cousin very much."

"I don't like it," Charles said. "Her things should be boxed up for her father, not discarded."

William nodded and went to the small circular window. "I have to think some bored student would have seen Agnes and her killer walking across the lawn."

"Out of a schoolroom window," Charles said agreeably. "Or each of them alone heading toward their fateful rendezvous, assuming the killer is part of the school community. I worry about that curate."

William shook his head. "We saw him at the end of the day. We know she died hours earlier."

"He might have been hovering around. Waiting for the drama to begin."

William pulled his shoulders toward his ears. "I hate to think a man of God could be so evil."

"Kate doesn't like the curate at St. Luke's very much," Charles said.

"Yes, because he has feelings for her but never expressed them openly, like a man should," William countered. "Therefore, he merely creeps around the corners of her life, staring."

"He can stop staring now," Charles announced. "Or I will deal with him."

William stepped to his side and opened the window, then peered out. "No obvious way to enter or exit by this window."

"You could put a ladder on that sturdy tree branch there," Charles said, pointing. "But no trellis to climb, and it's quite a way to the ground."

William nodded. "Right. It's the stairs or nothing, and only one set of them to this floor."

"Depending on the time of day, there would be a lot of people moving about here."

"Or a lot of people behind classroom doors." William wiped his nose with a handkerchief, then walked out without saying anything more.

Outside, they went to the craggy black poplar tree near Agnes's window. Charles stared up at it. "There is a myth about these trees, you know."

"What's that?"

"Phaëthon was a son of the sun god, Helios, and an Oceanid," Charles explained. "When he learned he was the sun god's child and not half-mortal, he demanded to drive Helios's chariot to prove himself. But he couldn't control the horses, and his erratic journey caused Earth to freeze and burn in turns, making permanent changes to the landscape. In order to stop the carnage, Zeus shot him down with a lightning bolt."

"What does that have to do with the trees?"

"His sisters were insane with grief, so the gods turned them into poplars." Charles shrugged.

"I'm not sure anyone mourns my poor little cousin to that degree," William said.

"Which brings up an interesting point. Doesn't it take strong emotion to kill? Love, hate, all of that? If no one loved her terribly much, then who might have hated her enough to take her life? A little motherless servant girl, sacrificed to her brother's expectations."

"And him too young for much fellow feeling." William shook his head. "Well, my uncle is understandably raw, but he has his farm to run, and my father is beset with the cares of the school."

Charles leaned his head against a branch, stretching his neck. "That blasted treasure map must be responsible. One of the older schoolboys or a man. One of the schoolmasters?"

"I know them all, and they are rather milk-and-water types. I can't imagine any strong emotion there." William's voice descended into a mutter. "They don't have enough ambition to work at one of the better schools."

Charles walked around the thick tree, generations older than he. He spotted a man, with gray hair threaded through black plastered against the back of his neck under his hat, kneeling at a garden bed on the edge of the lawn. "Hullo there. I think we've found our elusive gardener."

William shaded his eyes, despite the sky offering little sun. "Yes, that is Littlejack Dawkins."

They headed toward him. William offered a greeting to the man's back. He wore an ancient navy surtout, with stitching visible at the elbows and shoulder seams. His boots were brown with dirt.

"Master William." The man turned, spiked his spade upright into the dirt, and greeted him easily. "Allus a pleasure to see you."

"Hullo, Dawkins. We've been hoping to have a word with you."

"Oh? Why is that?"

"We're trying to establish what was happening here at the school yesterday," Charles interjected.

"Because of little Agnes." The gardener's gaze shifted from side to side. "Isn't that a matter for the coroner?"

"I think we all know he didn't do a thorough job," William stated. "Besides, he didn't have any suspects by the end of the inquest."

"Did you see Agnes yesterday? I could see you were around the property," Charles added.

Littlejack Dawkins spit into the grass. "I was trimming bushes in the front of the school all day."

"Did you see Agnes?" Charles repeated.

"I saw nothing, and Mrs. Bedwin knew it, so I wasn't called to testify at the inquest."

"Very well," William said. "Anyone suspicious coming onto the property yesterday?"

Littlejack Dawkins shook his head. "No. Hawkers know not to come to the school. Cook won't buy from them, and most of the boys don't have any pocket money until after Lady Day. Their Christmas money is long gone." He pulled out his spade and turned back to his work.

"Thank you," Charles said. He and William walked along the lawn to the edge of the woods. All was quiet again, except for the chittering of the birds and the rustling of squirrels and other small beasts in the underbrush.

"Thoughts?" William asked.

"I never saw Littlejack Dawkins yesterday, though I did see

cut branches littering the ground in front of the school. It's not as if he was out there every second."

"Does that count as a lie?"

"It counts as a hole in the story. I am, of course, curious to see what lies develop, but Littlejack is on my suspect list."

"We will need to narrow down the time of the abduction, if that is what happened, and murder, because, of course, no one was in the same place the entire day. Littlejack would have stopped for breaks at the very least."

"I had the sense from him that Mrs. Bedwin somehow dictated the interview list."

"That was odd," William agreed. "More proof of the incompetence of the local coroner."

"Or could it be a ploy, for some unknown reason? We both know the housekeeper could be in jail right now. Is there a link between her and the coroner?"

"Entirely possible, in a small village."

"For now, our best assumption is that Agnes's murder had something to do with the supposed treasure map, for there seems to be no other reason to kill a twelve-year-old girl," Charles mused. "So far, no one has expressed dislike of or obsession with the girl, nor has there been any indication that she was a thief."

"We must learn more about Agnes's map," William said.

Charles stared at the thick trees blocking the slope of the hillside. "I'm growing increasingly concerned that the mudlarks have not reappeared."

"They left before Agnes disappeared. It's not as if they have anything to do with the murder."

"Still, a circus is in town. What if one of the circus folk killed Agnes?" Charles inquired.

"We need to find it before they break down the show and leave town."

"We need to find John, Ollie, and Arthur," Charles said, wishing William would take the disappearance of the children more seriously. Of course, Agnes was his niece, but she was beyond help. Meanwhile, the boys were missing.

The notion that they were unaware of some pattern interlacing the death and disappearance troubled him.

Chapter 5

London, England, Wednesday, March 2, 1836

George Hogarth's office at 332 Strand, home of the *Morning* and *Evening Chronicle* newspapers, could be turned into quite a cozy dining chamber once the desk was cleared. Kate, his eldest daughter, spread a tablecloth over the scarred wooden surface, and her sister, Mary, set out crockery from the newspapers' own stores.

Kate glanced at her editor father as he entered the room holding a tray of meat pies collected from an errand boy he'd sent for them.

He set the tray down and handed Mary his shawl. "Warm in here."

"We left the door open to let the heat in for a few minutes," Mary explained, hanging the knitted fabric over his chair. Their bonnets and cloaks had taken up all the free space on the pegs.

"Is Mr. Dickens joining us?" Kate asked, anxious to see her busy fiancé for the first time in days.

Her father pressed flyaway graying hairs off his forehead and smoothed them over his scalp, then sat down and took up his pipe. "Charles went up to Harrow on the Hill yesterday, after William Aga."

Kate frowned. "After him? Has something happened?"

"William had an assignment there and no doubt took an opportunity to visit his father. Then yesterday Charles had a letter requesting he make his way there himself. No further explanation was in evidence."

Kate glanced at Mary, who looked equally concerned. "Has any word arrived from Mr. Dickens since?"

Mr. Hogarth took out his tobacco tin. "No, but I hope to have an article by one of them later in the day. I'll give ye an update at dinner tonight."

"Put your pipe away, Father," Mary chided, brushing ringlets, darker than Kate's blond ones, behind her ears. "We have a fresh pot of tea and these lovely pies."

He raised his eyebrows, normally seated low and dark over his eyes, then smiled genially. His tin went back into the drawer. "As ye will, Mary. I expect I don't have much longer to give into yer demands. Why, Kate will be married in a month, and I'm sure Charles will find ye a husband soon after that."

She blushed. "If only Mother can spare me often enough for suitors to visit at Furnival's Inn."

Kate laughed. "You look pitiable, Mary. Don't forget that Charles's brother Fred will be living with us there, too, and he's madly in love with you."

Mary shuddered. "He's a child."

"Ye'll be happy for a break when yer mother needs ye at home, then," their father said, his fingers creeping to his pipe again.

"Poor Fred," Kate murmured. She liked her fiancé's young brother, but if she were a year older than him, she might not appreciate his romantic attentions, either. It would be many years before he could wed, after all, since he'd only just embarked on his career as a law clerk.

"Where are ye off to after this?" their father asked.

"Furnival's Inn," Mary said.

"We took Charles's and Fred's mending home with us last week," Kate explained. "Neither of them ever has enough socks, so we wanted to return them as soon as we could. We didn't know he'd had to leave London."

"It will be delightful to properly live here," Mary enthused with a faraway look in her eye. "What larks we shall have."

"A lot of work, too." Kate straightened the green ribbon tied around her waist. "Running a little household of my own."

"I shall help, Mother willing," Mary said staunchly. "And never leave you."

"Until ye find a husband of yer own," their father said. His pie had already disappeared, as if by magic, and Kate had yet to pour the tea. She portioned it into cups before the entire pot could take on the flavor of tobacco.

After their father produced smoke wreathing his head in a color identical to his hair, he admitted he'd yet to receive an article from William Aga. He owed the newspaper an update on a gravel pit collapse.

"Is that troubling?" Kate asked.

Their father made a smoke ring and watched it dance through the air. "It's odd, since he did send that note to Charles. I hope there will be something for me on the stage tonight, so we can have it for tomorrow's paper."

Kate finished her tea. "Very well, then. Thank you for the pie. We'll take our bundle over to the rooms and then return home. It's easy to get a hackney from Furnival's Inn because of the cabstand right there."

"Hannah has been a bit inattentive lately, and I know Mother will need help with dinner," Mary added.

"Verra good," their father said. "Yer mother is a bit inattentive herself, with her nerves over yer wedding. The first of her chicks to leave the nest."

Kate felt her cheeks growing hot, though more from indignation than nerves. She and Charles had been engaged since last spring and ought to have been married before Christmas. One thing after another had caused delays. Now, though, the wait must be over, and her new life could finally start.

After a few warnings and admonitions, their father allowed them to depart, and they walked over to north Holborn. Charles's rooms were in a four-story Inn of Chancery, rebuilt about fifteen years ago as gentlemen's apartments.

They passed through the arched entryway that pressed out in rectangular fashion from the front of the flat façade. Kate had a key, though these current rooms of Charles's were not to be the ones they would reside in after the wedding, since he hoped to secure chambers with better light for them at the start of next month. He had furnishings on hold at fine secondhand dealers, and very soon, with luck, everything would be in readiness for their first home together.

She took the key from her reticule, but the door moved inward before she could even turn it in the lock.

"That's odd," Mary said.

"Hullo," Kate called into the dim room. She slid the key through her fingers. Charles had enemies, as they had learned over recent months. Listening carefully, she heard a snuffling sound, like the sound of an animal.

"What's this now?" chided Mary, peering around Kate.

Kate stepped through the doorway, untying her bonnet strings. The smell of sharp spirits hit her nose. As her eyes adjusted, she saw Charles's young brother Fred home from his workplace already. He held a bottle of gin against his knee. She marched to his side and pulled it from his fingers. "Fred! You shouldn't drink such strong spirits. And in the middle of the day? For shame." Fred wouldn't even be sixteen until the summer.

He snuffled. She identified the noise as the one she'd heard in the doorway.

She modulated her tone, reminding herself she would be his elder sister very soon. "What is wrong?"

Despite the gloom, she could see the gleam of tears in his eyes when he lifted his face to hers. "I was sacked from the law firm this morning."

"You were?" Kate exclaimed. "Whatever happened?" She pulled up a stool and sank onto it.

He shrugged and stared longingly at the bottle she held. "I'd rather do accounts, anyway."

"Have you had an offer in such a firm?"

"No, but I can find one. I'm sure I can, as long as they don't know what happened."

"What did?" Mary asked.

Kate shook her head. Mary was too much Fred's contemporary to get involved, no matter how superior she felt to him. "Take the mending into the bedroom and put it in the chest, please."

Mary walked slowly through the room.

Fred sniffled again. "I don't want to tell my parents, because Father will be harsh."

"They don't need to know. Your brother is master of this household."

Fred's full mouth worked. "Letitia is seriously ill."

"She is?" Letitia was a Dickens sister, engaged to be wed soon.

Fred nodded.

"I'm very sorry to hear that. But the truth is, it will necessarily limit contact between the households, anyway. Mrs. Dickens will need to nurse her." She didn't expect Mr. Dickens to be of much help. He never was. A pleasant and genial man, he was nonetheless something of a drain on the family.

"I've got to find another position right away," Fred said. "I'm sure you know how harsh I was on Charles when he was out of a job last year."

"No, I don't know about that, but Charles is resourceful, which you must be, as well."

"Do you have any ideas?"

Kate had only one. "If you really want to do accounts, you could ask Emmanuel Screws for employment. He thinks well of you Dickens brothers since the difficulties he faced over the holidays last year."

Fred licked his lips slowly. "I'll think about it."

Kate wondered if the boy was too deep in his cups now to recall this conversation the next day. For now, a nap might be the best solution for his problems.

He pulled a crumpled piece of paper from his pocket. "It's a note from the Furnival's Inn landlord that says we will be getting the new rooms we wanted before your wedding."

"That's wonderful!" Charles could delay their marriage no longer if the rooms were ready. They had been the last great impediment, as he'd insisted on their marital home being up to his tastes, which would never be possible in this present dark and crowded space. Of course, she'd do a better job of keeping it tidy. Charles and Fred had let their windows get sooty again, and they needed a strong application of vinegar and newspaper to restore the shine and visibility.

Mary came out from the bedchamber, her half-empty basket swinging at her side. "I heard you exclaim?"

"We are moving into the sunnier chambers," Kate explained. "The long delay is over!"

Mary clasped her hand. "I'm very pleased for you."

"What are we pleased about?" came a female voice from the doorway.

Kate turned and saw Julie Aga, William's wife. Ringlets of red hair curled around her cheeks, and the ribbon on her bonnet matched her hair. Her appearance had lost the willowy quality she'd possessed before her pregnancy became evident. She still had four months to go, by her estimate.

"The rooms," Kate explained to Julie. She and William had lived at Furnival's Inn when they all first met, and then had followed Charles to temporary digs near the Hogarth family home in Brompton before moving to a nice set of rooms in Cheapside, above a chophouse, the previous fall. "Thank you for meeting us here."

"My pleasure. I have my aunt's carriage waiting downstairs, so you have a way to get home."

"Thank you. Did you come in from Brompton?" Kate asked.

Julie laced her fingers together. "No, my aunt is downstairs. She wants to shop."

"Oh, goodness. Lady Lugoson is waiting upon us? We had better dash."

Mary came forward and offered the basket to the young matron. "Here are the dresses you wanted."

"Mrs. Hogarth is kind to lend them to me," Julie said, taking it. "I can't let out my own clothing anymore. The seam allowance is exhausted."

Fred's ears went red at the mention of Julie's pregnancy. A former actress, she was not a creature of great refinement. Her marriage to Charles's close associate kept her in their circle, however, despite her occasional clashes with decency.

"Before we go, I wanted to tell you some sad news," Julie said.

"What? Nothing with Lady Lugoson's impending marriage, I hope," Kate said.

"No, nothing has happened to Sir Silas. It's William's little cousin, Agnes. She's been murdered."

"Murdered?" Mary said. "Here in London?"

Julie dabbed at the corners of her eyes. "No, at Aga Academy. She worked there."

"That's terrible," Kate exclaimed. "Father said Mr. Aga had summoned Mr. Dickens to Harrow on the Hill."

"He w-won't be home tonight?" Fred slurred.

Julie shook her head. "I haven't had any more word. William wrote the note shortly after Charles found the body."

"There will be an inquest," Kate said, her pulse quickening. She did love a mystery. Could she help Charles figure out what had happened to the poor girl? He'd uncover the killer himself in time, but perhaps she could speed the process. The family needed resolution.

"Right," Julie said, wiping hair off her cheek. "Poor Agnes. My goodness, I am tired."

"We must get you home," Mary said, taking her arm.

"I wonder what we can do to help," Kate murmured.

Julie gave in to a yawn. "I'm sure more letters will come in the last post."

"If we have more information, perhaps some stratagem will occur to us." Kate pulled a blanket Charles's sister Fanny had knitted from a battered armchair and laid it over Fred. "Rest, Fred. I will take counsel with my father about what should be done with you."

Fred nodded and closed his eyes. "I didn't make any mistakes, but I was a bit messy with the ink. I'll be more careful next time."

She patted his dark hair, springy and almost alive under her glove. "I know you will. Sleep well."

"This is Toby Grimwig's boardinghouse. The students are in dormitories on the upper floor." William led Charles up the narrow front steps in the south house on the property the next morning. They had both done some necessary writing after breakfast, then had met to continue their investigation.

The higher they climbed up in the windowless space, the stronger the sharp, sweaty smell of boy became. The house had little light in general, as it was blocked by the larger school building next to it.

Charles felt suddenly cheerier about dear old Furnival's Inn, which did not smell pungently of the first sproutings of young manhood. "Rather miserable to be stuck here with a broken arm. Isn't there an infirmary? Some place with light and air movement?"

"No. If the school is overwhelmed by some sort of illness, they convert one of the dormitory rooms into a sickroom and move the boys around to accommodate it. I remember when I was about ten, we had a run of scarlet fever among the young boys, and one entire house was turned into the infirmary." They reached the upper floor landing. "Still," William continued, "they get a good deal of fresh air and exercise. The weather is quite reasonable here. It's really an excellent place for children."

Except for the food. Charles wondered if William was regarding the place with nostalgia, rather than how it presented itself at this moment, with limited rations, runaways, and a dead maid. His arm twitched involuntarily at the memory of that ghastly scene in the icehouse, the apron, the out-of-place skirts.

"Here we are." William smiled at Charles and, after stepping down the passage, opened the last door. "Grimwig is a special case, at any rate. He has a private room."

Charles saw four doors on this side of the floor. A row of iron bedsteads, the kind that could easily be disassembled for cleaning, were visible through one. Dust motes danced in the coldly bright winter sunlight streaming in through one window, though the floor held no hint of dust or fluff in the corners. The beds didn't appear to cover any sort of mess, either, as the limited bed coverings hid nothing of the floor. At the foot of each one was a chest, and discipline must be strict, for each bed was made neatly and nothing was out of place.

He followed William through the next door, into a smaller room with a number of small niceties in comparison to the barren dormitory.

A young gentleman sat propped against pillows on the only

bed in the room, his right arm encased in a heavy plaster of Paris cast from the wrist, past the elbow, and halfway to the shoulder. Underneath him was a red paisley-adorned velvet coverlet with a purple border, very luxurious and fashionable. A Greek primer lay in his lap, unopened.

"That must be a terrible injury, Grimwig," William said, flipping back his coat and seating himself elegantly on a stool next to the patient. "I'm sorry to see you laid up like this. This is Dickens, by the by."

"Broke my arm in two places," the boy announced with a twisting lift to his chin. He had the pale skin of someone who hadn't been out in the sun for a while, and his faded brown hair hung lank and unwashed. "The cast is so heavy that it's hard to balance."

"You can't write, either, I suppose." Charles walked over to the small fireplace, which had a cheery little wood fire going. A number of silhouettes were framed on the mantelpiece.

"A convenient excuse to avoid sums," the boy agreed. "I'm supposed to be learning Greek. The master says I should be able to read it by the time the cast comes off." His fingers, poking out from the cast, jerked.

"I hope you're applying yourself," William said sternly.

"I feel all right in the morning, but then the cast gets to me, and I have a dreadful headache by the start of the afternoon." Toby sniffed and tightened his lips.

"We won't bother you for long, then," Charles interjected. "You weren't at the inquest this morning, and we wanted to learn more about this mythical treasure map."

The boy snorted, his pale nostrils becoming even more translucent as the skin stretched. "Oh, it's real, all right." When he glanced into William's derisive face, he added, "I swear."

"You saw it?" William queried.

"Not clearly." Toby licked his lower lip. "Agnes had a way of flashing it around the school."

"What did you see exactly? From what you're saying, it could have just been a piece of paper."

Toby's gaze went to the side, then refocused on William. "No. It was parchment, kind of yellowed. With drawings on it and everything. Nothing a girl would have."

One thing this particular girl had was nerve. Why was she so foolish? Treasure maps should be secret by definition.

William glanced in Charles's direction. "It does sound real. Nothing she could have made herself."

"No." The boy blinked. "I don't think she was in cahoots with anyone, either, like her brother especially. He treated her like a servant, not his sister."

"What about Nancy Price?"

"I never saw them much together. I'm not sure they liked each other, but how would I know? They're just girls," the boy said scathingly.

"It would be an awfully deep game for such young people to play," Charles said. "But we are going to keep asking questions."

William patted the lad's shoulder. "Do you need anything before we go? Are you being checked up on regularly?"

"Could you refill my cup? It's warm up here."

William took the vessel. "Of course."

Charles followed him down to the kitchen. After William had finished with the boy's request, they went back to the main building. In the parlor, they saw the Aga brothers meeting with the curate.

Charles heard the words *family plot* and realized they were discussing Agnes's burial. Again, this was no time to confront the curate. He tugged William's sleeve, and they went out into the front hall instead, which was still dusty and cobwebbed.

Agnes's sad death had left one hole, at least, in the running of the school.

"Where to next?" William asked in a low voice.

Charles put up his hand when he heard the choking sound of a man trying to hold back grief. Agnes's father, he suspected. What a sad thing, to bury a child. His sister Harriet's death was one of the few times he'd seen his father not even try to be jovial. He was seven when she was born, a boy full of affection for an infant sibling, and though she hadn't lived for long, her memory remained.

William shuddered at the sound of his uncle's grief and opened the front door. They took possession of the front step and closed the door.

"Should we lie in wait for the curate?" Charles asked.

"I don't want to disrupt the planning for Agnes's burial," William said.

"I understand. Why don't we pause our investigation and attempt to track down Ollie, John, and Arthur? They deserve our attention, too." Charles buttoned his coat.

William nodded absently. "I'm sure the circus is where it always is. Let's stop by the coaching inn and find out who has horses to loan out today."

"A sound idea."

They walked through the front of the property. Charles noted that Littlejack Dawkins had cleared away the branches neatly and nothing remained of his project. Then they walked to the coaching inn. It felt like he had been there a week ago, not just a day.

"I forgot to send my article to the *Chronicle*," Charles exclaimed when the innyard jogged his memory. "Being called to the inquest so soon quite cleared my mind of it."

William clicked his tongue. "I took my quarry article to the inn before coming to you. Do you already have something finished on the inquest?"

"It's not much. Just the bare facts and the verdict. It's enough for now. I'll have them hold it for the next stage." Luckily, he had tucked it into his pocket at some point. William stayed behind to talk to a yardman while Charles went inside and made arrangements for his letter to be sent on to the *Morning Chronicle*.

When he returned, William had the name of a good stable. They walked halfway down the hill to where a side street led to a stable that had a blacksmith's forge next to it.

Charles nodded at the apprentice cleaning iron with a wire brush as they passed by.

"Nice day for a ride," the young man said, looking woefully at the sky. His skin stretched over his thin cheeks, and his Adam's apple jutted harshly from his tendon-rich neck.

"We're heading out to the circus grounds," Charles said. "Have you been out there?"

"No, sir. Too much work to do here." The lad was sixteen or so and looked much too lean for his broad shoulders. Lean all over, really.

"Your master feeding you enough?" Charles asked, concerned.

"Never enough." The boy coughed, a wet sound. "I just keep growing taller, anyways."

Charles nodded. "Best of luck to you." He followed William into the stable yard.

"Do you have a couple of hacks for rent today?" William asked a stable boy who was lounging with a pipe next to the barn.

"I'll get the master," the boy said after carefully setting his pipe on the side of a rusty water trough. A study in contrast to the blacksmith's apprentice next door, he waddled into the barn, the fabric of his coarse pants rubbing between his legs.

"That one doesn't appear to be working hard enough."

"I doubt the forge and the stable are owned by the same person," William remarked.

"I wonder if Fagin Sikes owns the forge," Charles muttered. "I don't understand how a young man is expected to do such hard work on small rations and survive."

"He could simply be growing," William said. "You know how boys are."

"I could see the shape of his skull under his skin," Charles retorted. "That's not a growth spurt. I bet if you lifted his shirt, you'd see lash marks. That boy had the signs of a fresh beating about him."

When he'd finished his short speech, the stable boy sauntered out again, followed by another man.

Charles guessed the stable master was the boy's father. They had the same bright red cheeks and heavy-bodied appearance. When the father removed his pipe from his mouth to speak, Charles could see the damage to his teeth where he kept his pipe clenched.

"We'd like a couple of hacks so we can ride out to the circus," William said. "Have you heard if it's still around?"

"Haven't heard that it left," the man returned pleasantly enough. "Expect it will be here for the rest of the week. They usually set up for about three weeks. They've used that land for years. Good place for them to make repairs. No one cares if they stay a bit."

"Thank you." Charles took in the scent of sweet smoke, not dissimilar to Mr. Hogarth's favorite. "You have any boys hanging around recently? We're looking for runaway students from Aga Academy."

"Don't know you," the stable master said, putting his pipe back in his mouth.

"I'm Charles Dickens. This is William Aga. His father runs the school."

"Didn't say I didn't know him." The man showed dimples as he grinned. "I heard as how Sikes got his hooks into the school."

"It gets worse," Charles said. "Poor Agnes Aga was murdered yesterday. Did you hear about that?"

The boy's plump cheeks puffed out. "Never! We saw her at church last Sunday."

"I'm afraid so," Charles said, putting his hand on William's shoulder. "Inquest was this morning."

"Just terrible. I'll go saddle the horses." The stable master started to turn, then straightened to look at William. "Why?" he asked simply.

William lifted his shoulders. "I'm sure you can imagine what a travesty the inquest was. Our only bit of information is that she was waving around a treasure map. Maybe someone killed her for it."

Chapter 6

The stable master considered William's words carefully. Charles could almost see the man flipping over each word before he nodded with great significance.

"Could be," he admitted. "Could be treasure around here."

"What?" William's brow knit. "I wasn't raised on those kinds of stories."

"Your pa is a practical kind of man." The stable master stuck his empty pipe in his leather apron pocket. "Not the fanciful type like your grandfather. I was sorry to hear he'd died. But I'm sure you know your local history."

"Thank you," William murmured.

"I don't know the history," Charles interjected. "Why do you think there could be a treasure trove in the locality?"

The man rubbed the bridge of his nose, then looked down at his son, who was finishing his own pipe. "Neddy, go saddle the roan and the bay for Mr. Aga and his friend."

Neddy disappeared into the barn. His father stared into the yard, his eyes unfocused. "I can think of three options."

"You don't say," William exclaimed. "Something a monastery might have buried during the Dissolution?"

"No. But think about that unfortunate king. If you remember your history, Charles I fled the Civil War and came through here on 27 April 1646."

"You think there might have been a treasure left from that misadventure?" Charles asked.

"Anything is possible. Something made his visit memorable. The actual date being remembered."

"Good point," William murmured.

"Going farther back in time," the stable master continued, "maybe every town has these stories, but I've heard rumors of an ancient king's grave somewhere nearby."

"Interesting," William said. "From one of the old kingdoms."

The man nodded. "Then, of course, there is a pagan temple from pre-Roman times at the top of the hill. There could be something left from the people who fought the Romans."

William's lips curved up slightly. "I think stories like that could be heard in just about any town, as you said."

Charles, on the other hand, found himself intrigued. He had found minor treasure from the sixteenth century before in London. He couldn't deny that artifacts could be under the soil, ready to be rediscovered. "It's a shame I can't bring Fred down. He'd love the hunt."

"You used to hunt for coins," William remarked.

"It wasn't that long ago," Charles admitted. "Those coins paid for my birthday party last year. Fred was willing to get dirty and hunt them up even after I was done with the business."

"It's a boy's business," the stable master agreed. "They have the speed to run from the night watch if they are caught."

All three men chuckled lightly just as young Neddy tugged one placid mare into the yard.

"Neddy is puffing for breath," Charles observed.

"Lung troubles," his father explained. "Doctor said the smoke would help with breathing. I don't see it, though, but I can't seem to stop the pipes."

"Try a different doctor?" Charles said. "There is always another one around."

"Maybe in London, but not here."

"Really? With all the students passing through? It's just that Dr. Goose?"

"Met him, have you? It's not a very large town, besides the students," explained the stable master. "But we get by."

Charles and William shared a glance of derision. Must be difficult to keep the townsfolk alive. Maybe they used the old ways.

As Charles took the reins of the relatively small horse, not much more than a pony, William followed Neddy into the barn to find a mount more suitable to his height.

The stable master led him to a mounting block, which Charles used only to protect the seams of his trousers. He hadn't expected to be here more than a day when he'd left London, and didn't want to have to repair his clothing.

He leaned down over the horse's neck when he was seated properly. "Where have you heard this ancient king's grave is?"

"I'm a good Christian," the stable master said. "But that don't mean the old curses don't work. Those folks didn't know any better, and I'm not about to go hunting up trouble."

"Not even when you were a boy?"

"The woods gave me the same breathing trouble Neddy has when I was a boy. I stayed out of them."

"The woods?"

The stable master shrugged. "I expect a lot of old things hide there."

William reappeared with a younger, larger horse. He used the mounting block while Charles asked, "How do we get to the circus grounds?"

"Go south through town, then angle east. Follow the road to Sudbury town, which is just two miles from here. You'll see the circus before you come into town."

"Thank you," the pair said in unison. They waved their good-byes and ambled out of the yard.

"I guess we didn't need the horses," Charles said as they started down the hill. "We could have walked."

"It's nice to see the town from atop a steed," William called as they passed a number of redbrick and stone school buildings.

"It's a good day for it." It had rained overnight, and the street was damp enough to kick up just a minimum of dust. Charles doffed his hat to a trio of girls chattering on the side, stuffed market baskets on their arms.

The road angled east after a few minutes, and they left the neighborhood of beerhouses, another forge, a butcher shop, and a chapel, then went past a row of neat terraced houses. They stopped at a sandwich seller hawking her wares at the edge of the road in front of a second terrace and bought ham sandwiches before continuing, then ate in the saddle. Parcels of unused land began to appear, not unusual in an area that contained less than two thousand souls.

The road remained busy. Charles counted nearly a hundred people walking alongside the road, which seemed odd for a Thursday afternoon. An expectant atmosphere hovered around the walkers. He could hear chuckles from shared jokes, and easy, happy chatter. "Do you think there is a circus performance today?"

William rode to the side of the road, where a half dozen men were tramping along, lunch pails in hand. After consulting with them, he returned to Charles. "Yes, we're just in time for a special performance of the Michielli Circus. A treat for one of the gravel pits, because it is the owner's birthday."

Charles couldn't keep the grin off his face. "There's a bit of entertainment we've been sadly missing."

"It doesn't seem right," William demurred. "Under my family circumstances."

"It's research," Charles coaxed. "It's not like you were seeking it out."

"Fair enough," William agreed equably.

"Additionally . . ." Charles's tone went grim. "This will put all the circus folk into one place. If the boys are here, we'll find them."

When they reached a crossroad, Charles could see men on horses coming their direction, along with an equal-sized crowd coming out from Sudbury town. The field to the east was trampled with beasts and human feet alike. A large barn, a permanent structure that was likely filled with harvest goods in the fall and emptied out over the winter to be rented out for a special event like this, was decorated with bunting. A massive temporary circle fronted the barn, constructed with hay bales.

They had erected bleachers made from rough wood, and temporary boxes had been built, too, to keep the gentlefolk separated slightly from the rabble.

A hundred feet in, a line had formed. Charles glanced around. They weren't the only horsemen.

"Paddock over there." William pointed. A little west of the barn was a fenced-in structure.

"Looks like that's where we can leave the horses," Charles agreed. They rode over and negotiated with a farmer's son to take charge of the horses during the performance. Then they walked back to join the line.

Charles kept an eye out for the mudlarks, but there were so many boys roaming about he probably couldn't have picked out any of them in a crowd. William and Charles surrendered coins when prompted and were pointed into the box queue.

A woman showed them into a box. She had long, curling blond hair and didn't wear a bonnet. Her lithe form was encased in a red military-style bodice complete with medals and epaulets, and her muscular legs were adorned in nothing but tight stockings, right down to her boots.

"You must be one of the performers." Charles's voice came out in a squeak.

"Helena Michielli," she said, with a quick incline of her pointed chin. "I am married to Baptista Michielli. This is his circus."

"Wonderful, wonderful," Charles murmured, unable to keep himself from stealing another glance at those scandalous legs.

"Have you hired any local boys?" William asked.

She shrugged. "We always bring in day workers for the run of the show."

"Even boys as young as seven?" William pressed. "One would be memorable. His name is Ollie, and he has only one hand."

"I am sorry, no," murmured Signora Michielli before turning away from William and taking the next party down the line to a box that held actual chairs instead of more hay bales for seating.

Charles and William were soon joined by a family party, a newly married coal merchant treating his wife and her parents and sister to a day out. William greeted them, polite though a shadow of his usually charming self, while Charles peered at the painted canvas hanging above the barn door. MICHIELLI CIRCUS proclaimed the banner in red, over a golden angel. BY APPOINTMENT TO THE KING read smaller text underneath. But what king? Crows were stenciled in a pattern under the eaves. He didn't care about any of that, as much as he loved spectacle. He wanted to catch sight of three boys and banish them out of the fresh air and sunshine, back into school.

His fellow circus goers chattered excitedly around him while he fretted, the air of anticipation mixing with the scents of hay bales and horses creating the unique flavor of the performance to come. If he couldn't turn Ollie, John, and Arthur into proper clerk material, he would fail more than just them. Arthur still had relatives they assisted with their charity.

"Look at this." William passed him a playbill, noting the delights they were to see.

Charles read aloud. "Signor Michielli respectfully acquaints the public that his unparalleled equestrian performance will commence on Thursday, the fourth of March, weather permitting, for the first time in England, at very considerable expense, a circus. The grace of Mr. Michielli, Jr., as he performs the *saut des rubans*, *sa de baguette*, and *saut devant-derrière* will bring tears to your eyes. He is an expert at Cossack riding, as well. Our ropewalkers and tumblers were trained by Spinacuta himself . . ."

"Sounds like quite a show," William said with a laugh.

"I am eager to see what they have to offer," Charles agreed.

"More beauties in stockings," William added hopefully.

A drummer appeared in cut-down British military garb, the tails of his red coat drifting through the dampened dirt. He stood in the center of the ring and beat a tattoo as the final remnants of the crowd filed onto the bleachers. The barn doors opened, and a group of riders came through, the grown men all dressed similarly. They were followed by five boys on smaller horses, in regular clothes.

"Jimmy!" the bride in their box called, waving.

"These must be the local students," Charles said. Circuses were always riding schools, as well.

The men dazzled on horseback. Even Charles's breath caught in his chest as Michielli Jr. finished his act by doing a double somersault down to the ground after a fantastic display of trick riding and juggling on horseback. After that, the woman they had met, along with two men and a child, did an extract of a traditional harlequinade, with Signora Michielli playing Columbine, while ropes were strung around the ring.

The ropewalkers and tumblers came out. The tumblers, probably the children of the ropewalkers, dressed in bright yellow costumes, were adorable as they darted around the ring, pulling the audience's attention in all directions.

A dilapidated clown came out to do a few tricks, performing the comic intermezzo, while the ropes were removed. Soon, though, all the performers appeared for "the spectacular." Signora Michielli, redressed in her original military costume, rode on her husband's shoulders as he galloped around the ring. Charles genuinely had his heart in his throat, but she didn't fall. By the end, he clapped as hard as anyone.

"There is something about a circus in broad daylight," William said with a sigh.

"It is not the time to see it at its best," Charles agreed. "Still, they undeniably have talent. Much of the performance was delightful, especially outside of London."

William nodded assent. "No sign of our boys, though."

"None at all. But they wouldn't be performing. They have no money for riding lessons." Charles scanned the ring and buildings, hoping to pick them out.

"Our boys don't know how to care for horses."

Charles turned back to his friend. "No, but they are quick studies."

"What would they do with Ollie?"

"The others might be working while he forages for food. Who knows what they might be up to? They are far from home, but they've shown themselves to adapt well to changing circumstances."

"We thought they had," William said under the roar of the crowd.

"Excuse me," said the bride. Her skirt scratched against the hay as she turned. "You are looking for some boys?"

"Runaway students from Aga Academy," William explained.

"Signor Michielli is always willing to speak to townsfolk," the groom said. "He wants riding students."

"Then we'll go see him." Charles inclined his head to their fellow box dwellers. "Thank you for the advice."

They both vaulted the hay bales around the edges of their box and stepped into the ring. The dirt had dried, and the vegetation had long since been destroyed by the horses. The clown came out of the barn pushing a wheelbarrow, a shovel over his shoulder.

Charles dodged a pile of dung. "I think we know what he's after."

"Horses," William agreed, dust trailing behind his boots as he walked toward the barn.

They went through the open doors, blinking at the sudden change from sunlight to the cool dimness of the interior space. The center of the barn had been turned into a staging area. Curtains along the passages formed a modicum of privacy.

Charles grabbed the arm of a skinny youth as he swaggered by. "Who are you?"

"I'm a juggler. They call me the Artful Dodger," said the lad, puffing out his chest. He wore motley and a top hat. At maybe fifteen years old, he still had a child's winsome full cheeks.

"You're one of the students? I remember you on horseback." Charles glanced around the barn. One of the horsemen narrowed his eyes in their direction, but plenty was going on in the horse stalls as the horses were relieved of their tack and wiped down after the performance. He kept walking by.

"No, not me. See, I'm one of the company." The boy's fingers twitched.

"The company dipper, no doubt," Charles muttered. The boy looked like a pickpocket and had been on horseback only during the procession.

Men shouted to each other as they pitched hay from the loft.

Other men carried in water through the rear door of the barn. A woman giggled inside the improvised dressing area.

"I'm insulted," the boy pronounced.

"Sure you are," William said. "Look, we're trying to find three boys, Londoners. John, Arthur, and Ollie. Do you know them?"

"My memory is poor," said the boy, lifting his sharp chin.

Charles pulled out a shilling and passed it under the boy's nose. "Does this help your memory?"

The coin disappeared so quickly that Charles scarcely felt it leave his fingers.

"How old?" asked the Artful Dodger, flipping the shilling in and out of his fingers.

"John is probably twelve," William said.

Charles displayed eight fingers. "Ollie is only eight. He's lost a hand. And Arthur is seven."

The boy fluttered his eyelashes. "Now you mention it, I do remember them. Close, they were, like brothers. All had straw hats with green bands."

"Yes, that's part of the school uniform," William said eagerly.

"Did they join the circus?" Charles asked.

The boy snorted. "Not just anyone can do that. You have to have talent to eat."

"But you remember them."

The boy focused on Charles as he spoke. "I'd like to take more coin off you, but the truth is, they ain't around here. They were in the audience a few days back, is all. They didn't hang around."

"Why do you remember them, then?"

The boy colored. "The oldest one, he saw me fumbling with a wipe. Gave me a bit of advice, he did. Don't fret your eyelids on that score. He didn't raise a hue and cry."

"I didn't know Poor John had those kinds of skills," Charles said. He batted at an insect passing much too close to his eyes.

William laughed. "Maybe he kept it in readiness for nights when the Thames had nothing to cast up. Do you know where they are?"

The Artful Dodger shrugged. "You can give me more dosh, but it won't change my answer. Sorry, friend."

William kicked at a streamer that had fallen from one of the horses. "We've spent enough time here. Nothing to do but retrieve the horses and come up with another plan."

Most of the clientele had left the bleachers and boxes, ready to return home for their dinner. Charles hoped they were well satisfied by their half day of adventure. Few of their fellow circus goers would ever get to London to see the superior entertainment available there.

The clouds darkened as they made their short trip back to Harrow on the Hill. The skies opened as they reached the outskirts, dropping a rainfall as reminiscent of November as it was of March. But by the time they passed the school, it had stopped again.

"We have to go back to the stables, anyway," William said after a longing glance at the front lawn.

Charles nodded. "We press on."

They rode through the town, attempting to keep the horses on the high parts of the road, and dismounted at the stable. Neddy had fired up a coal brazier and warmed his hands next to it. Charles and William shook off their hats and pulled off their gloves to warm their own chilled appendages.

"Think it will rain more?" Charles asked, glancing at the sky.

"Not for a while. I can see blue sky again." William rubbed at his reddened eyes with a pale finger.

"Let's go up to St. Mary's Church before we return home," Charles suggested.

"To light a candle for Agnes?"

Not exactly what he had in mind. "Certainly. We can also ask more about possible treasures in the area."

"What do you need to know?"

"Who might have been doing the same thing," Charles explained. "As soon as we light on some local authority who can say, 'Oh yes, young Noah Claypole asked the same question,' or 'That Littlejack Dawkins was by the other day on the same errand,' then we'll know who the murderer was."

William spread his fingers over the fire again. Neddy seemed to be in a snooze against the wall by his brazier, with closed eyes and mouth open. "Yes, I see what you mean. An excellent idea, if it works."

"What do you think happened to the boys?" Charles asked, hoping that, now that he'd shown he still cared about Agnes's death, he could return to the pressing matter of the mudlarks.

William sighed. "We know they went to the circus. Maybe they kept walking toward Sudbury town."

"We can't lose those boys, William," Charles said urgently. "We might as well have left them on the foreshore with Lack at this rate. At least they knew that territory."

"They'll turn up eventually," William said. "After a bit of a lark."

"I wonder if they could have seen the murder," Charles said, reluctantly pulling on his damp gloves. "Come back, then run away again?"

"If they did, we'll know who did it." William's response gave Charles hope that he would allow the search to continue.

In unspoken agreement, they rose, not disturbing the slumbering Neddy, and, after settling the horses, walked out of the barn. True to form, the sky shown blue over the street again. Fast-moving clouds didn't add more moisture to the humid air.

They walked to High Street, then to the top of the hill and St. Mary's, past the Harrow School buildings. The lead-covered spire, a landmark for miles around, guided them, though they walked past the actual ancient church, glowing angel white in the sun.

Behind the church lay the vicar's house, their goal. As they moved toward it, Charles could see down the north slope of the hill, covered in ancient oaks. A pond blinked blue light as the clouds parted farther, dappling the water, and he thought he saw movement around it. Though too early for the deer to foal, it could have been squirrels or field mice.

William marched up to the elegant stone house and rapped sharply on the door. Charles trailed behind, rather out of sorts. The door opened after only a few seconds.

Chapter 7

"Mr. Aga," said an elderly lady, her cheeks wrinkling into a smile. "I haven't seen you in months. Come in, come in!"

Charles followed William into the stone house. "I hoped we could see the vicar," William told the housekeeper. "Is he available?"

The cleric walked down the narrow front staircase, walking stick in hand. Charles recognized him from the school. "What brings you by, William? More about your cousin's final resting place?"

William flinched. "No, we're trying to sort out this business of her treasure map, with the thought that it might lead to her murderer. I understand there was a pagan temple here."

The vicar breathed loudly through his nose. "Ever the eccentrics, your family. I have to go to a bedside right now, and I don't really bother with these things, but my curate may have time for you. Mrs. Temple, why don't you take them up to my study? Mr. Wynd is there." He looked at William expectantly.

"A perfect solution. Thank you," William said. "I hope no one else is dying?"

"Someone always is, even in a village this size," the vicar said. "Don't hold my dinner, Mrs. Temple. This looks to be a long night."

He settled a muffler around his neck and went out as the elderly woman fussed at him. Then she turned back and smiled at Charles and William again. "Shall we go up?"

A couple of minutes later, they were ushered into a dark-paneled room on the first floor. The scent of cigar smoke hit Charles's nose as they entered, though nothing currently burned. He saw the vicar's imposing desk, over which a carved and painted cross, very detailed in its depiction of Christ's final agony, held pride of place. The curate sat behind a writing desk placed sideways under a window.

Charles recognized the eyebrows, which were so wildly tangled as to make the rest of the curate's features unimportant. The extreme baldness of his relatively youthful head explained why his hat had been tightly pulled down on the day they had met.

"More concerns about your cousin?" the curate asked, without rising or even setting down his pen.

"We have a number of questions," Charles said. "If we can have a few minutes of your time."

One of the curate's thumbs stroked against the grain of his eyebrow. "Who are you again?"

Charles took a chair from by the fireplace and placed it next to the writing desk. "Charles Dickens. The charity I share with Mr. Aga here supports three of the students at the school."

"What concerns do you have about Miss Aga?" the curate asked, setting down his pen and crossing his arms over his narrow chest.

Charles, feeling the man was being rude, chose to be blunt. "Why were you on the school grounds the day of the murder?"

"Oh that," the curate said testily. "I was checking red squirrel nests for deposits of hazelnuts. The nasty little beasts store them away."

"Did you have any luck?" Charles sat.

"I found a couple of nests, yes. Mrs. Temple made a lovely batch of hazelnut scones with them." He licked his lips.

"What about Miss Aga?"

The curate's nose wrinkled. "I didn't see her that day."

"When had you seen her last?" William asked, taking a seat on the nearest sofa and angling toward the curate. "Had you heard about the treasure map?"

"No." The curate's irritated expression cleared. "I'm from Roxeth, down the hill. My father managed the brickworks."

"We've asked around for lore about possible treasures that the map might lead to. Has anyone other than us been asking questions?" Charles asked.

"Interesting question, but no," Mr. Wynd said.

"Have you heard about anything connected to the church? It was a pagan site, correct?" William added.

He perked up. "Oh yes. There is documentation of a temple here in the seven hundreds, though surely it had been in the vicinity long before that. The original church was consecrated in ten ninety-four. We believe this current building is on ancient priests' land from an even earlier time."

"A great amount of history in these walls, then."

"In the land, at any rate," the curate agreed. "Is that what you think? That the map led here?"

"Or to something King Charles I left behind from his journey through these parts."

"On Grove Hill?" Skepticism showed in the curate's furrowed brow.

"Is that where the well is?" Charles asked.

"The well he watered his horse at, yes. But we have lots of wells. There was one here on the hill, dug by the Saxons in the five hundreds, it is said."

"How about burial sites? Ancient kings?" William suggested.

The curate spread his hands. "I don't have much of an interest in nature, except as a food source."

"Archeology is what we're after, I suppose. Know anyone who is an amateur digger?" Charles asked.

"No. The prominent families in the area, those who might have the leisure and family history for that sort of thing, have been superseded by the schools around here. I don't know of anyone."

"What about treasure hunters? Any of those around?" Charles inquired.

"Like grave robbers? No, we haven't had any of that body-snatching nonsense around here."

"Very well. If you think of anything suspicious, please let us know," William said.

"You've had plenty of time to think over that afternoon," Charles added. "Before you saw us, have you recalled anything else that happened? Anyone you passed in the woods? Any impression?"

The curate fixed him with a steady gaze. "No, nothing."

"Very well, then." Charles rose. He had little confidence in the man, but he knew when an interview had finished. "Thank you for your time."

The curate let them leave without the small courtesy of showing them to the study door or downstairs. William led the way out of the house.

"We might have been better to interview the housekeeper."

Irritation gnarled Charles's thoughts. "Is there any point in touring the well?"

"We need the map, nothing else," William said. "Let's get back to the school. I'm hungry."

They walked down the hill, sped along by the wind, both lost in sobering thoughts. Two days had passed, and Charles still had no idea who had murdered Agnes, not even a theory, really, or knowledge of where the mudlarks were. If they hadn't gone to work at the circus, there was no reason to think they would return when the circus packed up for its next town.

As the Aga Academy buildings came into sight, William said, "If we knew what was on the map, we could catch up with the murderer on the trail."

"But we don't know what is on the map, so we need to search the hard way." Charles dodged around a cart parked at the side of the road.

"Okay then." William slid his hands under his tailcoat and stretched his back as they reached the edge of the school property. "Treasure is money. Who needed it?"

"Your father must have, since he took on a business partner."

"That problem is solved, therefore," William said easily.

Charles picked a stray branch out of the hedge that Littlejack Dawkins had trimmed the day of the murder. "Any of the students might have felt the need for pocket money. Except the parlor boarder."

"He's out of it, anyway, with that broken arm. The mudlarks had already vanished."

"Yes, I don't think it was them. Those three are the softer lads. John and Arthur wanted to get away from Lack when he started his reign of terror on the Thames foreshore, ending their comfortable work under Lucy Fair."

"I agree. They are good lads at heart. You seemed concerned about Mrs. Bedwin."

"She found the body. The person who claims to find a body is often the murderer, and the reason they are usually taken to jail."

"Agnes could have threatened to tell my father about this affair Mrs. Bedwin is supposedly having." William's nostrils flared with distaste.

"It sounds like an open secret," Charles protested. "But I agree that your cousin sounds like a girl who would act before she thought. Maybe something happened that morning specifically that led to her death?"

"Is there any other reason Agnes might have been killed?" William mused.

"I think Barney Wynd was lying about something," Charles said.

"I agree." William adjusted his hat as a splatter of rain dropped between them.

Charles squinted at the sky. He still saw blue among white clouds with only a little gray in them. "Returning to an earlier point in the discussion. Shortly after Mr. Sikes came into the enterprise, Agnes died. Are you sure he's a good man?"

William shrugged. "My father has known him forever. No hint of scandal at the workhouse. No sign of dastardly secrets."

"Or a penchant for young girls?"

"No, not that I've ever heard." William leaned toward Charles's ear. "I think we need to keep a close eye on the students."

"And Mrs. Bedwin," Charles agreed. "What about the gardener? In a place like this, there are many suspects."

"I hope we can figure out the puzzle quickly. I don't want my father to have any further threats to his livelihood." William tightened his jaw and marched up the front steps of the school.

As soon as they entered the front hall, they saw Mrs. Bedwin bustling toward them. "Letters came for you gentlemen."

"The mail coach must have come and gone," Charles said, taking his. "Thank you. I hope my article will be to Mr. Hogarth's satisfaction."

William chuckled. "I'm sure it will. He is one of your biggest literary supporters, even if other aspects of your personality don't always make him happy."

Charles set his hat on a step, then leaned against the newel post. "I'm a different generation. Here, there is a letter from Kate."

William took his own correspondence from the housekeeper. After she walked back toward the kitchen, Charles sighed loudly after he read Kate's letter. Nothing but irritation today, it seemed.

"What's wrong?"

"I'd better write back immediately and run the letter down to the inn."

"Oh?"

Charles stared at the letter. "Our Fred has lost his job."

"He's young. Not quite responsible yet?"

"Sounds like clumsiness that did it. Poor penmanship."

"What will you do?"

"I'll tell her to send Fred to Mr. Screws. He's claiming he wants to be a man of business instead of a lawyer."

"That's a good idea."

Charles sat down on a stair tread and put his head in his hands, forcing himself to think. The application of a hot cup of tea would help, but he did have one thought. "What if we ask Julie to send Lucy Fair here to help find the mudlarks?"

William tilted his head. "She was their gang leader until a few months ago."

"Exactly. She would know how they think. If we have to stay at the school to watch over all the suspects here, we can't wander the county, trying to find the boys."

"You're right." William made a fist and thrust it into his other palm. "I'll write my wife, and you write your fiancée. Different post offices, so who knows who will get our missive first?"

"Do we need to send anything else to the *Chronicle*?"

"I haven't had the time to write anything more. I'll have to check in at the quarry again. We don't have any further update on the inquest."

"We aren't going to be able to stay here much longer if there is nothing newsworthy."

William nodded. "Then it's time to make every second count. When we go to the inn, let's ask if there are any political meetings happening around here. That might buy us a day."

On Friday morning, Charles woke in his comfortably warm borrowed bed with the bitter taste of hops and cigars in his mouth. He had found a political meeting to attend in the hopes of getting an article out of it, and it had gone much too late, thanks to the free ale and tobacco. He stumbled to the scarred writing desk in his room and forced his eyes to open enough to translate his notes, then quickly wrote an article about the conversation regarding the restrictions of the Poor Laws.

After that, he folded it up and went downstairs to the dining room. William and his father sat in silence, bowls of oatmeal mostly untouched in front of them.

"Good morning," Charles said in a suitably somber tone. "I need to head to the inn to make sure my article goes in the mail coach."

William offered a tight-lipped smile. "Good idea. After, I was thinking we ought to go out to the farm and talk to my uncle."

"Why?" his father asked.

"He might know something we don't. Like the origin of that treasure map."

"You can't think that is what the murderer wanted," his father said, setting down his unused spoon. "Her skirt was, err, not where it should have been."

Charles poured a cup of tea and sat opposite Mr. Aga. "What do you think happened?"

The schoolmaster's cheeks flushed a sickly peach. "Some vagrant came across her in the woods. When he was, err, finished, he tossed her in the icehouse to hide the evidence of his evil deed."

"Everyone in our society wants to blame vagrants or servants for everything that goes bad," Charles said. "But in my experience, truth is usually found much closer to home. If it is poison, it is a woman in your life. If it is violence, then it is a man, likely someone under your very nose. Besides, someone was able to access the locked icehouse."

Mr. Aga pulled off his spectacles and rubbed the bridge of his nose. "I know you have gained some experience with these things, but the alternative is to blame one of these boys I am responsible for. How can I think one of these tender youths killed my own niece, our spirited Agnes?"

"Was she especially close to anyone?" William asked.

"No. We wouldn't have allowed much familiarity."

"Mrs. Bedwin seems a distractable sort," Charles suggested.

"I took her on when her husband died," Mr. Aga confided. "It's the responsibility of the community to take care of such women, widowed and childless. She knew how to run a home and did it well. Her husband was involved in a bank. But I fear she is more interested in her next husband than in her work. She announced her engagement to me last night."

"To whom?" William frowned.

"One of the masters." Mr. Aga forced a weak smile. "It seems I am to lose a teacher as well as a housekeeper."

"You won't keep them on?"

"No. His father is ailing, and he has a farm to manage for the Earl of Northumberland. The master will take over from his father. Our Mrs. Bedwin has done well for herself, given that I happen to know she's half a decade older than her betrothed."

"He doesn't know that?" Charles asked.

His smile grew feral. "I'm not about to tell him."

Charles considered what this new information might mean as he spooned oatmeal into a bowl. Mrs. Bedwin might not be entirely honest, but she was leaving her kingdom here. Was there any way in which a servant's death might smooth her path? Surely her swain wasn't also involved with Agnes Aga. It seemed terribly unlikely. What if Agnes knew the secret of Mrs. Bedwin's age? While he didn't want to spread the truth about, it was something to consider if nothing else bore fruit.

Twenty minutes later, they went to the inn so Charles could send on his article, discussing the Bedwin matter the entire way. Afterward, they rented horses again and rode to the dairy farm, which was on a side road southwest of the circus grounds. Charles kept an eye out for signs of vagrants and rough living, in the hopes he'd find someone to question about the mudlarks, but he saw nothing in the early March chill.

"Here we are," William said, pointing to a sign that said AGA DAIRY. He turned his hack onto a wide dirt road and led Charles down a hill onto a farm property.

Charles saw bluebells and Queen Anne's lace on one side of the road, a patch of snowdrops on the other. Bright yellow daffodils signaled that spring was on its way, giving hope to a day marred by yet another conversation about death. The sun had not appeared from behind the clouds yet, but they'd completed their ride without suffering through more rain.

William rode past the cottage. The windows were dark, and no smoke puffed from the chimneys. He dismounted in front of a small barn. The larger barn took pride of place, freshly painted, with doors open to the world. Charles could see rows of cows. It was hours past milking time, but men were inside tending to the stalls while the cows ate in the pasture behind.

"Is Uncle George inside?" William asked, calling to the first man he saw, while Charles took the reins of both hacks and led them into the smaller barn.

He found stalls for them and settled them in, explaining to the stable boy that he would be back for the horses in an hour or two.

"He's out in a field," William reported when Charles found him. "He grows feed here, as well."

"Should I retrieve the horses?"

"No, we can walk out. We wore our boots."

Charles adjusted his coat and thrust his hands into the pockets, then trudged behind William through the damp muck of the barnyard. Luckily, George Aga wasn't too far into the field. Instead, he was consulting with an older man at the edge of fresh plow marks. Charles was impressed that he had the fortitude to continue his daily labors despite his troubles, but he supposed the work of a farm couldn't ever stop.

They waited patiently until he had finished his consultation. When he turned, he saw them waiting and came toward them, unsmiling. Though William had told Charles that his uncle was a couple of years younger than his schoolmaster brother, their appearance made them seem the opposite. The work of a farmer had carved the flesh off his body, giving him the appearance of bony bird legs, especially since his legs were out of proportion to his torso.

"Nephew," George Aga greeted them. "What brings you by? We deliver to the school, you know."

"We just wanted to speak to you, Uncle George. This is Charles Dickens, who works in London with me."

William's uncle inclined his head. "Pleased to meet you."

"The same," Charles said. "We have some small experience in, err, resolving situations for grieving families. We hope to do the same for you."

He stiffened slightly. "Oh, is that what this is about? Young Agnes?"

William nodded. "When did you see her last? She seems to have gone missing after breakfast on Tuesday. We know she went to her room, and then she disappeared."

"I don't know nothing about that," Uncle George stated. "I

saw Agnes only at church on Sundays. Sunday is when I saw her last."

"You didn't like to come to the school?" Charles asked. "With both of your children there?"

"I'm a busy man, and I don't do our deliveries." The older man stared at Charles, hard, as if assessing what was worth sharing. "Besides, Mr. Sikes didn't see the need to give Agnes time off, believing she would merely get into trouble."

"She's your brother's niece. Didn't he get a say?" Charles asked.

Uncle George wiped his nose with his coat sleeve. "Sikes is a harsh taskmaster. Don't imagine he treats Brother any better. Everyone is afraid of the workhouse."

"Of course everyone should be afraid of the workhouse," Charles said. "I hear all sorts of dreadful stories when I'm covering meetings on the subject. Is the workhouse here worse than average?"

"Don't know," came the laconic reply. "Haven't been anywhere else."

"How would you describe your daughter?" Charles asked gently.

"Headstrong," Uncle George said promptly. "Didn't like to mind me. Thought she'd do better with a woman's hand."

"Mrs. Bedwin, you mean?"

He nodded. "Who else? I ain't got a wife or a housekeeper. She were a danger around here. Farm equipment can get you hurt real bad. I thought the school was safer. The boy's done well enough out of it."

Charles could see the picture developing of an impetuous, reckless young girl. No wonder her father had persuaded his brother to employ her, with the hope of a familial eye over her workplace and a woman's touch to guide her. "There was no hope of her safely becoming a dairymaid? You must employ some women here."

"If she stayed here, the best to hope for was her marrying some farmhand. I always thought she might pick up a bit of learning at the school, not too much for a woman, mind, but something. Meet a different sort of young man. With her being the master's niece and all." The farmer kicked a dirt clod.

Charles nodded. "A sensible plan. I am sorry it went so terribly wrong."

Uncle George spat into the greening grass at his feet. "Me too. Don't know what we did to deserve this."

William patted his uncle's shoulder. "Nothing, Uncle. Just the worst sort of bad luck, running into evil. We'll figure out who did it."

His uncle shrugged. "No point in that. Won't bring her back."

"But we'll have justice for her," Charles said. "That is important, too."

"Think she'll sleep any better in her coffin if her killer's been punished? I doubt it," Uncle George said, the shadows under his eyes seeming to deepen.

"We can't know the answer." Charles used his gentlest voice. "All we can do is try."

Kate held Fred by the coat sleeve in front of Mr. Screws's countinghouse that afternoon. In her other hand, she gripped Charles's letter. She'd worn her warmest cloak and bonnet, remembering Charles complain about how tightfisted the man of business was about coal. Despite her fear of the chill, she could see sunbreaks in the sky. The foggy season had passed, and London burned less coal than in previous weeks. A sense of optimism took hold here.

When Mr. Screws had been through his troubles some months before, Charles said he had claimed he would retire and spend the rest of his life in prayer. But he had rallied after a couple of weeks and returned to the office. Since he had not been able to persuade Charles to remain in his employ, he had combined his business with the rival countinghouse one floor up. The sign above the door now read SCREWS AND SOWERBERRY.

Kate had never been inside, though she had passed by before. Fred, next to her, visibly steeled himself before opening the front door and walking in. A sign in the front hall told them that Mr. Screws's office was on the ground floor and Mr. Sowerberry dominated the first. Kate opened the door to the ground-floor office.

A small anteroom held a coat-tree and a tray-sized desk with a stool tucked underneath. The desk was empty, and no one sat at it. Kate peeked through the open door into a much larger room. An old cast-iron stove hulked in one corner. Chests and shelves covered the walls. Three men worked at desks in the center of the room, and she saw three doors in the right wall. A fourth man, better dressed in old but brushed breeches and a bottle-green coat, pointed to something in a ledger.

She couldn't say the space was cozy, but it was warmer than the outdoors.

"Can I help you?" The green-coated man looked up from the ledger with a gentle smile. All of them had a careworn air and wore shawls, hats, and fingerless gloves. They didn't appear unhappy or half-starved, as Charles had described the countinghouse employees back in December. Mr. Screws must have improved their pay and added a bit more coal to the stove's allowance. Mr. Sowerberry's influence?

"Yes. Are you Mr. Cratchit?" she asked uncertainly. "I'm Catherine Hogarth, and this is Frederick Dickens." Fred shifted from side to side next to her.

The man blinked; then his face wreathed in a smile. He walked to them, holding out his hand. First he pumped Fred's hand, then Kate's, then laughed aloud. "What a pleasure to meet you! I know exactly who you are."

"And I, you," Kate said, blushing. "Mr. Dickens told me

how very helpful you were to him when he acted as Mr. Screws's secretary."

"He was very helpful to me," Mr. Cratchit agreed. "Mr. Screws discovered he enjoyed having a secretary and promoted me to the position!"

"Congratulations," Kate exclaimed.

"Yes, it takes me out of doors when he remains at home. A pleasant change. I was able to hire my son as our newest clerk." He indicated the youngest careworn man, who Kate now realized was no more than Mary's age. The contrast between that young shaver's appearance and Fred's rosy cheeks could not be more apparent.

"Oh." Kate saw the disappointment in Fred's eyes.

Fred steeled himself. "I saw you had an empty desk in the other room."

Mr. Cratchit nodded. "We are planning to hire an errand boy to staff it. Mr. Sowerberry's son emigrated to Australia over the holidays, so we're having to adjust."

"Interesting," Kate murmured, wondering how to turn that fact to their advantage.

Chapter 8

Kate heard the thump of a cane behind one of the doors in the countinghouse before it opened. A gray-haired figure in old breeches and a new black tailcoat stomped out, relying heavily on the cane, though his eyes burned with the fire of a much younger man.

"Mr. Screws," Kate exclaimed, happy to see the elderly man looking well, relatively speaking.

The countinghouse owner looked down his nose at her. "I seem to recall you."

"I'm Catherine Hogarth," she said helpfully.

"Ah, I remember young Fred here. You must be the future bride."

"Yes, sir. We met a few months ago. More than once, in fact. I was one of the carolers that horrible night." She was certain he was playacting his dawning look of recognition, for he had the merest twinkle in his eye.

"Horrible night indeed." Mr. Screws fixed his gaze on Mr. Cratchit, who gave a visible shake, then nodded vociferously. "What can I help you with? A loan for the wedding? Has Mr. Dickens been overspending like his father before him?"

"No, no, of course not," Kate assured him. "We're here on behalf of Fred. You have an open position?"

"For an errand boy. That goes to a younger lad, normally."

Fred puffed his chest out. "I'd like to train as an accounts clerk, sir. Would you take me on?"

Kate held her breath as Mr. Screws looked him up and down. She'd always liked the old man, or at least she'd liked him more than Charles did, but they had come to an understanding over time. While Mr. Screws had claimed he would retire after all the shocks around his partner's death, he didn't seem to have done so, and she was not surprised, somehow.

"I suppose, when there are no errands, Mr. Cratchit can train two boys as well as one," Mr. Screws said.

Kate clapped her hands. "How very kind! Did you hear that, Fred?"

He nodded and pumped Mr. Screws's age-spotted hand, then Mr. Cratchit's thin one. "Capital, sir. Thank you very much!"

"I suppose you want to start next week?" Mr. Screws said with a sneer.

"I'll start right now," Fred said, taking up the challenge.

The sneer turned to a smirk. "Very well. Mr. Cratchit will have the making of you."

The new secretary cleared his throat. "I will show you around the office. We still have half a day of work before us."

Mr. Screws regarded Kate. "And what about you, Miss Hogarth? What do you do now?"

"I'm not sure what to do," she confessed.

"Come with me." He raised his voice. "Young Mr. Cratchit can bring you a cup of tea."

He led her into his office, a cheerless place that at least had a window, and offered her one of the chairs. "What is on your mind? A loan for your wedding finery?"

Kate sat and arranged her skirts. "Mr. Dickens has mixed himself up in another murder."

"I haven't read about one in the paper." He lowered his brows. "Of course, I don't take the *Morning Chronicle*."

Kate suddenly remembered the amount of patience that had to be applied in dealings with Mr. Screws. Would it hurt this tightfisted man to take the newspaper? She supposed it had the wrong sort of politics for one old and wealthy. "If you did, you would have seen the notice about a death at Aga Academy in Harrow on the Hill."

"Well, that does not concern me. That is miles from here."

"Yes, but the girl who died was William Aga's niece. He is a dear friend of ours and works at the newspaper with Charles."

"Aga Academy has been in operation for twenty-five years," Mr. Screws said.

Kate wondered about the extent of his knowledge. She knew Mr. Screws had had dealings with the Dickens family, but with the Agas, too? "That long? I am surprised. I thought it was founded by Eustace Aga, William's father. I suppose he must be in his fifties."

"I would not have backed the operation," Mr. Screws said, taking his seat behind his desk. "But yes, I believe he started it upon inheriting some property. Hired older men to be the masters. I have met a couple of the alumni."

That explained his command of the history, she supposed. "Do you remember any of the names? It might help Mr. Dickens."

"James Maylie," Mr. Screws said promptly. "I've given a loan to him. He mentioned his school days fondly."

"What did he need the loan for?"

"Quarry," Mr. Screws said. "Common business in that town. Very profitable."

"A good man?"

"I've no reason to doubt otherwise," he said, planting his hands on his desk and leaning forward. "Now, tell me about this wedding you are still planning. Why have you not brought Dickens to the altar yet?"

*   *   *

Charles and William decided to finish matters with his uncle's family and interview Monks Aga, Agnes's older brother, as soon as they returned to the school. They found the student in a private tutoring session, though the tutor readily agreed to find himself a cup of tea so they could speak to Monks.

Charles took the seat behind the master's desk, and William perched on the desk's edge. The fifteen-year-old didn't display the same marks of grief on his attractive face that his father had. He had a calm, respectful demeanor, however.

"Your cousin William has all the facts," Charles said. "But please walk me through how you and Agnes came to be at the school. How old were you when you came under your uncle's care?"

"I have attended classes here since I was eleven," Monks explained. "But I came to board only last fall."

"Why did you leave the farm? It isn't far." Charles spread his hands over the desk.

"I didn't like having to do chores before school started. I was tired. Agnes was old enough to be trained. My father made a deal with Uncle. Agnes was employed at the school to cover my board."

Charles shifted on the hard seat. "Couldn't she have stayed on the farm and learned that work?"

"It's going to be mine someday," Monks said carelessly. "I won't want my sister to be a dairymaid."

Charles frowned. It would be better to have her as a servant? He could see that Monks saw nothing wrong with the situation. Perhaps it was only his youth and inexperience. He might have wanted his sister nearby, used as he was to seeing her every day.

A bell rang under the floor. Monks jumped up, pulled like a puppet on a string. "That's tea," he said. "May I be excused, Cousin William?"

Charles stared at the back of William's head as he inclined it. His friend needed a haircut.

"Do you miss her?" William asked, as if he'd read Charles's mind.

Monks rubbed the back of his hand under his nose. "She was just a maid. I hardly ever saw her. May I go?"

William gestured at the door without his usual vitality. The boy, on the other hand, sped into a trot and was gone before they could have called him back.

"I hope that was the end of his tutoring session," Charles remarked. "Would they ever run into teatime?"

"Poor Agnes," William said in a low voice when the door had slammed shut. "I think we have our suspect. No feeling whatsoever, and him my own cousin."

Charles cleared his throat. He could do with a spot of tea himself, though bread and butter sounded utterly parsimonious for a grown man. "Isn't it in Monks's best interest for his sister to live?"

William took Monks's chair and rubbed his eyes. "How so?"

"His sister's labor paid for his boarding. Can his father afford to keep him here now? He's lost two workers for his farm in his children, and now school won't be paid for."

"My father can take him as a charity student."

"Who will pay for that? He must have been hard up, to bring in Mr. Sikes."

William licked his lips. "Our charity—"

"Is not for the son of a farmer. We can't take on any more fundraising. We are frequently overstretched as it is."

"Our charity students have vanished." William rubbed the space between his eyes. "You are right, though. We never discussed what to do if we lost our students. Do we keep supporting Arthur's mother and siblings? Their wage earner is still gone."

"Our duty was to the mudlarks," Charles said. "Not that I

want to send any family to the workhouse, but our offer to Arthur's family lasted only as long as the boys were students. I can only hope the family was preparing for this day. We gave them some time."

"The boys were not thinking of their own responsibility when they ran." William stood and paced in front of the desk. "Just like my cousin. To be honest, I think Monks is a bad 'un and unpredictable."

"What?" Startled, Charles stood, as well. "What brings you to that conclusion?"

William paused in his perambulation to face him. "Though I have lived in London for a decade and don't know Monks that well, I've had enough exposure to him to be concerned."

Charles cocked his head. "This concern existed before Agnes's death, then."

William clasped his hands behind his back. "Monks and Agnes grew up basically motherless, since their mother died giving birth to a stillborn child. Their one stepmother lived only a year, and even she has been dead for seven years."

"No softening effect of maternal love, then," Charles said.

"It's far worse than that." William stared at the desk. "It pains me to reveal a family secret, but Monks was removed from the farm to the school for a reason."

"Something happened?"

"More than one something. Many an animal has gone missing over the past five or six years. Agnes had a habit of bringing home strays, taking them into her bedroom instead of leaving them around the barns, but they always disappeared. Sometimes the bodies were found."

"It was assumed that Monks killed them?"

William nodded. "The bodies were tortured."

Charles winced. "Did he do it to hurt Agnes?"

"No one thought he had any particular animus toward his sister. From the earliest days when he could hold a slingshot, he enjoyed knocking birds from trees. He'd stomp on their wings if they were injured. He pulled dogs' tails, was bitten a number of times. He wasn't allowed to milk the cows, because he was so rough."

"This was a lot more than not liking farmwork," Charles observed. "Did he treat people as badly as animals?"

"He didn't form many attachments. He had one friend, a follower, really, but he died four years ago, when the boys were eleven."

"Did Monks kill the boy?" Charles wondered aloud.

"There was no question of that, I believe. Some sort of wasting disease. Bone pain . . ." William's hand went to his chest. "But Monks lost his closest companion. He amused himself by designing mouse and rabbit traps."

"I haven't seen any animals around the school. No mousers prowling."

William winced and resumed his pacing. "I think we need to watch Monks. The boys aren't given much leisure. It's not useful to give them time for mischief. But we had better know his movements."

"To see if he returns to the scene of the crime?" Charles suggested. "As is common?"

"I wish I could see more abnormality in his utter lack of sadness over the death of his sister," William confessed. "That doesn't surprise me at all, given his age. But is he responsible?"

"We can search for another icehouse key. Also, we need that treasure map," Charles reminded his friend. "If we find Monks on the trail, then we have nothing left to question."

Fred's last act as a free man was to call a hackney cab for Kate before he put himself under Mr. Cratchit's tutelage. Kate felt very bold when she took the risk of riding alone to Cheapside. Thankfully, she didn't think her parents would see Fred anytime soon and learn that she'd been in London on her own.

She kept herself very upright in the seat and out of the view of the windows. Between that and her bonnet, she saw nothing of the city herself, but it couldn't be helped. Julie Aga would never trouble with being so respectable, but she'd lived an unconventional life. It troubled Kate's parents when she spent time in Julie's company. Everyone knew she'd briefly had feelings for Charles.

Unlike her parents, though, Kate knew Julie loved William, and while she might flirt with Charles, she valued her marriage and her coming child.

The cab let her out across the street from St. Mary-le-Bow Church in Cheapside. The Agas' building had a chophouse on the ground floor, then three floors of apartments, and a half attic on top. Though a step up from Furnival's Inn's dark bachelor rooms, Charles had his heart set on a house once he could afford the rent, so they wouldn't be moving here.

She went up the steps to the rooms above the chophouse, her stomach grumbling at the smell of high-quality roasting meat. Heat did not rise with the smell, and she knocked on the Agas' door with her hands still in her muff.

The door opened promptly, and a pointed-chin face poked out, looking wild eyed.

"Hello, Lucy," Kate said. "I've come to see Mrs. Aga."

Lucy Fair, the maid of all work in training, had been a mudlark in her previous career. Charles and William had begun to worry about her fate, despite not having recognized the saintly beauty of the girl until she'd bathed. They guessed her to be fourteen already once they'd had the dirt and baggy rags off her.

Lucy opened her mouth to speak, but her lips trembled, and no sound came out.

"I have no word about the boys, I'm afraid," Kate said gently.

"'Ow could they?" Lucy said after working her mouth. "A free education thrown away?"

"We don't know what happened," Kate said. "But it's very

cold in the passage. Would you let me in, please? Mrs. Aga doesn't need bad air drifting in."

Lucy stepped back, then slammed the door as soon as Kate was in. She clutched at her skirts to make sure they had survived the violence of the moment. Lucy stared at her.

"Will you announce me, please?" Kate said gently. "Mrs. Aga might not be receiving." She knew it was likely that Julie could hear every word, since the entrance hall was nothing more than a space with a boot bench, off the parlor.

"Mrs. Aga," Lucy called from the hall into the parlor, pronouncing the names very carefully. "Miss Hogarth to see you."

"Come in," Julie offered.

Kate stepped past Lucy into the parlor. Julie, round with pregnancy, sat in a giltwood chair in front of the fire, her feet kicked up on the decorative grate. Since Kate had been here last, a number of watercolors had been framed and placed on the walls, not much improved from the previous handpainted display. Julie had been taking lessons with her aunt and had yet to attain proficiency.

The decorations were very fine, with a focus on painted wood. Like William, Kate's fiancé liked the rich sheen of good wood and had been buying the best furnishings he could find at secondhand shops, preparing for their marriage. Their rooms would be more elegant than Julie's cozy abode and probably less expensive. She did hope he would purchase a cunning little game table like the Agas had, though.

Kate noted that Julie had remained undressed, despite the time of day. She wore a dressing gown, and her fiery red hair flowed everywhere, like that of a drowned Ophelia.

"You've caught me recovering from my bath," Julie said. "Bring another cup, would you, Lucy?"

Lucy bobbed and dashed off.

"She's terribly upset at the news of her missing mudlark friends," Julie confided as Kate took the opposite gilt armchair.

"It's best to keep her busy. Washing and drying my hair is quite the chore."

"It's very thick," Kate agreed. "It's kind of you to think of Lucy."

"I try to keep enough distance to train her properly," Julie said with a sigh. "But it's just the two of us much of the time."

"And, of course, you know the boys, too."

Julie nodded. "What do you think has happened?"

"Nothing good. I'm glad they were well away before the murder."

"I've never heard about any scandal at Aga Academy." Julie frowned. "Both circumstances must be connected."

"What about this partnership? Charles wrote that Mr. Aga had a partner now. Were you aware? Is that connected, as well?"

"We knew about Mr. Sikes, though I've never met him. However, he's a leading citizen of the town." Julie shrugged. "Is Charles suspicious of him?"

Kate bristled at Julie's familiar use of Charles's name, but the ex-actress did not bother to follow convention. Really, Kate despaired of Lucy's future prospects with anything but an unconventional family. Hopefully, Lucy would stay with the Agas for many years. "I don't know, but he thought enough of the new regime to mention it."

Julie shifted in her chair as Lucy brought Kate a matching black transferware cup. She admired the scene of a couple walking toward a manor house. "Charles would like to own a house like the one on this someday."

Julie drained her cup noisily and looked at the design. "I would prefer to have our own carriage first."

"That would be nice," Kate agreed with a chuckle, then glanced at the teapot on the table between them.

Julie touched her hair and made a face. "It will take all afternoon to dry, and me with no husband ready to appreciate all this glory."

Kate blushed, but Julie plowed on, not noticing. "When have our men ever solved one of their mysteries entirely without our guidance?"

"Never," Lucy said stoutly, as if she were part of the conversation and not the maid.

"I believe we should hie to Harrow on the Hill." Julie grinned. "'Despising, for you, the city, thus I turn my back. There is a world elsewhere.'"

"What are you quoting?" Kate asked.

"The Bard, of course." Julie leaned over her belly. "Listen, Kate. You are marrying Charles next month, and while it isn't completely inappropriate for you to make the trip, you have a chaperone in me. Lucy too."

"If he's gone much longer, it will impact the wedding." Kate had to admit her frustration. She loved a mystery, and here was one, the tragic death of a young girl connected to Charles's dear companion, and yet she was stewing some twenty miles away. "However, you should remain safely at home."

"Never," Julie declared. "I have some four months yet with this belly. I am carrying forward, you see."

Kate's cheeks went hot again. "Really, Julie. I am not married yet."

"By the time this baby is in the world, you shall be in the same condition yourself," the actress pronounced. "Mark my words."

"Good heavens." Kate stared at the manor house on her teacup again, trying not to think of the reality of that prediction. Not surprisingly, neither Lucy nor Julie had thought to offer to fill the cup.

"Very well." Julie set her cup on the tray and hoisted herself to her feet. "Help yourself to a hot drink while Lucy helps me dress. We will take a hackney to Brompton to see your mother and then borrow my aunt's carriage for the last ten miles of the journey."

Charles and William walked back to Mr. Aga's house for dinner that night after a fruitless series of chats with the school's staff, hoping to learn if Agnes had a hiding place somewhere on the grounds. They had made a quick search of Monks's shared room, and no key had been found. No one had any ideas, and frustration ran high as they walked into the dining room. Surprisingly, they found Eustace Aga just sitting down next to his brother.

"Hello again, Uncle. Father." William greeted them, taking a seat, as if tension and sorrow didn't hang like a red kite over the proceedings.

"Mr. Aga," Charles said, nodding at both. "I hope we aren't interrupting."

"No, no," the schoolmaster said with a forced smile. "We expected you both. Was your day productive?"

"Not terribly," Charles admitted as William poured wine into their glasses from a decanter. "We did speak to Monks to see what he might know."

"He told us about the financial arrangement," William broke in.

His father nodded. "In the past I took payment in milk from Brother's dairy, but when he asked me to remove Agnes from the farm, we took her labors in payment instead."

"Had something happened?" William asked.

"She didn't like farm life," Eustace Aga said laconically. "Thought there was something better out in the world. I didn't know a better place for her."

Mr. Aga's cook came in with the food. Charles cleaned his plate of its lamb, cabbage, and potatoes in minutes. When the men rose, he and William declined the offer of port in the study and went for a walk instead.

When they were outside, Charles tapped William's arm. "That was a very important conversation."

"How so?" William asked, adjusting his hat against the light rain.

"I now realize Monks didn't have the need to keep Agnes alive that I'd expected. Your father seems to have been perfectly willing to take another nonmonetary form of payment. Therefore, Monks is still a suspect in his sister's death."

"I am sorry to be vindicated," William said. "I would prefer my own family to be above suspicion, but I do not see how that is possible."

"I am all the sorrier for it." Charles stared at the darkened sky. The clouds were moving fast enough that stars still peeked out here and there. "I hope tomorrow brings solutions for all of you."

"Tomorrow is Saturday. What is our first point of investigation?"

"We need to keep looking for the map. One of the kitchen girls mentioned a friend of Agnes's up the hill. We'll call on her first. She might have the answers we need."

Chapter 9

The next morning, Charles and William went to a newer row of terraced houses in the upper town and inquired of the stout, dark-skinned maid at the door if Mrs. Maylie and her daughter would receive them.

The maid left them in a small front hall. Charles took one look at the dizzy-making black-and-white pattern of the tiled floor and closed his eyes. He suspected he'd not slumbered sufficiently.

When he heard footsteps again, he opened his eyes and saw William looked a little green himself.

"Was the sausage bad?" William whispered.

"I think it's the floor," Charles said.

The parlormaid returned and bobbed in their direction. "Mrs. Maylie will receive you in the parlor. If you will follow me."

Charles cleared his throat. "We particularly wanted to see Miss Myrtle Maylie, if that is possible. Agnes Aga is Mr. Aga's cousin, and we understand the young miss was her closest friend in town."

"If you'll follow me," the maid said again and walked across the floor.

Charles noticed the sharp-cheekboned maid didn't glance at the dizzying front hall tiles, either. He and William followed her into the parlor, which had decor more extravagant than the typical stained wood floor and a few rag rugs. She lit the fire, then departed.

"I doubt Mrs. Maylie will know about the treasure map," William said grumpily.

"We'll clear it up. Just employ your usual winning ways with the lady. I already feel better, just being away from that floor."

William shook his head, then winced. "I haven't recovered yet."

They sat in silence. Charles rubbed his gloved hands together periodically until the fire caught. William endured in obvious discomfort.

Ten minutes later, a lady entered the room, followed by a girl in the late stages of childhood. Their familial relationship made itself known in wide-spaced eyes and identically fluffy bird's-nest hair. They both wore serviceable navy gowns without adornment. Mrs. Maylie's gown looked new, and the girl's had probably been cut down from an older gown of her mother's. The top of the girl's head didn't reach much past her mother's chin.

The men rose. As Mrs. Maylie introduced herself, Myrtle lifted her face and stared directly at Charles. She gave him a saucy smirk. Now he believed she was a friend of the wayward Agnes.

As soon as the Maylie ladies had cleared the doorway, the maid returned with a tea tray. The ladies sat on the sleigh sofa, and their guests took the unmatched but highly fashionable pointed arch–backed armchairs. All three pieces were upholstered in the same cream fabric with a small red flower decoration. The maid placed the silver-plated tray on a fragile cabriole-legged table in front of the sofa.

Mrs. Maylie poured tea serenely, while William forced a smile and explained their mission.

"I've always liked your father," Mrs. Maylie said. "Mr. Maylie would never have the patience to run a school. His rough crew at the quarry tries his patience enough as it is."

Myrtle giggled at her mother's side and took a cup of milk laced with an ounce of tea.

"How did you come to know Agnes?" Charles asked. "I assume she would have been busy at the farm until she came to work at the school."

"Church," Myrtle said. "We've walked in the graveyard after services since we were little girls. I've always known her."

Mrs. Maylie patted her daughter's hand. "Such a tragedy. So sudden."

"Have you any notion at all of what might have happened?" William asked, staring into his teacup.

"You know as well as I that she was a lively girl, but not a lick of malice in her." Mrs. Maylie shuddered. Her tea sloshed and dribbled down over the side into the saucer. She set it down with a clatter. "You can see we are not quite ourselves just yet."

"Of course," Charles said soothingly. "You know of nothing that happened in the days leading to the tragedy?"

"We saw her only on Sundays," Myrtle said uncertainly.

Charles suspected she wasn't telling the truth.

"Some vagrant," Mrs. Maylie insisted. "There are woods behind the school, you understand. Someone living rough perhaps came upon her at the icehouse."

"I understand Mrs. Bedwin doesn't feel it is safe to have anyone out there but herself," William commented.

"And now we see why. She's not the most sensible of women, but she has a good heart," Mrs. Maylie agreed.

"What of Agnes? What was her character?" Charles asked.

"She had a mischievous streak," Myrtle announced.

"How so?" Charles asked before her mother could intervene.

"She managed to find plenty of time for herself one way or another," Myrtle said with a little smirk. She bent her head to her tea.

What a sly little thing. Charles glanced at William, who still looked unwell. "When she was at the school? Or at the farm?"

"Mr. Aga was much too busy to supervise his niece, and none of the other servants had control over her," Myrtle announced.

"Not even Mrs. Bedwin?" Charles asked.

Myrtle rolled her eyes.

"Clearly not," William murmured, then set down his tea saucer, his tea untouched. "May I?" He pointed to the small plate of shortbread biscuits.

"Of course." Mrs. Maylie lifted the plate. "I'm sorry I didn't offer them. My nerves, you see. I'm terrified."

"You think this vagrant you suspect will attack the ladies in town next?" Charles asked blandly.

She put her hand to her mouth. "Who can say?"

Charles nodded and pasted a pleasant expression on his face. If the girl had had no real supervision, any of the numerous disasters that could ruin young women might have occurred, especially in a school full of males. Something had been bound to transpire, if not her death. "Miss Maylie, were you acquainted with Ollie, John, and Arthur? Boys at the school."

"The London boys," Myrtle said. "I've seen them at church. Agnes said they were treasure hunters before."

"In a way," Charles agreed. "We understand she rather boldly flashed around a treasure map herself."

"It was those boys that reminded her," Myrtle revealed. "Yes, she said John liked to boast about the jewelry he found on the Thames, and she thought, Why not find a little treasure for herself?"

"Where did the map come from?" William rasped.

Myrtle lifted her hands slightly. "I don't know, but I saw it once."

Charles was startled enough to spill a little tea on himself. "She showed it to you? Did she bring it to church?"

Myrtle glanced at her mother. The sly look was back. "We had a place we met in the afternoons sometimes."

"Where was that?" her mother asked sharply.

"Just a field, Mother. In between here and the school. She'd get away before tea, and I'd be taking my walk with Luysa. We'd take a few turns around the field before she went back to serve."

Mrs. Maylie relaxed. "I'll have a word with Luysa later. Agnes was very naughty to leave her duties like that."

"Did she run off at other times of day?" Charles inquired. "We know she went to her room after the servants' breakfast, then was never seen again."

"I saw her only in the afternoons, sir," Myrtle said.

"Do you know if she had a secret way of leaving her chamber?" he asked.

William nodded at the sensible question. Unfortunately, the girl only looked confused.

"She went to her room," Charles expanded. "We've found the proof of that, a stained apron. She was known to have dropped oatmeal on herself. But no one saw her come downstairs again, even though she was eventually found out of the school, as you know."

Mrs. Maylie's face went pale, and she swallowed hard. She squeezed her daughter's hand. "Please tell these gentlemen what you know. We must help them sort out this tragedy."

"I was never in her room, Mother. I don't know anything about the school."

"Of course not." Mrs. Maylie patted her hand. "Well, gentlemen. I don't know what else we can do to help you. We will pray for your success. I would comb the woods for unsavory individuals if I was you."

"Very useful, ma'am," William said.

Charles shook his head at William, who ceased his summing-up. Myrtle had licked her lips, and he had a feeling she was about to offer something useful.

The girl's eyes brightened, just as he had suspected. She sat up a little straighter. "I remember the first point on the map! That isn't revealing a confidence, is it, Mother?"

"Not if it will help these gentlemen," her mother said.

"Please tell us," Charles urged. "It is possible that the villain is following the map as we speak."

Myrtle clasped her hands together. Her tongue appeared to lick the corner of her mouth, then disappeared again. "There is a spot in the woods where an old chimney from a vanished house still stands, and the trees have grown so densely around it that they've formed a protective spot, which has been used for many a romantic liaison."

Mrs. Maylie's eyes went wide. "Myrtle!"

"I'm sorry, Mother, but it's true. Agnes said—"

"I don't want to hear what Agnes said," her mother insisted.

"But we do," William said gently. "It could be that this murderous tramp made camp in the ruined foundations."

"Indeed," Charles added. "Agnes could have come upon someone."

"Who then plotted to kill her later, before she could tell anyone," William said, then looked quizzical.

"Well," Charles said hastily, "the tale needs refining, to be sure, but it is an excellent clue. It also tells us that the map really does exist."

"It does," Myrtle assured them. "Agnes said it would be the making of her."

"Rather the unmaking," Charles murmured in a low voice.

*   *   *

Lady Lugoson had a very good carriage, yet the bumps of the road were still trying Kate's nerves when they turned off a main road into a coach yard early Saturday afternoon. The early March day had warmed as much as the late winter sun made possible, but the wind was enough to turn their bonnets into kites as the trio were helped down into an innyard, if the bonnets were less securely fastened.

Julie supervised the collection of their carpetbags, quickly packed, as Kate surveyed the area. She couldn't see much, as the road was on a slope extending up and down a hill.

"Where is the school?" she asked Lucy.

Lucy held on to her bonnet and pointed south. "Down the hill. It will be hard to walk in this wind."

"Maybe we can find a cab or a cart." Kate walked over to a yardman and shyly addressed him, then made arrangements.

"What are you doing?" Julie asked, following her.

Kate grabbed for her bonnet on both sides as a gust went past her, rustling her skirts alarmingly. "We can't walk in this wind."

"It isn't far at all," Julie said, just before a gust hit her and set her cape whirling around her. A yard boy walking by fixed his eyes on her belly, his mouth going round. She grabbed at the fur-lined wool and clutched it to her. "Very well. Heavens, I think we've arrived in a storm."

They were ushered into the inn while a horse was harnessed to a cart. About fifteen minutes later they were on their way, their bags in the back along with Lucy.

Kate looked with interest at the buildings as they passed. They mostly seemed to be part of a venerable school. As they traveled farther south, they reached a residential area. She saw a familiar figure, walking the same way as they were headed, in a very nice felted beaver top hat cut in the Regent style. Dark curls tousled in the wind. Next to him, a taller figure, in a similar hat, with lighter, closer-cropped hair, provided accompaniment.

"Mr. Dickens," she called, her heart going light for the first time in days. "Charles!"

"William!" Julie shrieked, then laughed. "Husband!"

The cart pulled alongside the men. "Hold up," Kate ordered.

The men turned as the driver called to the horse. Kate saw the very gratifying light go on in Charles's eyes as he recognized her.

"Miss Hogarth?" he called, his expressive mouth breaking into a smile. "Whatever are you doing here?"

William reached up to Julie, clasped her hand warmly, then kissed it. "What are you up to, my girl?"

Julie laughed. "Climb into the back. Come along."

Charles gave Kate a wink and hied himself into the cart. She heard the faint words of the men greeting Lucy as the driver clucked to his horse again. Julie clutched Kate's hand as they began to descend the slope.

"They had better not be mad at us," she hissed in Kate's ear. "The boys have been missing for days, and we have to find them."

"They must be on a lark," Kate said, resurrecting her part of the same argument from the coach journey. She still couldn't believe her mother had let her come, but Julie's cries of "Life and death!" had put her into quite a tizzy, until the kitchen maid had needed to pull out the smelling salts. They'd less been authorized to go than waved away.

A few minutes later, the cart pulled off the road in front of a much more modest set of buildings in a more modern style than that of the upper town. Kate noted the grounds were well kept, with freshly trimmed hedges.

As the driver helped first Julie, then Kate down, she could hear Lucy demanding to know what was being done to find her young dear ones.

Julie marched to the back of the cart to berate her maid. "Lucy, you haven't even offered your condolences. Mr. Aga just lost his cousin."

Lucy's chin wobbled; then she straightened her back. "The dead are dead, but my friends must be found."

Julie seemed to have lost a little of her certainty. Kate patted her arm. "We're here to help," Kate said. "The men have their priorities, and we shall have ours. All will be resolved."

Charles jumped down from the cart, brushing straw from his trousers. "You couldn't miss the mystery, darling?" Gladness lifted her heart as he took her hand, a little more easily than he might have in town.

"You have a wedding to get to, Mr. Dickens. I'm merely try-ing to speed up the proceedings."

He chuckled. "Let's take all of you into Mr. Aga's house so you can settle yourself. I believe there will have to be some re-arranging of the, er, chambers."

"Very good," Kate said with a blush.

"Ahem." Julie cleared her throat. "Not to be insensitive, but Lucy is right. The boys need to be found."

"We agree with you, my dear," William said, "and we have been searching as time allows."

"We were misled," Charles explained.

"By whom?" Kate asked. "Have the mudlarks made enemies at school?"

"In what way?" Julie asked at almost the same moment.

"It was suggested to us that the mudlarks had run away to the traveling circus that is in town," Charles told them. "But they had only attended it, not joined. They scarcely made an impression on the circus folk at all."

"You said something in your letter to Mrs. Aga about a trea-sure map," Lucy said.

William nodded. "Yes. We just had an eyewitness tell us the first point of the map."

Lucy worried at her lip, looking all the more like a frightened angel. "If a treasure map had been found, they would undoubtedly be following the treasure, since the circus turns out not to have claimed their attention."

Charles put his hand on William's shoulder. "It's easy enough now to check. Do you ladies want to go to the first location with us?"

"Absolutely," Kate said.

"Julie should rest," William said.

"Julie should not rest," Julie interjected. "I napped in the carriage. I slept most of the way."

William glanced at Kate, and she nodded. It was true, sort of, but she'd seen how Julie looked when unwell, and at the moment, her eyes sparkled with life.

"We'll have to do some rough walking," Charles warned. "Is everyone in boots?"

"Yes," Kate assured him. "The stagecoach is too cold for mere shoes."

"Very well," Charles said. "We'll take you to Mr. Aga's house, leave your things, then go on our tramp. The old property in question is in the woods behind the school."

An hour later, Charles herded the group onto the school grounds. William had been unable to persuade Julie to stay behind, and Julie had been unable to persuade Lucy that the purpose of a maid was to perform chores, like unpacking for her mistress, so all five of them were on the hunt. Charles had to admit it had a little of the air of old times, or at least happier ones, when they had walked down the road in Brompton to visit the blacksmith family who had lived on the street behind his rooms. Or when they'd gone Christmas caroling together.

"How did Fred do with Mr. Screws?" he remembered to ask when his brother's presence at last year's deadly caroling party came to mind.

"They were planning to hire an errand boy," Kate explained. "Not a clerk position, but they promised to train him. He's Mr. Screws's employee now."

Charles frowned as they stepped between buildings and crossed the lawn toward the outbuildings. "Should we look at a different firm?"

"It's nicer now than you described," Kate said. "Mr. Screws has partnered with another firm."

"I did wonder why he was staying in business," Charles said. "He'd been ready to give it all up not too long ago."

"He seemed very well, younger even," Kate said. "He has some contacts here and gave me the name of one, a James Maylie."

"We've already spoken to the Maylies, the women at least," William interjected. "That is how we learned of the first point on the map."

"If the female Maylies were so useful, maybe Mr. Maylie will have something to offer, as well," Julie suggested.

"Mr. Screws had a good opinion of him, which is rare enough," Kate added.

"We're about to the icehouse," Charles said. "Where Agnes perished, or possibly was carried after the tragedy. We don't really know."

They stopped at the small clock-shaped building to pay their respects. After a moment of silence, Lucy tightened her lips and muttered, "The living."

Charles despaired of the Agas turning her into a proper maid at that moment. They would have to find something else for her, though there was little enough for a woman with no capital to do to earn her living.

"Do you know the woods well?" Kate asked William.

"I don't know every tree and dip in the land like I would have, but I know the general area. People have lived here since before Roman times. You never know what you are going to come across. We're looking for the remains of an old house, but if the chimney is still standing, I don't imagine it's more than a hundred years old."

"Where is the chimney from here?"

"As I recall, we'll walk down a slope, then wind through the woods for a bit on an old path, and then we'll see it. It's not too far away, or even too wild and overgrown."

Julie took her husband's arm. "The return trip will be the hardest part, I expect."

"It's uphill," William agreed, with a hint of his usual cheer. "I am glad to see you, Mrs. Aga, even if you should be in London, resting."

She grinned back.

Charles caught Kate's eye and, with a nod, held out his arm. "Shall we, Miss Hogarth?"

She slid her small hand around his forearm. "Indeed, we shall. I want to come across living children this time."

Lucy forged ahead, taking direction from William. The slope had slippery elements, though rocks and undergrowth increased its overall integrity. The men kept the women on their feet. Charles expected that Kate clung close merely for the pleasure of it, though Julie was legitimately a bit more ungainly, given her condition.

After about ten minutes, they reached the flat part. William pointed at the visible dirt path between trees. "Probably cut through by whoever owned the house back in the day, and maintained by some little traffic ever since."

Lucy darted forward. Charles grabbed her arm. "I know you are looking for the boys, but we've no reason to think they are aware of this spot. This is the first clue of Agnes Aga's treasure map. We don't know who all has seen it or what danger we might be facing."

Lucy's gaze, so intent on the journey, flickered to Charles's. She blinked, then seemed to be restored to sense. "You don't think the boys are 'ere?"

"It's not a bad guess, treasure map or no," William said. "There is shelter in the trees, but we don't know what caused the boys to run in the first place. It's close, though. Friends could even sneak food to them."

"I don't know that they would have friends," Lucy said doubtfully. "They have each other."

"Ollie was here first. I hope he had chums," Charles said.

Lucy worried at her wind-chapped lip. "He's a quiet sort, but boys can change quickly, and I haven't seen him since Christmas."

Charles walked alongside her, leaving Kate in the protection of William. The path wasn't quite wide enough for multiple people, so he had to brush branches away from his face. He saw the starts of spring buds around them and the not yet unfurled tender leaves. Soon this path would be a bower of delights, a fitting walk to a place where trysts were conducted. At this time of day, he hoped the ladies wouldn't be exposed to anything unseemly.

"Chimney," Lucy said, pointing as a rectangle of fieldstone became visible past a trio of evergreen trees, which had formed a screen.

"That will be it," Charles agreed. "I wonder who used to live here."

"Someone who thought to farm it," Lucy said, with the disdain of a city dweller for a humble farmer.

Charles reached for her arm when she gathered her skirts to run. "I'll go first, Lucy. Stay behind me." He reached for a stout stick in the underbrush and wrapped his fingers around it, then moved forward with caution.

He heard voices a second later, boyish chatter. After returning to Lucy, he whispered, "We've found someone, and they sound cheerful enough."

Lucy listened intently; then a smile spread across her angelic face. "That's John's voice! I'd recognize 'im anywhere." She reached for her skirts again, shook off Charles, and dashed into the clearing.

Charles broadened his stride to follow, though he kept his stick in hand. The former house had been reduced to nothing more than stone foundations and what was left of the chimney. He saw bits of pottery stacked on a couple of the rocks. They had dark pigment painted onto them in the shape of birds. Visitors had been excavating, or maybe it was some kind of shrine. None of the shards were big enough for reuse.

Three child-sized figures huddled in the ruins. The boys, found at last. Relief rushed through Charles's veins, weakening his knees momentarily.

Lucy dashed up to her protégés, who were sitting on larger rocks in front of the fireplace. Charles saw heaps of crunchy dead leaves to the side, makeshift beds.

In a second, the boys had leapt up, cries of delight emanating from each throat. Ollie, who had been mostly parted from Lucy since the previous summer, rushed into her arms, followed closely by John and the smallest and youngest of the boys, Arthur. Little Ollie, Poor John, and Cousin Arthur, as they had been known on the Thames foreshore.

Only a few joyous moments of reconciliation passed before Lucy began to scold them. As Kate and the Agas reached the ruins, she boxed John's ears, as if he wasn't nearly her height.

"'Ow could you be so cruel to the Agas and Mr. Dickens?" she cried. "Running off, ignoring your education, worrying everyone!"

The boys glanced between each other as John rubbed his ears. "We left fer somethin' better," Ollie reported.

"Something better? What can be better than an education?" Lucy asked. "Clean clothes, good food?"

"Not very good," Arthur piped up. "Pickings are slim since that Mr. Sikes took over. Can't wait until there's rabbits in the woods again."

John licked his lips loudly.

"It's a couple of months until there will be a solid new crop," William said. "What have you been doing for food?"

"There's nuts, if you know where to find them," John said.

Charles remembered the curate in the woods. "Has someone been feeding you? From the church maybe?"

"No," Ollie said loudly. "We're independent men."

"What did you leave for?" Charles asked in a hearty manner. He echoed, "What is better than an education?"

"Treasure," Arthur piped up. "We'll be rich!"

William nodded somberly. "You have a treasure map?"

John was old enough to be sly, but the younger boys nodded eagerly.

"How did you acquire it?" Charles asked. Surely, the youngsters hadn't killed Agnes for her map. Though, after Lucy left the Thames foreshore, they had led a hardscrabble life without the maternal warmth of their leader, looking for bits and bobs cast up by the river, and John and Arthur had run with a very tough crowd for a while.

"That'd be telling," Ollie said.

"Agnes, who I would guess owned the map previously, is dead," Charles said. "What do you know about that?"

"Dead?" John asked with a frown.

Arthur put his hand in Lucy's. "We don't know nothing about that."

"Did she have a fever?" Ollie asked.

Charles recalled that Ollie's father had died of one. "No, someone strangled her. The map went missing. You see how that looks, don't you, boys?"

"Someone killed her?" John asked, the lines in his forehead increasing.

"Did you do it?" Julie asked.

John shook his head. "We're innocent."

"We didn't kill nothin', not even a rabbit," Arthur said with disgust.

Lucy smiled fondly at him and picked a twig out of his hair.

"Do you have anything to eat?" Arthur asked plaintively.

"No," Charles said. "When did you leave the school?"

"Sunday, after church again," John said, rolling his eyes. "It's so boring."

"How did you get the map?" Charles inquired.

Ollie shifted from side to side.

"Did you take it?" Charles asked.

Kate stepped to Ollie and put her arm around the boy's grimy shoulder. "Where did you find it?"

"We just found it," John said.

"Why would you steal it?" Charles asked.

"We borrowed it," Arthur piped up.

"We were tired of the food," John explained. "And she was always waving it around and not doing her work."

"She didn't scrub out the privy," Arthur said.

"It stunk," Ollie added. "And our beds have been damp all winter."

"I had the terrible sniffles," Arthur added.

"It doesn't matter, anyway," John said, kicking a rock. "We can't understand the map."

"I'm sorry there have been problems at the school," William said. "I promise you I'm going to become more involved."

"It was in an empty crock," Ollie admitted.

"Where?" Charles asked.

"In the pantry. There weren't any kitchen people around on Sunday night, and we were hungry." Ollie fixed his large eyes on Charles. "At tea, I asked for more bread and butter, and Mr. Sikes said no."

"We knew housekeeping was lax, but it sounds like the kitchen is a problem, as well," Charles told William.

His friend shut his eyes for a moment. "You went to steal food?"

Ollie bit his lip. "We just wanted some of the dried fruit. They never give it to us."

"The fruit was all gone, anyway," John added, visibly disgruntled. "But the map was there. We grabbed it and went hunting."

"School isn't fun now," Ollie complained. "The masters just tell us to memorize this, memorize that. An' the food is terrible now. Only gruel for breakfast. No seconds, and no butter on the bread at tea. Mr. Sikes says meat makes too much spirit and soul."

Did Mr. Sikes think the school was a workhouse? And why had Mr. Aga permitted so much change? What had William's father distracted?

Chapter 10

"Sit down, boys. We might as well make use of these old stones." Charles stared at his charity students. On one hand, he wanted to hug them, grimy though they were; on the other, their reappearance created as many questions as answers. Agnes, for one, had been smarter than he expected to hide the map away properly. Most of the students wouldn't have been daring or resourceful enough to attempt to steal food. More important, the fact that they'd been told the boys had joined the traveling circus might have been to send them on a wild chase in the wrong direction, away from the murderer or the treasure hunters. Where did the rumor originate?

He took his own spot on a stone, along with everyone else. "William, who told you the boys had joined the circus?"

"Nancy Price, the servant girl, told me, I think." His friend, after wiping off a stone with his handkerchief for his wife, screwed up his forehead in concentration. "But I can't quite remember."

"Did you have the notion that your father had come to that conclusion on his own?"

"It doesn't seem like he'd be talking to Nancy," William admitted.

Charles shifted as a sliver of pottery poked at him. "No, he doesn't seem to have involved himself in the hunt for the boys at all. Which makes me wonder if other children have disappeared over the years."

"Hold on there," William said sternly. "I won't have you insulting my father, and if you think for one second you're going to look at him as a murder suspect, I'll ask you to leave Harrow on the Hill now."

They stared at each other. Charles realized his breaths were shallow. He forced himself to slow down his exhalations, then took a deep breath. "Not spoken like a true investigator, William. We have to follow any clues where they lead us."

Kate touched his arm softly. "I don't think Mr. Aga had anything to do with his niece's death. But it is possible that someone will try to frame him."

William half turned away. "They should have hauled off Mrs. Bedwin."

"Sacked her, at any rate," Charles agreed. "What a ghastly housekeeper for an establishment like this. When all this is over, you need to explain that to your father in the harshest terms."

"She'll be married and gone soon enough. Maybe it is time for him to sell the school, though," William said. "Perhaps that is even what he is trying to do in sharing the burden with Mr. Sikes."

"Horrible Mr. Sikes," Ollie complained. "I'm too hungry to learn anything now, and I had all my letters and numbers before he came, anyway."

Charles looked at the boys with fresh eyes. They didn't have the emaciated appearance of workhouse folk or the desperate appearance of the inmates of Newgate Prison, who were fed better, if not well. But they were not ruddy specimens of boyhood, either. Had they ever been, though, since he'd met them more than a year ago? Ollie with his missing hand? Arthur, who'd been little more than a baby when he'd been pulled into the mudlark gang with his older brother?

He patted his pockets. "I'm sorry, boys, but we came without victuals. Not very smart planning with ladies in tow."

Lucy's hands darted into the mysterious recesses of her skirts and reappeared with a squashed ham sandwich. "For emergencies," she explained as Julie laughed.

She portioned it out to the boys as Charles, full of thoughts he could not make into anything coherent, walked around the ruined house with Kate. It seemed that over the years, students had amused themselves by whittling away at the surfaces.

"What do you make of this?" he asked, fingering the rough carving of a cawing crow cut into one of the chimney rocks. "A good spot to spend the week after our wedding?"

"A little too rustic, Mr. Dickens," she said. "For all that I'd follow you anywhere."

He chuckled. Then he noticed a clearing with a lot of large flat stones at the far end of the rocks, behind the chimney.

Kate's gaze followed his. Her chin jutted forward. "Look. Some of the stones are still standing."

Charles pulled her past the house, and they walked around the clearing. He kept her steady as they wove through a collection of scattered smaller rocks and sparse vegetation. When they had made a complete circuit, he stared at the pitted gray stones, which rose a little taller than he was in some places. "They form a rough circle of about three yards."

Kate set a gloved hand on one of the tall stones, wonder in her gaze. "I wonder what that means. It would be a lot of work to build this."

Charles tilted his head at her, and they walked between two of the stones into the center of the circle. Half buried in the dirt lay another flat stone. A deep divot held muddy water from the earlier rain. "Based on what we heard at the church, I wonder if it's the site of an ancient king's grave."

Kate's eyes went wide as she stared at the flat stone. "Truly?"

He grinned at her and stomped the ground with one boot. "Imagine what treasures may hide under my feet. Along with a skeleton, of course."

"Alas." She sighed. "It is only the first stop on the supposed treasure map, not the final one."

"That is an excellent point and reminds me that we'd better take a look at the map. The boys need to give it up."

Kate's brow rose. "Lucy should have traded it for the sandwich."

"Oh, they'd give it to her for nothing. She's their Boudicca." Charles leapt onto the central flat stone.

"She's the closest thing to a mother any of those boys had last year. What a life for a child. I hope the masters aren't too hard on them."

"They are imperfectly civilized wild animals," he proclaimed from his mount. "They might not see the value of all this educating until they have work that pays better coin than mudlarking ever could."

"In that case, the school is going to have a most difficult time with them." Kate circled him. "I do hope our children will have the benefit of a mother, and a father, too."

"Oh, Kate." Charles jumped down, took both her hands, and looked into her eyes. "We'll be fine."

"I'm frightened, Charles. We are about to take such a big step, and it's a dangerous time in a girl's life."

"Our mothers were fine, and you will be, as well," he assured her. "Don't you want a sweet little family as much as I do?"

"Of course." She gave her shoulders a little wriggle. "It's just that out here in this windy place, probably standing on a grave, it gives one queer thoughts."

He pulled her close and rested his cheek on her bonnet. "It will feel very different back at dear old Furnival's Inn. We won't honeymoon here, I promise."

She looked up at him, eyes alight with new excitement. "Have you made plans?"

"I shall, now that our rooms are coming available. We're very close, Kate. I predict this shall be our last escapade before that biggest adventure of all, matrimony."

Her lips curved up, and ignoring all propriety, he bent his head for a kiss. Her lips were chilled and windswept, but her breath warmed him right up. Her hands tightened in his, and her little gasp sent his senses whirling. The kiss intensified dangerously until the spell was broken by a gust of cold wind.

Charles ended the kiss. "Even nature insists that duty calls."

She nodded. "There is much to do before we return home, but it must happen fast, lest we anger my parents yet again."

He loosened his grip on her hands slowly, then gently tucked one of them into the crook of his arm. "We won't think about that now. First the mystery."

"And the murder," she said softly. "That poor girl, and here we've been enjoying ourselves like characters in a novel."

A drip hit Charles's nose. The skies opened, and rain poured down. Kate squealed and grabbed at her bonnet. He pulled her toward the old chimney and pressed her against a tall evergreen that could provide some coverage. The others jumped up from where they'd been lounging among the foundations and did the same.

"Where is the map?" Charles called.

William, who was closest, Julie in his arms under a large bird's nest that remained in a leafless tree, shrugged at him.

John had tugged Lucy into the shelter of a stand of trees that had interlocked branches and provided a kind of tunnel of wood.

"Which of you has it?" Charles demanded.

"I do," John admitted. "It's wrapped up in a handkerchief."

"As soon as it stops raining, I want it, and then we're going back to school," Charles shouted over the drumming of the rain.

It poured down. Some of the pottery pieces that had been gathered on the foundations slid off the stones. The ground around them turned to mud in minutes.

"Perfect time for a hot cup of tea," Charles said in Kate's ear.

"Wouldn't that be lovely," Kate agreed. "Or a cup of chocolate, all tucked up under the blankets."

"A blazing fire," Charles added. "All the papers."

She giggled. "We'll be the most decadent young couple imaginable."

"I'll stay home with you," he declared. "We'll live on chocolate and news."

"Are we going to be able to get back?" Julie called from the next tree. "This is awful."

"It will stop," Ollie said from where he was huddled with his fellow runaways. "It never lasts forever."

"I'm amazed they aren't ill with these weather conditions," Kate murmured.

"Only the hardiest of souls survive the lives they've led," Charles said with confidence. "Barring accidents, they will see their three score and ten."

He enjoyed the excuse to hold Kate in his arms and took full advantage of it until the downpour slowed to a steady rain, then indeed trickled away, as Ollie had predicted. They all bunched together as best they could under the branching shelter the boys had found, and John handed over the map, which had been rolled up under his school-issue coat.

"Parchment," William said as he and Charles spread it open between them.

Charles stared at the map, confused, until his brain made sense of what he was seeing. "I'm surprised to see it is composed of symbols rather than being something like a regular map with landmarks."

"Agreed, but why should a treasure map be any one thing or another?" William said.

"Where would you say the map begins?" Charles asked John.

The boy pointed to a symbol with an outline of a house topped by a rectangle.

"I suppose the little bumps on it represent the fieldstone," Charles opined.

"How would anyone guess what this is if they didn't know already?" Julie asked, frowning.

"That's a good point. Why was Myrtle Maylie so sure this was the spot?" Charles asked.

"We figured it out, too," John said.

"If it was easy, it wouldn't be a treasure map," William said, then glanced at his wife. "We need to get you in front of a fire. This isn't good for you and the baby."

"I am used to London streets, not tramping in the woods," Julie admitted.

"Your hems are very damp," Charles said, surveying both Kate and Julie in turn. "We'll sort out the next symbol when we're safe in front of a fire."

"You aren't eager to find the next clue?" Julie asked. "I'm shocked, Charles, I really am."

Lucy giggled as Charles shook his head. "We've found the boys. They didn't kill Agnes."

"We didn't kill *nobody*," Arthur insisted.

"She died sometime on Tuesday," William said.

"We were 'ere," John confirmed. "Nowhere near the school. We tramped in the woods until we found this place, and then didn't know what to do next."

"We've been 'aving an 'oliday," Arthur said.

"Mr. Aga and Mr. Dickens are afraid the map 'ad something to do with Agnes's murder." Lucy gave them each a stern glare.

Their eyes opened into identical circles, making them look like a trio of brothers.

"Like we stole the map, so she got killed?" Ollie said with a gulp.

"We don't know," Charles said. "But it is possible."

"And time to face your punishment like men," William added. "Come along now."

"But we don't want to go back," John protested.

"It's nice 'ere," Arthur added.

"I'd be happy to eat real food again," Ollie said. "Even if it's starvation rations."

"Come now," William chided. "It's not that bad."

"It isn't that decent, either," Charles pointed out. "We will have done some good here if we can sort out this business with inadequate rations for the students, even if it means we have to increase our charitable donations."

John went back into the ruins to pick up their sole treasure, a filthy handkerchief with a handful of knots tied into it, including one holding a few coins.

The group had just started in the direction of the school when Charles heard a branch breaking a few feet ahead of them. He stopped and put out his hand to hold back the rest.

"It's probably just an animal," Julie said.

"No." John looked very wise. "It's a person."

A boy stepped out from the trees, in the same Aga uniform the mudlarks wore. Charles recognized him from the inquest, despite the cap he wore pulled down over his curls.

"What are you doing 'ere, Claypole?" John said, puffing up his chest and stepping away from the younger boys.

"Thought you joined the circus, Smith," said the newcomer in a superior tone.

"Who told you that?" William asked.

Noah Claypole smirked. "It was all these foundlings could talk about last week. Figured they couldn't come back after they spent all their pocket money on it. Smith owes me tuppence."

Charles knew the boys still had money in the handkerchief. "Why does he owe you money?"

The boy's eyes shifted from side to side.

Charles turned to John and repeated the question. "Why do you owe him money?"

John's upper teeth went down on his lower lip. He worried at it for a moment, staring at the ground, then looked up at Charles with an air of contrition. "We had a bet."

William frowned. "About what?"

"The map," Arthur piped up.

"The map?" Julie asked, rubbing her belly. "What about it?"

"Who could find the starting point first," John mumbled.

That was why they had stolen it, then. John had lost a bet, and he had taken the opportunity to cure his wounded dignity.

"Did you know where the map was, Noah?" Charles asked. "Were you sneaking around the school, as well?"

"No," he said sullenly.

"Then how?"

He shrugged. "Agnes waved the map around one day, and I had a better look at it than most."

"Was this before or after you made the bet with John?" William asked sternly.

The boy's cheeks lost a little of their ruddy tone.

John's mouth dropped open in outrage. "You knew before you made the bet? You're no gentleman."

"Smith here no longer owes you tuppence," William ruled. "And no pudding after dinner for either of you for a week."

Noah snorted. "We haven't had pudding since Christmas."

Julie's forehead wrinkled in concern. Charles knew his expression was similar. Why were they running Aga Academy like a charity institution? This was unacceptable.

"We will have to deal with the issue of pudding later," Charles said, taking Noah by the collar. "Come along. We need to get the ladies to somewhere dry."

They walked back through the woods, seeking intermittent shelter, though that often backfired due to the trees dripping wherever there was vegetation to do so.

After Charles figured there had been enough silence for the boys' wounded dignities to calm, he opened up the questioning.

"Where did you come across the map in the first place?" he asked. "She really just waved it around the school?"

"Grimwig was allus complaining about how boring it was at the school," Noah said. "But Agnes, she had some pride in the place 'cause of her uncle being the owner. She said there was treasure around here. That perked up old Grimwig, until he broke his arm, at least."

"That indicates she had had the map for a while, or had known of it," William said.

Noah shrugged. "Never saw it until last week."

"Who was the most interested in it?" Charles asked.

"Him," John snapped. "He talked about it all the time. He got the ruler in Latin for talking in class."

"You were plenty interested," Noah sneered back. "Betting me money you don't have."

"I have tuppence," John said. "I just intended to beat you, is all."

"John?" Charles asked. "When did you first hear about the map?"

"From him," John said. "I never saw it."

"Then how did you recognize it when you found it?" Kate asked.

"It was obviously a treasure map," the boy said.

"No one killed her for it?" Noah asked, then brightened as a terrible idea seemed to strike him. "Or did you rob her body, Smith?"

"We didn't know she was dead," Ollie said in a dark tone. "Did you kill her?"

"No!" Noah shouted in a tone of outrage.

"To be clear, did anyone tell you the boys joined the circus, or did you start that rumor yourself?" Charles asked.

Noah shrugged. "Maybe. I told the lads I thought they had gone off to join up."

"Did you tell the headmaster?" Kate asked.

"No, but he hears everything eventually."

"Then who did you tell?" Charles demanded.

The boy shrugged. William put up his hand. "Let it go for now. I don't like the look of those clouds."

"A gusher is coming," Arthur said happily. "We'd find all sorts of good stuff by the bridge after one of these, wouldn't we, Lucy?"

She squeezed his hand. "Indeed, we would. I'm so 'appy to see you again, my lad."

When they arrived at the boy's boardinghouse, they immediately crossed the path of the master, who was seated in his office with Mr. Aga. The master's face lit up, but Mr. Aga remained stern.

"I'm very happy to see you have been found safe and well," enthused the master, a reedlike young man not much past his own school days.

"'S math sin!" said a boy in Scottish Gaelic, walking past them. He wore a school uniform that looked fit for a larger child. "Nice to have you lads back."

"We didn't run off to the circus, sir," John said, glancing at the headmaster. "We just needed a bit of rough living."

"You aren't here to do what you like, Mr. Smith," the young master said after a glance at the headmaster. "You are here to learn and to be molded as a British gentleman."

"Indeed," Mr. Aga said, his features stiffening in a way Charles hadn't seen before. "Fanciful behavior is unacceptable. It was not end of term, and you had no business disappearing from school. Your town privileges are revoked for the month. Remain on the property."

As the boys' expressions went grumpy, Mr. Aga glanced around the group, and his gaze alit upon Julie.

"My dear," he exclaimed. "We must get you in front of a fire."

"You can use my study," the young master said.

"No, no, let's remove you to my house," Mr. Aga said. "Have the boys bathed and fed. Tomorrow is soon enough for formalities."

"The map?" Charles said. Somehow, John had kept possession of it when the downpour began.

"What?" John said suspiciously.

"I'll keep it as a curiosity,'" Charles said. "It will too easily be stolen if you keep it, and you stole it in the first place."

"What?" Mr. Aga said, startled.

"They were very naughty," Julie confirmed.

"It was in the larder, not in someone's room," John protested.

"That makes it Mr. Aga's," Lucy told John. "Not just anyone's. This isn't the foreshore."

"What about this one?" Mr. Aga asked, pointing at Noah Claypole.

"After the treasure himself," Charles said heartily, placing a warning hand on the boy's shoulder. "Seems to have come by the information honestly enough. If he had privileges in the woods, he's fine."

Mr. Aga did a double take. "No one has privileges in the woods. Your town privileges are revoked for a week, Mr. Claypole. It's not safe to wander there. Could be poachers or vagrants."

"You'd disappear and never be found again," Ollie said hopefully.

Noah made a face at him.

"Let us remove Julie to that fire?" William suggested. His father nodded, and the adults, minus the young master, left the boardinghouse and walked through the predicted heavy rain to the school.

Charles kept Kate upright and free of the puddles as much as possible, thinking about his future investigation of the treasure trail. He supposed his fiancée would want to come along. Not only were they both fascinated by it, but also Agnes's murder might be connected somehow.

Chapter 11

That afternoon in the graveyard, the rain dripped off Charles's hat. Gusts of wind muffled sound, but water bounced off his nose, slid down his chin, and eased under his muffler to dampen his clothes. The vicar kept his stately tone as he spoke the prayers meant to lay Agnes Aga to rest.

As was common, only men were huddled around the grave, though the truth was, few women were a part of Agnes's life. It could be argued that Julie was her closest female relative, by marriage at any rate, and he'd had no indication that Julie knew Agnes at all. Mrs. Bedwin and Nancy Price, the cook and the kitchen girls might have been Agnes's closest companions, but they wouldn't be welcome here and, in any case, were busy with duties burdened further by the girl's death.

Charles stared across the open grave at the curate, Barney Wynd, who stood as far away from the vicar as possible, while still looking to be part of the same religious service. The distaste in the curate's eyes for the vicar was obvious whenever the older man wasn't looking.

What was the story behind that? Instinctively, Charles turned to William, but his eyes were red rimmed and unfocused. Probably from the wind, but who could say? Beyond him, the middle-aged Aga brothers stood stalwart, much closer together than the vicar and curate.

The vicar finished the service. The first shovelful of dirt was thrown onto the simple coffin. Charles turned away to allow the family to say their good-byes privately. He wanted to take shelter in the church, but that might be insensitive. Instead, he bent and stretched his chilly fingers in his gloves and tried to focus on the gravestones around him, looking for interesting epitaphs. He saw several with crow motifs, which must be a local custom.

On Sunday, after a return to St. Mary's for services, the women went inside the church while Charles and William lurked in the front, hoping to find James Maylie. Charles had taken in Kate's information from Mr. Screws. The men stood out of the wind on the flagstones in front of the decorative iron-studded door, in a small vestibule, waiting for the Maylies to appear.

Charles looked for Myrtle Maylie around the church grounds, until he spotted her coming up the hill between her mother and an older man, who was likely her father.

Charles and William watched through the arch as Mr. Maylie clapped a man, warmly bundled for the weather in a black wool coat and red muffler, on the shoulder and came toward them. The quarry owner seemed a popular sort, with a mix of equals and subordinates greeting him as they approached the door.

"Mr. Maylie," William called just as the man passed through the door and reached greeting distance. "I'm William Aga. Might we have a word?"

His daughter shyly waved at them. Mrs. Maylie nodded politely and took her daughter past them as her husband stopped.

The middle-aged man gave him a pleasant smile. "How can I be of help, Mr. Aga? I know your father. Fine man."

William introduced Charles, who said, "We have another acquaintance in common. Emmanuel Screws of London?"

"The name is familiar to me. My father had a loan from Mr. Screws not too long ago," Mr. Maylie said easily. "We own a quarry together. You visited with my wife and daughter recently, I believe."

Charles stepped against the wall to allow another family to pass into the church. "We're trying to sort out this tragic business with Miss Aga and understood your daughter was her close friend."

"She's very upset," Mr. Maylie confirmed. "Poor child. Such a grisly end, Agnes had. I couldn't be at the funeral."

"Were you near the school at all that day? Do you recall anything unusual going on the day she died?" Charles asked.

"I suppose I ride by it every day," Mr. Maylie said. "But no, I cannot recall anything special."

"When I came," Charles said, "Agnes must have already been dead, her body freezing in the icehouse. I did notice the work of the gardener in the front. Branches were everywhere. I didn't see him, though."

Mr. Maylie's head bent to the side as he considered. "I take it that you suspect Littlejack Dawkins in her death?"

"Is there a reason we should?" William asked.

The man sighed loudly and ran his fingers along his watch chain. "It's possible."

"Was there some kind of relationship between the gardener and my young cousin?" asked William.

"Not that I'm aware. My daughter has never made such a comment, and she will prattle along on any subject, as I'm sure you noticed." He gave them a wry smile. "Her mother has not been able to train her out of the love of the sound of her own voice."

"She seemed a very pleasant young lady," William said blandly.

"Well," Mr. Maylie exhaled. "The truth is, I wouldn't trust

Littlejack Dawkins around young women. He interfered with a young servant a decade ago."

"At my father's school?" William asked, his eyes narrowing.

"No, he was working at Harrow School then. I expect he came cheap for your father, who does tend to see the best in everyone." Mr. Maylie shifted his stance. "Perhaps he was right, for I haven't heard a whisper of trouble since."

"Until now," Charles said. Had they solved the mystery? Had Littlejack Dawkins killed Agnes either in the commission of a rape or after it?

"I would not want to condemn a man on no evidence," Mr. Maylie said, "but I cannot think of anyone else connected to the school with that sort of history."

"Mr. Sikes is a newcomer to the school," Charles said in a low voice. "The children don't seem very fond of him."

"He is not an indulgent man," Mr. Maylie admitted. "But I do not think there is any reason for concern."

"Perhaps something in the changes he made when he came to Aga Academy led to this disaster," Charles suggested.

"If Agnes was selling food to the boys out of the kitchen door?" Mr. Maylie raised an eyebrow.

Charles saw that the man knew very well how parsimonious Fagin Sikes was. "Certainly. Something of that sort."

"I cannot imagine how that would lead her to her doom in the icehouse," said the quarry owner after a pause. "But I admit I can see such a thing happening. The rumor is that the servant class at the school is lax."

"The housekeeper," William murmured. "She is a subject to bring up with my father."

"I've heard the rumors, passed from Agnes to my daughter." Mr. Maylie cleared his throat. "I'm surprised Mr. Sikes has not done something there, but perhaps his agreement with your father does not involve managing the staff."

"I was surprised the coroner didn't jail her." Charles was jostled as a large family thundered into the vestibule and pushed past him.

"I believe they are cousins." Mr. Maylie tilted his head as voices lifted in song at a distance. "I expect he's known her every day of her life. Female hysteria, but not a bad woman. I believe I should join my family, gentlemen. I hear the choir."

"Thank you for your insights," Charles said. Then they followed him into the church.

Charles and William joined their party, seated at the back instead of in the area set aside for the school. Despite the beautiful surroundings, Charles found the service less than uplifting. Barney Wynd was given the honor of preaching the sermon, but it sounded like he'd merely stolen some text from the Elizabethans, talking about Moses and monarchs in a way that was quite unbecoming, given that they had an elderly, sick king on the throne.

The curate made a long list of points in the most flowery language, pressing back his fingers on his left side with the fingers on his right until the joints popped. Charles saw Kate's face go rigid with distaste.

"Must have the joints of a circus performer," Charles whispered in her ear.

"It looks painful," she whispered back.

Charles forced himself to stay upright in his seat as the man pressed on to a third list, popping his fingers as he broke into Latin. If it wasn't for the warm press of Kate's shoulder next to his, he would have spent the time drifting entirely out of reality and might have solved the murder right there.

Instead, he endured the service, though he might have drifted off just before the last hymn. His eyelids startled open when the choir began. Kate, staring at her borrowed prayer book, didn't seem to have noticed anything amiss, however.

Not too much later, they processed out of the church but found themselves in a knot of people walking past the vicar and curate, who were holding court not at the main door but at the edge of the cemetery.

"I hope you enjoyed the sermon today?" Mr. Wynd said to Kate. His face was pink from the cold.

"I appreciated your final point about living with joy," she said. "I do hope we are led safely to the fruition of His promise."

The vicar smiled, satisfaction imbedded into his well-fed face. Mr. Wynd, though, didn't react.

William stepped close to Charles. "We need to feed Julie," William said in Charles's ear.

He stammered his excuses, and the quartet headed down the hill. "I think we're going to have to walk."

"I'm fine with this," Julie said, pulling what looked like a knob of yellow cheese from her pocket. "The road is downhill in this direction. Where did the curate find that sermon? In Shakespeare?"

"It was very odd," Charles agreed.

"The sentiments were well enough," Kate said, "though largely irrelevant to the parish. He is positively off-putting as a person, however."

"You know he is one of our suspects," Charles told her. "He's the curate we found coming out of the woods that day."

"I'll give him this much criticism," William added. "He might as well have pulled that sermon out of some dusty old book. It had absolutely nothing to do with what has happened here locally. No hint of the murder or a lost child or anything relevant. Which makes sense if he's the murderer himself and wants Agnes's death forgotten."

"What is it about curates?" Kate asked. "How do any of them turn into the vicars we so admire?"

"Do we?" Charles murmured. "I thought we admired men of action, like reporters."

She giggled and grinned at him. "Well, reporters most of all. But churchmen deal in words, as well."

"Is that Littlejack Dawkins down the hill a ways?" William asked. "Let's catch up and have a word with him."

"Go on," Kate said, releasing Charles's arm. "I'll take Julie back to the school."

Charles tipped his hat, then followed William across the road to a public house. A number of men were loitering in the doorway of the closed building. He spotted the Aga Academy gardener.

"We'd like to have a word, Mr. Dawkins," William said.

"Nothing doing, unless it comes with a wee drop," the gardener said. "I'm parched."

"I've a bottle in my bag," William said. "Come along."

The gardener shrugged. "Fair enough."

They finished the walk down the hill together. By the time they reached William's father's house, Julie and Kate had disappeared upstairs. William went to his room, while Charles settled the gardener in the parlor.

"I never thought to see this room until the day I retired," the gardener said, pulling off his cap and twisting it in his hands. "It's not for the likes of me."

"Where else would we go?" Charles asked. "One of the classrooms?"

"No better than this, I expect. What do you want with me?"

"Have a seat," Charles invited. "I just want to go through your movements about the grounds the day Agnes died again. Who did you see? Was it a normal kind of day? Did you run across the curate? That sort of thing."

The gardener kept a stubborn silence until William returned with a squat green bottle of rum. Charles decided to ignore the gardener and busied himself with pouring water from a can into a kettle and setting it on an iron hook over the fire.

"I hope you'll forgive me for skipping the ceremony of mixing punch," William said, pulling three small rummers down from a shelf by the fireplace. He poured rum into each glass, then added hot water from the kettle that Charles had prepared.

"I don't know why you keep questioning me," the gardener complained once he'd drained his first glass and held it out for a refill. "I was nowhere near the icehouse."

"Where were you, then?" Charles asked. "I didn't see you at the front of the house."

"I have a little spot between the bushes on the side lawn," he admitted. "I keep a bottle there."

Enlightenment dawned. "You didn't see the curate at all?"

"No," the gardener grumbled.

"What about Agnes? When she went from the school building to the icehouse?"

"I would have been in front then. I worked diligently enough in the morning," he insisted.

"Then in the afternoon you were closeted off in those bushes."

"Saw nothing, heard nothing," he confirmed. After finishing his second glass, he leaned forward. "Now, I'll admit the coroner is a little too obsessed with his dinner and likes a fast inquest, but the man has neither malice nor brains."

Charles saw the hint of intelligence lurking in the gardener's face. "What's your point?"

"I know you suspect me because of the inquest, but no one was left out of the inquest to hide anything," he confided. "What happened was an operation built wholly in the interest of concluding it as quickly as possible."

"We understand Mrs. Bedwin is a relative of the coroner," Charles said.

"True." The gardener fingered his chin and held out his glass again. "I'd look at Nancy Price or that student, Noah Claypole. They both have that sneaking way about them. Wouldn't trust either of 'em."

William filled the gardener's glass again, and Charles added the water. "I'm glad we are friends now. Are you sure you don't remember anything else? Anyone who paid too much attention to my cousin?"

"Oh, she was always fighting with her brother. Those two were like a pair of starving dogs. I saw that Nancy in the middle of it with them one time." Littlejack Dawkins shrugged and poured the third glass down his throat. "That's enough for me." He slapped his cap back on his head and walked out of the room, whistling like he didn't have a care in the world.

"More unpleasantness with Monks," William said, then tossed back his first glassful. He winced, as if the rum was caustic, though it had slid down the others' throats easily enough.

"True," Charles agreed. "But there are plenty of other suspects. We'd best find out what they were fighting about, though."

William set his glass down on the table and closed his eyes. "I'm glad you are here, Charles. I would think you would have had enough dealings with murder by now to have left me to my own family drama."

"You've been at my side during my own pains." Charles poured him another shot of rum and doctored it with the cooling water, then restored the kettle to the hearth. "I came here for the boys, but we still have some investigating to do. Right now, though, let's get our writing done for the day."

"How are you feeling?" Kate asked Julie. Lucy had placed a stool under her mistress's feet in the room she and William were sharing in Mr. Aga's house and then had gone after a pot of tea.

Kate liked the room. The wallpaper had Egyptian floral motifs in red and tan, perhaps out of style now but very pretty, along with a large feather bed and comfortable fittings. She thought guests staying in the comfortable chamber might think the school rather nicer than it was.

"Fine," Julie insisted. "I'm used to long walks, and I'm recovered from the journey here. Really, you mustn't coddle me."

"We're coddling the wee bairn," Kate said, intensifying her Scottish accent to make Julie smile.

"Then let's go downstairs before the tea is served, so that we aren't stuck up here," Julie said. "Otherwise, we will miss all the fun. I'm quite sure this bairn loves a mystery."

Kate grinned and held out her hand to aid Julie in hoisting herself to her feet. "You have a good life, Julie."

"Well, I know it. Finding William was the good-fortune stroke of a lifetime." Julie put her hands on her back. "Do you feel the same way about Charles?"

"Of course," Kate said automatically. "It's not the same, though. We aren't married yet."

"Soon," Julie promised. "And then you might be longing for your engagement again. He's going to be demanding."

"I'm ready," Kate said softly.

Julie stared at her a long moment, then caressed her stomach and nodded. "Will you come when the baby does?" she asked. "Mrs. Herring promised to be there, and the midwife she uses will attend me, as well."

"I should be living in London by then," Kate said. "I'll come."

Julie nodded. "Then we'll say no more about it." She lifted her chin and strode out of the room.

Kate followed her, considering how much easier this friendship would be once she was no longer her father's responsibility. She smelled rum as they walked into the parlor, where Charles and William were sitting with their writing desks.

"Has the gardener gone?" Julie asked.

The men jumped to their feet. William walked his wife to the sofa and lit the fire.

"Yes, he's gone," Charles said. "What shall we do with the remainder of the day?"

"I'd like to see the treasure map," Julie called.

Kate disagreed. "We had better focus on solving the murder. We can't stay here for long. There is too much to do in London."

"The map is the key," Charles said, gesturing Kate to an upholstered chair by the fire, rather rubbed down on the arms by years of use. He sat on a straight-backed chair next to her.

"That means Noah is the killer," Kate said. "Is that what you think? He was chasing the treasure, after all."

"I hate to say this, but I must favor Monks for the killer," William said somberly.

The men exchanged glances.

Kate cleared her throat, wishing for the tea that Lucy had probably taken upstairs. "We need to lay out a case for each of them, if you disagree. That way we can keep all the points in our heads."

"We cannot leave out the gardener, no?" Julie asked. "Or did you absolve him?"

"Not really," William said. "He claims to have been drinking in a hidey-hole for all the important parts of the day and saw nothing."

"I liked him," Charles admitted. "But there is an issue of past behavior there. We need to know where everyone was when Agnes left her bedchamber."

Lucy, with flushed cheeks, appeared in the doorway, holding a heavy tray.

Julie waved. "I am sorry, Lucy. Just bring the tray here, will you? We decided to join the men."

Lucy set it down, then rubbed her hands together. "Do you think the students are back from church now?"

"They would be in the boardinghouses, not here," Charles told her. "Do you want to see them?"

"I'm sure they were lying about something," Lucy said. "I'd like to get the truth out of them."

"Something about the murder? Do you think they were on the school grounds that day, after all?" asked Kate, startled.

"I dunno, miss," Lucy said. "But it's important to know, right?"

"I agree," Julie told her. "You are dismissed, Lucy, but keep your wits about you. You aren't much older than poor Agnes, and I don't want anything happening to you."

William gave her instructions to the boardinghouse and wrote a note to the master so that she could gain admittance.

"I will go with her, if that is all right with you," Kate said to Charles. "Two of us together will be fine."

Charles glanced at William, who nodded. "Very well, my dear. We can work on the timeline here and consider the map."

"Yes, spread it out on the table here, please," Julie said. "I'll have the tea poured straightaway. Then William can put the tray out of the room."

"Mind any spills," Charles cautioned. "The last thing we want is damage to the map when we went to all this trouble to get it."

Chapter 12

As soon as they walked in, Kate recognized the boarding-house smells, a combination of her brothers' room and the family kitchen when cabbage or fish were cooked.

"I'm not sure where to go," she said uncertainly, staring at the staircase in the small hall.

"At least it is clean. I'm glad I work for the Agas and not in a place like this," Lucy confided, glancing at the spotless walls. "Tidying up after a great lot of boys who have the money to come to a school like this?"

"Some of them are charity students," Kate pointed out.

Lucy shuddered. "Yes, but they pick up airs quickly. It's been only a few months, and I don't think our boys could go back to mudlarking. Did you see? They were still wearing shoes and seemed to feel the cold at their campsite."

"I'm glad you all have a better life now," Kate ventured.

"We had freedom then," Lucy said. "For a time. When Lack and the boys came, that was the end of it. I know the Agas saved me, and Charles rescued as many of my boys as he could. But I have good memories."

"I know you do. I see the love you all have for each other."
Kate broke off when a maid holding a broom bustled by, a
cloth hanging out of her apron pocket.

"Oh, 'ello," she said with a smile. "Can I 'elp you? You're
the 'eadmaster's guests, ain't you?"

Kate inclined her head. "Yes. We need to see the boys who
have just come back. Err, Mr. Smith and his friends?"

"Up in the attic room." The maid grinned. "Those rascals.
Glad they made it back safe. Just go up the steps to the top."

"Thank you." Kate hesitated. "Did anyone think their disappearance had anything to do with the murder?"

"No. Them boys 'ave good 'earts."

"No one must have worried that they killed her, then. Did
anyone worry that they had been killed?" Kate asked.

"Some boys 'ave a swagger about 'em, like they can take care
of themselves." The maid hoisted her broom handle over her
shoulder. "No, I don't think anyone worried."

"That's a good and a bad thing," Kate said with a sigh. She
gestured Lucy to the stairs, and they began the climb up.

The stairs were also tidy, the risers swept free of mud, and
the walls mark free. Someone kept a tight ship, for all that the
maid looked well fed and content.

"A lot different than Blackfriars Bridge, where you used to
live," Kate suggested gently as they reached the top.

"We were 'appy enough under there," Lucy said, opening
the door at the top of the stairs. "Needed nothing, wanted
nothing."

Light swelled into the staircase, coming from the doorway.
Kate blinked until her eyes adjusted; then they walked through.
She saw eight iron bedsteads pushed against the walls under the
eaves. Cozy enough. An open crate rested at the foot of each
bed, and the coverlets, of thin gray wool, were pulled tightly
over the beds in a militaristic style. Few secrets could remain
hidden in this spartan space.

"I wonder if this is for the charity students or if all the boys sleep in rooms like this," Kate whispered. She hadn't known what to expect in a boys' school. Were they allowed any leisure? Or would they be in the chapel, having additional services, or doing other sorts of projects, like working in the school's garden plots?

Whatever they were supposed to be doing, John, Ollie, and Arthur were sitting on a moth-eaten rug in the center of the room, playing knucklebones. Lucy, forgetting any sort of maidenly dignity, dropped down on the rug and started a game with the boys after they greeted her. Kate smiled benignly and went to the window, where she checked the angle of the view. If anyone had been up here, might they have seen Agnes's fatal walk across the lawn?

As Kate expected, after a couple of minutes playing the game, with shouts of "Ha, you only got the dog," and "Hey, horses in the stable," Lucy began to speak in a soothing tone.

"When did you boys start liking fruit?" she asked.

"Fruit?" Arthur stuck out his tongue. "I only like apples."

"Are your teeth feeling better?" she asked John. "One of your front teeth was very loose when I saw you at Christmas."

"A little," he muttered.

"And you, Ollie?" she asked. "'Ave you learned to manage well enough that you can open casks now?"

His head dipped. "I guess."

"I was surprised to 'ear you'd been trying to steal dried fruit from the larder," she said conversationally. "Crackers, maybe. A pie, or something off a joint. But 'ard, chewy fruit? Why, Arthur doesn't have the teeth for that, even if John's are better."

Arthur's head hung as low as Ollie's. "We were going to 'elp you out, too."

"'Elp me?" Lucy asked. "What kind of 'elp do I need?"

"A job," he blurted. "You could keep the shop for us. You know sums."

Kate frowned. *A shop?*

"You're learning sums, aren't you, boys?" Lucy replied. "I bet you are pretty good now."

"I can hardly even read the alphabet," John reported.

"Numbers are confusing," Arthur said, piling up the bones until they fell into an untidy pile.

"I'm pretty good," Ollie said, lifting his head. "But you're a lot older than me. You'd do well in a shop, Lucy."

"If I worked in a shop, who would take care of Mrs. Aga?" she asked. "She gets 'erself into a lot of scrapes, you know." She reached out and tickled Arthur's knee.

He giggled. The boys were thoroughly distracted by now and didn't overreact when she said, "Where did you find that map, Ollie?"

Kate stepped quietly toward them, careful not to squeak the floorboards. She saw Ollie's face color.

"We fibbed," Ollie muttered.

"Ollie," John said. "The code of silence."

"It's Lucy, innit?" Ollie mumbled.

"We stole it from Agnes's room," Arthur said, defiant.

"But I swear we didn't lie about anyfing else," Ollie muttered, visibly upset and rosy with apology.

"Why did you do that? It might have been that poor girl's only portable property," Lucy asked softly.

Ollie's mouth worked.

"The school has changed a lot," John said.

"We wanted to find the treasure so we could start a pawnbroker's shop," Ollie said. "We could all 'ave a business together and not work for anyone but ourselves. The mudlarks could sell to us."

"And we'd stay clean," Arthur added. He began to pile up the bones again.

"You shouldn't steal," Lucy scolded. "It's against the Bible. You have a lot of religion now."

John's cheek twitched as the bones tumbled.

Lucy patted Ollie's knee. "I am 'appy you 'ad an idea for your future. Dreams are important."

"You can have a pawnshop," Kate added. "That dream can come true if you work hard. You can learn sums in school and pay attention to the value of things, so you learn how to buy and sell, but you can't steal, or your lives will be ruined. You'll end up in Newgate, and as Mr. Dickens can tell you, it's not a very nice place."

"We're 'onest boys," Ollie assured her, then considered. "Mostly, at least."

Kate took an empty crate from one of the beds and flipped it over, then gingerly sat on it. "Improve from mostly honest, please. Now tell me all about when you took the map."

"There's nothing to tell," John said. "I kept lookout after tea."

"What day?" Lucy asked, moving near him on the floor, as if her presence might coax the truth from him.

"Monday," John said. "Ollie and Arthur went up."

"Agnes 'ad an attic room, too, but the attic at the school is bigger," Ollie added. "I kept watch at the top of the stairs while Arthur looked for it."

"How did you know where her bedroom was?"

"Easy," Arthur piped up. "She's the messiest girl in the world, Monks said, an' 'e was right."

Monks. What part had he played? "You looked through all the servants' rooms until you found the messiest one?"

He nodded. "It was only the second one I tried. The door wasn't even shut, and I looked in the box with the things spilling out of it, and there it was, the map."

"She disappeared the next morning. Do you think she went looking for the map?" Kate replied.

"With 'er mess, she probably wouldn't have noticed for days," Ollie opined. "Arthur said her box smelled bad."

Kate worried at her lip. "None of that is an excuse to blatantly steal from her."

"Do you think we caused her murder?" John asked, shamefaced.

"I don't know." Kate squeezed his shoulder. "I hope you'll promise to help figure that out, without doing anything more secretive or dangerous yourselves."

"We aren't those sorts of boys," Ollie confided. His voice had the pure tones of innocent youth, but the delivery indicated the life experience of the average foreshore veteran.

John lowered his head. "Rules are different in school, ain't they?"

"Ain't they indeed," Lucy echoed.

William held back a yawn in his father's parlor. Charles refilled their glasses from Mr. Aga's collection of spirits. They had both cataloged the symbols that made up the map, but had not come to any agreement on what their next step should be.

"The next day is the beginning of the workweek," Charles ventured, leaning forward on his elbows. The map swam in front of his nose. How had he been here nearly a week?

"We've sent in articles. Our duty to the *Chronicle* hasn't been shirked."

"You know better than that," Charles chided. "We can't make up our own assignments forever. I can't take all this time away from London."

"I can take leave. My cousin died, after all."

"You can, but I want to take time off after the wedding, and I am afraid Kate's parents will be furious that she is away. She has many younger siblings requiring care, as well as duties around her father's house."

"You'll be wed in a few weeks."

Charles stared into his glass until the rum blurred. "There is no expectation of her being released from any of that until the wedding. We need to return to London."

"What about your moral commitment to help me sort out what happened to Agnes?"

"It might be easier for you to focus on that if I escort Kate and Julie back to London," Charles suggested.

"My wife belongs here with me, and I can assure you that Kate is perfectly happy to tend to her and help us with our inquiries," William snapped.

Charles began to retort back, but he refocused his eyes and saw the high color on William's cheeks. When had his friend become so pale? He had a feverish look about his eyes and dots of moisture on his forehead.

"I'm going to open a window." Charles stood. He felt wobbly from the rum. "I'll pen an obsequious letter to Mr. Hogarth explaining the situation. It will buy us another day or two."

"Good," William said in a morose tone most unlike him. "We've found the mudlarks. Only one mystery left to go."

"We'll sort it out." Charles forced confidence into his voice. "It's a school. How many people might there be who wanted to kill a young girl?"

Kate and Lucy walked back to Mr. Aga's house, both lost in their thoughts, and said nothing until they had returned to Julie's room.

"I'm going to rest now," Julie said, offering a pained smile at them after they caught her holding a novel called *Cloudesley* instead of napping.

"I don't blame you for finding it hard to rest," Kate said after relaying the conversation she and Lucy had had with the boys. "The news of the boys stealing was hard to hear."

Julie sighed. "I hope the theft had nothing to do with poor Agnes's death. I won't rest easy until the truth is uncovered."

"Do you want me to help you with your clothing?"

"No, Lucy shall manage me," Julie said with a fond glance at her maid. "Then, do you want to return to the boys?"

"I'm that upset with them," Lucy said with a shake of her head. "What's to be done? Will Mr. Aga send them packing? Arthur has family, but the other two do not. Will they have to go back to the foreshore?"

"It's very bad what they did," Julie said.

"No one needs to know but us," Kate interjected. "As long as they never do it again. The stakes are too high for them. All boys do foolish things sometimes, but telling the truth could ruin their lives."

"What about right and wrong?" Julie asked.

"John and Arthur have only just started at school," Kate reminded them. "They've scarcely settled in. Give them time. I'd suggest more religious education, but I'm not sure the staff here is equipped to teach them any better."

"I'll speak to William," Julie said. "Maybe there is another church with better curates."

Lucy glanced at her mistress. "Let's get you under the covers. You're very tired, I can tell."

Kate wondered if they should be trusting Lucy quite so much when her gang of friends was capable of committing larceny. She went downstairs, unbuttoned her cloak, and tucked it over a peg in the front hall, then stepped into the parlor, where they had left Charles and William.

She found her fiancé at a writing desk, while William paced next to him, muttering something, his face red. Neither of them noticed her. She went to the table, where the treasure map still lay open.

The sought-after item was a piece of parchment, tan in color and quite tattered around the edges. It did appear very worn, and she could see faint markings close to the tears, as if it had once been some other sort of document. The map did not look as any of them had expected. In fact, would they have called it a map at all if they hadn't heard it referred to as such? Instead of some sort of landscape rendering with a line and landmarks, it was merely a list of pictographs, one after another from the top of the page. The only reason they could be certain what was the top and what was the bottom was the second marking, a head.

The first marking, now that they knew what it was, or at least what everyone perceived it to be, was a rendering of the chimney in the ruined house. Kate picked up the map, took it to the window, and stared at the second symbol, the head.

Her intent focus, with the sunlight streaming through the window, gave the image a strange sort of animation. It came to her what the head might represent. She'd been exposed to the life of that person a couple of months ago.

Could this head really represent the late poet Lord Byron? She traced the curly hair with the distinctive receding hairline, indicated by a side part, the thick eyebrows and molded lips. Whoever had designed the map wasn't much of an artist, but she couldn't deny that Byron had ties to Harrow on the Hill, having come here in 1801 to attend Harrow.

She'd learned a lot about the poet from Thomas Moore's *The Works of Lord Byron*. It had been published in recent years, and Lady Lugoson had some of the volumes. After having met Lord Byron's widow a couple of months ago, Kate had been curious enough to seek out the new volumes about him.

Based on what she had learned, the treasure map symbol just might lead to St. Mary's churchyard. When Lord Byron was a student at Harrow School, he used to lie on John Peachey's grave in the churchyard, and his illegitimate daughter was buried there in an unmarked grave.

Kate shivered. The poor child had died in a convent in Europe, far away from either of her parents. Such a sad end. While she didn't understand why Lord Byron would insist on having her coffin transported all the way here to that quiet graveyard, it did mean he had strong ties to the place.

"Why are you shivering, Kate?" Charles asked, a solicitous hand on her arm.

She forced her body to settle and smiled up at him. "Just terrible thoughts. No parent should have to bury a child, and yet it does happen."

"All too often," Charles said, bitter memory etched across his brow. Not all his siblings had survived their early birthdays.

"I know you've had such losses, dear, that are difficult to bear. For now, I think we should go to the churchyard," Kate said, holding up the map. "Don't you think this looks like Lord Byron?"

Charles's mobile features worked; then he nodded. His ink-stained finger pointed under the man's head. "I do see what you mean."

She nodded, satisfied, and recited the two biographical facts that linked the great poet to the churchyard. "It could also be Harrow, of course, but that's a very large place."

"Like his lodgings when he was a student there?"

"Yes, that is a possibility, but my mind ventures to his daughter's grave. Or his place of solitude on top of a certain grave? That feels right to me." She smiled up at him. "My feminine instinct."

"Let's go back there," Charles said. He lowered his voice. "William doesn't look well. I think the strain is getting to him. I'm having trouble enough getting any work done, but he has his cousin's death and concerns about his father's business practices weighing on him, as well."

"When is your next *Pickwick* installment due?" Kate asked, wondering about the state of his well-paid literary endeavor.

"Mid-month. The sheets are a weary length," he confessed. "I had no idea there was this much to do."

"You had said you wrote more for the first one than you needed."

"Yes," he agreed. "I am to do twenty-four printed pages, and

I wrote a story that doesn't fit. So that goes in this one, which saves a bit of time."

"I know you will manage everything," she assured him. "I have complete faith in your skills. But no one expected you to solve a murder at the same time. I do hope I can be of some little help in the matter."

"Just seeing your face helps a great deal," he assured her. "For now, I think a walk is just the thing we need. It will clear both of our heads, and who can say, maybe we will find something in the graveyard."

Chapter 13

When Charles and Kate strolled past the Harrow buildings on the way to the graveyard, he saw a familiar shock of russet hair and the skinny form of the boy he'd come up from London with, clad in a much less tidy set of clothes than nearly a week before. He and another boy were kicking a glass bottle down the street.

"Hullo again," Charles said.

The boys looked up, guilt etched on their faces. "Oh, it's you," said the one Charles had met.

"Do you have any idea where the John Peachey grave is?" Charles asked.

"It's a tomb, not a grave," the second boy said. "It's flat." He leveled his hand parallel to the ground to demonstrate.

"Where is it in the churchyard?" Kate asked.

"Go through the west entrance and then walk south. You can't miss it."

"You following in Byron's footsteps?" asked the russet-haired boy. "My father knew him at school."

"Really?" Charles said, interested. "My fiancée here has taken tea with Lady Byron, his widow."

The boys regarded them as Kate smiled benignly. "It's not the same, though, is it?" said the russet-haired boy.

"No, your story is much better," Charles assured him, holding back a laugh. "Thank you for the information."

They climbed the hill, Charles solicitously holding Kate's arm, and went through the west gate. Broad vistas spread out majestically around them, a feast for eyes long turned to dust. The Peachey tomb turned out to belong to more than just the one man. John Peachey had merely been the first sibling to die, expiring close to sixty years before, though the fourth sibling had died in this decade.

Kate shivered. "Not an especially old grave."

"No. It's been opened since Byron's day, but William Peachey must have been a very old man, given how much longer he lived than his siblings."

"I think it's sad to be buried like this. Where are their wives and husbands?"

"I'm glad not to see any children," Charles returned. "For they should still be alive."

"Do you see anything that might help us with the treasure map?" Kate asked.

Charles pulled out the map and consulted it. "After the sketch of a possible Byron, there is a formation that might be a broken heart."

"Or wings," Kate said, tilting her head in various directions.

Charles looked at the surrounding jumble of stones and tombs. "It means nothing to me. I don't see a monument in this shape nearby."

"If it isn't the Peachey grave that is indicated, there is still poor little Allegra's grave."

"No one knows exactly where Byron's daughter is buried." Charles surveyed the graveyard.

"She is supposed to be near the entrance, right?"

"We can walk over there and see if we can find a monument that looks to be in the right shape," Charles suggested.

"I don't have any other ideas," Kate confessed, then smiled up at him. "But I am glad to be here with you."

For a moment Kate thought he might steal a kiss, but then his gaze bounced from her to a gravestone, and she saw the moment he changed his mind. Instead, he strode briskly through the green space, holding her arm. She stayed alongside him until they were at the front of the church.

"Allegra's grave is meant to be around here somewhere," Charles said.

Kate walked down the path leading out of the churchyard, then back in again. The grave wouldn't be very old, and thus not sunken, like it might be in a very old graveyard, but it would be old enough that the grass grown over it would not look any different than the surrounding vegetation. Allegra had been born in 1817 and had died in 1822, making her younger than both Kate and Charles. If she'd lived, she'd probably be a very grand young lady.

Kate remembered her conversation with Lady Byron and how her daughter, Allegra's half sister, now Lady King, had gone from first meeting to wedding her husband in only six weeks, whereas she'd been waiting for Charles to afford to marry her for nearly a year now.

Frustrated with her irritated thoughts and knowing how disappointed Charles became when she went into one of her sulks, she walked nearly as briskly as he up and down the paths. The steepness of the hills had her catching her breath at times. How had the coffins been sunk into the hill? Were they tilted, the bones bunched in some disgraceful heap at one end, or had the gravediggers dug into the dirt at an angle?

"Kate," Charles called. "What a little Fury you are."

"It isn't right that her grave is unmarked," Kate said. "Whatever Byron did himself, it wasn't a five-year-old's fault."

"That's not our concern," Charles said. "Today we are focused on the injustice done to another young girl."

"I know you are right," Kate said. She spun around slowly, her eyes unfocusing as the vast landscape spread out around the hill moved in bands of green around her.

"Wait a minute," Charles said, pointing across the north side of the vista.

Kate stopped. "I see it, too. The trees!"

They gazed down the hill, standing next to each other. A stand of trees stood in the broken-heart or wings formation that appeared on the map after the sketch of Byron. Kate had no idea of distance from up here, but it didn't seem too very far away.

"It's the clue!" Charles exclaimed. "By Jove, you were right, Kate." He grabbed her arms and spun her around.

Quite forgetting where she was, and giddy with excitement, she put her hands on his chest to steady herself. He stopped moving, then crushed her to his chest.

"Oh, darling." His hands stole to her cheeks, and his mouth dropped to hers.

She felt his warm breath against her wind-chilled face and let him kiss her for a long, delicious moment. "We have only a few weeks left to wait."

"Very few," he murmured and kissed her again, a tender brush of flesh on flesh that made her knees tremble.

Giddy with anticipation, she nodded. "We have to find the killer so we can return to London. You have to finish furnishing our rooms. My mother and Mary will help you, but there is a lot to do before the wedding."

He chuckled in a very knowing tone. "Let's sort this out quickly, then," he said, his hands stroking down to her arms again. "We have rooms to sweep and furniture to pick up from the dealers and kitchen stores to lay in and buckets to buy and broomsticks and boots and . . ."

She laughed as he ran out of breath. "My own dear boy, it is a good thing you have more energy than any man I have ever met."

"I wonder if you can keep up with me," he said suggestively, clasping her hands.

"Mr. Dickens," she said reprovingly. "Is this really the time to doubt my abilities?"

"I never do," he assured her. "You saved my life this year, after all."

"Indeed I did." Her tone was pert. "Shall we take a very long walk down this hill and see what might be special about that wing-shaped grove of trees?"

"A veritable genius of an idea." He dropped her hands as a middle-aged couple came into the graveyard. They exchanged quiet greetings; then Kate followed Charles to the north side of the graveyard, as they made their way down the hill.

"So much delicious fresh air," she panted as they reached the flat ground again some tens of minutes later. "This is nothing like London."

"You can see why I dream someday of living in Kent," he told her. "Out of the fogs of London. As much as I love it, someday I dream of living at Gad's Hill Place."

"Why is that?"

"I was a child when I saw it, just nine years old, and my father told me if I worked hard, I could live there someday. In fact, I hope to own the house we saw, or something similar. That day stuck with me, and I mean to accomplish my dream."

Kate watched the trees disappear as his mind's eye turned to Kent. Her gentle squeeze brought him back. "I believe you can manage anything you can dream, Charles, as long as you steer clear of your enemies."

"I shall have to take you to see it," he said, guiding them across a field that seemed to be free of livestock. "It is a nice brick abode with bowed windows in a pleasantly bucolic setting."

"Indeed, you must, if I'm going to live there in the future."

He nodded thoughtfully. "An excellent point, Kate."

They reached the edge of something that resembled a meadow or path. Kate's boots held up. Being raised in Scotland meant one knew how to protect oneself from the elements, but she was starting to wish she'd worn warmer stockings. This adventure would have been more pleasant in a couple of months.

"I've lost track of where we are," she admitted to Charles. Behind them was a blackthorn hedge, its bare branches covered with white flowers. Ahead, the forest seemed to be a mix of oak and poplar trees. "How are we to recognize the formation of the trees from here, now that we are level with them?"

"I believe we are in the right spot." He gestured up to the trees. "The broken-heart formation was at the edge of the woods."

Kate turned in a circle, staring up at the hill behind her and the woods before her. She recognized a large rowan tree at the edge, its branches just starting to twig. The thought of the jam she could produce from the berries later in the year made her mouth water slightly. "My parents would lock me in the attic if they knew I was alone out here with you."

"Only until the wedding," Charles said with a chuckle. "It's too late to worry about that now. Worry more about the long walk back to school."

"It's excessively cruel for you to mention that," she said.

"And not a muffin man or hot potato cart in sight for miles," he agreed. "Now, what are we going to do?"

"Look at the map. We need to see if we can sort out what the next clue might be from here."

"Good point. It's not as if we're going to find treasure here, just something that leads to the next point of interest."

Kate heard a branch break somewhere in front of them. She grabbed Charles's arm. "What wild animals might there be around here?"

"Nothing too frightful. Mostly birds, I would think. Hedgehogs might be awake? Rabbits?"

"The noise seemed to be coming from higher, Charles. Maybe it was just a bird, but it sounded larger than that."

Charles stilled. She could see he was listening intently to something. What?

A moment later, she heard what he had. Voices floated on the wind. Charles relaxed as the sound became more obvious. "It's humans, darling. Not a wild boar or a wolf."

"Ha. Humans might be equally deadly. What are they doing out here? Following the map?"

Charles turned in a circle. "You know, I expect we are behind the school, as the crow flies. What do you want to bet if we walked that way, we'd wind up back at the icehouse where Agnes's body was left?"

"Do you think she might have been meeting someone to follow the map?"

"Why not?" Charles said. "Anything is possible. At least it is an idea. Anyone who knew the map might have seen the tree formation while wandering through the graveyard."

"Especially if they were there deliberately, following the map. Put it in your pocket," she suggested to Charles. "We don't want to give the game away."

She stepped away from him as the first dark shape emerged from the woods, not wanting to give the slightest hint of impropriety. How she wished William and Julie were with them to chaperone. Even Lucy Fair would have been more than welcome at this moment.

Unfortunately, a member of the Aga family emerged from the woods, albeit a young one, with black hair and a decided resemblance to his cousin William. She calculated the odds of news of her sojourn with Charles reaching back to her parents. She'd met Monks Aga when he'd been invited to his uncle's dinner table the night before. But then she saw who clung to Monks's arm, and knew she had nothing to fear.

The youth had a girl in the school's servant uniform with him. No older than Lucy, this girl had nothing of the other girl's beauty.

"Nancy Price, dressed in her work clothes no less," Charles muttered. "I remember seeing how she looked at him at the inquest, and I'm not surprised."

Monks wore his school uniform. "A couple of wicked children out for a lark," Kate whispered back.

But of all the people that might know the map, they were so very likely.

"Something tells me the pair of you aren't out here on school business," Charles said, stepping in front of Kate.

Monks caught sight of Charles and did a double take. Instead of speaking, he turned to Nancy with sudden violence and pushed her away from him, hard enough that the girl sprawled onto the branch- and weed-covered ground.

"Get away from me, you slag," he snarled at her. Then he turned back to Charles. "She's always following me, like a bitch in heat. I can't get any peace."

Kate saw the servant's expression go from shock to anger to a sort of acceptance. She wanted to help the girl up but didn't like the idea of getting too close to the tall, volatile youth.

Nancy scrambled to her feet without help, revealing a tear in her skirt and dirt down the side. "I apologize, sir," she said with a tone of utter falsehood. "Mrs. Bedwin asked me to fetch her, umm, from the woods, and I had something in my shoe, so I held on to you so I could fix it."

Monks's upper lip curled. "Don't do it again."

Kate felt her hands shake. She tucked them into her muff. The casual violence against Nancy had been such a sudden thing and was indicative of the boy's character. She could think of a number of ways he could have dealt with the embarrassing situation without resorting to hurting the girl.

"Why are you walking out here, Aga?" Charles asked. "Shouldn't you be at a prayer service?"

"It's teatime," the boy snarled. "I wasn't hungry."

"Students are allowed to roam freely like this?" Charles inquired.

"I'm family." The boy's tone flattened.

Kate wondered if there was any discipline at the school. Charles had said school life seemed to be deteriorating. This might be another sign of it, whatever Monks was up to.

"We're going back to school," Charles said. "Nancy, come stand by me. Monks, you lead the way."

The boy didn't even glance at his victim, merely turned on his way and marched off. With a warning glance at the servant girl, Charles followed Monks, the others at his sides, Nancy limping slightly.

Though it had seemed like the trail had ended at the rowan tree, Monks's feet soon found a well-trodden path.

"Nancy," Charles asked, "do you remember the day of the murder very well?"

"A little bit, sir," she said, rubbing her side.

"Mr. Aga and I searched the school for any sign of Agnes. We noticed that you seemed to have a missing apron. What has happened to your spare?"

Nancy gave Monks's back a nervous glance. "I—I stained it, sir. It was soaking in the washhouse, but it's clean now."

"What did you stain it with?"

Her cheeks colored. "Blood."

Kate saw Charles was going to ask a follow-up question, but she gave him a wide-eyed shake of the head. The way the girl had said *blood*, Kate suspected the apron issue had been a personal matter, not anything to do with Agnes.

They had been only about fifteen minutes beyond the icehouse, walking at a fast pace. Charles stopped Kate there and sent the other two on, admonishing Nancy to return to her duties immediately.

Kate glanced around the clearing as they departed. "Was Agnes killed in the icehouse?"

"Maybe, or dragged there immediately afterward."

"Was she, err, violated?" Kate asked. "That boy." She shivered.

Charles patted her shoulder. "I agree. That disturbed me, as well. And honestly, I don't know. Her skirts were disarranged, but no one could have managed such a delicate matter in an icehouse."

She blushed and realized she probably looked as Nancy had when her apron had been mentioned.

"We didn't see any sign of struggle out here. We still don't know how Agnes came to be at the icehouse. She wasn't doing an errand. The truth is entirely obscured, still."

"They didn't say at the inquest?"

"The doctor barely examined her until afterward. Coroner Bumbleton is no Sir Silas Laurie, that is for certain."

Kate glanced at the low building. It looked only half raised from the earth. The light was starting to fade, giving the clearing a sinister appearance.

"What is next in this landscape?" she asked.

"Some sheds."

"Have they been searched for signs of a struggle?" She coughed. "Or an assignation that went sour?"

"Good question. William and I have been most distracted between the mudlarks and the murder. Why did you want me to cease my questioning of Nancy? A bloody apron on that day."

"Was the timing suspicious?"

"Agnes had been missing for hours before we discovered Nancy's apron missing, but that may not be suspicious in itself."

"I had the sense it was a personal matter," Kate said steadily. "Among other possibilities, she might have been interfered with. It's not as if we think Agnes died in her room."

"No, you are quite correct. Surely someone would have noticed her killer carrying her dead body across the back lawn, even if they don't remember the usual sight of her living self walking there." He nodded, as if coming to some decision. "I will take you back to Mr. Aga's house now. William and I will have a look in the buildings and then return to the clearing in an attempt to follow the treasure map."

Kate had no interest in searching the sheds herself, but she suspected the men would need her help with the treasure map. As brilliant as Charles was, she'd figured out the clues herself. "I am certain Monks is capable of murdering his sister, Charles."

"I will also speak to Eustace Aga about the safety of his female servants," he agreed. "Let's go back. Hopefully, there are still some tea things at Mr. Aga's house."

"Always ruled by our stomachs," Kate agreed cheerfully. "Oh, Charles, I cannot wait to have full command of our kitchen."

"The first thing I shall order is your treacle tart," Charles told her. "I have dreams about that."

"I am glad to hear it, and we will have solved this business all the sooner if I peruse the map while you and Mr. Aga search the sheds."

He laughed at her hopeful smile. "Do you think so? I suspect the clues are discerned only by standing in the landscape. It would have been impossible to understand that broken-heart shape without being in the vicinity of Allegra Byron's grave."

"In other words, we're going to have to go back through the woods," Kate said. "Charles, you are right. What a lot must be done before we can leave."

They walked back to the school, trying to wrap their heads around the various mysteries.

When they arrived at Mr. Aga's house ten minutes later, the back of the house was shut up and locked, not a bad notion when a killer was roaming around the school. Charles checked his appearance and Kate's. They both wiped off their weed-dotted, dirty boots with Charles's handkerchief, then walked around to the front.

A landau, both of its hoods raised to keep out the weather, was at the edge of the street. A pair of matched black horses were still in harness, though a coachman in a smart blue coat was seeing to them.

"Mr. Aga has visitors," Kate said. "I wonder who?"

"Someone visiting a student?" Charles guessed. "It is Sunday. I don't know the procedures. A parent might have to visit the headmaster before being allowed onto the grounds."

They walked inside. Charles saw Mr. Aga in the parlor, seated in the chair closest to the door. Beyond him stood Mr. Sikes, leaning against the mantelpiece. Also standing was a man of some forty-plus years, still dressed for the outdoors in a new, shiny top hat and a deep brown cloak with a fur collar. He leaned on a walking stick, as if he had a weak leg.

As Charles hovered in the doorway, the man twisted and lifted his chin in such a way that Charles recognized the motion. This man must be Toby Grimwig's father, come to check on him. Unfortunate for the wounded boy that his father seemed such a forbidding sort, but at least he had come.

"Go upstairs," he whispered in Kate's ear. He couldn't have her tramping through the boardinghouses, and he hoped to join the school owners for the conversation. He might learn something more about the history here.

"Am I interrupting?" Charles asked, stepping in boldly. He saw no sign of William.

Mr. Aga turned to him with a gentle smile. "Ah, it's Mr. Dickens, our guest. Mr. Grimwig, this is Mr. Dickens, who works with my son in the London newspaper trade."

Mr. Grimwig's eyes narrowed as he lifted his chin in that twisting way, then inclined his head in greeting. "I wonder if you, as I do, Mr. Dickens, smell Sodom and Gomorrah at this school."

"Sodom and Gomorrah," Charles said, startled. "I should hardly think so. There are rather a lot of children here with high spirits, you know. Your son seemed well enough when we visited him in his very nice room."

"This gentleman"—Mr. Grimwig twisted his chin at Mr. Sikes—"tells me that young Toby is finally able to return to the classroom."

"Is he?" Charles asked. "The cast is of an intimidating weight."

"Dr. Goose comes tomorrow, my dear," Mr. Sikes soothed. "I'm convinced that he will be able to reduce the size of the cast. Young Mr. Grimwig is a keen enthusiast of learning and is eager to reenter his studies with his fellow students."

Charles doubted that, though there seemed nothing wrong with the boy's intelligence. "I must have had the erroneous impression that his fall took place more recently than it did."

"February," Mr. Aga said.

"Late January," insisted Mr. Sikes.

"Of course, of course," Mr. Aga agreed.

Charles glanced between the two men. He hoped they weren't risking the future strength of the boy's arm in order to keep him as a student. "Surely another week or two will do no harm, either way. I'm certain that Dr. Goose will have the answer." He thought nothing of the sort, in truth.

Mr. Grimwig sighed and fluttered his eyes closed. "My son will not be seeing the local doctor. While, as you know, my wife has gone to her glory, my aunt has agreed to take him on and place him in the care of a tutor for now."

"My dears, my dears," Mr. Sikes cried, "let us not be hasty. The boy needs the companionship of others."

"I had not understood there would be quite so many charity students here, or quite so much disruption. While I'm sure that servant died through her own misadventures and her death does not reflect on the school, I nonetheless would like my son to have peers, if not equals."

Mr. Aga had gone very white, but his voice was composed when he spoke. "My dear sir, we have made every alteration to our practices that you required. Indeed, this school has become a testament to Grimwigian principles for the sake of your son. Surely this is the best place for him. He will not be shut up in his room past tomorrow, I assure you."

Charles realized what the cost of bringing on a high-caste student had been. Mr. Aga had seen a chance to elevate his school and couldn't afford to do so. He'd brought on a new partner, changed the educational practices and, ironically, lowered the food quality, all in the hopes of attracting Mr. Grimwig's like. Perhaps young Toby had a selection of younger siblings and other connections who might have come here once the school had been remade in his father's philosophy. Toby had been the sole parlor boarder here at the school for now, a little prince. Had he been taken down on purpose by the other boys? His thoughts went to Monks Aga. Was it possible for another boy to rule the school when the headmaster's own nephew was such a strong personality?

As the men discussed the situation vehemently, Charles considered that Toby's departure might cause the educational system at Aga Academy to change for the better. That would only benefit John, Ollie, and Arthur, who needed adequate nutrition and a little whimsy in their educational pursuits. His own temperament had been saved in his youth many a time by a bedtime story or an amateur musical.

In truth, he had let the boys down by blindly trusting Eustace Aga. He resolved to pay attention to more details in the future, in any endeavor.

With his new prominence, he might even be able to find Mr. Aga a new parlor boarder. Nothing was more likely.

"Surely you don't want to pack the boy into a coach with such an uncomfortable inconvenience as the cast," Mr. Aga stuttered. "Why do you not return in a week and see how things have improved for young Master Grimwig?"

"I think not. I'm taking him into London and having a doctor I've heard of look at him. I believe Dr. Manette has treated boys at your school before?"

"Ollie," Charles said aloud. All three men glanced at him. "Pardon me. Yes, he treated Ollie for his terrible hand injury. Ollie even lived in his surgery for a time. He has recovered beautifully."

Mr. Grimwig nodded. "Yes, I believe he is an expert in limbs. Those Frenchies have to be, with all the wars they inflicted upon humankind in my youth."

Mr. Sikes inclined his head obsequiously. "I cannot guarantee we will be able to keep Master Grimwig's very fine room open for long, but if it is just the matter of a week or two for you to seek the counsel of Dr. Manette, we will make do. His fees are paid until Lady Day and are nonrefundable, of course."

"I will write," Mr. Grimwig said in a distant tone. Then he

sharpened his words. "If you will ring for your housekeeper to have someone pack a bag for him? We will call for the rest at another time."

Mr. Aga bent his head in defeat, while Charles suspected Mr. Sikes did not think all hope was lost. Of course, he was used to the workhouse, where many who departed were able to do so only for a time.

Chapter 14

Mr. Sikes had remained for dinner. Charles had been frank, asking questions about what Toby Grimwig's departure meant for the fate of the school. Mr. Aga and William had both been rather quiet as Mr. Sikes defended a series of his actions in the tones of moral imperviousness.

"We need to question that girl," Julie insisted as she and Kate went into the parlor after dinner. The men were having spirits and cigars before joining them. Lucy had been sent to eat with the household servants.

"It might be early enough," Kate admitted. "I don't think Mr. Aga wanted us to linger long over dinner."

"It was not a feast," Julie agreed. "Though the roast was excellent. Given how fiery Charles is, he probably unleashed his opinions on Mr. Sikes as soon as we left. They will be in there for an hour if William has the energy to engage in the discussion. He's had a bit of a headache, and no surprise."

"Your poor husband." Kate went to the parlor windows and pushed a curtain back. While no one would go to bed for hours yet, the sky had completely darkened. "I remember there is a lantern on the table near the door in the school's front hall. It is only across the street. Nancy's room is in the attic. I could send Lucy to bring her down to the school parlor."

"No." Julie worried her lip. "It's the scene of the crime, isn't it? Nancy's bedroom, I mean. We've been thinking all along that Agnes was removed from it forcibly, in some fashion."

"There won't be anything to see there now."

Julie's skirts rustled, displaying her restlessness. "I'm curious, and I know you are, too. We're going to turn into murder tourists."

Kate smiled. "Or lady detectives. Can you imagine?"

They both laughed. Kate thought Lucy might be a welcome addition, in truth, but she respected Julie's wishes and went to light the lantern, then came back with their cloaks, which were in a closet under the stairs.

In a couple of minutes, they were on their way to the school, making sure not to lock themselves out of the headmaster's house in the process. They only had to dart across the street after waiting for one carriage to pass.

The trimmed hedges were ghostly blocks as they passed through them, the bobbing lantern in Kate's hand catching black shadows, looking first like boots, then like the bottoms of cloaks. She shook her head and tried not to give in to fantastical thoughts. Rather, she reveled in the adventure and wondered what sort of trouble Julie Aga was capable of getting her into as the years passed. They reached their first snag at the school's front door. It was locked.

"Do we ring?" Kate asked.

"I'm not sure anyone would answer, with a housekeeper as incompetent as Mrs. Bedwin," Julie said. "Let's go to the servants' entrance. Maybe someone will still be in the kitchen."

She was correct, and after they tramped around to the side of the school, the cook did let them in.

"What are you doing here at the school?" she asked. "Pudding at the headmaster's table too soggy for you?"

Julie laughed and replied in an equally teasing manner, and Kate realized she and the cook had interacted before. If she had thought to mention that fact, Kate would have had calmer nerves.

"I'll take you upstairs myself," the cook said in response to Julie's query. "I'm done here. I just like to do a bit of organizing after dinner, once the scullery is tidy."

She took off her apron and led them up the servants' staircase, then pointed to the left side of the attic. "That's Nancy and Agnes's room." She colored. "Well, just that Nancy's now, until Mrs. Bedwin hires a new girl."

"Thank you," Julie said graciously and knocked on the door.

No one came to the door. Kate put her ear to it and didn't hear anything.

Julie shrugged and opened it. She and Kate stood in the doorway. The only light came from a window, and that wasn't much, but Kate could discern a lump on one of the beds.

"Nancy?" Kate asked. "Do you have a candle?"

Nothing but a sniffle came in response.

"I'll see if Cook can lend me one," Julie said and returned to the hallway.

Kate sat on the empty bed opposite the lump to wait. She heard a couple more sniffles but nothing more until Julie returned, holding a rushlight in a handled clip. "Not ideal, but it will do."

"Now, Nancy, what was going on today?" Kate asked. "Surely you don't have permission to be stepping out with one of the students on a Sunday afternoon."

"He is the headmaster's nephew," Nancy said in a tone that held grit.

"That may give him privileges, but not you. In fact, it means you should be all the more careful." Kate paused. "Especially since he behaves like quite a violent person. Why did he push you?"

Nancy heaved a long sigh, punctuated by a hiccup. "It hurts."

"What hurts?" Julie said sharply.

"Where the stick stabbed me as I fell," the girl whispered.

"Did it cut your skin? Are you bleeding?" Kate asked.

"I don't know." The girl's tone was full of misery.

Kate glanced at Julie. "We'll get a better candle so we can see the injury."

"Oh, I couldn't. It's . . . it's on my lower parts."

"This is a fine time to be delicate," Julie said acidly. "If it's not a part of your body you can see, then someone else will have to do it."

"After you answer a couple of questions," Kate said. "What were you doing out there with Monks Aga?"

"He's courting me," Nancy whispered.

"Courting you?" Julie said, her voice rising to stage strength. "He's fifteen!"

"It doesn't matter. He says he's going to be rich."

"How old are you?" Kate asked.

"Fourteen."

Kate swallowed hard. The girl was young, likely low class and poorly educated. Agnes might have had a path out from menial work if she had lived, but this girl would be left behind. The only path to real advancement for her was to stay unmarried and rise to the position of housekeeper, if she had the brains, which she did not seem to. Otherwise, looking for a husband was a good idea, but not for a few more years, when bearing a child would be a safer occupation. And certainly not among the students, to whom she couldn't possibly be anything but a vulnerable mark.

Kate didn't scold her, though. She merely asked, "Does he claim to have his sister's treasure map?"

"Yes," Nancy said in a small voice.

"Agnes's map or a different one?" Julie clarified.

"Agnes's map. He said he inherited it."

"Where does he say he found it?" Kate asked, keeping her tone even. In addition to being a seducer, Monks was a liar, because Charles had the map.

"He didn't say."

"Don't you think it would have been here, in your room?" Julie asked.

"You didn't let him in your room?" Kate demanded, horrified, remembering the bloody apron.

Nancy waved a tired hand. "No, it was never 'ere. Agnes liked to wave it around the boys, but never to me."

"Where did she keep it?"

"I don't know, but Monks did."

"He might have at one point," Kate said, deciding to reveal some of the truth. "But someone had taken it the day before Agnes was murdered."

"Monks?" Nancy asked, her voice squeaking.

"Thankfully, no," Kate said. "But still, he lied to you. He has never had the map since at least the day before Agnes's death."

"Lied," Nancy whispered.

"I'm afraid so," Julie said, with a hint of sympathy. "You must avoid him, Nancy. He is in no position to wed you in any case."

"He's the heir to a dairy farm," Nancy said faintly in a tone of wonder.

"Yes, and no match for the likes of you," Julie snapped. "Now, we're going to get a lamp and take a look at your backside. You'll mind us, because otherwise you won't be able to return to your duties tomorrow, and I know you don't want to be sacked."

*   *   *

On Monday morning, Charles stepped into the dining room in Mr. Aga's house to find Kate and the Agas assembled. He had done his best to dash off a couple of slips of *Pickwick* that morning, after rising early. Chapters Three to Five of the project were due, and not at all completed, no matter how much confidence he displayed to Kate. At least his imagination never deserted him. He had far more control over that than the toll of hours passing.

In the dining room, he found the remnants of the morning meal rather more dismal than he might have hoped, but Kate rushed to pour him tea, cover some toast with the stringy remnants of a nearly empty jar of marmalade, and dish out oatmeal.

"Not what you will feed me after we are wed, eh, Kate?" Charles said.

"No, I'm sure we can do a bit better than this, especially just before a long walk," she assured him.

"Are we walking?" Charles asked. "Just the thing."

William set down his teacup. He still looked a bit peaked. "I'd say we should wait and do our work for the day first, but the sky has that rainy look."

"Are we going to find the next spot on the map?" Charles asked, then spooned oatmeal into his mouth.

"Yes. It was well done of you to uncover the second and third clue on the map," Julie praised. "I just wish we knew if Monks had done the same."

"We can't assume he hasn't known the answers all along," William pointed out. "I'm sure Agnes, however she obtained the map, would have shared it with her brother."

Charles wanted to leave aside the doings of the Aga family. Otherwise, they would fall back on the murder investigation, and he wanted to put the matter of the map to rest. "What is the fourth clue?"

"A couple of wavy lines with dots," Kate reported. "But you have the map."

"And so I do," Charles replied, remembering the map's whereabouts. "Excellent memory."

"William, dear, will you fetch our boots while Charles slowly finishes his breakfast?" Julie asked.

William smiled in a half-hearted way and rose from the table. "I'll pull all our things out of the closet. Eat up, Snail Dickens. We'll never solve our mysteries if we relax half of the morning."

Charles threw his crust at William as he walked past. William fumbled and let it drop to the floor, but he chuckled as he walked out.

Julie and Kate shook their heads in tandem. "You would think they were a pair of wayward brothers, rather than professional men."

"No different than my younger brothers," Kate agreed. "I quite despair. My mother is not going to know what to do with herself when two of my brothers go off to school soon, but then, she is losing my help, as well."

"And Mary's?"

"As much as she can be spared. Soon she'll be old enough to find her own husband, but for now, she can help me set up my household."

"That will be a good education. I had little idea of what I was doing, especially after we moved to Cheapside," Julie admitted. "I did quite a bit of household work in my mother's house, but I also was very busy on the stage."

"I cannot imagine how you could ever successfully apply yourself to two spheres," Kate said.

"I do miss the stage, though." Julie gave a forced smile. "The applause, the rich language in the speeches."

"The costumes?" Kate asked.

"No. They aren't nearly as nice as they look, and always smell of either sweat or mothballs."

William poked his head in the door. "Boots are assembled. Come along."

Charles thought William looked a little unsteady on his feet as they tramped through the woods in the bright spring sunlight. They had paused for a moment at the icehouse out of respect before continuing on their way, giving his friend the opportunity to steel himself.

He kept an anxious eye on William, and Kate and Lucy flanked Julie as they followed a winding game trail down the hill until they found the stand of elms that had looked like a broken heart from the cemetery.

"You have an excellent memory," Kate complimented him. "I didn't think about identifying the trees from this angle."

"The question is, What can we see next?" Charles asked.

"We still are at a degree of elevation," William said. "Maybe the next clue is also downslope."

Charles pulled the map from his coat pocket and spread it out over the limb of one of the barren trees. "You see the wavy lines we are looking for?"

"With the little dots," Julie clarified.

Lucy stepped out from the chilly shade cast by the large trees, hugging her arms around her shawl. "It's really only clear on two sides."

Kate followed her and pointed up. "We came from there. The cemetery is above us, starting on the slope."

William pointed behind them. "That's the footpath to the school."

Julie pointed south. "That looks to be more woods."

"Which leaves us with west." Charles walked with the map to the outer rim of the center of the broken-heart formation and stared west down the hill. "We're looking for wavy lines, with dots between them."

"Who has the keenest eyes?" William asked.

"Me?" Kate said doubtfully. "I spotted the trees." She came up alongside Charles.

He wanted to spot the clue himself, but he spent a lot of time peering at his writing under candlelight and couldn't deny it probably affected his vision. "Take a look, darling," he invited. "Fix the shape of the symbol in your head, and then scan the down slope."

Kate nodded. She looked very intently at the map, focusing her pretty blue eyes, then resolutely gazed westward. Charles saw her head move to the left, then to the right, then back again, and pause just right of center.

"What's that?" she asked, pointing.

William came up next to her. "I can't make it out."

"Too many late nights with candles like me," Charles said.

"I think two hills are overlapping," Lucy said.

"Yes, I agree," said Julie, whose nights performing in theaters didn't seem to have harmed her vision any. "It appears there are some sort of earthworks in front of the hills."

"A gravel pit," Kate breathed. "The dots . . . That must be it."

"It makes sense," William said. "We definitely have those here."

"We met the Maylies," Charles added, remembering their conversation. "They have a gravel pit."

"Maybe they are involved in the mystery," William mused.

"Could your cousin have stolen the map from her friend?" Julie asked.

"I think Myrtle would have told us," Charles interjected. "If it had originally belonged to her family. If it was a Maylie possession, she would have known about it."

"Besides," Kate added, staring keenly into the middle distance, "it's a middle clue on the map. The Maylies are unlikely to have anything to do with the mystery."

Julie shivered suddenly.

Lucy put a solicitous hand on her shoulder. "Are you cold?"

"Did a goose just walk over your grave?" Kate asked.

"No." Julie frowned. "I feel like we're being watched."

William turned in a circle. "It's certainly possible, since we can't be sure that we aren't being followed."

"The mudlarks?" Kate guessed.

"Or Monks," Charles said. "Probably not Nancy, at this time of day."

William shrugged. "Let's walk down to the quarry and see if we can spot the next clue. We can outbox any of the most likely suspects."

"William," Julie chided. "We won't be boxing John, Ollie, or Arthur, thank you very much."

A bit of William's usually easygoing levity showed as he grinned. "I wouldn't mind taking a swing at Monks, however."

Kate knew the other three were slowing Charles down as they walked to the quarry. An indefatigable walker, he loved to tramp the London streets at night when his brain was too full of ideas to permit him to rest.

It took most of half an hour to reach the sand quarry. Men were pushing wheelbarrows between a warehouse and a brick-works on the far side. A horse hauled a wagon full of sand, which sparkled a bit in the sun.

It seemed a prosperous enterprise, the sort of thing from which Mr. Screws had become rich by supporting with loans. She wondered how Fred was doing at his new job.

"Here we are," Charles said. "It's not a small place. How are we going to sort out the next clue?"

A man who'd been directing the wheelbarrow pushers spotted them and walked in their direction. The backs of his hands were permanently darkened from the sun, but the palms didn't bear the marks of hard labor. He had a decade on William, judging from the creases around his eyes. "No offense, but this isn't a place for young ladies. State your business, gentlemen."

Charles didn't answer. Instead, his attention had moved to a man standing in the shadow of the warehouse.

William spoke instead. "We're just taking a country walk. I'm sorry to have interrupted your work."

"We're associates of Mr. Screws," Kate blurted. "He's done business with the Maylies."

"Up from London, are you?" the man said in a tone of greater curiosity.

William nodded. "We've met the family in town."

"Did they invite you to see the quarry?" the man asked.

"It seems like visitors aren't rare," Charles said abruptly. "What kind of business does Aga Academy have with the quarry?"

The man opened his mouth, then closed it, looking confused. "I suppose we might sell bags of sand to the school for the garden or such. Mostly our sand is used for foundations, and we have the brickworks on-site. Maybe the school buildings need repairing? I don't know any more than that."

William looked at Charles, who lifted his chin in the direction of the warehouse.

Kate took a closer look and saw whom he had noticed, a man in the rough clothing of a day laborer. He had a little round belly and rather stooped shoulders. "Do you recognize him?"

"That's Littlejack Dawkins," Charles said.

"The gardener?" William asked.

"He's right over there." Charles indicated with his chin.

"What is the gardener doing here on a Monday?" An expression of irritation on his handsome face, William stalked toward the warehouse.

Did it have something to do with the treasure map, or was he here on the school's business? Were there two copies of the map? Kate couldn't say anything to Charles in front of the quarry worker, but her worries multiplied. Might there be three copies, and Monks had one, too? Or was the gardener's appearance a coincidence?

She suspected that if there was more than one copy, it meant they were on a fool's errand, and the map led to something of no value. Of course, that didn't mean Agnes wasn't killed over it, because she clearly believed it did have value.

"We need to walk around the entire quarry to figure out the next clue," Julie whispered to Kate.

Kate gave her a warning look. She didn't want the worker to know they had any purpose. "Mr. Dickens, perhaps you should join Mr. Aga? Mrs. Aga and I will continue our walk."

Charles nodded and engaged the workman in a bit of idle chatter about the weather as Julie took Kate's arm and they walked through the gateposts leading to the main road, followed by Lucy.

"I have no idea what direction to go in next," Kate confessed.

"What have you done to sort matters before?" Julie asked, scanning the area, with her hand flat over her forehead.

"Fixed the symbol in my head and then just sort of unfocused and refocused my eyes, I suppose."

"Very well, then. What is the next symbol?"

"It is an arch with a wide base."

"As simple as that?" Julie asked. "Nothing more?"

"Not as I recall. Charles has the map. There are some specks of dirt on it and a water spot or two, but I don't remember being concerned that anything was obscured."

Julie nodded and screwed her eyes up in concentration. A large wagon pulled by four oxen in yokes appeared from another gate along the brickworks, kicking up dust as it trundled by.

"This is a terrible vantage point," Kate said, "and nothing looks remotely triangular shaped."

Julie pointed at a large tree in the distance, on the top of a small rise. "You could call that a triangle, the hill and the tree, but it's the wrong shape."

Kate coughed as a second wagon followed the first. "Let's

walk along with the wagon and turn left when we reach the edge and circle the entire operation."

They paced the entire business, avoiding depressions, which were probably dug by wild animals, and a couple of spectacular anthills, but didn't see anything exactly shaped like the symbol.

"This is concerning," Julie said as they walked in through the gates to find Charles and William. "Where else could we go?"

"I don't know." Kate rubbed her boot against the gatepost to dislodge a chunk of mud. "I'm afraid we've hit a dead end."

"Well, if investigating the quarry area doesn't give us any clues, what do we do? Start over?"

Kate waved to Charles, who was still talking to the workman in the quarry. Maybe it hadn't taken as long as she'd thought to circle the quarry. He shook the man's hand and came toward them.

"William went to the well house to find some water, and then he said he would ask at the office for a ride back to town for us."

"They aren't suspicious of us?" Kate asked.

"I've been telling them we are lost," Charles said with a shrug. "I like a good ramble, but you three must be exhausted."

Julie smiled wanly. Lucy led her over to the warehouse so she could lean against the wall. The sky had darkened with William's predicted rain. At least it wasn't warm.

"Any news on the gardener? How did he come to be here?" Kate asked as she and Charles followed.

"He had a pony trap, and if it fit more than one person, I'd have had him take Julie back. He was picking up sand for the garden. Though I have to say I don't like the looks of William, either."

"Why not?" Kate asked.

"He just doesn't seem himself. Maybe it's sorrow over Agnes. I don't know."

William appeared after a couple of minutes. "He needed to improve the drainage of the back lawn, fill up the depressions," William explained. "He has trouble with field vole barrows."

"That's a dead end, then," Julie said.

"At least he doesn't have a copy of the map," Kate said. "Let's get all of you back to the school and sort out our thoughts. I don't want any of you tramping in the rain if we can avoid it."

Chapter 15

"What do you think we should do now?" Kate asked Charles as William helped Julie down from the wagon they had rode on, joltingly, to the school. While it had been kind of the driver to take them right to their destination, Charles was afraid the bricks they had sat on had permanently damaged their attire.

At least Kate, an expert needlewoman, would be his next month and in charge of maintaining his wardrobe. He'd be happy to turn over the responsibility for difficult washer-women and clothing repair to her.

"Lucy and I should take Julie across the street to rest," William said as he gave the driver some small coins in thanks.

"I want to see the boys," Kate announced, turning toward the school building after she waved at the driver.

"Now? Why?" Charles asked, tugging at his coat to set the fabric back into place.

"The map has stumped us," Kate said. "They've been here, especially Ollie, for months. The triangle may make sense to them."

"I'm inclined to start back at the beginning," Charles told

her. "What if we chose the wrong set of locations to match to our clues?"

Julie sighed. Her skin seemed more translucent than usual, and she worried harshly at her lip. "Charles, if you want to return to the cemetery by yourself and look again, that is your business, but the rest of us are tired. I trust Kate's vision, however."

"What're the chances of finding two right clues in a row if the first was wrong?" Lucy asked.

"Probably rather good," Charles opined.

"I disagree," Kate said stoutly. "The wing formation of the trees was really very specific."

"Exactly," Julie said. "Why don't you talk to the boys, Kate? I'm going to lie down." She put her hand protectively at her midsection.

It was clear that this represented a signal to William, who tipped his hat to Kate, then took his wife's arm and led her across the street without another word. Lucy followed.

"I am afraid to check the post tomorrow," Charles said. "I expect your father will order us back."

"You must call the banns the instant we are back in London, Mr. Dickens," Kate said with a sweet smile. "Or Calvinist fire will rain down on your curls."

Charles grinned. "I live for danger. Let's have a word with the boys. I want to make sure they are in their room, to be honest. They had plenty of time to memorize the map and might have run away again. This is that dangerous time between classes and the next meal."

They crossed the street to the main school building. They knocked and were given entry by Nancy, who looked very put out.

"We're just on our way to Alpha," Charles explained in his best soothing manner. "With the gates around the front all locked up, I didn't know how else to get to it."

"It's because of the murder," Nancy said frankly. "But it doesn't help. The woods are open."

"Maybe they think someone could have come in straight from the main road," Kate suggested.

"It wasn't attended," Charles said. "When I came in, no one was at the front."

"When you came, sir, no one knew she was dead yet," Nancy blurted out. She covered her mouth with her apron. "It's such a 'orror, it is. She'd 'ave been my sister when Monks married me, and now I'll never 'ave, either." She burst into noisy tears and ran up the stairs.

"That's a different side to Nancy," Kate observed as the girl disappeared from sight. "I hope she hasn't, well, found herself in an interesting condition thanks to her fascination with Monks."

Charles had observed that women waxed and waned like the moon in their moods. Best ignored when inconvenient. "Let us do this quickly. We missed luncheon, and I don't want to disregard tea in such a disdainful matter."

"No," Kate agreed. "My stomach is glued to my spine already."

He showed her how to thread her way to the rear door; then they went to the boardinghouse and were let in by the same master. He looked askance at the pair of them. "I must insist that you leave the boys to their peace for now. They are in quiet contemplation with their Bibles until tea."

"Truly?" Charles said pleasantly. "As their benefactor, I must insist I see this Christian miracle for myself."

"Very well," the master sighed. "I was busy with a good book of sermons myself." He flounced off to his right.

Charles inclined his head to Kate. "Up the stairs. After you, my dear."

When they reached the attic dormitory, Charles saw that, indeed, no Bible reading was on the menu. Most of the boys were on the floor, playing games with pebbles. He counted them.

"Ollie?" he asked.

"Over here," came a weak voice.

Charles went toward the bed in the far corner, under the eaves. "What's wrong?" he asked when he saw the lump of blankets on the cot.

"My 'ead 'urts," Ollie said, his voice muffled by the covers.

"Is the light bothering you?" asked Kate, who had followed Charles.

Charles, worried about mumps, motioned Kate back with his hand. He gently pulled back the covers and looked for telltale swellings. While he found none of those, the boy kept his eyes tightly shut.

"Are your eyes hurting?" Charles asked gently.

"No, it's my head." The boy touched his forehead.

Charles touched it lightly. The boy felt warm, but not hot. "Let's open a window and let in some fresh air. You aren't used to being shut up indoors."

"And drink something," Kate advised. "That always helps." She went to the ewer and brought it back, then helped Ollie drink some of the water left in the bottom.

The boy looked small there, bundled in blankets. He kept his stump hidden and used only his other arm. Charles hoped the muscles of the arm weren't atrophying. He'd have to speak to Mr. Aga and make sure Ollie was using both sides. This wasn't the time to mention it, though, with him in pain.

"Is there anything else we can do?"

"I'm sure Mrs. Bedwin can make willow bark tea. I'll find her," Kate said. "That will fix you right up, young Ollie."

"Is there a housemistress or someone who takes care of you in this boardinghouse?" Charles asked.

John stepped up next to him and peered at Ollie. "No, just the lower master in charge."

"You know how to find Mrs. Bedwin, don't you, Mr. Dickens?" Ollie asked.

"Of course, and Cook, as well. We'll fix that headache." Charles tried to smile, but something about the look of the boy had him worried. An odd listlessness, combined with restlessness, concerned him.

Eager to have Kate safely away from a possible illness, he took her arm, said good-bye to the boys, and pulled her out of the dormitory.

"What's wrong?" she whispered as they went down the stairs.

"I had the memory of my sister Harriet," Charles whispered back. "And I don't like that."

"Oh, Charles."

He couldn't see her face, but he understood the tone of her voice. She knew his little sister had died young. "Yes. I know you and I will face such hard times throughout our lives. This should be such a happy year for us both."

"He only has a headache."

He heard fabric brushing against fabric.

"It's not like Christiana Lugoson," Kate said.

"It doesn't have to be, does it? We all stand in the company of the dead whether we know it or not."

"He's just a child," Kate said fiercely. "Don't wish it upon him, Charles."

"I do not," he said with just as much temper. "I just recognize danger, that is all. Let us get the housekeeper." He stomped down the rest of the stairs and opened the front door harshly enough that it banged against the wall.

Kate hurried after him, holding her cloak tightly about herself. They had only a few steps to make before they progressed to the back door of the school. Charles had a moment of worry that the door might be locked, but it was not. He made sure to lock it behind them, however, then went into the kitchen, where Cook and her kitchen maids were busily slicing bread and passing a breath of butter over the slices.

"Can you make willow bark tea?" Charles asked. "Or is that an item that Mrs. Bedwin controls?"

"I have a bit laid by," Cook said. She set down the ladle she was holding and wiped her forehead with her forearm. "Who needs it?"

"Ollie, in the boardinghouse. He has a bad headache, and I don't like the looks of him."

"Can you wait? I don't know where Mrs. Bedwin is. I'll make it for you."

"We'll take it to him," Kate assured the cook.

Charles pulled Kate against the wall so that a maid could pass by with a tray. She had a cloth tied over one eye in piratical fashion and, as a result, hadn't even seen them. He heard Kate's stomach rumble. Her face colored, but she said nothing. They would probably miss this meal, as well.

Cook disappeared into a pantry, then came out again with a crock. She tapped willow bark into a small teapot, then poured in water from a kettle hanging over the fire.

"Just give it a few minutes to steep," she said. "And mind that you don't burn yourself."

"We'll be careful. Thank you," Kate said.

The kitchen door opened. Mrs. Bedwin bustled through, her eyes a bit wild. Her hair had frizzed out of its neat style, as if she'd been working in the hot kitchen, as well.

"I'm afraid we have a serious issue," she announced to Cook, not noticing Charles and Kate. "The first house has arrived for tea, and the lower master told me that he's missing one of the boys."

"Not one of the charity students again," Cook said.

Mrs. Bedwin twisted her hands together. Her voice cracked. "No, Monks Aga is the pupil missing this time."

Kate turned to Charles. He knew what she was thinking before she spoke. "He's not with Nancy this time."

"What?" Mrs. Bedwin turned to them.

Charles explained. "We saw Monks with Nancy in the woods, but not today. And we just saw Nancy. She opened the door for us."

Mrs. Bedwin's lips tightened. Despite her own peccadillos, it did not appear that she appreciated the romantic yearnings of others. "When was this? I will speak with her immediately."

"Yesterday," Charles told her.

Mrs. Bedwin marched out of the room. Charles followed her, trailed by Kate. He puzzled over what this might mean. Was it as simple as the headmaster's nephew romanced more than one girl? Maybe this time he was with someone who lived in town? The housekeeper was rather alarmed, though, so it didn't seem like his wanderings had been noticed by the adults.

Also, the fact that his sister had been murdered made the situation concerning.

Either Nancy worked on a short leash or Mrs. Bedwin had recently given her orders, because the housekeeper beelined straight to her, to where she was dusting a series of silhouettes on the parlor mantelpiece with a feather duster.

"Has Monks Aga been courting you?" Mrs. Bedwin demanded.

The feather duster caught on one of the silhouettes. It lifted from its leaning position and crashed to the floor, the wood cracking on one side against the decorative fire screen as it fell.

Nancy gave a little shriek and dropped the duster into the fireplace as she grabbed for the silhouette.

"Have you seen Monks today?" Charles asked, deciding to take charge of the interrogation.

"At 'is meals," Nancy said. "Cook asked me to serve because that Betsy 'as a boil next to her eye."

"Did he say anything to you?"

"In front of the h'other students?" Nancy's tone was shocked. "Of course not. 'E'd never."

"How does he usually communicate with you?"

She colored. "He talks to me. In the odd moment, when 'e sees me in the 'all or such."

"Is he courting anyone else?" Charles asked.

Her face crumpled a bit. "No, I—I don't think so."

Mrs. Bedwin narrowed her eyes. "You are not to leave the school, Nancy, without written permission from me, do you understand? What I mean by that is, you are not to leave this building."

"B-but the boardinghouses," Nancy stammered.

"Written permission," Mrs. Bedwin repeated. "You have no business anywhere but in this building."

Nancy's gaze lowered. "Yes, ma'am."

"Does he have anywhere he likes to go? Just that spot in the woods where we found you? Anywhere else?" Charles asked.

"We just walk," Nancy said, with a nervous glance at her superior. "In the woods, like, but nowhere special."

"We will have to search the grounds," Charles told Mrs. Bedwin. "Can you speak to the lower and assistant masters and have them make inquiries with the students who are particularly friendly with young Aga?"

"I shall," Mrs. Bedwin promised.

"I'll take the lantern in the hall," Charles said. "We'll take the tea to Ollie, then take a turn around the grounds and, finally, return here to confer with you."

"Thank you, sir." She clasped her hands together again. "I do hope we can find him before Mr. Sikes learns about this."

"I'll need keys to open the outbuildings," Charles said.

Mrs. Bedwin nodded. She walked into the pantry, and he heard some rattling and a door banged. Soon she was back with an iron circle of keys. "Do you see the labels?"

"I do," Charles said, a bit of dread solidifying like old stew meat in his stomach at the sight of the one that read ICEHOUSE. "We shall report in to Mr. Aga when we are done. I suggest you do the same."

The housekeeper replied with a bob of the head. Her lips were white with tension. Charles gestured to Kate, and they left the parlor.

"We have a little daylight left," Charles said. "Though I do wonder if our time would be better employed in speaking to the students as they file in for tea."

"I could do that," Kate said. "And you could search the grounds. Unless you think we should stay together."

He smiled at her, then lit the lantern. "If it wasn't for the sake of Agnes, I would suggest we separate. However, we don't know where the danger lies at Aga Academy. I cannot, in all conscience, leave you alone."

They spent a few minutes transporting tea to Ollie; then they went outside. Charles led the way to Littlejack Dawkins's secret place, but other than the bottles, nothing was hidden in the bushes.

"I had hopes that Monks was a secret stealer of gin," Charles said, disappointed. "Our next best hope is that some prankster locked him in one of the outbuildings. Let us take a turn around the lawn, and then we'll go into the woods."

They walked around, both peering into the gloom, but found nothing. Finally, they began to check the sheds on the outskirts.

"You aren't going to go in?" Kate said, horrified, when they reached the icehouse.

"It is the last thing I want to do." Charles stared at the clock-shaped structure with a feeling of nausea. "But I must."

"Stay at the door," Kate urged. "Simply shine the lantern in and don't go through."

"I have to kneel down first. This door is suitable only for fairy creatures." He unlocked the door and pulled it open.

Kate shivered. "It just radiates malice."

"Don't blame the ice," Charles said. "Wonderful thing for headaches. I wonder if we have time to bring Ollie a chunk."

"He is our friend, not Monks Aga," Kate said. "Chip off a bit and wrap it in your handkerchief."

"Do you see that stone vase? Grab the ice pick for me?"

Kate rustled around a bush, then, momentarily, handed him the sharp instrument. He felt better once it was in his hand. Scanning the cold, dark lumps of icehouse ice with the lantern, he assured himself that none were human. He chose a spot and pushed back a bit of hay, then set down the lantern and dug in with the ice pick. A chunk of ice came loose. He wrapped it in his handkerchief.

Kate handed him hers, as well, and he knotted the ice into both, then quickly shut up the space again.

"It's like a tomb," Kate said after she'd set the ice pick back in its vase again.

"Indeed. Let's take a look on this side. There might be more buildings. I definitely have more keys."

After a while, Charles heard the church bells again. They needed the lantern to see much of anything now. "We had better go speak to Mr. Aga."

"It's very disappointing. If someone killed Monks, too, we have to persuade Julie and William to return to London."

Charles's eyebrows rose. "In case someone is targeting the entire family?"

"It's not worth the risk for them to stay here," Kate said with a shiver. "I'm frightened."

Charles tucked the ring of keys into his pocket so he could put his arm around her. "I'm here. You're safe."

She leaned into him, her bonnet pressing against his neck.

"It's quiet here, but I must say the atmosphere has quite lost its romance."

He chuckled. "I agree. Let's hurry across the street now and confess all, as soon as we deliver the ice to Ollie, poor mite."

"He has lost a lot for such a young child, what with being orphaned," Kate said. "But he has a future now, so he is fortunate indeed."

Charles thought about that while they returned to the boardinghouse. He saved Kate the climb to the attic and brought the ice himself. Ollie said he had drunk the willow bark tea, but he still looked unwell, restless and in pain. Charles left the handkerchiefs knotted around the ice and helped him set the lumps over his forehead as John hovered nearby; then he and Kate returned to Mr. Aga's house.

They found the headmaster in the parlor with William.

"Where have you been all this time?" William asked.

"I'm afraid Monks has been reported missing," Charles said in his most noninflammatory tone. "Have you been informed here yet?"

"What?" Mr. Aga ran his hands through the hair above his ears.

"Yes. Mrs. Bedwin told us. We searched the yard and the outbuildings."

"Even the icehouse." Kate gave the conversation a sobering touch as she untied her bonnet.

"Good heavens," Mr. Aga said faintly.

"Did he go to Uncle George's farm?" William asked.

"I will send someone to check." Mr. Aga rose.

"Have you eaten?" William gave them a wan smile.

"Not since we breakfasted," Charles confirmed.

William rang the staff bell for provisions to add to the tattered remnants of food on a plate placed near the fire. He insisted Kate be seated and take the last morsel of ham sandwich.

*   *   *

An hour later, after they had eaten, Kate sat in front of the parlor fire with a linen panel in a frame that she was embroidering for her future home. Julie and Lucy had joined her, and William had disappeared. His father had gone across to the school. Her dear Charles bent over a slip of paper next to the best lamp, working on the second installment of *Pickwick*.

"Should we go over to the school?" Julie asked. "I'm concerned about William's father not having returned by now."

"It will take time to send someone to the dairy farm," Kate soothed. "Especially now that it is dark. How is your knitting?"

Julie stared at the mass of wool in her lap. "I'm trying to make an infant blanket, but I seem to have dropped some stitches."

Kate set down her embroidery and lifted her candle over the blanket. "I'll help you pick them up."

Lucy knit on with nimble fingers. Just as Kate had finished helping Julie with her repairs, the front door opened and closed. Charles's head went up, like that of a hunting dog pointing at game. He set his pen next to the inkwell on his travel desk and stood.

His shadow on the wall moved gruesomely as he stretched; then a lantern joined the light already in the room and changed the dark shapes as Mr. Aga entered.

"Monks does truly seem to be missing," he said, his voice rather devoid of emotion.

Julie set down her knitting and pushed herself to her feet. Her usual fluidity of movement was diminishing as her body changed. "How dreadful, Father Aga." She went to him and patted his arm.

Mr. Aga nodded. "Where is William? I thought he might help me do a bed check tonight. I want to make sure every student is accounted for at the end of the day."

"A wise notion," Charles said. "I would also ask each and

every student as they are ticked off your roster to say when they last saw Monks and where."

"Just like with a crime," Kate added. "We can retrace from the last place he was known to be."

"An excellent notion. Julie, dear, can you tell Cook we are ready for supper? I can use a good meal before the evening's activity," the schoolmaster said.

"Of course." Julie patted his arm. "And then I will go upstairs and find my Mr. Aga. He is probably writing."

"I'll go upstairs," Charles offered. "I need a fresh handkerchief from my luggage, anyway. I've spilled ink all over this one."

Kate, Julie, and Charles remained at Mr. Aga's house after supper, while he and William went to perform the bedtime checks. Julie dozed while Kate embroidered and Charles wrote. Lucy was upstairs, tending to Julie's wardrobe.

Kate felt drowsy herself after quite a substantial meal of roast and potatoes with a salad of chicory and lamb's-quarters, followed by a stodgy boiled pudding.

Charles had moved to the chair by the fire where Julie had sat earlier, and balanced his writing desk on his lap while he wrote. He had finished his daily words for *Pickwick* and now had moved on to a review of the circus he had attended with William, in the hopes some newspaper would be interested. He often did theater reviews in London.

The needle had just dropped out of Kate's hand when a commotion in the front hall exploded the evening's peace. Kate blinked to full consciousness as Charles set his writing desk on the floor.

"What is that?" he exclaimed.

Kate stood in tandem with him. He held up his hand and rushed out of the room, taking a lamp with him. She followed more slowly with a candle.

In the hall, Mr. Aga was breathing hard. William looked wild eyed. The hat rack had been overturned and had knocked the umbrella holder on its side, as well.

"You haven't found Monks?" Charles asked in a quiet tone.

"No, and it gets worse." William righted the hat rack and set his dripping hat on it, leaving a puddle on the floor.

"What?" Kate asked, clutching the back of Charles's coat.

"Cholera," Eustace Aga said, his face gray in the light of the lantern he held. "One of the students who shares a room with Monks is terribly ill."

Chapter 16

"Cholera," Kate whispered, horrified. The disease spread through households and killed in as little as a few hours. With Agnes dead and not replaced, the servants were spread thin. Who would care for the afflicted? She set the umbrella holder in its place by the hat rack, and William stuffed two umbrellas and a walking stick back into it.

"Who?" Charles asked.

"The Field boy. He represented his name well. He and Monks loved to tramp around the area together. Kept them both fit, I thought." Mr. Aga rubbed his hands together, then interlocked his fingers at the knuckles.

"My wife cannot stay here," William said, plucking the hat from his father's head and carefully placing the dripping felt onto the hat rack. "I'm going upstairs to pack her bags."

"Where will you go?" Kate asked. "There is no coach at this time of night."

"The inn," he said, starting for the stairs.

Charles nodded to Mr. Aga, then followed William up. Kate joined them.

"Pack your things," Charles told her.

"I should help Julie."

"William will do that," he said.

"Are you going to come with us?" Kate asked.

"Of course. You'll need help with the bags. Julie can't carry anything. Now hurry," he said in urgent tones.

Kate bustled into her room. She stayed in her gown, since everything she'd brought was practical, without her sister Mary to help her dress. After changing from shoes back into walking boots, she tossed everything into her carpetbag, then took it down and packaged up her embroidery. She cleaned Charles's pen and settled everything carefully into his writing desk.

When the others came down, she was ready, with Julie's knitting placed in her bag, too.

Mr. Aga must have returned to the school, for he was nowhere to be found as they bundled up in their outerwear and opened the front door for the walk uphill to the inn. Julie appeared the most exhausted Kate had ever seen the usually vibrant girl. Both William and the faithful Lucy took her arms for support.

Kate would rather have been sleepwalking, too, as they stumbled through the center of the town. Charles enjoyed such perambulations mightily, as they provided him both time to think and fodder for his stories. For herself, she'd rather be peaceful in a warm bed, but then, their labors were not the same.

When they arrived at the inn, William woke the sleeping attendant, who had one room available. Charles pulled Kate aside as William helped Julie up the stairs.

"Tomorrow please escort Julie and Lucy back to London," Charles said.

"Won't William take her? Under the circumstances? What if she becomes ill?"

"She is the least likely to have been exposed. The afflicted student is not in the same boardinghouse as the mudlarks. He's in Beta."

"I see."

Charles rubbed his eyes. "I'm sure Julie will be fine, and she has Lucy to care for her in any case. William needs to help his father with the problems at the school."

"I don't like any of this," Kate said. "I know I cannot stay here, but you shouldn't, either, not really."

"I need to return to work." Charles sighed. "I had the fore-thought to place my newspaper work into my pocket." He reached in and pulled out a sheath of papers. "Take this to your father? I can't leave here just now."

"Of course." Before Kate could say more, William clattered down the stairs, followed by Lucy.

He looked exhausted, with deep shadows under his eyes, which Kate thought were likely to remain there whether or not there was daylight.

"Julie refuses to return home," he reported.

"You can make her," Charles said.

Kate didn't like his flat tone, but the hour was late. None of them were in good spirits.

"I have the baby to think of. If she spends the entire carriage ride crying or railing against me, she might hurt the child," William said. He put his hand to his forehead.

"I still have responsibility to Miss Hogarth. What would her father say? Then there is Lucy, as well." Charles nodded at the girl. "I can take Kate and Lucy to London."

"I won't leave my mistress," Lucy said. "It ain't right. She's too tired to think right."

"I won't leave her, either," Kate agreed. "We'll stay at the inn and follow developments. Just this walk through the night ought to keep her in bed for the day. She can't risk the baby coming early."

"You think the coach back to London is too dangerous?" William asked.

"A short night of sleep after a late-night walk through a hilly town?" Kate said. "I do think she should rest instead of traveling, if you don't think we have to outrun cholera."

"We don't know where it came from," Charles said. "Cholera is a dangerous beast. It would be wisest for you all to go."

"We'll wait another day, for Julie's sake," Kate said. "But we can get your articles on the coach in the morning."

Charles nodded and asked the attendant for paper and ink, then wrote a note to Mr. Hogarth and wrapped it around his articles. "I don't know what more we can do."

"We'll check on you tomorrow afternoon," William said. "With any luck, another day will help us solve Agnes's murder. The cholera will throw everyone into a panic."

"Yes, someone might think it best for their immortal soul to share what they know," Charles agreed. "We can make an announcement and demand information at breakfast. The students are all together then."

"If the school isn't shut down," Kate said. "Or the children aren't too frightened."

William ran his hands over his face. "If the students leave the school, they will take the disease with them. It is a most terrible situation, and I do not know what to do."

Charles leapt across a mud puddle in the innyard, dimly illuminated by a brazier, after they left the women.

"Are we sure Julie hadn't been exposed? What about Lucy? What about Miss Hogarth?" William fretted. He sloshed directly through the mud puddle and didn't notice.

"Julie can't stay at the inn alone, and Lucy and my fiancée are very tidy young ladies," Charles soothed. "I can't deny that Miss Hogarth or even Lucy has been more among the denizens of the school, but they haven't been in the afflicted boarding-house."

"Right," William muttered and put his hand to his head. "Oh, my head is such a muddle, I can scarcely think."

"If that's the condition you are in, I feel true pity for your poor father," Charles said. He took William's arm to lead him down the street, staying close to the school buildings. Harrow did not completely douse their lights, and they had enough illumination to steer free of refuse that had been swept to the edges of the road.

Eventually, William lifted his head, and Charles released him, taking comfort in his own thoughts. He didn't want to be at the school during a cholera outbreak, either, but what could he do unless his editor ordered him back to town?

He forced his thoughts to the treasure map, dread weighting his belly when he thought of his utter lack of comprehension. Where had they gone wrong? It had been making sense until their failure at the quarry.

When they returned to Mr. Aga's house, Charles and William went into the parlor. Charles stirred up the fire and put the kettle on. "Find a bottle of something," he told William as he lit two candles in front of small mirrors on the mantelpiece. "We need to take another look at the map."

William rummaged in a cabinet, while Charles took off his coat and reached into his pocket for the map. His gloved fingers returned from their quest empty.

"Behave, you monkey's paw," he muttered, then tugged off his gloves and tried again.

William set a bottle of gin on the table. He stared at it. "No, I'd prefer rum." He sighed and picked it up.

Charles set down his coat and patted the rest of his clothing. "The map was in my coat, correct?"

William placed a half-empty bottle of molasses rum on the table. "I saw you put it there."

"It's not there now."

"You lost it?" William asked.

"I know I didn't take it out," Charles said, lighting the lamp. "It was in the inner pocket, secure. Did someone steal it?"

William's eyes moved from left to right as he calculated. "We weren't near enough to anyone for you to have been pick-pocketed in our recent perambulations. It must have been earlier in the day."

The front door opened and closed again. William returned to the sideboard to fetch glasses as his father came into the room. His steps were slow, and the lamp cast grotesque shadows over his face.

"Father?" William asked, setting glasses on the table. "You look in need of some rum punch."

"We did a thorough bed check," Mr. Aga said in a hollow voice.

Charles came forward. "More cholera?"

Mr. Aga rubbed the side of his nose. "Not yet, but Nancy Price isn't at the school."

"She returned from Uncle George," William said, confused.

"Yes, but she's gone now."

Charles winced. "Has she run off, or has someone taken or lured her like Agnes?"

"I simply don't know." Mr. Aga passed his hand over his eyes. "Punch will take much too long to make. Just pour me some rum and hot water, please. A large one. First, Monks goes missing, now Nancy. And cholera. Whatever am I going to do?"

Kate dropped another lump of coal into the fire, then returned to the bed. Julie lay on one side, using Kate's cloak for a pillow and her own to attempt to provide some comfort for her ungainly body. Next to her, Lucy smiled drowsily and rolled over, then emitted a faint snore.

"Is it hard to sleep?" Kate whispered.

"The baby seems to press on everything at night," Julie said in a similarly low tone. "But it is a comforting feeling, as well. I haven't felt any movements yet."

"Is that normal?"

"Mrs. Herring said I should feel the quickening any day now." Julie yawned.

Kate searched her face uneasily for signs of unusual skin tone or shadows underneath her eyes. William had looked unwell, though she thought Julie looked fine for a woman more than halfway through carrying a babe.

Was William fighting the disease without realizing it or admitting it? Cholera cared nothing for babies coming or accomplishments. Murder didn't matter to her anymore. They could all die.

"Go to sleep, dear," Kate said.

"Aren't you?"

"I'm just going to sit up in front of the fire for a minute. Warm my hands."

"Hmm." Julie closed her eyes.

Kate, seated on one of the low stools provided, tucked her feet under her skirts after removing her boots. The bed would be warm, but she couldn't lie down yet.

After a few minutes she heard the sheets rustling. When she looked around, she saw Lucy slide out of bed and come to the fire.

"I thought you were asleep," Kate whispered.

"It helps her sleep if she thinks I am," Lucy said softly, sitting on the other stool. She shook her head.

Kate had stayed away from any sort of frank discussion of the situation at the school, because she didn't want to scare Julie, but she could see Lucy was concerned, as well.

"But I'm not asleep," Julie said crossly from the bed. "What are we to do? The school is doomed without the murder being solved."

Kate blinked. At least Julie wasn't focused on cholera. She glanced at Lucy, who tilted her head.

"Very well," Kate said. "Lucy, would you please help me with my hair while we consider the suspects?"

"Yes," Julie agreed loudly. "Who is most likely?"

Lucy picked up Kate's hairbrush. "That Monks is a scary sort."

Kate nodded and pulled the first pin from her hair. "With Nancy as an aide or alone?"

"Oh, they would be in it together," Julie said. "But what about that gardener?"

"Littlejack Dawkins," Kate said. "I don't think I like a drunk for a murderer."

"There 'as been no sign that 'e's incapacitated by the drink," Lucy said, taking over removing Kate's hairpins. "And a man like that, no wife. 'E might well assume privileges with a female servant."

"And kill her accidentally?" Kate asked.

Lucy ran the hairbrush lightly over Kate's tumbled hair. "'Id her away, didn't 'e?"

"Not somewhere she'd never be found, though," Julie said in a tone of reflection. "Then you'd put the body in the woods."

"Might 'ave been a temporary place," Lucy said, deepening her brush strokes.

"A good point," Kate said, holding her head straight. "What if the killer was about to be discovered, so he stuffed Agnes into the icehouse?"

"It has a lock, though," Julie said. "Someone had to have the key."

"That would require planning, then," Kate suggested. "There is that curate we don't like. He's been in the school enough to know where the keys might be."

"One of the older students?" Julie said through a yawn. "Like that Noah Claypole? William said he wasn't a very nice sort of boy."

"He's all of thirteen, I believe."

"Not too young to kill." Lucy set the brush down and braided Kate's hair.

"You would know," Kate said, standing to fetch a ribbon to tie the end of the braid. "But she'd possibly been trifled with, and thirteen seems too young for that." She unbuttoned her simple blue dress, and Lucy took it from her.

"Housemaids are strong," Lucy said, setting the dress aside and starting to untie the laces of Kate's top petticoat. "She'd 'ave an 'arder time fighting off an older man."

"Good point," Julie said. "We really have no clear answer."

"We've listed off everyone we can think of." Kate slipped out of the petticoat so that Lucy could untie the next layer. "Maybe the most likely candidate will become clear after a night of rest."

Charles yawned the next morning, as he attempted to write with his portable desk balanced on his lap in bed. He'd managed a few words of *Pickwick*, but he needed food and tea before his brain gave him the rest. After he cleaned his pen and secured his ink, he put his desk aside and performed his morning ablutions.

He forgot about food as soon as he entered the passage. The next guest room was inhabited by the Agas, just William now, and then his father's room was next. An unmistakable miasma of human misery hung in the air. Someone had taken ill, and from the particular stench, Charles suspected cholera.

Run. The thought came to him, a child's reaction to something he couldn't possibly understand. But his friend had brought him into this, and in turn, he'd brought *Kate*.

He stepped down the passage, the few steps to the next room feeling like miles, and pushed open the door. *Don't let it be William. Let it be the next door, or some door I never saw, with a guest that I haven't seen.*

God, however, did not hear his prayers. William lay in the bed, pale and shivering. The cloth that normally covered the chamber pot was draped over the floor, and the pot hadn't been pushed under the bed. As Charles looked at William, his friend covered his belly with a groan.

Charles swore. "Has the tweeny been in here?" He ran to the curtain and pulled it open, then went to the water jug. Thankfully, a couple of inches of water remained. He poured them into the bowl and brought it to William.

"Drink," he urged, lifting his friend's head to receive the fluids.

William still had the strength to do that much. When the water was gone, he settled back onto the pillow. "Protect Julie. No matter what Hogarth says about her."

"I will," Charles promised.

William gripped Charles's arm. "At all costs."

"Of course," Charles insisted. "But you're strong, William. You'll get better."

William clutched his stomach again. "I have cholera."

"I know, but you can get through this." Charles's arm shook under William's feverish hand.

William chuckled, a strange, giddy little sound. "Half die, they say. Why should I be spared?" His face contorted, and he used his washing bowl mightily.

Charles remembered Mr. Hogarth talking about a Scottish doctor and his insistence that hydration was the cure to fighting cholera. Since Charles couldn't imagine that God wanted to kill the prosperous father of a soon-to-be-born babe, he knew he had to make William fight.

"I will do everything in my power to help Julie, and Lucy and Kate, too," Charles said. "But you have to promise me that you will drink all the water I bring you. It might help you survive this day."

William's lips were already cracked. Charles touched his neck and found his skin disturbingly cold.

"I'll fill the jug and be back," he promised, then grabbed it and ran for the water can in the parlor.

After that, he pounded on Mr. Aga's door, shared the terrible news, then bullied the servants into restoring the necessary hygiene equipment in William's room.

Charles prayed that Heaven would spare him from illness so he could help others. If William had cholera, who else might be afflicted?

Julie had woken, clear eyed and healthy, as had Lucy. Kate had asked Lucy to help her dress, then had sent her downstairs for news and breakfast.

She'd returned with porridge and sausage. No panic existed in the public room. No one seemed aware of the cholera patient at the school.

"Do you think we've panicked too soon?" Julie asked, tucking into her bowl of porridge from the bed. "Maybe the child had just returned to school and picked up his illness elsewhere."

Kate took her bowl to a stool in front of the fire, which had been built up by the inn's tweeny. "Even if he had, the disease is at the school now. Only that one boy had a room to himself."

"At least he's unlikely to have taken the disease with him when he departed, since his broken limb isolated him."

Kate sighed as she set her spoon into the oats. "What are we going to do today?"

"Write down everything we know about the murder and the

suspects," Julie suggested. "Like a play. Maybe the motivations of the people will become clear."

"Maybe we'll create a complete fantasy," Kate countered. "It's facts we want. Agnes's biography, however pitifully short it might be. What little disagreements might she have had that surged into something horrid."

"Like what?" Lucy asked, sitting down on the other stool and pulling the last bowl into her lap. She'd cut her sausage into pieces and mixed it into the porridge.

Kate rose, having decided to do the same thing. Julie saw her pick up the knife and held up her bowl hopefully. "Like she could have stolen the treasure map from Monks, who didn't tell anyone, just resolved to kill her."

"An interesting thought," Julie said. "Where did it come from?"

"The farm?" Lucy offered. "Because no one has said they had heard of the map at the school until Agnes flashed it around."

"Excellent point." Kate slid cut sausage into Julie's bowl, then set the knife against hers. "What do we know about the farm?"

"Her father didn't want her there," Julie said. "She wasn't cut out for farm life."

"Maybe she stole the map from her father?" Kate suggested. "He's busy with his farm. Has anyone asked him about it?"

"It's a good question. I have no idea." Julie chewed thoughtfully. "But if I was a farmer with a treasure map, I'd have been hunting for the treasure for years."

"I don't think the business of a dairy farmer ever stops. It's not like crops, where there is a lull in the winter."

"Still, you aren't going to just lock up a treasure map in a chest and leave it for years without doing anything."

"You might," Kate said. "What if he couldn't figure it out?"

"If you'd lived here all your life, you'd probably have recognized that chimney from the ruins. You'd certainly know where Lord Byron's haunts were."

"Right, but you might be as stymied as we are by this point in the map."

"Exactly, but everyone would know the clues. If Uncle George had the map, Monks would know the clues. Agnes would have known them. That's not the story as we understand it, though."

"Not at all," Kate agreed.

"Agnes had that friend, the Maylie girl," Lucy ventured.

"Mr. Dickens and Mr. Aga have spoken to the entire family," Kate said. "No, I'm still focused on that farm. A young girl's world is generally a very small one."

After they finished their breakfast, Lucy piled up the dishes and took the tray back to the public room. Kate opened the window and looked out at the yard. She saw the stagecoach pulling in. Hostlers rushed from the various buildings to tend to the horses, their hats tilted to keep the light rain out of their eyes. The coachman climbed down, nearly falling. From the bowlegged, meandering way he walked, Kate suspected he'd drunk too much of whatever he kept at his side to warm him. She hoped they used a different driver for the return trip to London.

Passengers jumped down from the top of the coach. Three men appeared to be together. They both stood for a moment, kicking out their legs and stretching their backs to reverse the effects of the ride. A quartet of people exited the coach as someone pulled off bags that had been tied to the back. Kate didn't recognize any of the travelers.

As she stared out at the scene, she shifted her gaze from the yard to the town, which spread downward from their vantage point, below the church at the top of the hill. The buildings of

Harrow School, mostly redbrick, looked neat and pretty. A child appeared on the street, into Kate's view, and walked into the yard.

Kate frowned and leaned out the window. She recognized the child. It was Cousin Arthur.

"We have a visitor," Kate announced, turning to Julie.

"William?" Julie asked hopefully. "Can you please help me dress?"

"No, it's Arthur."

They had left Mr. Aga's house before the Monday laundry had been returned to their rooms, so Julie was forced to stay in her shift. Kate found her stays in her luggage and helped her into them. She looked critically at the laced side slits, which provided the ability to adjust as the baby grew. "Do we need to fix the sides?"

"No, they are fine for today. I guess little Aga Junior didn't grow overnight."

Kate nodded and went to Julie's back, pulled and tied laces until Julie was satisfied, then helped her with the other details of her wardrobe.

"I've become used to spotless clothes," Julie said. "This is not up to my usual standards."

"We'll send Lucy to Mr. Aga's house to pick up our clean clothes. I'm sure they've been ironed by now," Kate said. "We can't return to London without them."

"It ought to be safe," Julie said. "The cholera is at the school, and Father Aga's house is across the street."

Kate opened their door when she heard a knock, to find Arthur and Lucy. "Oh, I wasn't expecting that," Kate said as Lucy hoisted in a bundle. "Arthur has brought our belongings."

"Mr. Aga said as 'ow you should take the coach this morning," Arthur said, self-important. "It will leave soon, but 'e gave me the money, so I'm to tell you and then go make the arrangements."

"We can't," Julie said, spreading out her skirts and coming to the door. "I'm not leaving without my husband."

"Dreadful news about that," Arthur said, flushing.

The world whirled around Kate for a second, then righted itself. She already knew what the boy would say.

Julie went pale. "What is it?"

"Your 'usband, 'e's been taken by the dread disease," Arthur said, puffing out his slight chest.

Kate clutched Julie's arm, hoping to keep them both upright. "Just the one student and Mr. Aga?" She felt Julie vibrating under her grip.

Arthur shook his head. "Ollie too. That 'ead pain 'e got is cholera now. That's what the schoolmaster said. 'E's been taken to the other boardinghouse. We've got the sick ones in there, and the 'ealthy ones in with us. Proper mess, it is."

"I'll go back to the school with him," Lucy said instantly. "Mr. Aga must be nursed properly."

"I should be the one," Julie said. "But William would never allow it, not with the baby coming. You cannot, either, Lucy, though I do appreciate your dedication."

"Then who?" Lucy asked.

"Mr. Dickens," Kate gasped. "He must be helping Mr. Aga."

Julie's eyes seemed to have sunk inward just in the past minute, aging her. "Oh, Kate."

They clutched at each other, matching tears in their eyes. Julie could be losing her husband this day, and Kate might never have one at all.

Arthur pumped his arms. "We'll fight our way to the sickroom," he promised. "John and me. We'll take care of Ollie and Mr. Aga."

"Don't go anywhere near them, do you hear me?" Julie released Kate and put her hands on Arthur's shoulders. "We don't want you taking sick, too, a healthy specimen like you."

Arthur worried at his lip. "Ollie isn't a very 'ealthy specimen."

"God will protect him," Julie said. Her voice caught. "And William, as well. Say your prayers as you walk down the hill, Arthur. And go exactly where you are told. If you can, clean your dormitory with carbolic acid and water, anywhere that Ollie has been. It will help protect the rest of you."

Chapter 17

"We can't sit in this room all day," Julie said suddenly a couple of hours later.

"I don't think we have a choice." Kate tossed her embroidery to the side and stood to stretch her aching back. "What if we are infected, too?"

"I don't think we're ill," Lucy said, setting the shirt she was mending on her lap. "We would know, wouldn't we?"

"If we had cholera? Yes, I should think so," Julie told her.

"William and Ollie both seemed unwell this past day or two," Kate pointed out.

"I don't have a headache. Do you?" Julie asked.

Kate shook her head. Lucy followed suit.

"We have to do something." Julie slid off the bed and began to pace from there to the door. Her feet made unladylike thumps on the uncarpeted inn floor.

Kate, used to distracting younger siblings, cast about for something to do with the limited resources they had. "Do you have any paper?"

"I do, and a pencil, too," Julie said. "I always keep them

handy in case William runs out. Do you want to write Charles?"

"No, I do not want to write Mr. Dickens," Kate said severely. "But I thought I could re-create the map. I think I remember it all."

"Oh, good idea." Julie went to her carpetbag, put her hand in, then her arm up to the elbow, and dug around. She pulled out a stationery wallet. Lucy took it and undid the lock with a small key from Julie's ring.

"I never keep a pen box set with my clothing," Julie said. "It's much too fine to risk, but there is a pencil and a knife."

"It's rather dull," Lucy said, picking up the pencil. "But Mr. Aga showed me how to mend the tip."

She set to work while Kate did her own bit of pacing, trying to remember each mark. When Lucy handed her the pencil, she sat on a stool and placed the wallet in her lap.

Ten minutes later, she thought she had all the markings in order on a piece of letter paper. Six of them descended in an orderly line down the page. First of all, the barely sketched outline of a house, just five lines, with a triangle to indicate the roof, and a rectangle for a chimney. The second, a head, a recognizable portrait of Byron. The third, a pair of wings, or a broken heart, as Charles had said, if you ignored the rough outline. Then the wavy lines with dots, their dead end at the quarry. The next symbol was an arch with a wide base, like the apse of a church. After that, a tall, sharp-pointed triangle, with one line up the middle and one across, a cross, really.

Julie leaned over her. "You don't suppose there is anything around the sides of the original map?"

"How?" Kate huffed as another unpleasant thought struck her. "Also, Charles might not even have the original. For all we know, the symbols were copied from something else."

"We have to assume it is. I don't know how. Invisible ink or something? I remember that from a play I was in."

"I think the markings we can see are enough of a mystery," Kate said dismissively.

Lucy set down her darning and knelt next to Kate. She ran her finger down the page, symbol after symbol.

"Can we skip all the others and just focus on this one?" Kate asked as Lucy's finger hovered over the sharp triangle overlain with the cross.

"The biggest thing in the landscape here is the church," Lucy ventured. "Do you think you need to go back to the church?"

"Anything is possible," Kate said. "But the next symbol is an arch. Besides, the church can't be seen from the quarry. It's sort of nestled in a rise."

"The other issue is that your map is wrong," Julie said.

"It is?"

"Yes. You forgot the last symbol."

Kate stared at the page. "That's right. My goodness, there was a seventh symbol. What was it?"

"A rather odd one, sort of like three triangles knotted together," Julie said.

Kate thought, then shook her head. "It isn't really coming to mind."

"If I might." Julie took the pencil, carried the page back to the bed, and began to sketch. "It's a very complicated one."

"At least you remembered it exists," Kate said ruefully. She watched her friend bend her head over the page, the light shining in through the window highlighting the glorious fire of her hair, and was grateful that Julie had a moment's ease from the fear of her husband's illness.

William had insisted on leaving his father's house. Charles could not believe he found the stamina to walk down the stairs, given his ordeal, but after drinking several cups of water and some willow bark tea, he said he felt well enough to be transported to the boardinghouse holding the two sick students.

Charles and William's father helped him across the street. Arthur helped as best he could, since he had returned from the inn.

When the trio had William settled into a narrow iron bed in a makeshift sickroom, he smiled sweetly, then slid into sleep without saying another word.

"I'm going to check on the other boys," Mr. Aga said.

"Run back to the schoolroom," Charles told Arthur.

"What if I'm needed for messages?"

Charles considered. "You may be right, but sit outside with a book. There must be one around here somewhere."

"I'll find one," Arthur said.

Charles followed him into the passage and hunted through the vacant rooms until he found a stool.

Arthur returned with a Latin text. "The lower master 'ere who runs this dormitory teaches Latin."

Charles shook his head. "Have a seat. Maybe you'll learn something."

Arthur frowned and looked at the book as if it were in, err, Latin.

"I'll return as soon as I can. I want to see if I can find Nancy, that maid who is missing."

"'Ow are you going to do that?"

"Check with her parents. I have directions." He patted Arthur's shoulder.

"Am I going to die?" Arthur asked.

"We all die someday," Charles said as gently as he could. "But no one understands cholera, why it touches some and passes over others. It's best to think about other things."

"What about Ollie?"

Charles pressed his lips together. "Sometimes people rally. It doesn't kill everyone."

Arthur straightened his thin body. "What are 'is chances?"

"I believe about half survive. It can't hurt to pray for him, when you are tired of Latin." He patted the boy's shoulder and departed. Who knew how long he had before he needed to help nurse the students or William or even Kate? Or became afflicted himself. Cholera tended to be a rather unhurried disease, treading on heavy, methodical feet through neighborhoods. Devastation stretched over time.

Charles walked out into the sharp-needled late winter rain. It felt unusually welcome, because of the way it would cleanse the air, even as it soaked him through. If the rain brought cholera, all of England would be dead, so he wasn't worried about the droplets hurting him. Perhaps it would wash the miasma away. One theory was that dirty air caused cholera, but despite Mr. Aga's poor luck with servants, the school had a solid cleanliness to it.

Charles followed directions, turning past a tailor's house, then right into a courtyard after a pharmacy. Nancy's family lived in a sagging three-story house, on the top floor.

A female child, maybe a year older than Arthur, opened the door and gave him a suspicious look.

"Is your mother home?" Charles asked.

The child shook her head.

"I'm here from Aga Academy," Charles said, in case the girl had been told to turn away anyone who looked like a bill collector.

"Don't care," the child said rudely, then started to close the door.

Charles stuck his foot in and spoke into the opening. "Cholera has struck at Aga Academy, and I'm trying to find Nancy to make sure she isn't ill."

Satisfaction hit as he heard rustling in the back of the room. Would the mother appear? Or the missing Nancy herself?

Nancy appeared after a minute, wearing her maid's uniform, probably her best clothing.

"You ran away from your work," Charles said mildly.

"Not surprised by the cholera," Nancy said, her upper lip twitching.

"Is that why you fled?"

"I 'ad to tidy the rooms in the boardinghouse where your little friends live. Three boys were complaining about their stomachs."

"You didn't suspect a bad meal?" Charles asked.

"I'd eaten the food myself. I knew it was fine that day."

"As a result, you went straight to fears of cholera?"

"It's been only three years since my father and two sisters died of it," she said simply. "I know what it looks like."

"Was Ollie one of those children?"

She nodded.

"Who else?"

"Two in the dormitory, on the next floor down. I don't remember their names."

Not John or Arthur, then. One small relief. "Did Monks flee, as well?"

"I 'aven't seen 'im. I don't know where 'e went."

Charles narrowed his eyes. "How about Agnes's map? It was stolen from me."

She snorted. "Some clever little bugger took it? Well, I never. I 'aven't seen it."

Charles put his hands on his hips. "You are a coward, Nancy, but I can understand why. You'll have to pay your respects to Mrs. Bedwin when the illness passes and see if you still have employment."

The younger girl wrapped her arms around Nancy's waist. "She 'as to work. Otherwise 'ow will we all eat?" She let go and pushed Nancy a little.

Nancy tightened her jaw and stood her ground. "I'm not going back there, Lolly. I'll find something else." She shut the door in Charles's face.

As it happened, he had moved his foot away just in time.

While he wasn't convinced he knew everything Nancy did, his assessment of her countenance when she spoke of her family losses from cholera rang true.

Charles girded his confidence with a meditation on the irregular nature of cholera outbreaks as he returned to the school. The disease could kill half the people in one house, skip over the next, and kill a third of the next household after that, rather in the manner of a Biblical plague. If only he knew which animal's blood to smear on the sides and tops of each Aga Academy doorframe to spare the occupants.

When he reached the boardinghouse being used for the afflicted, he found John and Arthur loitering in front.

"Why aren't you in classes?"

John yawned. "Canceled. The lower master has pains in his stomach. Mr. Aga made him go to bed and told us to leave Ollie to rest."

"The Latin master?" Charles asked.

Arthur nodded. He still had the Latin text.

"Do you know anything about the present whereabouts of the map that had been in my possession?" Charles asked. "It has been stolen."

Arthur scrunched up his young features. "I swear we didn't steal the map this time."

"We have it memorized now," John added. "We don't need to."

"I wonder who was interested enough in the matter to take it," Charles murmured. "How many patients now?"

"Five, I think," John said, his expression going bleak. "Two students from this 'ouse, our Ollie, the master, and young Mr. Aga."

"Three total from this building, then," Charles said. "I wonder what they have in common with Ollie and William?"

"We'll 'ave it next," John said dolefully.

"You just never know with cholera." Charles patted his shoulder and went inside.

He ignored all propriety and went to the kitchen to retrieve a jug of water, then began walking the rooms. The earliest afflicted, Ollie and the first patient from this house, were desperately thirsty. Charles did not at all like the looks of the other boy, whose skin was taking on a bluish, leatherish cast.

All five of the patients were lucid, though. Lucid and terrified. William begged Charles to help him into the room with Ollie, so he could comfort the boy he'd helped through the terrors of having his hand destroyed in an accident on the Thames foreshore less than a year before.

Charles ran downstairs to refill the jug, then helped William assuage his mighty thirst before allowing him to stand. His taller friend tottered against him and cast up his accounts into a pot as they walked, but they made it to a spare bed next to Ollie's.

Charles pushed the slight boy's bed close to William's, so they could talk if they found energy; then he served them water yet again.

A kitchen girl arrived with lemonade, saying Mrs. Bedwin hoped the patients could drink it. Charles dosed all five of the afflicted with it, knowing that if the school was overrun, such niceties would disappear quickly.

When he went downstairs for more water, he slipped outside for a minute to check on John and Arthur and steal a breath of fresh air. He found them with the curate.

"Take these students and get some dinner for yourself," said Barney Wynd. "I will watch over the house for an hour."

"You'll take such risk upon yourself?" Charles asked.

"It is my Christian duty," the curate explained. "This school has few enough to give care."

Charles bowed his head. Perhaps he and his friends had misunderstood the mysterious man of God. He thought the curate might offer a prayer, but he didn't. Charles handed over the jug after a pause. "I suggest you keep water plentiful to aid the patients' colossal thirst."

"They are in that phase of the disease?"

"I see you are familiar with the course of it."

The curate nodded. "I was at school during the last outbreak."

Charles worried at his lips. All this talk of fluids made him thirsty himself. He didn't feel any sort of stomach discomfort, however, and he'd noticed William looked unwell for days leading up to the diagnosis. "I will return with beer if I can."

"More nourishing than water," the curate agreed pleasantly, then went into the house.

Kate kept busy with ordering Lucy out and about on various little chores, like running to purchase a new skein of black thread for her embroidery and fetching meals for them.

Julie slept for a couple of hours in the afternoon but otherwise fretted. She wrote letters to her aunt and the newspaper, to inform them of William's illness. From time to time, she glanced at the re-created map and paced, muttering lines of Shakespeare to herself.

Late in the day, Lucy returned from the inn's kitchen, where she had taken their tray.

"Are you feeling well, Lucy?" Kate asked. The girl had a little flush.

"Very well, yes, miss," Lucy said.

"Why are your cheeks pink?" Julie asked sharply.

Lucy put her hands to them. "One of the stable boys was teasing me."

"We won't stand for that," Julie said. "Do I need to have a word with the stable master?"

"No." Lucy smiled faintly, still holding her cheeks. "He was making love to me, not being cruel."

Julie and Kate exchanged a glance. The Agas had taken Lucy

into training as a maid because they had been afraid for the young girl's fate on the rough Thames foreshore, as older, nastier youths had moved in on her territory. She had turned out to be a lot more beautiful, and a little older, than they had realized, but still, she was only around fourteen.

"It's much too soon for that sort of thing," Julie said, echoing Kate's thoughts. "You must ignore such a boy, pay him no mind. He has nothing to offer you."

"No, ma'am," Lucy said quickly.

Julie shook her head a little, distracted, then reached for the map again and took it to the bed. "How could Agnes have acquired a map tied to the church in the first place?"

"We don't know for certain if the triangle with the cross means the church," Kate said. "And the churchyard clue of Byron is a cultural, historical sort of clue, not a religious one."

"She went to the church every Sunday her entire life," Julie muttered. "Mr. Aga is quite an ordinary sort. There's been no hint of anything irregular with him or the family that I've ever heard."

"No pirates in the family?" Kate asked. Treasure seemed to equal pirates, somehow.

"I really have never inquired. William's mother died young, of course. I've never met Mr. George Aga or been to the farm."

"You haven't been married very long."

"No, and it was a short courtship. We had our lives in London, and my relatives there. Harrow on the Hill seemed distant."

"William's always busy with work."

"Very true," Julie said. "Now his family has become interesting in the most gruesome way. I don't want to be the wife that loses her husband, instead of the other way around." Her voice clutched as her hands went to her belly and surrounded it protectively.

"We'll sort it out," Kate said, rising from her stool and going to comfort Julie. "But it is harder with only the three of us, all trapped here."

"We aren't really trapped here," Lucy nearly whispered, as if afraid Charles or William would hear. "There's no cholera anywhere but at the school."

"We could have it, however," Julie said flatly.

"Does your stomach hurt?" Kate asked.

"No, and my bodily functions are entirely normal," Julie answered.

Kate flushed. Well, she had cared for enough children to be comfortable with the topic, more than a man might be. She straightened her back. "Mine as well. You, too, Lucy dear?"

"I am very well."

The trio glanced among themselves and nodded at each other.

"Very well," Kate said. "It has been most of a day. If we are all still fine tomorrow, we run little risk of being ill, I'd say. As long as we stay away from the school."

Pain pressed the front of Charles's skull against his brain as he walked through the door of the boardinghouse the next morning. Mrs. Bedwin had done her duty, sending him home late the previous night to sleep for a few hours. He'd protested, saying he should sleep in the house with the afflicted, but since he'd had no symptoms, she'd disagreed.

He had no clothing that did not smell like a sickroom, after just two days, but at least his pain was in his head and not his belly. When he reached the door of William and Ollie's room, he set the full water jug on his hip and opened the door.

The smell of the rice-water illness hit him. He shuddered a little, taking it in, and walked in, forcing a cheerful smile onto his face.

"Good morning, patients," he said softly.

William turned away from the light in the doorway and coughed weakly. Ollie was still just a dark lump in the blankets.

"Thirsty?" Charles said to his friend.

"Yes," William croaked. "Thirsty."

Charles drew the curtain slightly, enough to see that thank goodness, William did not have a bluish cast to his features. That would probably be the end stage of the disease many did not survive.

"I cannot stop drinking," William rasped.

"That is because it comes out again so quickly." Charles filled the cup on the windowsill meant for William and helped him to drink, then woke Ollie and did the same.

Death could come in sleep just as easily as in wakefulness.

When he'd finished with the lad, he repeated the motions until the jug was nearly empty. Then, as predicted, he had to help both of them with the consequences.

Both of them were weak and shaking by the end of the operation. Charles went downstairs to fetch more water and see if any servant could be found to help him tidy up and supply him with any news.

He went back up with his jug again and heard stirring at the end of the passage. Dr. Goose was leaving a room, shaking his head.

"Bad news?" Charles said in a low voice.

"The first patient has died," Dr. Goose whispered. "He will not be the last."

"The student? Field?"

"Yes," the doctor responded absently. "Children die faster, I observe."

Charles saw muck on the doctor's hands. The stench, though he tried hard to breathe through his mouth, was more than he could take. He poured half the jug over the doctor's hands right there. The water dripped down the wall and puddled on the wood floor. He didn't care. "Don't bring the stench of death in to see my friends," he said fiercely. "They must have hope."

The doctor made no response, only wiped his hands with his handkerchief. "Any news on the Miss Aga matter?"

"None," Charles said. "Tell me, Doctor, did you examine her again in your offices?"

"I did, yes."

Charles swallowed hard, suddenly wanting some of the water himself, but he felt too nauseated to drink. "Was she still a maid? I've never known for certain."

"Will you not let the dead have their privacy?"

"No, Doctor. It might be important. A woman would have left her a maid, but a man?"

The doctor nodded. He put his hand to the side of his face, and his fingers spread across his temple and down his cheek. He considered, then nodded when he'd come to a conclusion. "Yes, young man. Miss Aga died a maid. No sign of interference with her body."

"Then why were her skirts rucked up?"

The doctor shrugged. "The evildoer was interrupted? The skirt slid up when she fell? You yourself interfered with her?"

"I never touched her," Charles snapped. "How dare you suggest such a thing."

"We cannot know," the doctor said mildly. "There is no ability in science to discern who might have touched her."

"But I have witnesses," Charles said. "I was partially in view, and both my friend and the housekeeper would know I did not venture far enough into the icehouse to touch her."

"We do not have the same witnesses for the killer's actions," the doctor said. "Your friend may not survive the day. Mrs. Bedwin risks her life to care for the afflicted, as do you, for that matter. In a few days, this poor child's death might be past anyone who might care, everyone joined together in the Lord's merciful embrace."

Charles didn't know if he should take that as a comfort or a threat. But he wasn't willing to let his friends go easily to their heavenly reward, either. He let Dr. Goose pass him in the hall and followed him back into the sick chamber with his half-full water jug.

Chapter 18

After Charles emptied what was left in the jug into the parched, suffering throats of Ollie and William, he went downstairs again to refill it. When he passed through the front hall on the way to the cistern, he heard a knock on the door.

Hoping help had arrived from somewhere, he opened it. He found John and Arthur on the step. John balanced a stout stoppered jug on his shoulder.

"Beer," Arthur piped. "We fetched it from the brewer this morning. Mr. Aga said it's William's favorite."

Charles leaned against the doorjamb, weak with gratitude. "That was kind of you. William and Ollie both seem to be holding on. All the news is not good, however. There has been a death, the first student who became ill."

"Richard Field is dead?" John asked incredulously.

"I never knew the boy's first name. I imagine so." Nausea pressed deeper into Charles's stomach. Disease dehumanized in the same way death did. "I should return swiftly to attend our friends. Thank you for the beer."

"We'll get more," John promised. "I could carry only that one jug."

"Reach into my pocket," Charles said. "Take the coins to pay the brewer."

He scarcely felt the boy's touch. His purse winked into John's hand, and the boy offered a rare grin.

"You've had training," Charles observed.

"I liked digging in the muck on the foreshore better," John said. "Less chance of being 'anged compared to a fingersmith."

"Who taught you?" Charles asked, his brain, even in these circumstances, turning him toward thoughts of details he could add to his chapters. Might Mr. Pickwick have his purse stolen by some light-fingered child?

"An old man. 'E runs a school for children, sort of like this," John told him. "In Limehouse. 'E's an odd 'un. I 'eard he was a Hebrew. Allus wore a flannel gown, ever so greasy."

"A kidsman," Charles said thoughtfully. "I always wondered how such men found their young charges."

" 'E lived right in the building we did when my pa was alive," John explained. "I was 'ungry one day, cuz Pa drank our food money, and one of the old man's fingersmiths invited me for a meal. Good it was. I still remember." He rubbed his belly.

"What did 'e feed you?" Arthur said, licking his lips instinctively.

"Sausage an' bread an' butter," John said wistfully. "Remember when they served sausage 'ere?"

"They did that before Mr. Sikes took charge of the kitchen?" Charles asked. Did the deterioration in the student menu play some part in the fatal illness sweeping the school now?

Arthur nodded eagerly.

"I remember something else," John said. "About the old man. 'E tried to get me to drink a pot of hot gin and water. Said it would 'elp me sleep. I thought about upstairs, and what Pa's drink did to me mum, and I said no and ran back to her."

"Very wise," Charles said. "You must have been no older than Arthur at the time."

"Mum told me to stay away from 'im. Said the sausage was probably made from ground-up little boys who ran away."

Arthur's eyes grew round.

"Now, that was just meant to scare you," Charles admonished, adjusting his grip on the beer jug. "The Jewish people do not eat children. They are quite nice when you get to know them, the ones who aren't kidsmen, at least. Now go make yourselves useful to Mrs. Bedwin." He shut the door with his foot and climbed the stairs with the beer.

He wished he'd been able to save a mouthful of the excellent brew for himself after he'd tossed the contents of fouled pots out the window into the hedges below and given them back to his suffering friends. Happily, they had the energy to drink the beer.

Ollie teared up when some splashed down his nightshirt instead of into his mouth, but Charles shushed him and calmed him down with a comic song about an expiring frog he was formulating for *Pickwick*.

When Charles had finished and Ollie was calm, William croaked for him to come near. "Do you have paper and pen?"

"It's back at your father's house. I have a pencil and a scrap of paper, though."

"It will have to do. I want to make out my will," his friend rasped.

"Very well," Charles said somberly. "Let me just fetch some water first."

"No, let's do it now, while the beer is working." William blinked dry eyes.

"Are we going to die?" Ollie asked.

"You are doing well, my strong lad," Charles said. "Our prayers are being answered." Privately, though, he knew chances were that one of them would not survive, though neither of them was in the fatal phase of the disease for now.

"Right," William said wearily. "You know what a will ought to say. Sound mind and such."

"Of course." Charles put his paper against the wall and wrote with his pencil.

"I want you to keep Julie away no matter what to protect the baby," William said. "That child is my last and best legacy."

"I'll tell her it is your wish," Charles said.

"The fumes from our bodies could sicken them, even after we're dead," William added.

"So they say, but you know no one really understands cholera," Charles said.

"All the better reason to keep her away." William's voice cracked. "To think we wanted the intellectual and moral satisfaction of sorting out what happened to our poor Agnes, and it has come to this."

"I 'ope 'er killer dies of cholera, too," Ollie insisted. He began to cough.

"Now I must really insist on fetching the water," Charles said after Ollie's cough led to all the beer leaving his body.

After a half hour of tidying up and giving water to both of them, Charles finished William's will and watched as he signed it.

"Can I make a will, too?" Ollie asked.

Charles had one more slip of paper. He turned back to Ollie and did not at all like what he saw. The recent bout of illness seemed to have sunken the child's eyes into his head. "First, you must drink more water," he said, desperation seizing him. "More beer, too. Oh, John needs to come back with it."

"Then you'll 'elp me?" the boy pleaded. "I have a few things for my friends."

"Of course, dear child," Charles said, smoothing the soft pale hair back from the boy's forehead. "I will write it all down."

A knock came at the door. Mr. Aga had a jug in his hands. "A delivery from the boys. I came to visit my son."

"Wonderful," Charles said. "They need to drink constantly. It's the only thing that seems to comfort them."

"They must have stew downstairs," Julie said impatiently, throwing her blue calfskin-covered copy of *Ivanhoe* onto the bed.

"I'd rather have bread and butter. You want something hot?" Kate asked. She'd stirred up the fire a little too high when Lucy had delivered fuel.

"Both," Julie said. "This baby does insist on growing."

They sent Lucy on the errand. When she'd left, Julie rearranged the blankets on the bed. She'd been using them behind her lower back.

"I'm not really hungry," she confided. "I just want Lucy to stay active."

"We should send her on some errand regarding the mysteries," Kate said. "I don't know what, though. It's not safe for a pretty young maid to tramp through graveyards and the woods alone."

A knock came at the door; then Lucy peeked in. "You have a visitor downstairs," she announced. "I didn't have time to order any food."

"Is it Charles?" Julie asked. "I don't mind if he comes upstairs."

"No, it's someone we saw at church."

Kate glanced at Julie. "I can go down if you'd like to rest."

Julie swung her legs to the floor. "No, I'll come. We don't appear to have anything to worry about here."

They went downstairs into the public room and found a gentleman waiting for them. He inclined his head on his short stub of a neck when they entered.

"Which one of you is Mrs. Aga?" he asked pleasantly.

"I am," Julie said grandly.

"Please allow me to make myself known to you," he said. "I am James Maylie."

"Yes, of course," Julie said. "My husband spoke to you at St. Mary's last Sunday. Please allow me to introduce Miss Catherine Hogarth, Mr. Dickens's fiancée."

Kate smiled at him. "We know your name through Mr. Screws of London."

"Indeed, I do know the man."

Short, round, and bald, Kate thought him a generation too old to be the father of Agnes's friend, but these things were ordinary enough. "Have you been to the school?"

Julie gripped her hand. "Have you brought news?"

"I have indeed. I was just at the school, and as I had to come into town for supplies, Mr. Aga asked me to visit with you." He shook his head. "Terrible news about young Richard Field."

"What happened?" Julie asked.

"That is the boy who took ill first, yes?" Kate said.

"From what the schoolmaster said. I'm afraid the boy has gone to his reward."

"The first boy dead," Julie whispered. "Such a shame."

"Perhaps you would care to sit down?" Mr. Maylie said.

Kate had the feeling he wanted them sitting for more bad news. But it wouldn't be about William; this wasn't how Julie would be told. She nodded and led Julie to a table with benches far enough away from the fire that they weren't near strange men. They both sat, with Lucy hovering nearby.

"Please, sit and give us the rest of the news," Julie said. She had gone very pale, perhaps not having worked through Kate's logic.

Kate squeezed her hand under the table as Mr. Maylie fluffed out his coats and sat on the opposite bench.

"I'm afraid there has been another death," he began.

Julie's entire body shuddered. "No," she said. The word came out as an eerie sort of crime.

"The terrible news is that we found a body this morning."

Kate frowned, holding tightly to Julie. "Found?" she queried.

"At the quarry, yes, miss," Mr. Maylie confirmed.

Julie didn't relax, like Kate had hoped.

"Was it another cholera death? Has it started to sweep through your employees?" Her voice trembled only a little. They had been at the quarry.

"Yes, it was cholera. The state of the body is quite unmistakable," he said soberly. "It wasn't an employee, though. It was another student."

"Monks Aga has been missing," Kate remarked, remembering. "Was it he?"

"Yes. And yes, that is what his uncle said." The quarry owner shook his head. "I wonder if he'd been taking a walk when he took ill. The quarry isn't on the path to his father's dairy farm."

Kate guessed he'd been following the map. She didn't think he'd been around to steal their copy, so he must have seen it by way of Agnes before she died. Not surprising given that she'd been waving it around. "It doesn't matter now, I suppose. Poor boy. The Agas have been very hard hit now."

"And Mr. William Aga is ill, as well." Mr. Maylie clucked his tongue. "He's heir to both the school and the dairy farm now. George Aga has no one left. He's just lost both of his children."

"My child is left," Julie said, lifting her chin. She stretched her right arm across her body and gripped Kate's arm with her hand.

"Do you have news about Mr. Aga?" Kate asked. "We do not know what is going on at the school today."

"I understand he is sharing a room with one of the charity

students who took ill," Mr. Maylie said. "They are still conscious, in full possession of intellect."

"That is common until the end, no?" Kate said.

"It is a disease that can kill in hours, which is probably what happened to Monks Aga, or the course of the illness can be up and down for days," Mr. Maylie explained. "Many do survive, of course."

"How many?" Julie asked.

He spread out his hands. "A third? A half? You hear about entire families dying in the same room, but if most of a family stays healthy, they can often nurse the afflicted back to health."

A serving maid walked by with a tray of steaming pots. She looked at them curiously, then brought her drinks to a table near the fire.

"Monks may have been the first local victim of the terrible disease," Kate said. "He went missing on Monday. William Aga was not quite himself, but it wasn't obvious he was fighting the disease until yesterday afternoon."

"We knew Richard Field had it Monday," Julie said. Her voice sounded constricted.

"He and Monks were in the same dormitory room," Mr. Maylie added. "I understood that from Mr. Aga when I told him the terrible news."

"Does Uncle Aga know?"

"Yes. I went to the farm first."

"Poor man," Julie murmured.

"It's heartbreaking," Kate agreed. "Will you be riding toward the school on your way back to the quarry?"

"I don't live far from there," Mr. Maylie explained. "Would you like me to take a message?"

"I would," Kate said. As the serving maid came back their way, she asked Mr. Maylie to call for pen and paper.

He drank coffee while they waited; then she penned a note to Charles when her writing implements arrived. After inquiring about the health of William, Ollie, and everyone at the school, she added a line. In the course of his nursing, he must find out how Agnes acquired the map. What if the source of the cholera had something to do with it? She didn't know anything about Richard Field, but Monks could have caught the disease while hunting the treasure and given it to Richard.

Kate's thoughts tumbled over Agnes, who'd been murdered, not killed by cholera, but still. Monks had been found at the quarry. They had met him and Nancy in the woods. That made her afraid that he'd figured out the next symbol.

Had he discovered it because he'd followed them there? Or because he'd sorted out the next clue? Or, like them, had he figured it out wrong?

She knew she ought to be more sorrowful about the boy's death, but he'd been a nasty piece of work, and a little too old to be likely to grow out of his malignant treatment of girls. For now, she just wanted to solve the mysteries that swirled around.

When she wasn't praying for William and Ollie, of course.

Mr. Maylie left them with a cheerful smile, which was both out of place and soothing, promising to deliver the letter to Charles.

"We have to return to the quarry," Julie said.

"I shouldn't think so," Kate responded. "My thoughts are not quite formed, but Monks died at the quarry like a wounded animal. What if he acquired the disease there?"

"Experts seem to think cholera is transmitted by miasma," Julie pointed out after a moment of thought. "If we stay in the fresh, clean air, we will be fine."

"It is a disease that only poor people get," Lucy suggested.

"We know that is wrong," Kate said. "Mr. Aga has it at this very moment. And our Ollie may be poor, but what about Richard Field? He was a fee-paying student, I imagine. That means his parents are well off enough."

Lucy chewed at her lip. Julie glanced between the two of them. "Lucy, fetch our cloaks. We are going for a walk."

"A drive," Kate demurred. "It sounds all very well to walk, but we are at the top of the hill, not even at the school. The quarry is far away."

"I used to walk London all hours, just like Charles," Julie said. "Running errands for the theater."

"You aren't Mr. Dickens," Kate said sharply. "Matrons with expectations do not wander the countryside. Besides, once we leave the inn, no one will know where to find us. What if news comes about your husband?"

Julie set her jaw, then rose and went to speak to the serving girl, out of earshot of Kate.

When Lucy returned with their garments, Kate hissed at her and pulled her close. "Pretend to turn your ankle a couple of streets into our walk so we can return to the inn."

Lucy nodded. "If you think it's best, miss."

"Julie must take her condition more seriously. Mr. Aga would want that."

"Yes, miss."

Julie returned, a triumphant gleam in her eyes. Lucy dressed her while Kate draped her own cloak over her shoulders and tied her bonnet over her cap.

They went out into the yard. A four-wheeled trap waited in the yard, with seating for four. Two horses were being harnessed to it.

"You rented us a trap?" Kate asked.

"I did," Julie said. "You can't object to that."

"You are impossible," Kate hissed. "We shouldn't be leaving the inn."

"We will simply pay our respects," Julie said disingenuously. "Monks was my husband's cousin, after all. I wonder if they searched him."

"Julie!" Kate exclaimed.

"I'd like to know if he had the map." Julie's voice was calm.

Kate exchanged a glance with Lucy, but the girl merely helped her mistress into the cart. A stableman helped Kate in, as well; then a driver climbed on, not much older than Lucy.

"The Maylie quarry, if you please," Julie said.

Kate held on to the side of the trap as they rumbled out of the yard. Julie had started to throw money around as if she was the baroness, rather than her niece. Maybe she did have that kind of pin money. Kate certainly didn't.

She did enjoy the view of the town from the trap, however. The buildings of Harrow were quite pretty, and once they were out of town, the countryside had a pleasant almost-spring hum in the air. Birds called over the jangling reins.

Kate tried to stay focused on the landscape, keeping the arch symbol from the map in mind.

"I'm looking for other quarries," Lucy said in her ear. "What if we saw the wrong one from the woods?"

"All the clues could be interpreted wrongly," Kate pointed out.

Lucy shook her head. "Never believe it. What else could the Byron 'ead be?"

"The school he attended? His boardinghouse? His favorite pastry shop, for all I know." Kate pressed her lips together. "We cannot assume we have anything correct."

The ride became bumpy again as gravel from the quarry dotted the road. Kate had a white-knuckled grip on the trap's side when they turned in.

"Gate is closed," the driver announced. "Are they expecting you? I can climb down and see if anyone is here."

Kate turned on the seat, surveying the surrounding landscape. Her mouth dropped open. She pointed.

"What?" Lucy asked.

Julie, seated opposite them, turned around.

Kate pointed north. "Look at the shape of the hill. It's an arch!"

"Why didn't we see it before?" Julie asked.

"We were on foot and looking from the quarry, not the road," Kate explained. "This has to be right. We weren't lost, after all."

"That means the sharp triangle is indeed the church spire," Julie said. "Well done, Kate. We have only one clue left to solve."

Lucy's eyes went wide.

"What should I do, ladies?" the driver asked. He took his hand off the reins to rub at the side of his mouth, where a sore crusted the skin.

Julie shuddered. "Take us back into town. We should have realized they would close the quarry out of respect."

"But first, a moment of prayer," Kate said. At Julie's look of confusion, she added, "For Monks, of course."

"Yes, of course," Julie murmured. She put out her hands, palm down. "One minute for poor Cousin Monks."

Charles dumped his dirty clothing into a heap on the floor in the guest room of Mr. Aga's house. He couldn't wear his trousers or coat again until they had been cleaned. The house-keeper would have to add a washing day that week, thanks to cholera.

He dressed in the spare clothing the housekeeper had brought him from Mr. Aga's chest, grateful for it despite the large size. Happily, it all fit around the middle, and she'd sup-plied pins so he could take up the sleeves and the trouser-leg hems.

He expected he looked like a boy dressed as a man when he was done, but it couldn't be helped. Now that he was decently dressed, as much as could be expected, he had to go to the greengrocer's. Ollie had started to cry piteously for ginger beer, and his mudlark friends were off to the brewery to get ale for William.

At least his afflicted friends both still cared enough to ask for their favorite beverages. Charles chose to take that as a good sign.

Offering up a prayer for the Lord to keep his friends safe until he could return, he left the house and walked up the street in the direction of the store, taking great gulps of fresh air. His stained clothing had affected the air in Mr. Aga's house, and most great minds believed that miasma in the air caused cholera. The fouler the air he breathed in, the more likely he would be afflicted himself.

He stood at the entrance to a court, not sure if he should turn. The opening between buildings seemed narrower than he'd expected. Up ahead, he saw a trap turning to the right. The bonnets of the passengers looked familiar. What were Kate and Julie doing? Abandoning his plan, he resumed his normally enthusiastic pace to follow the trap.

Chapter 19

Charles closed his aching eyes and opened them again, checking to make sure the vision of the trap ahead of him on the street was real. What were Kate and Julie doing outside the inn, in a trap with a driver? Was he hallucinating? He followed, passing a clothing merchant and a coal merchant, then a more genteel newsagent and a coffeehouse. The trap stopped in front of the very greengrocer's he'd gone to find.

He watched half a building away as a very young driver helped down Kate, then Lucy, and then all of them assisted Julie, who seemed to have grown more ungainly than he remembered.

A man came out of the shop as Julie reached the road. He looked familiar, as well, though Charles couldn't quite place him. The sleep deprivation of recent days plagued his memory. Irritation sped him up again.

"Charles?" Kate said uncertainly as he approached speaking distance.

"I thought you were remaining safely at the inn," he said, his words appropriately harsh.

"We needed fresh air," Julie explained in plaintive tones.

"You went for a drive?" asked the other man, glancing between the two parties.

"Yes, Uncle Aga." Julie put her hand on the man's arm. "I felt utterly restless when I heard the terrible news. What can we do to help?"

Charles finally recognized George Aga, from his very long legs more than his nondescript face. His thin-lipped old man's mouth hung slightly open, as if his jaw had forgotten how to close. A change had come over his posture. He didn't remember the man having such a pronounced stoop when he'd seen him previously, but grief did such things.

"Terrible news?" Charles asked. "I've just come from the school. William and Ollie are no worse."

The door opened again, and the schoolmaster came out, holding a crate of foodstuffs.

Charles blinked. "I thought you were at the boarding-house."

The man nodded wearily at Charles. "I am picking up food supplies myself since most of my staff is ill or has vanished."

"Where is Mr. Sikes?" Charles asked. "I thought he was in charge of the food stores."

"Mr. Sikes is nowhere to be found," said the schoolmaster. "He left a note saying he was urgently needed upon workhouse business."

"Put it all in the trap," Julie said. "We can take the supplies to the school."

"You'll do no such thing," Charles insisted. "You can't go anywhere near there."

Kate's bonnet inclined. "Julie and I can walk back to the inn from here. It's not far. You take the trap, Mr. Aga. That way you can fetch more at once."

"We have to go to St. Mary's." The schoolmaster sighed heavily.

"My son, you know. We must make arrangements," George Aga said.

"What?" Charles asked, bewildered.

"My son has been found dead." He hung his head.

How had he missed the news? "Monks? How?"

"The cholera. It must have taken him so suddenly that he—" George Aga's mouth worked.

Julie patted his arm. "Monks was dead, you see. It's a terrible business."

Charles glanced at Kate. She didn't gesture in any way. Could the story be true? He didn't see how murder could be disguised as cholera, so he decided to take the information at face value. "The school is sorely afflicted. But I've seen the maids. They were still working."

"It's the cook," Mr. Aga said. "She has taken to her bed with the vapors. And Mrs. Bedwin didn't have time to replace Agnes before our trials worsened."

"Oh, dear," Kate said. "The school needs a very thorough cleaning. There must be someplace where the air is bad."

"My father used to wander about town muttering such things," George Aga interjected suddenly. "He hated any sort of puddle, any uncleared cistern. He used to pay the nightsoil men to come twice as often to our property that was normal."

"He lived to be a very old man," Eustace Aga added. "He was doing something right."

"He blamed my wife's death on bad air. She liked keeping windows closed, whereas my father wanted them open all year round," George Aga said.

"Where was Monks?" Charles asked. "We couldn't find him."

"He was found at the quarry," Kate said. "Mr. Maylie came to the inn to tell us."

Charles's eyebrows rose. "The quarry?"

Kate nodded.

"You went there, I suppose."

Julie took Kate's arm defiantly. "We went for a drive and nothing more."

"We figured out the clue," Lucy said, bouncing on her toes. "The quarry is the fourth clue, after all. We realized it from the road."

"This is not the time," Charles said severely.

To his surprise, George Aga's lips flexed slightly, almost as if he'd started to smile before realizing the horrors of the day.

"What are you reminded of, sir?" Charles asked.

"The map. The treasure map, yes?"

Charles nodded. "We've thought that if we solved it, we'd uncover the sad truth about Agnes and give your family the answers about the tragedy."

George Aga quirked his cheek. "My father, who died only recently, was an antiquarian. He either bought the map somewhere or made it up."

Charles vaguely remembered William taking one of his occasional trips here just before they had all moved to Selwood Terrace for the summer months. He'd told Charles about his grandfather, a very eccentric old man.

Kate gasped. "The map came from your family?"

"Yes, the silly old thing. Father loved to tell tall tales. He must have given it to her, or she found it after he died. I hadn't thought of it in years."

"It wasn't real," Eustace Aga said. "And not important now."

"No," Charles agreed. "The afflicted are our focus. I am here to pick up ginger beer. Ollie was begging for it. Let's finish our buying and get back to the school."

George Aga coughed, or possibly covered a sob by coughing. "Is my nephew going to die, as well? My entire family and possibly your entire school are going to be wiped out in the course of a week."

"Brother," said Eustace Aga heavily. "William is not gone yet."

Charles's gaze had gone to Julie. Her face had paled from its normal exuberance when William's uncle spoke, almost as if her skin had been covered with stage makeup. "By no means," he added. "Given the circumstances, one could say he looks rather well. Many recover."

George Aga shook his head. "Don't offer false hope to the ladies, Mr. Dickens. We're going to lose them all. Why should my nephew be spared when my children are dead? No, there is a curse on this entire family."

Eustace Aga frowned at his brother, though the hand he held out to Charles shook slightly. "Mr. Dickens, would you please finish the arrangements here? We have an account. I will walk with the ladies and my brother to the inn and then to the church. All the better to return to my school more quickly."

Charles nodded and tilted his head to Kate in such a manner that she turned to Julie and Lucy and started to return to the main street. Julie seemed confused and unsteady when Kate spoke to her, but with the help of Kate and her faithful companion, Lucy, she started up the hill. Soon he was left in front of the store, with no one but the driver staring at him.

"Strange doings," Charles said.

"No one wants to stay near a house of sickness," said the youth wisely. "But it's sad to see even a father desert a sick son."

Charles kicked a rock. "No one is thinking clearly. I must get back."

A man appeared, carrying another crate of food. He stopped, confused when he saw Charles.

"Load the trap. I'm taking it back to the school," Charles said, then went inside to add ginger beer to the order.

"I will not sit in this ghastly room for another minute," Julie said, pulling her arm out of Kate's grasp that evening. "If we're all going to die, we might as well do it singing and dancing."

The expectant former actress executed a turn that moved her past her maidservant and out of the room.

Kate could do nothing but look at Lucy in horror. In the hours that had passed since their walk back to the inn, Julie had been in a strange mood, muttering bits of Shakespeare to herself and giving in to short bursts of laughter.

"I think she 'as lost her mind without 'er 'usband to 'elp 'er," Lucy said.

"Mr. Dickens and my father have never trusted her," Kate responded. "Is that because they have seen such dramatics as this?"

"No, it's because they both think she wanted Mr. Dickens to marry her first," Lucy said. "They think William was her second best, but they are wrong about that."

"Oh?"

"I don't know what might 'ave 'appened," Lucy said. "But she loves 'er 'usband. That uncle of 'is was downright cruel."

"I noticed the change, as well." Kate shook her head. "The sad truth is, many people with cholera do die."

"Not our William Aga," Lucy said, with fierceness in her tone. "He's strong and not old, and he's well cared for."

"What about Ollie? Richard Field is dead, and Monks Aga."

"It can be laid at that Mr. Sikes's door," Lucy insisted. "Making the food so poor. You cannot take sausages out of a boy's diet."

Kate's jaw trembled when she tried to speak. She leaned against the fireplace, not yet lit for the evening with all the emotional drama. "Then you think poor Ollie will die."

Lucy hung her head. "I don't like 'is prospects, miss. I've seen lots of little ones go. Both of my brothers, even."

"What do we do?" Kate whispered.

"Pray our Mr. Dickens 'as the strength to nurse all of 'em, and not take ill 'imself." Lucy sniffed.

Kate felt tears forming in her eyes, as well. "Mr. Dickens has charge of the patients. We have charge of Julie, and the Lord has charge of all of us, I suppose. We had better do our part."

"Yes, miss." Lucy wiped her eyes with a mostly clean handkerchief, tightened her mouth, and marched through the door.

A couple of minutes later, as Kate reached the bottom of the staircase, followed by Lucy, she heard male laughter in the public room, then a snatch of singing.

As she and Lucy stepped into the room, she saw a man take up a fiddle to the left of the fire and strike up the notes of a tune that sounded vaguely familiar from her childhood in Scotland. The public room seemed unusually well lit. Not only was the fire stoked high, but each table had a candle, too. It made for a cozy space.

Then Julie, with a wineglass glinting firelight in her hand and no sense of propriety whatsoever, moved in front of the mirrored mantelpiece and began to sing for the twenty or so men in the room.

> *A rose tree in full bearing,*
> *Had flowers very fair to see,*
> *One rose beyond comparing,*
> *Whose beauty attracted me;*
> *But eager for to win it,*
> *Lovely, blooming, fresh, and gay,*
> *I found a canker in it,*
> *And threw it very far away.*
>
> *How fine this morning early,*
> *Lovely Sunshine clear and bright,*
> *So late I lov'd you dearly,*
> *But now I've lost each fond delight;*
> *The clouds seem big with showers,*
> *The sunny beams no more are seen,*
> *Farewell ye happy hours,*
> *Your falsehood has changed the scene.*

Applause and cries for more greeted the performance. As Kate stood at the back of the room, aghast, Julie bobbed a little curtsy and started to sing something much bawdier.

"What does she think she's doing?" whispered Lucy.

"Taking her life into her hands," Kate snapped. "She's not a tavern performer. She's the niece of Lady Lugoson. We have to get her out of here."

At the end of the second song, Julie gave a little cough, then drained her entire glass. Her cheeks went pink, and a man in the front gave her a pot of some steaming liquid.

"That might be gin," Lucy said, scandalized. "She can't drink that."

"She just wants to be in her cups," Kate responded. "Her fear for William's health is just too much for her."

They watched as if paralyzed as Julie took a request to sing another song, which was an upbeat version of the first, with almost the same tune.

"How does she keep all these old songs in her head? You don't even have a piano."

"She sings all the time, and her aunt has a piano," Lucy said. "I think she misses it, the stage, you know."

"I thought she spent all that time at her aunt's house taking painting lessons, but that wasn't all."

"No. She treats the music room like a stage." Lucy took a deep breath. "I'm the only audience, usually."

"If William dies . . . ," Kate said, and then she couldn't finish the thought.

"I expect she will." Lucy finished the thought. "Go back onstage in some capacity. Unless Lady Lugoson can talk 'er out of it."

"Her sister is an actress, so she can hardly insist Julie desist on grounds of propriety."

Julie took a sip from the steaming pot and began to cough.

Kate didn't know if she had reacted because she was unused to hard spirits or because there was something even worse in the drink. She rushed up to her friend and grabbed the pot, then dashed it against the table.

As the men laughed, Kate felt cornered. Julie was the daughter by marriage of Mr. Aga. She wasn't a stranger in this town. Kate couldn't let this continue.

"This is unseemly," she hissed. "Come upstairs with me right now."

Julie looked at her with eyes glazed by grief or wine. "Very well. It does not matter."

"Sing us another," one man called. Another sang a snatch of a bawdy song.

Julie turned to her crowd and lifted one hand, then gave an elaborately saucy bow. The men hooted and cheered, and a smattering of them applauded. It seemed to satisfy the actress, and she joined Kate.

As they walked out of the public room, Julie snatched a wine bottle off the serving girl's tray and wobbled off with it.

As soon as they were safely back to the staircase leading upstairs, Kate grabbed the bottle from Julie's hand.

"You do not want the effects of a hard night's drinking tomorrow, Mrs. Aga," she hissed as soon as they had reached the first landing. A few steps up, it had the feeling of a stage over the inn's front hall.

"She is right," Lucy said. "All the vomiting you might do could hurt the baby."

Julie's lips puffed into a pout. "Very well. I just wanted to forget for a little while, remember what I was."

"You still are a great performer," Kate assured her. "But you've chosen a respectable life. You have a husband and a child coming. What more could any woman want?"

Julie swallowed hard, staring at her. Kate realized what she'd said but stood by it.

"Let us spend the rest of the evening praying for William," she said. "Prayer is a good place for us to find solace."

Lucy patted Julie's arm, but her mistress brushed it off. Kate sighed and picked up the bottle again, then went back down the three steps to hand it to the serving girl. She didn't want it added to their bill.

Kate stood at the edge of the smoky room and tried not to cough as she searched through the gloom for the girl. It seemed like a dozen men had lit cigars in the few minutes since Julie had finished singing. Finally, she spotted the blur of a person with a tray and approached her.

"Here you go," Kate told her, holding out the bottle. "It's still sealed. We didn't drink any of it."

"Mrs. Aga is a bonny singer," the girl said, taking the bottle. "She's good enough to be onstage."

"I'll tell her you think so," Kate said, realizing that Julie was indeed known in this town, but not by her former career. How easily she could leave her past behind if she wanted to.

When she reached the door out of the public room again, she heard a bark of a cry, then a girl's shout. Lucy! Had Julie fainted?

She sped out of her usually sedate pace. The front hall had little illumination, but she saw the candle Lucy had been holding bobbing down the staircase.

Kate crossed the floor in an instant and saw Julie huddled on the floor.

"She threw herself down the stairs," Lucy cried.

Kate used the newel post to help her kneel. Just then, Julie broke into sobs.

"She's conscious," Kate said. "Come now, dear. You have to fight for your baby."

"What about my William?" Julie said in the most tortured tone.

"He is in God's hands. It's your duty to protect his child. What were you thinking?"

Lucy reached her and knelt at Julie's feet. She set her candleholder on the first step. "Thankfully, she only tumbled down a three-step staircase."

"Tumbled by accident or threw herself down?" Kate asked. The story had changed.

"I don't know." Lucy ran her hands down her mistress's face and clothing. "She isn't bleeding."

Julie batted at Lucy's hands. "Don't worry. The baby is still moving. That's all anyone would care about."

"How can you say that?" Kate asked. "You just had a room full of men clapping for you. Not to mention how you would break poor Lucy's heart if anything happened."

"You must stop risking your 'ealth," Lucy said. "What if the cholera came over you while you were in a weakened state?"

"Then I'd be dead," Julie said dully. "What does it matter? If William dies, I want to be dead, too."

"You are needed," Kate said. "You are the closest to a daughter that Lady Lugoson has now. Your husband needs your prayers. And the rest of us, we need your friendship." She reached for Julie's hands and clasped them.

Julie responded by turning to her side. "I do not feel at all well."

Kate jumped back when Julie cast up her cups. Her pulse fluttered when she recognized that it could be a sign of cholera, but for all that it could very well be nothing but too much gin. Holding back her own bile, she felt Julie's forehead, which felt cool.

"Just the wine, then," she said aloud. "Come, Lucy. We have to get her upstairs. Then you can tell the serving girl to clean up this mess."

Twenty minutes later, they had Julie upstairs and back in bed. Kate stirred the fire.

Lucy took her arm and led her to the door. "Was it rice water?"

"It wouldn't be regardless, not when she had a bellyful of wine," Kate whispered. "We'll know what the reckoning is soon enough."

"I'm going to the church in the morning," Lucy said. "I don't know how to deal with 'er fear. We need a priest's guidance."

"Not if she really is ill," Kate cautioned. "We will be fighting for all our lives if she has cholera."

Kate stirred early the next morning. Neither she nor Lucy had wanted to share the bed with Julie, so they had taken turns in the early night, alternately sitting anxiously by the bed or sleeping on the floor in front of the fire.

Julie had become sick once more, still smelling of wine; then they all had settled into uneasy slumber.

By morning, though, as filtered light came through the shuttered window, Kate saw that Julie's color appeared normal. When she touched the younger woman's forehead, it felt cool.

"What do you think?" Lucy asked, stirring from her cloak.

Kate stepped to the fire, which they had kept going through the long, restless hours. "I think it was just the wine, laid over with gin or whatever was in that pot last night."

Lucy sat up and tucked stray hairs behind her ears, then started to coil her braid into a knot with the pins she'd removed the night before. "I will see what they have to break our fast and then go to the vicarage. Someone can provide Julie spiritual guidance."

"Keep it light. Dry toast or something of the sort," Kate advised. "Julie will probably be very sensitive to smells this morning."

"Yes, we do not want a repeat of last night." Lucy stood and wrapped her cloak around her again. "More coal, too. We are nearly out."

Kate rubbed her arms and nodded her thanks. Her neck and back were sorely kinked, but the patient was no worse.

Lucy and Kate ate their porridge and drank their tea as silently as they could, but Julie woke up before they were done, complaining about the light. Kate checked on her again, while Lucy brushed Julie's dress, and they helped her prepare for the day. All the while, Kate wondered who might perform such services for her, as she might very well be in the same state at Christmastime. Would her mother really spare Mary to be her helper until Charles could offer her space and money for a maid?

When Julie had been made comfortable, Lucy left to inquire at the vicarage and returned within an hour with Barney Wynd. Kate hadn't liked him when she'd met him before, but now she was grateful for any aid.

She thanked him for coming, then went outside for a short walk to the greengrocer's while he talked to their wayward young matron.

When she heard the church bells tolling the next hour, she returned to find the curate still there, drinking tea Lucy must have fetched. Julie's cheeks were pale, but Kate detected no hint of illness in the air.

"Thank you for coming in our time of need," Kate told the young man.

"It is perilous days, these," the curate said. "We have the same milkman as the school, and he was able to tell our housekeeper that no one else has come down with cholera overnight."

"That is wonderful news," Kate said.

"Yes." He shook his head, as if beset by some inner dialogue. "What is the latest about poor Agnes Aga? I know her brother has been found. Is it thought he was to blame?"

"I'm sure that would be the easiest solution for everyone," Kate said thoughtfully. "There is no doubt he had a tendency to violence. We saw him push his sister's fellow maid out in the woods."

"The easiest solution," the curate echoed. "You do not think he was responsible, though?"

"I could believe it," Kate ventured. "I would just want some sort of proof."

"What would that be?" Julie queried. "The actions of one dead person against another dead person are unknowable. And I don't think Monks was the diary-keeping sort."

"He had a boastful air," Kate ventured. "Might he have told one of the other boys?"

"We can have William interview them all." Julie paused, then continued in a whisper. "If he recovers."

"More people survive cholera than you might expect," the curate said quickly. "He is being well nursed. Most people around him have not been afflicted, which I believe makes all the difference."

"You've ministered to the school," Kate said. "Is there anyone you might expect would have been capable of violence toward a servant?"

"The wealthier the boy, the most likely he would treat a servant as nothing more than a beast of burden. But the wealthiest student by far was Toby Grimwig, and with his broken appendage, he couldn't have done much, especially given how the girl was found."

"You really heard nothing that day?" Kate asked. "I know you were in the woods." A frisson of unease slid up her spine as she recalled that fact. At least they were three against one if he turned out to be a killer.

She was pleased to see his expression did not change, however. He remained thoughtful, rather than becoming suspicious of her question.

"I really did not," he said. "Certainly, I heard birdcalls as I checked the usual squirrel caches, and a human can imitate such things. I believe I heard a sort of howl once. It could have been a person, I suppose. Nothing recognizable. I saw no one."

"Very disappointing," Julie said baldly. "As you must have been the closest person to the murder."

"I recognize that." The curate winced. "If it was not the richest boy, and therefore the most arrogant, you can look to the next wealthy student."

"Who is?" Lucy asked.

"Noah Claypole."

Kate nodded sharply. "I would believe he was mixed up in the business, as young as he is. We know he had some knowledge of the treasure map Agnes waved around before she died."

"I do wish that would be forgotten," the curate said.

"Why?" Julie asked. "It's tied in to the murder. What do you know of it?"

"I know you should not search for the treasure," he returned. "No one should."

"Why?" Lucy asked.

"Because, dear child, it is protected by the Morrígan."

Kate had no idea what he was talking about. "I don't understand."

"That is good. Following that map is a mistake. Speak to the servant. If Monks's violence hurt her, it ought to have opened her mouth. If she really seems convinced of the boy's innocence, then look very carefully at Noah Claypole."

"What about the masters? The other servants?" Kate asked.

"What would any of them have to gain? They would lose their positions. A student in late boyhood, however, he would think he was invincible, and a chance at a treasure map might be enough to kill a servant." His nostrils flared. "Scarcely human at that age."

"An interesting point," Lucy said, sounding so matronly Kate had to hide a smile. "I do agree with you."

The curate nodded. "I must leave you ladies. I am glad I could provide you comfort."

Kate thanked him and escorted him to the door, then returned to her companions. She had stopped caring about the treasure as soon as illness struck the school, but she had to keep Julie's mind busy.

"Do we leave off the hunt?" she asked Julie.

"No," Julie said promptly. "Even if Mr. Wynd is correct, we can't question anyone at the school right now. The map is all we can work with for the moment."

"I agree." Kate felt satisfied at the way Julie's brain moved to action, rather than inaction. Now, if only her husband could fight off his illness.

Chapter 20

"Are you sure you feel well enough to go to St. Mary's?" Lucy asked in a rather squeaky voice as she finished perfecting Julie's hair. Her natural curls took well to the current elaborate styles, though Kate had seen a French fashion magazine that indicated a simpler mode would be coming soon.

"Fresh air would be delightful. I'm right as rain."

"Really?" Kate didn't quite contain her skepticism.

"I didn't drink nearly as much as you think last night," Julie insisted. "I don't think the baby likes me singing. It gave me indigestion."

Kate inspected her. "Your eyes are clear, and your skin is rosy. I cannot imagine you are ill in any way."

"Exactly. Blooming health." Julie gave her a bright smile.

Now Kate knew Julie was acting. No one would normally smile like that with a husband fighting cholera. Still, she wanted to leave the room, as well. Letting the fire go out and opening the window would do wonders to clear the air of last night's drama and the heavy smell of coal that lingered.

They drew on their cloaks and went downstairs. In the innyard, a coach had arrived, though it was not as full as it often was. Had word reached the surrounding towns that Harrow on the Hill had a cholera outbreak?

Kate glanced around, taking in the midday sun, the smell of the horses, the bustling of the passengers, and the inn's servants. Charles loved this busy life. He'd told her they would travel to all sorts of interesting places. Sometimes, he seemed to forget she had been born in Scotland and wasn't quite so innocent of the world as some young women would be.

"Kate," Julie said urgently, dragging her out of the way of a stable boy pulling one of the heavy coach horses toward the water trough.

"Sorry. Woolgathering."

"I can see that. We should go to the church before anyone stops us."

"Who would do that?" Lucy asked.

"It's not such a large place. One student out running errands, or a servant. They'll report our movements to Mr. Aga."

"And Charles," Kate agreed. "He wouldn't want us out, but even here in the yard, I feel better."

"Exactly. The room is much too close. My head is much better," Julie said absently, admitting she didn't feel as wonderful as she'd claimed.

As they climbed to the top of the hill where the church was, they discussed the clues again, agreeing that they were looking for some representation of the final clue on the map, a curious interlocked set of three knotted triangles.

"The curate gave us a clue, as well," Kate said, remembering, stopping to stare out over the gravestones on the hill as they closed in on the church. "Do you think he knows where the treasure is?"

"Maybe he is the treasure's guardian," Julie said.

"Oh." Lucy's eyes widened. "Do you think we need to fight for it? I'm quite good in a fight, but I don't think either of you would be."

"At the first sight of danger, we'll go," Kate explained calmly. "I agree that the curate acted suspiciously."

"Are we still thinking he might have killed Agnes, I wonder?" Julie asked.

Kate stared up at the church spire, which rose through the thick evergreen trees that dotted the hill. "He might have done it, if he'd thought Agnes close to the treasure, but no one has ever indicated she was hunting for it, merely waving the map around."

"Like it was a toy," Lucy agreed. "To get attention."

"Yes," Julie agreed. "I believe she was that sort of girl. I remember her asking me dozens of questions about my hair and clothing when I met her. She kept touching her own hair and face, as if imagining my styles on herself."

"Boastful, fanciful," Kate murmured. "More likely to talk about the map than hunt for the treasure."

"I still think someone killed her for it," Julie said.

"Which means the killer isn't the curate, if he already knows where it is."

"Oh, yes," Lucy said. "That makes sense. I wonder about that Noah Claypole. He's big for thirteen, and I know how bad boys can be. I don't think Lack at the foreshore was more than fifteen, and you remember Brother Second, how easily he took to that vicious life."

"And he's not much more than a bairn," Kate agreed. "I remember Charles telling me about their violence toward him, and Charles was bringing blankets and food."

"Some poor souls cannot see 'elp when it is offered," Lucy said. "I was sore afraid when William suggested I come with him, but still, I believed him about the little baby needing 'elp. 'E'd 'elped Ollie before."

"Yes, you knew you could trust us," Julie said gently. "Look how well it's turned out."

"I miss the old life, I do," Lucy said. "As it was before Lack came." She stared up at the church, visible now at the end of the path. The ancient stone spire seemed to rise into the heavens, as if inviting everyone who came there to imagine greater things than what lay in front of their feet, which was a sea of bodies in most directions, buried in the quiet churchyard.

"Mortality and eternity," Kate said, looking around. "Where should we hunt for the symbol? There are an awful lot of graves."

"What about the church itself?" Julie asked. "I wish our men were here to help."

"And the entire student body of Aga Academy," Lucy added.

"We would have separate," Kate said. "If we're to inspect every gravestone. That seems unwise."

"We know William's grandfather had the map," Julie pointed out. "It won't be a new gravestone, right? If the clue is on a gravestone."

"That's an excellent thought." Kate tapped her finger on her lips. "We should start with the Peachey grave, since it has the Lord Byron connection."

"Where is it?" Julie asked.

"It's south of the west entrance. The view is amazing from there."

"It doesn't sound far. We can start there."

"I can walk around the outside of the church and see if I can find the symbol," Lucy offered.

"Let's stay together," Kate suggested. "I don't think young girls should be wandering around the church alone."

"Why? Agnes didn't die here." Julie scanned her surroundings and walked west.

Kate and Lucy followed while Julie spoke. "No, but both of the Aga children are dead, and we don't know why really, except because of the map. I don't want anyone else to be hurt."

"Monks didn't die from murder," Lucy said. "He might even have killed his sister."

"It's where he died that concerns me," Kate explained. "What else could he have been doing but chasing the clues?"

They reached the grave where Lord Byron had so poetically taken his leisure in a more romantic era. Kate circled it, looking for the strange symbol of interlocking triangles. Julie checked the stone vaults nearby, while Lucy bent over each gravestone.

"I don't see anything here," Kate said, kneeling to look more closely. "Not even in the scribbles people have carved into the stone."

"Byron enthusiasts?" Julie asked.

"Yes," Kate agreed. "Silly people." She stood up and ran her hands down the back of her skirts to straighten them. Below them on the hill, she saw a man hunting for something. Looking for the grave of a loved one?

As she watched, the man straightened and pressed his hands into his lower back, not unlike what she had just done. Something about him seemed familiar. When he moved away from an upright stone marker, she saw his entire body, and even from the back, she recognized him from his long legs.

"What is William's uncle doing here?" Kate asked. "Do you know if his wife is buried down there?"

Julie moved next to her and put a hand over her eyes to shade them as she peered down. "No, none of the graves down there are modest. She has just a flat stone in the ground."

"Dear me," Kate murmured. "Does he have another copy of the map?"

"He was very dismissive of it," Julie said.

"He might have had second thoughts, now that his children are dead."

"He might know something we don't," Julie added. "Should we confront him?"

"Certainly not," Kate said. "We'll tell Charles, and he can do it."

"Let's wait for him to leave and then look around that spot ourselves." Julie scratched her cheek.

"Only if he heads south." Kate scanned the horizon. "We don't want him spotting us, in case he really is being suspicious."

Julie sat on a low stone and watched while Kate went to retrieve Lucy, glancing back every few seconds to make sure they remained alone.

When George Aga had gone out of view down the hill, without having shown any signs of paying respects to any particular grave, or having generally acted like he'd found something, they made their way to the general vicinity of where he searched, using the shapes of the graves and the large trees as markers.

They searched until the church bells rang again but saw no sign of the strange symbol.

"I'm ready to rest," Julie announced after the bells stopped.

"Lucy can find us some dinner while I write Charles," Kate said. "I'm sure one of the stable boys will take a note for me."

Charles thanked the yard boy from the Crown and Anchor, then closed the boardinghouse door. He leaned against it wearily and put the cool paper to his forehead. Was he losing the battle for William's life? Ollie had continued to drink eagerly from every vessel Charles brought to his lips. William seemed to have lost interest. His lips were cracked and dry, but he didn't have a bluish appearance, not yet.

The other astounding news was that no one else had taken ill. No one knew which boy had sickened first, Richard or Monks. Mr. Aga thought they had probably contracted cholera from a low spot in a field, or some similar miasmic place, while out exploring. Charles wasn't so sure, since he had the feeling that both William and Ollie had been sick for longer than anyone realized. They had just taken better care of themselves than the unfortunate deceased.

He remembered that stone circle in the forest, by the ruined chimney, where they had all been chasing the treasure, and wondered if some moldering old bones had harbored disease. Or even if they had been cursed. Mr. Aga had said Monks and Richard Field loved to tramp around together. Ollie had been there, as well, as had William.

The rest may have been lucky or may have missed breathing in the vapors somehow. By some mysterious mechanism, not everything sickened the same people.

But enough woolgathering. He was so tired that he found it difficult to focus. He opened the intricately folded note and immediately recognized Kate's handwriting.

"What the blazes?" Charles muttered after he'd read it. The question of what the three young women had been doing in the graveyard aside, this was not good news. "Now George Aga is after the treasure his children might have died for?"

He stomped upstairs. Did William's uncle think his children knew something he did not? Or had he decided to believe his deceased father had owned a real treasure map all along? Could Kate be wrong, and he was merely visiting a grave?

When Charles went into William and Ollie's sickroom, the smell of violent illness swept through him like a cannonball. "Oh no," he cried and went into a flurry of providing ale and water to his two thirsty patients and then doing what he could to clean up the messes, once again throwing chamber pots of waste out the window into the hedges below.

"You were doing better an hour ago," he said to Ollie.

"Waves go through me," Ollie whispered. "More water."

Charles continued to give him sips, then applied salve to the boy's sadly cracked lips when he had fallen asleep. He wiped his fingers on a rag, then turned to William.

"I must perform the same duty."

"Ale. I'd rather die drunk," William said, his words slurred.

"I don't blame you," Charles said and performed the same services for his friend.

"Have you heard from the inn? Julie?"

"A stable boy brought a note from Kate. They are well and even took a walk through the graveyard earlier."

"That seems unwise." William coughed.

Charles waited until it had subsided and offered more ale. His pot was running low, but as soon as William slept, he could refill the water can from the butt outside the kitchen. He'd love to have someone scrub down the floor and change the linens, but he suspected the patients were too ill for that.

"Kate wrote that she saw your uncle George in the cemetery, too, hovering around graves below the Peachey tomb. Is your grandfather buried there?"

"No. Buried near my aunt. All the family is in a group."

"I see."

"Bury me there, too. But not with Monks. Don't want to share his grave."

"I'll apply to Lady Lugoson for funds to get you a nice tomb of your own," Charles said, trying to joke.

"Good. Don't make Julie do it. Be my friend to the end."

"Of course," Charles promised. "Julie and the baby will want for nothing if it comes to that, but I still think you will recover."

"That makes one of us." William lifted his weak and shaking hand from the blanket.

Charles gave him the last of the ale. "Now, let us distract you. Do you think your grandfather could have made two copies of this treasure map?"

"You think he made it up," William said flatly. "Don't know. Liked secrets."

"Your uncle? Does he like secrets, too?"

"Maybe. He answers to no one."

"Did he feel like his children were merely workers, too?"

"Likely so. But he sent them to school."

Agnes went to work, not learn. But fathers did worse things to their daughters than let them out as servants. "I hesitate to even suggest it, but do you think your uncle George could have killed his own daughter?"

William's eyelids flew up. He leaned slightly to the right of the mattress and was noisily sick.

Charles flew into action, cleaning up the rice-water mess. He couldn't get William to drink more water. Like Ollie, it seemed he wanted only to sleep, though he kept muttering something through his cracked lips.

Charles leaned his ear closer to William's mouth, trying to understand. After a few syllables, he recognized the quote from Psalm 137.

> *Daughter Babylon, doomed to destruction,*
> *happy is the one who repays you*
> *according to what you have done to us.*
> *Happy is the one who seizes your infants*
> *and dashes them against the rocks.*

Charles stared down at his friend. Did he mean that his uncle really did kill Agnes? Slowly he went to the door and leaned against it. He needed more water, rags, a change of bedding. Was there any hope of help left in the house?

No matter what, he knew he couldn't deprive them of liquid refreshment when they woke again, if only in an attempt to keep them drunk. From the state of their lips, he knew their bodies were parched from the insides out.

Later, after he'd found John and Arthur, he scribbled a note to be taken up to the inn for Kate and also sent them for more beer.

His note, written with trembling hands, said that he was afraid William wasn't going to survive. At the same time, he told them they could not come. It simply wasn't safe. He folded it so that the boys couldn't see the letter's contents.

"Don't dawdle," he instructed. "Walk to the brewery and order the beer. Then, while one of you waits, the other must take this up to the inn."

"Yes, Charles," John said. He didn't ask questions.

He likely didn't need to, from the smell of Charles's clothing alone.

The next morning, Kate sat on a stool in front of the fire, with Charles's latest missive in her lap. She felt numb horror at the idea that he didn't think William would survive his illness. He hadn't even mentioned poor Ollie. Did that mean the boy would survive? Charles couldn't know, in any case, unless the boy's face had turned blue. She tried to imagine healthy, handsome, ever-smiling William in such a state and could not. Ollie had been frail ever since he'd lost his hand, but William? There was no heartier soul than he.

She hadn't told Julie about the letter. After her drunken flinging herself about two nights before, and with a room full of men in the public spaces below, she didn't dare risk another dangerous display.

Lucy knocked on the door. Kate rose and undid the latch to let her in. Lucy set down the tray of porridge and coffee on one of the stools.

"We've had better accommodations," Kate said.

"It isn't bad," Lucy said. "I've lived under Blackfriars Bridge."

Shame swept Kate when she realized how much easier her life had been in comparison. She bent her head. "At least that life is over."

Julie stirred as Lucy clanked the coffeepot against a cup. Kate debated what to tell her and when.

"Have we had any word from the school?" Julie asked, wiping sleep from her eyes.

Had she read Kate's mind? "Yes, they delivered a letter with our water this morning."

Julie sat up, cradling her belly with one arm and her back with the other. Her braid slid down one shoulder, the coarse strands of her hair sticking out like a brush at the bottom. "It's not good news, is it?"

Kate's lower lip trembled. "They are still alive, Ollie and William. No one else has taken ill."

"How dire is it?"

"Charles wrote that they are sleeping a lot."

Lucy came to the bed with a cup of coffee and cream for both of them. "Drink this while it's hot. There's a chill in the air this morning."

Julie took a sip, making a face. "No tea this morning?"

"Different cook on duty. This is what they gave me. I'm sorry," Lucy said, her eyes lowering.

"No, it's fine," Kate assured her. "The cream is fresh. They must keep a goat in the barn here."

"Did Charles write anything else?" Julie asked, her gaze meeting Kate's. "Can I see the letter?"

"He's very concerned about William's prospects," she whispered.

"Why?"

"He was muttering a psalm, which doesn't seem like William at all, and then he went to sleep, with his lips so parched. Charles is afraid."

"He is burning to death from the inside," Lucy said. "That's cholera. My parents died of it four years ago."

"Oh, Lucy," Kate exclaimed. "I didn't know that."

"I wasn't that different from you when I was young," Lucy told them. "But it all ended. I was ill, too, but I recovered."

"You didn't have other family?" Kate asked.

Lucy shuddered. "I was taken in by cousins, but they were cruel. I became sick again with something, and I had such a high fever that I had convulsions. I ran away when I recovered."

"We never thought you knew even how old you were. I thought you grew up on the streets," Julie said.

"It hurts to remember my parents. Sometimes I see their faces in dreams, but I forget when I wake up," Lucy whispered.

"I'm sure they would be very proud of you," Kate said. "You've done very well for yourself, and you're a credit to them."

"Thank you." Lucy's lips trembled. "If your baby won't have a father, Julie, what are you going to do?"

Julie scratched her cheek, then twisted her fingers together. "I have a trade, if it comes to that. Many babes have been raised on an actress's pay long before now. My child will be fine."

Kate finished her coffee. "We should eat to keep up our strength. My, it is stuffy in here."

"I agree," Julie said. "I crave cow's milk."

"It would be a nice change," Kate agreed, noticing that Julie had left a red line on her face.

"Let's walk to the dairy farm," Julie suggested. "We can air out this room and get milk."

"Do you think Mr. Aga will want us coming to the farm?" Kate asked. "We don't know what he was up to at the cemetery yesterday."

"It doesn't hurt to ask," Julie said. "If he's decided to take the map seriously, we can join forces. It may very well be an Aga treasure, and he ought to know about my husband's condition."

"Very well." Kate acquiesced, realizing they had to do something with their day. Julie was not the sort to sit quietly, making baby clothing, if she could find literally anything else to do with her time.

*   *   *

A couple of hours later, the trio arrived at the dairy farm. They had started walking there but had come across a milk wagon just finishing up deliveries for the day, and the driver had offered them a ride the rest of the way.

"I hope Uncle Aga might have workers to spare," Julie told Kate, holding her belly against the jolting ride. "They must be rather desperate at the school. If he could send a couple of people to help in the kitchen and the boardinghouses, it might make all the difference."

"They must keep the rooms clean," Lucy agreed. "Dirty things can add to miasma. They need to do laundry every day right now."

"They don't have the staff for it," Julie told them. "I know they have several fewer students than they did, between the deaths and that boy whose father took him away, but with Agnes dead and the illnesses . . ." She trailed off without completing the thought.

"He might offer help," Kate agreed. It might not have occurred to him to suggest it. The running of households was not in the male purview. They really needed to speak to George Aga's housekeeper.

As Kate recalled, a dairy operation had two busy periods, because cows needed milking twice a day. They arrived at the farm during the quieter period in between, late morning.

"Where is Uncle Aga at this time of day?" Julie asked the driver.

"He'll be eating," the driver said. "You came at a good time. The victuals are a treat here."

"Thank you for allowing us to ride with you," Kate said.

"Of course, anything for an Aga." The driver jumped down from his seat and helped all three of them. He had stopped in front of one of the barns.

They walked across the muddy yard, delicately holding their

skirts above the muck, until they reached the corner of the yard where the modest redbrick house awaited them.

The maid who opened the door recognized Julie and invited them into the parlor to wait for her master. Kate sat on an uncomfortable overstuffed horsehair chair, while Julie paced, saying her legs had cramped. Lucy stood by the fireplace and watched them both.

"I thought we would be offered food," Julie fretted.

"The maid can't do that. We have to wait for your uncle-in-law," Kate said, feeling like she ought to use child-soothing tones.

Julie stopped in front of a smoke-damaged portrait of a woman in an old-fashioned cap. She had William's generous mouth and rounded chin. "She could have offered tea."

"They might be much more used to tradesmen appearing, rather than guests," Kate said, then pointed to the covered mirror over the fireplace. "Also, this is a house of mourning."

"It's also a farm. The operation stops for nothing," Julie snapped.

"That is true," said a weary voice from the doorway.

Chapter 21

George Aga came through the doorway into his parlor. His breeches had dark stains at the knees. He had a black armband over his coarse corduroy coat. Circles surrounded his eyes, as if they were banded in mourning, as well.

"Hello, Uncle," Julie said, turning.

"I thought you were meant to stay safely at the inn, Mrs. William?" he said, walking across the room.

"Come sit," she said, going to the elderly green velvet sofa that was placed at the edge of the rug, in front of the fire. She patted a worn armrest, then sat in the middle of the sofa.

He considered her, then took a seat on the side she'd patted, and sat very straight on the edge of the cushion. "What is the matter? I need to get back to the barn."

"We thought you ought to be aware, in case you hadn't had a letter from Father Aga," Julie said. "William is very bad." She said the words as if giving a speech, but then her lips trembled, and she dropped her head into her hands.

"In the final stages?" he asked after a moment's heavy pause.

Julie sobbed instead of speaking. George Aga sat with his hands in his lap, a tormented island of pain.

"No, not quite that," Kate explained from her uncomfortable seat. "He'd been conscious, and he isn't blue."

"But he's not conscious now."

"That's what the letter from Mr. Dickens said. Have you heard anything more?" Kate asked.

He shook his head. "No, but I cannot hold out much hope. I'm sure your man is doing his best, but two of the children are dead already."

"A grown man can live when a child does not," Lucy ventured.

Mr. Aga didn't look at her. Kate had the sense he was not pleased to be addressed so familiarly by a servant. Julie hadn't trained Lucy out of speaking her mind.

"I wonder if you might be able to spare someone, even yourself, to go up to the school and help your brother and nephew?" Kate asked.

"Spare someone?" His voice snapped at her like the mouth of a crocodile. "I have already lost my children."

"They weren't employed here," Kate said in her most soothing voice. "Surely you have employees who could assist at the school?"

"Send your maid," he snarled.

"She's my maid, Uncle Aga," Julie said, lifting her head. "William wouldn't allow it. Isn't there someone who could help?"

"No, we have all we can handle here. I won't have someone bring the contagion to the farm. We are past it here."

Julie tilted her head at Kate. Her eyes seemed very clear now, not the least bit despairing. Kate began to realize that Julie had been acting when she broke into sobs.

"That isn't how the disease works," Kate said, taking Julie's seat on the sofa after the actress slid to the far end. Kate began to explain the theory of miasma while Julie quietly rose.

Kate talked on and on. Julie tilted her head to Lucy, and she moved forward, just enough to block an easy view of Julie while she poked through the single bookcase in the room.

Kate took a breath after the first ten minutes. George Aga responded to her theorizing with a grunt, but he stayed where she was, so she resumed her talk, rambling through various Greek views on the nature of illness that she'd heard her brother Robert talk over with their father when he'd studied the language.

She glanced away from the farmer once, to discover Julie had quite disappeared. Kate resumed, asking him what his theory was. He didn't like that, so she went back to talking about the 1832 cholera outbreak in London, which struck not long after her family had moved there from Edinburgh.

Just when she was running out of the facts as she remembered them, a bell rang in the farmyard.

"You'll have to excuse me," George Aga said. "It's time for me to return to my workers."

"Of course, sir. Thank you for allowing us to visit." For all that, it was a very poor showing. He'd been patient enough, but he hadn't even offered tea.

Where was Julie? Kate was thinking of how she could delicately indicate that Julie had some sort of feminine issue, when the actress appeared in the doorway.

"How will you go back to town?" George Aga asked as he rose.

"One of your drivers conveyed us here," Julie said.

He seemed unamused. "They have other duties at this time of day."

"The weather is very fine for March," Kate said quickly, as it was obvious he would not offer them return conveyance, not even for a pregnant niece. "We will enjoy the stroll. Thank you for your hospitality, and if you see anyone who is unoccupied among your workers, I do hope you'll send them up to the school." She bobbed a quick curtsy and pulled Lucy away from the fire, desperate to get outside and find out what mischief Julie had managed.

They had nearly reached the door, with Mr. Aga watching them closely, when the maid appeared next to the actress.

"Is there something I can do for you, Mrs. Aga?" the maid asked. "I saw you in the pantry."

George Aga's eyes narrowed.

Julie touched her belly. "Desperate for a bit of dried fruit, I'm afraid. This baby has me doing the oddest things."

Kate, in utter shock that Julie would say such a thing in front of a man, swept past her out the door. Behind her, she heard a swish of skirts as Lucy followed.

"Do not come here again without your husband, Mrs. William," George Aga said.

"Perhaps you didn't understand why we had come," Julie said sweetly as Kate stood behind her. "Mr. Dickens doesn't seem to think my husband will ever rise from his bed again." Her voice trembled on the last words.

George Aga lifted his chin. "I don't want hysterical women here, whatever the cause."

Kate tugged on Julie's arm. She had gone very pale, and Kate didn't know how she would cope with the deadweight of a swooning Julie. Luckily, Julie turned, as if in a trance, and followed her out the door and into the yard.

"No hysterical women," Julie whispered.

"Agnes doesn't sound like the calm sort," Lucy added.

Kate moved in between them both and, holding their arms, tugged them through the muddy yard. "I hope you can walk, Julie, because you're going to have to."

"I don't mind the fresh air, especially after that horrible visit," Julie said.

Kate shushed her, increasing their pace until they had achieved the road. "I know you two are thinking what I am," she said.

"It's 'im who's done it," Lucy said. "'E killed 'is own daughter."

"Why?" Julie asked, cradling her belly. "I believe he's capable of it. His eyes were pure poison when he heard what his maid said to me."

"He doesn't like hysterical women," Kate repeated, the words tolling in her head.

Julie scratched her inflamed cheek. "What does that have to do with Agnes?"

"Maybe he wanted her to leave the job at the school?" Kate suggested. "Or he demanded the map from her?"

"Do you think something 'ad 'appened to make him think it was real?" Lucy asked.

"She'd been offered money for it." Kate glanced up at the sky. Ominous dark clouds were filling in the blue. "We don't have long before rain."

"William won't like me being out in a storm in my condition." Julie scratched again.

Kate sighed and pulled her friend's fingers from her cheek. "You are the storm in your condition. I cannot believe you were caught in the pantry."

"I cannot believe a maid thought to tattle on me," Julie groused. "I'm Mrs. William! I'm carrying the only living heir to the family."

Kate didn't think she could stand a bout of Julie's genuine hysterics, especially when they needed to return to the inn before the weather turned. "Do you think he might have killed his wives, back in the day?"

"He could have smothered the first one after Agnes's birth because she screamed too hysterically," Julie suggested.

" 'Died in childbirth' can cover a lot of different tragedies," Kate added, pulling her along the lane. "We could find out if anyone was present to know what really happened."

"If they weren't, then no one will ever know," Julie said. "Even if there was someone, no justice will come of it now. Just as well. Who would want to be tormented by Uncle Aga for all these years?"

"Someone who would rather not be dead." Lucy grabbed at her bonnet as a gust of wind swept past her.

"We are going to pass by the school if we keep walking this way," Julie said.

"We can't risk going there." Kate grabbed at her own bonnet. "I'm so sorry, Julie. Let's cut through the woods. It will be a little faster, and the trees will protect us from some of the weather."

Mrs. Bedwin straightened a sheet over William's foot and set down a water can. "You had better sleep, or you will find yourself ill, as well."

Charles rubbed at his eyes and leaned his head against the wall. He'd placed a chair between both beds. An empty jug of beer kept his feet apart. "I think Ollie looks pretty well, all things considered."

Mrs. Bedwin touched the boy's forehead. "His skin feels soft and moist, like it should. I think he may recover. Mr. Aga?"

"I was sore afraid for him yesterday. He babbled and fell unconscious. But later he did wake again, ferociously thirsty," Charles said.

"That is good."

"Yes. I don't know that he's safe, but he isn't in the final stage, as I'd feared."

"Go sleep before I change my mind," Mrs. Bedwin said.

Charles could see the smell was getting to her. "If you sit

right where I am, the draft from the window will send clean air right to your nose."

"Good advice."

Charles lifted the jug and edged around the housekeeper. The light had dimmed as the afternoon came to a close. "You look tired yourself," he said when he noticed the shadows under her eyes.

"Mr. Aga, the elder, is ill now," she said softly.

Charles's eyebrows lifted. "Oh?"

"He's in the room next door. He agreed to come over here so we could nurse him better. His staff is all over here. You can catch your rest in a quiet house, but food will be offered daily in the main school building."

"Oh, dear."

"I don't like the looks of him at all." She pressed her lips together. "And you, Mr. Dickens, you have been as close to the patients as him."

"I feel fine," Charles said. "I'm getting married next month."

Mrs. Bedwin glanced at William, still but for the rise and fall of his chest. "And he has a baby coming. God doesn't care."

"He does," Charles said. "We just don't understand Him."

He went downstairs, attempting not to be shaken by Mrs. Bedwin's unchristian notions. On the table in the small front hall, he found a letter in Kate's handwriting. He took it outside to read.

He laughed a little when he read it. The ladies thought George Aga had killed his own daughter. Well, why not? The man seemed odd enough. He would have had the power to entice his daughter from her bedchamber. Surely, though, any number of people would have seen him that morning. He would have needed to sneak away from the dairy farm and go to the school.

"Charles!" John called, his too-short-for-his-age body appearing around the side of the house, trailed by Arthur. "What's the news?"

"I'm sure you heard about your schoolmaster." Charles handed the ale jug to John.

"He cast up his lunch right at my feet," Arthur said proudly.

"Stay far away," Charles advised. "I don't want you ill, as well."

John hoisted the jug. "Should we run away again?"

"No." Charles hesitated. "At first, I thought the miasma must have been at the ruined chimney. I saw what might be a burial stone nearby."

"The air smells good there," Arthur assured him. "But the back 'edge, the one the boys use as a privy sometimes? That is foul."

"A back hedge, eh?" Charles thought about his own casting out of chamber pots from the sickroom. "I'll ask Littlejack to clear them out."

"Behind the boardinghouses," Arthur clarified.

"Yes, I assumed so." Charles yawned. "Very well, boys. If you can fetch the beer for Ollie and William." He stumbled over his own feet as he moved forward, then righted himself and walked in the direction of the schoolmaster's house.

Charles woke when someone touched his shoulder. He blinked and rolled over. His neck ached from whatever odd position he'd been sleeping in, though he had slept in Mr. Aga's comfortable guest bed. "What?" he mumbled.

"Coffee and toast for you, sir," said a girl.

Charles wiped sleep from his eyes and recognized Mr. Aga's kitchen girl. "Why?"

"Mrs. Bedwin sent one of the students over to have you woken up." She curtsied and hurried out before he could ask another question.

He didn't think the housekeeper would dare disturb a guest of Mr. Aga's without extreme provocation, so despite his spinning head, he rose and dressed in his stained clothing.

He checked the window as he downed his coffee, and through blurry eyes, he saw the sun was quite high in the sky. It must be close to noon.

Half an hour later, he'd found Littlejack Dawkins in his spot tucked into the hedge that ran along the side of the back lawn, and told him to clean out any bad-smelling areas behind the boardinghouses, making sure to keep a scarf over his face while he did it.

At the boardinghouse, he said hello to John and Arthur, on guard duty. "What's the word, boys?"

"Mr. Aga is very bad," John said, looking grave.

"The senior or junior?" Charles asked.

"Our schoolmaster," John clarified.

Charles winced. "So soon?"

"It happens that way sometimes," John said slowly.

Charles blinked. He saw exhaustion etched around the boy's eyes and wondered if the children had slept. "What day is it?"

"Saturday."

"And Richard Field was visibly ill on Monday." Charles shook his head. The week had vanished. Did he even have a job at the *Chronicle* still?

He went into the boardinghouse and upstairs. An astonishing sight met his eyes. William was out of bed and leaning against a wall.

"What is going on?" Charles demanded, going to his friend.

"My father," William said. He had deep circles under his eyes, and his smile was completely gone, but his eyes were clear. "He's very bad, Charles."

"You are too weak to nurse him," Charles said. "Come, I must help you back to bed."

"No." William shook off Charles's guiding arm with a shaking hand. "I must stay with him."

If his taller friend collapsed, Charles didn't think he could carry him back to bed, but he liked William's show of strength. He supported him through the door into the new sickroom.

On one bed, student Noah Claypole, once so self-assured, lay pale and sweating. "The chimney, the chimney," he muttered as he tossed his head.

William shuffled to the other bed. Charles turned and saw Mr. Aga, in the condition he'd been fearful of before. Had no one been tending the schoolmaster?

William attempted to bring a cup to his father's lips, which looked blue in the daylight. His skin looked as if it had been tanned against his skull. Charles saw all the hallmarks of severe, deadly illness on the man.

He helped William lift his father's head and tried to get him to drink, but the water dribbled out.

"Ale," William cried. "We need ale."

"He's unconscious," Charles said softly. "It works only when they feel thirst."

"Beer," croaked Noah Claypole.

Charles didn't see a jug, but there was still water in a ewer, so he poured that into Noah's eager mouth while William prayed over his father.

"It was the chimney, wasn't it?" Noah gasped after repeated rice-water explosions and a renewed application of water.

A maid came and went, taking out cloths and bringing in water.

"John and Arthur insisted the air was clean," Charles told the boy. "Did you go to John Peachey's grave?"

"Why would I do that?" Noah asked, then lost his drink again.

Charles registered that Noah truly had seen only the one clue on the map.

Hours passed. Beer arrived from someone, somewhere, at some point as the sun began to descend in the sky. Neither William nor Charles could get any into Mr. Aga, but Noah and Ollie drank a couple of glassfuls, and Charles made sure William did the same. He believed his friend had passed any danger point, weak as he was.

Charles opened the door into the passage as the long shadows across the room joined. "Is anyone there?" he called. "We need candles."

Mrs. Bedwin brought a candle just as Mr. Aga stopped breathing. As Noah asked what was happening, William sobbed tearlessly over his father.

"We must get you away," Charles said gently, pulling the filthy sheet over the kind old schoolmaster's face. "We can't risk you being infected again."

"It's just me now," William said, his shoulders sagging. "I'm the only one."

"It's not. You have Julie, and the baby coming. They need you. And your uncle needs you. And the school."

"You can't leave me here with a corpse," Noah shrieked, the cry oversetting his stomach. More rice water.

William melted onto a chair in the corner as Charles did his best to clean up, then called into the hall again. Mrs. Bedwin came, looking much the worse for the day.

She and Charles supported William down the hall to the bed in the room he shared with Ollie. Charles checked the boy and then hoisted the empty jugs.

He met Mrs. Bedwin in the hall. "What do we do about Noah?"

"We can't take young Mr. Aga back to his father's house. He's too weak," the housekeeper fretted.

"And the other rooms are up the stairs," Charles said. "We'll have to remove Mr. Aga."

"We need the doctor's men for that."

"I'll run down and tell John and Arthur to go for him," Charles promised. "Keep a close eye on Master Claypole. We don't want him to go mad. It would be poor legacy for the school, if he survives his illness."

When he went downstairs, he barreled straight through the door without pausing, desperate for fresh air.

The boys were there, faithful despite the hour. Charles shared the news. The boys were very solemn as they took the ale jug and handed him a couple of letters.

"Mr. Dawkins cut down all the hedges with an ax," Arthur said in a small voice.

"I didn't even hear the noise," Charles said. He put his hand to his forehead. "I can't believe Mr. Aga died."

Arthur's lips trembled. "Will we all die?"

"No. Just stay away from most people until the contagion passes."

"That's three people dead and only three sick," John stated. "The odds are very bad."

"You have to have faith," Charles told him. "I know that sort of thing has not much been taught in this school for some time, but you have enough religion to understand. No one cared for Monks. Mr. Aga took ferociously ill very fast. And no one knew at first what was wrong with Richard Field. Ollie and William have been properly cared for all along, and they seem to be recovering."

"Why them and not us?" John asked.

"I hope men of science sort it all out very soon. Please go fetch more ale before the brewery shuts down for the night."

The boys obeyed. Once they were gone, Charles leaned against the wall and opened his letters. The young women at the inn were fine and wanted news. He also had a letter from his brother. Fred sent word from London that their sister Letitia had survived her harrowing illness. Charles closed his eyes and let his hand drop to his thigh. His sister had been spared.

The next letter that must be written was one to George Aga. But when he shared the news, was he inviting a killer to the school?

Chapter 22

The next afternoon, Charles walked over to the late Mr. Aga's house after being released by Mrs. Bedwin from sickroom duties. He supposed the house belonged to William now, assuming he lived long enough to claim it. Would his friend survive? Could the improvement Charles had seen be temporary, or could his father's corpse reinfect William?

He wished he understood more about disease, but as far as he knew, no answers existed. Give him a London street and a couple of people walking down it. He could think of a dozen notions of what they were doing and why. But an illness? He saw no patterns.

One thing he knew, though, was that he couldn't go up to the inn or over to the farm in his physical condition.

He climbed a staircase that felt like it rose all the way to heaven, then went into his room to change his clothes. His brain had a hard time comprehending that no clothing was to be found. Nothing of his original possessions were in sight. His carpetbag had been emptied, and no evidence of his limited wardrobe existed in the room.

Had someone chosen a Saturday to do washing, or had someone stolen his clothing? He stared down at himself in the darkening light. His attire, borrowed from the dead man's wardrobe, was in a most dreadful state, holding the stains of a dead man and much else. He was a carrier of his own dreadful miasma. His hands trembled from the very horror of it.

Today was Sunday. He supposed one of the servants might have thought to do the washing so that anyone who was able to leave would have something to wear to church, but if that were the case, the clothing should have appeared by now.

Charles turned around the room, but not even a rough towel remained. When he went to the bed, not having noticed before in the dim light, it had been stripped, as well. If not for his bag and his writing desk, he'd have thought he'd left this place. Maybe instead, the servant had thought he'd died?

He rubbed his hands over his eyes. The situation with Noah Claypole and Mr. Aga's body had been too critical to send news to the inn. He hoped no one had sent word to Kate and Julie that he had died.

He went to William's room. Julie had taken everything of hers when she'd gone to the inn, but it seemed someone else had taken most of his friend's possessions, as well. Charles found William's writing desk, a copy of Ainsworth's latest novel, and his empty carpetbag. No clothing remained here, either.

Charles stood in the center of the room. If someone had decided to do laundry yesterday, they probably wouldn't have it ironed until today, after services, perhaps. He could search the house and see if a basement room held the drying racks, or even the yard, and find a shirt to dry in front of the fire. He must attempt to sponge the worst stains from his borrowed coat and trousers. It would have to do.

He couldn't find anything, though. It seemed someone had taken everything off the property. Perhaps they had contracted to a laundress somewhere in town. He stood in the empty kitchen after he'd come up the stairs and saw that while he searched, it had become full dark. Where was he even to sleep? On the parlor floor, in front of the fire, covered with the miasma of death?

Charles had a woozy feeling, like he couldn't quite control his body from inside. He had worried about Noah Claypole's madness, but what about his own?

Just then, he heard footsteps above him. He considered the layout of the floor above. Not his room or William's. He had just heard someone in the rooms belonging to Mr. Aga. Had his ghost come to haunt?

No, someone was stealing. His nerves steeled as he recognized the likelihood of that.

Moving slowly with numbed feet in the gloomy kitchen, he reached for an iron pan that hung on a wall. The long-handled pan weighted down his arm, making his wrist ache, but he couldn't leave the empty house to a robber.

He went up the stairs slowly, turning over the possibilities. Was it some random person taking advantage of the news, which even now John and Arthur would be sharing at the brewery, or perhaps the washerwoman had told, or was it someone after something closer? The map or evidence of some kind that would solve Agnes's murder?

When Charles reached the upper hallway, he lit a candle on a table between the guest rooms to fight the lack of light and tiptoed down the hall, the light casting sickly shadows on the Paris-green wallpaper.

The door to Mr. Aga's rooms was closed, which was probably why Charles hadn't heard anything before, assuming the interloper had been there all along. Charles didn't even know what exactly made up the man's suite. A bedroom, certainly. Perhaps a dressing room? A study?

He went to open the door and realized he had no hands free.

What was he to do without? A candle could also be a weapon as well as a source of light. He set the pan gently against the wall and turned the doorknob.

The door opened. He held up the candle and saw a modest bed, a simple chair, a table with a ewer and basin. The scent of illness hung faintly in the room. Here the bed had been stripped, as well. Whatever had happened, Charles would find no warmth of blankets in the house tonight.

He recognized the room was empty and enacted some geometry that would tell him the kitchen layout in comparison to the space here. Two doors were closed, flush against the wall. Behind which would he find the source of the footfalls?

He could not believe he had imagined the noise. After regathering his pan weapon, he crept fully into the room and went to the first door.

He leaned his ear against the door and listened. Hearing nothing, he slowly turned the knob and peered inside as soon as he'd opened the door a crack. He saw an untidy desk and a couple of shelves. Cold air blew against his face. He saw the single window was cracked open.

After fully entering the room, he hunted to see if the wind might have pushed books off the shelves or desk, creating some noise that his tired brain might have interpreted as footsteps. While the desk was untidy, with evidence that Mr. Aga had not been fulfilling his duties to pay off tradesmen lately, nothing littered the floor.

Very carefully, he stepped across the room and closed the window. When he surveyed the space, he did not think the footsteps had come from here. He had not been near the outer wall of the kitchen when he'd heard them.

After inching through the room again, he went back into the bedroom, then steeled himself to enter the last door. He turned the knob and opened the door a crack.

This appeared to be a lumber room. Charles pushed the door

fully open, holding the pan behind him. His wrist clicked from the weight of it.

When he lifted his candle high, he saw George Aga sitting on a wooden crate in the middle of the half-full room.

"Mr. Aga," Charles said, remembering the letter from Kate. Caution was needed. "What are you doing here?"

The farmer, for all intents and purposes, might have been in his own tomb, surrounded as he was by earthly possessions. Crates were stacked against one wall. Three chests were lined up against another.

George Aga spread his arms. "My family is here. My mother's wedding chest, and her mother's. My father's telescope, my uncle's books. Everything comes here to be buried in this room."

Charles's natural sympathy was dampened by the other man's dull tone. "And you? Why are you here?"

"To be buried." The man rose.

Charles had never before realized the farmer beat him in height. Farmers were a strong bunch, but he kept himself fit with walking and riding. He could survive this encounter. His fingers clenched around his pan, still out of sight.

He set his candle on a shelf in front of a mirror, no doubt fashioned for just such a moment. The other man had a lantern at his feet. Charles became very aware of the palpable taste of old, dusty paper in the air. All it would take was a knocked-over flame to turn the space into a tomb in truth.

"There are people who think you unnatural enough to kill your own daughter," Charles said evenly.

George Aga reached for his lantern and swung it up to illuminate his own eyes. Yellow flushed over his face, creating highlights and deep shadows. "Then they recognize a man in despair."

"You did kill Agnes?" Charles asked.

The farmer's voice lowered to a rasp. "I never meant to lose my entire family."

"Just her? Was the girl so insignificant?"

He grunted. "I always believed that map was real, because it was already old when he was a child."

"I thought it was your father's creation."

"Father kept it locked away, but it wasn't in his strongbox after his death." George Aga pointed to a large flat box with a broken lock on top of a chest. "Everything that was his came to this room in the end. I would have kept the map if I'd found it. I tore his room apart but never had satisfaction."

"Agnes already had it?"

The man turned to a cloth bag on the floor. Charles saw a stained apron half-folded at the top. He imagined he could still smell the faint odor of burned oatmeal. Agnes's sad possessions, not even meriting a box, had come to rest here, as well.

"When I saw that map, Father's pride, in Agnes's possession, I realized my father never loved me." He turned directly to Charles. "Eustace was the oldest. He had all the property. I had to build a life from nothing. I had to house and tend to Father to pay for my farm. I had to work for all of it."

Charles thought of the unpaid bills on Mr. Aga's desk. "Did you beg money from your brother, as well?"

"What if I did?" the farmer sneered.

Charles wanted to cry foul on the man for his self-pity. If all he had to do was provide a home for his father in return for the funds to start a farm, he had everything, not nothing. "Your father must have loved your family. If he gave the map to Agnes, well, that was your daughter, not Eustace's. William wasn't given the map."

George Aga sputtered, flecks of spittle appearing at the corners of his mouth. "He gave it to her, not me. It was her prize! He loved her!"

Charles took a small step toward the door, hoping it was fully open. "Your daughter. You could have given her a little money and purchased it from her. She was a silly, boasting girl. A little dowry money and you would have had the prize."

He laughed. "You think so? You think I could take my father's love from her? My dead father?"

Charles's throat felt very dry. Love, that difficult emotion, was the true prize here, not the map. Though George Aga had been searching for the treasure regardless, according to the women. He could trust nothing the man said. "I'm sure your father loved you. I know mine loves me dearly, despite the occasional taunts when I stumble."

The other man snorted as Charles continued gamely. "As for the map, well, it was just symbols. You must have memorized them. My fiancée saw you at the cemetery. My friends think the church is the second to last clue."

George Aga thumbed his nose with his free hand. "Do they? I never saw it clearly. That morning I went to see her. I thought I would reason with her. I thought she could tell me my father did love me best. I thought I could make her tell me he did. She would give me the map to prove it."

"It was gone. The map, that is, not your father's no doubt warm feelings for you," Charles suggested.

He nodded. "Yes, she said she thought she had lost it. She'd taken it out to a shed to show one of the students. I said I would help her look for it. We were in the shed, in the dark. I asked her why Father had given it to her. I thought she might tell me she had stolen it from the strongbox." He sniffed.

"What did she say?"

"That it was their secret. Their special secret, her dowry. She'd wed an important man, not a farmer like me. I wasn't to know." George Aga paused, his eyes wide. "As if I wasn't worthy of the map! As if he didn't love me."

Charles waited for more; then, when the farmer said nothing, he prodded. "You had gone into a shed with Agnes, where she had met a student, to search for the map."

"I met her by the rear door of the school," George Aga said. "She was beating out a dustrag. Everyone had gone to their classes. It was quiet. When she saw me, she said she'd searched her room, but she hadn't seen the map since she'd showed it to Richard Field."

"The first cholera victim," Charles noted.

The man cleared his throat. "I must have been fighting cholera myself, a milder case, and brought it into the school that day, killing my son and my brother and probably destroying my brother's school in the process."

"You think you had cholera?" Charles imagined the man's defense at the trial. Was he making it up as he went along?

Aga's next words left Charles wondering. "My stomach hurt. I had a fever in me, but I wanted that map."

"How did she come to leave the schoolhouse and go across the lawn with you to the shed unseen?"

"We walked along the hedge," he answered, recalling that day. "She liked to brush against them, silly thing, and thought a branch could have hooked the map out of her pocket when she returned."

"But you didn't see it, and so you both went to the shed."

Aga gestured. "We looked around inside. She was growing frustrated with me. Said Mrs. Bedwin would be cross with her."

Charles kept an eye on the lantern on the floor. "You wouldn't let her leave?"

"My lantern went out. She bumped against me when she backed up." George Aga's gaze was vague with memory. "My arm went up from the impact. It landed upon her neck."

Charles recognized, from the memory of her injuries, what had happened next.

"I didn't mean to do it. I just wanted Father to say he loved me."

Didn't mean to do it. He'd snuffed out his own daughter's life, and it had been nothing but a chance accident. So he claimed. The truth was, he'd strangled her in a fit of rage, then dragged the poor girl's body into the icehouse.

Charles's stomach churned at the thoughts of the poor girl's naked thighs, the rucked-up skirts. Her father hadn't tried to make it look like an accident and confess to having been involved. Had he attempted to create a fiction of a rape, then murder? In any case, he'd wasted the time and attention of the authorities of the town and thrown his brother's school into an uproar.

He'd caused his own nephew to come here and be stricken with cholera, and possibly caused his great-nephew or niece to be fatherless. He'd killed his son, his brother.

"You have a great deal to answer for, Mr. Aga. Why did you even have a key to the old icehouse?"

"Well, I know it," the other man said quietly. "My father's key, you know. A keepsake."

"I'm going to take you to the coroner's house now," Charles said. His tone left no room for maneuvering, and his heart had no room for patience with the man. "I'm sure Mr. Bumbleton can decide best how to proceed with you."

"Leave me here," George Aga said. "Allow me to hang myself in my brother's room." His gaze swept through the room. "The trellises are sound. Littlejack takes great pride in them. Just a little rope, and I will jump out the window." He went to it and opened the latch, then pushed the window up.

Cold air rushed in.

"Mr. Bumbleton must hear your confession from your own lips, sir," Charles said severely. "Come with me now."

"No." The farmer looked down. "We are far enough up. Maybe a mere jump would kill me."

Charles had studied a little of the scientific principles of boxing. He judged the distance between them; then quickly moving forward with a fist raised, he delivered a paralyzing blow to the older man's chin.

When George Aga staggered back with a grunt of surprise, Charles, irritated that the blow hadn't felled him, nonetheless jumped forward quickly and tripped the man onto the floor. He trussed him up with the curtains until he was docile. The farmer began to cry.

Charles saw Arthur and John out the window when he peered out, unsure what to do next. "To me," he called.

The boys looked up.

Charles gestured. "I need help!"

While the farmer moaned, "Let me die," over and over again, to Charles's unsympathetic ears, sounds of the boys tearing through the house reverberated.

Eventually, they both ran into the room.

John put his hands on his hips. "Rather disappointing. I thought a schoolmaster would live in a much nicer house."

"It's nice," Arthur said, then coughed.

"Why is Mr. Aga on the floor?" John asked.

"He has confessed to killing his daughter," Charles explained. "Do you know where Mr. Bumbleton lives? We need to take him there."

"It would be easier to fetch the coroner here," John said. "We'll find him and bring him."

"We'll run all the way," Arthur promised. "Can you sit on him until we come back?"

Charles looked at the quivering, sobbing lump of Aga manhood, lying like more Aga rubbish among the remains of his family possessions. "We'll manage. Run along, boys."

Chapter 23

Once the coroner arrived and heard George Aga repeat his confession, his men bodily removed the farmer and took him by cart to the local authorities.

"I thought you were wrong not to detain Mrs. Bedwin at the start," Charles told the coroner as they stood in the street, watching the cart move slowly up the hill, lanterns swaying from the sides.

Tobias Bumbleton gave him a complacent smile. "She's a silly woman, but she had complete power over the girl. If Agnes had irritated her, she'd have sent her home to her father in disgrace, not strangled her."

"Did you suspect the father had done it?" Charles asked, switching his lantern to his non-throbbing hand.

Mr. Bumbleton rubbed his bulbous nose. "I would have thought a dairy farmer too busy to come up here and chide his silly daughter. He was out of his mind with the cholera, I suspect."

"You think he really had it? His son and brother died of the disease, but he doesn't look ill to me."

"No way to know, except by talking to the man's servants." The coroner lifted his watch from his waistcoat pocket. "Mrs. Bumbleton will be holding the roast for me, Mr. Dickens. Mr. Aga has confessed. All that is left for you to do is help William Aga bury his dead. I assume you'll return to London soon?"

"After the funeral," Charles promised. He'd lost his taste for treasure hunting. William was the only one left who might care about his grandfather's map, and he would be an invalid for some time yet.

Charles saw the servants returning as the cart trundled off, carrying George Aga. The man still sobbed. Mr. Bumbleton lit a cigar and climbed into his trap. His driver flicked the reins, and he set off, as uncaring about justice as ever. Though perhaps not as much of a fool as Charles had initially feared.

"What happened to my things?" Charles asked.

"I'm terribly sorry, Mr. Dickens. We didn't know what to do with ourselves," the late schoolmaster's housekeeper apologized profusely. "I'll have your clothing brought to your room immediately, and then we'll take what you have on."

Sometime later, they returned his clothing, still damp.

He insisted they iron a clean shirt dry for William while he dressed, and then he took it over to the boardinghouse. William dictated a note to him for Julie after he'd helped William and Ollie wash up a bit.

He persuaded William to rest, as he didn't think he could safely get him down the stairs and across the street.

Finally, quite late in the evening, he had time to go to the inn. Charles climbed the hill with John and Arthur at his side. He shivered at times from his still-damp attire. Certainly not from the effects of his encounter with George Aga.

They entered the front room of the inn, and Charles sent Arthur up to fetch the young women while he and John went into the coffee room. He called for the genial beverage, knowing the hot rum and water he'd prefer would send him right to sleep. How long had it been since he'd written an article or sketch in one of these smoky rooms, a hot drink at his side?

Coffee arrived in two large pottery mugs. He saw John beam with pride at his own vessel.

"Go easy," he told the boy. "You'll be up all night."

"It's even more bitter than ale," John declared after his first sip. "I never use my spending money here."

"You have spending money?" Charles asked, knowing their charitable funds did not spread that much.

"Mr. Aga gave us ten shillings each at the beginning of term," John explained. "To teach us money management, he said."

Charles blinked hard. "He was the best of men."

John lifted his mug. "To Mr. Aga."

Charles followed suit. "To Mr. Aga."

John drank deeply, then set his mug down. "What will happen to us now? School days are over?"

"That is not up to me," Charles explained. "William has escaped with his life. I hope all the troubles of his father's death and his uncle's treachery do not weary him overmuch. And there is Mr. Sikes. I do not know what kind of arrangements were made with him."

"If he stays in charge, we're leaving," John said.

Charles nodded. "We'll find you a different school. You don't have nearly enough education to be out in the world yet."

"We did just fine before," John said.

"Only until bigger, crueler boys moved in. Don't worry, John. There's a better life out there for a man of education."

Charles turned when he heard footsteps in the doorway. Kate, Julie, and Lucy entered, with Arthur close behind. Forcing his weary bones to rise, he bowed extravagantly to them. "I come from the wars, ladies."

"Oh, Charles." Kate quickened her steps until she reached him, then curtsied. "I'm glad to see you, and well."

"William?" Julie asked in a low voice.

"Better," Charles assured her. "I had him in a clean shirt just a little while ago, and he dictated a letter to you."

"Oh." Julie held out one hand. The other held her belly.

Charles gave the letter to her. "Poor child will never know much family."

"No," Julie agreed.

"We will be your family," Arthur said, leaning against Lucy.

John jumped up, with a guilty expression on his face. "Yes, me too."

Lucy smiled and rumpled Arthur's hair. "Well, you're all my family, and you're good enough for anyone."

Charles, for the first time, noticed a resemblance between the girl and boy. "Are you related?"

Lucy nodded. "Not sure how, with my parents and Arthur's father dying before they could tell us, but I know we're cousins."

Charles sent John to fetch enough chairs for all of them, and they settled in a circle near the fire.

"What has been happening?" Kate asked.

"I feel disrespectful, knowing this is William's family I'm speaking about," he started.

"Just tell the facts," Julie said.

Charles nodded. "George Aga wanted the map. It seemed to have been given to Agnes by her grandfather as an inheritance."

"He died not long ago," Julie stated.

"Yes, and that started this disaster, along with the cholera, of course," Charles agreed. "But Agnes no longer had the map in her possession. She and her father went to look for it in the shed where she had shown it to Richard Field."

"Oh," Kate said. "Do you think Agnes had cholera, as well?"

"Impossible to know." Charles shrugged. "But George Aga killed his daughter there in a fit of rage when they couldn't find the map—though, of course, it was never really about it—then hid her in the icehouse. It seems that the denied love of his father drove him mad."

"Jealousy," Kate observed. "He was in a murderous rage out of pure jealousy, that Agnes had the time with and love of her grandfather that her father did not."

"If one is lucky enough to have grandparents living, how nice that they have time to spend with their grandchildren in a way that would not have been possible when they were busy young parents," Julie said. "What a fool Uncle Aga is. Besides, it's possible the map doesn't really lead to anything, anyway, given George Aga Sr.'s character. Love was the prize all along, not a treasure, and you can't receive the love of a ghost."

"We were not so lucky in my family," Charles said. "But I imagine grandparents can soothe many deficiencies if they are present."

"I think love lasts," Kate said. "I have to feel that way, with most of my family so far away in Scotland."

Charles patted Kate's hand. "You'll have a new family soon, and no doubt a nursery full of children to adore you."

Kate blushed. "God willing."

Word arrived at Mr. Sikes's safe home somehow, and he appeared at Mr. Aga's house to take charge of the situation from that freshly cleaned house.

Charles kept Kate informed of developments at the school by letter since the women continued on at the inn.

William improved rapidly, enough to be taken by trap to his father's funeral and brought haltingly into the church with support from Charles and Mr. Sikes. John was at his back, to grab him around the waist if he should stumble, though they left Arthur at Ollie's side. The boy's illness had subsided, though he was still too weak to leave his bed.

Though women didn't often attend funerals, Julie insisted on coming since Mr. Aga had so few family mourners. Mr. Sikes didn't want the students there for fear some could still carry the contagion.

Kate had been in many old churches, but nonetheless, a seven-hundred-year-old one was worth investigating. Her gaze roamed over stained-glass windows, many markers both placed on the walls and cut into them, along with various pieces of furnishings, such as small tables with relics on them. The church narrowed at the front, and she saw a small marking carved into a pillar near where she sat.

Her eyes widened as she realized what it was: the interlocked triangle symbol. She nudged Julie and pointed with a toss of her head.

Julie nudged her back. "It's the final symbol on the map."

Kate wondered how they could possibly investigate the church. Perhaps, the entire map was a religious allegory of some kind, though she hadn't heard that Mr. Aga's character lent itself that way. Only William would know.

By the end of the service, she'd come to the conclusion that the symbol was some sort of Holy Trinity representation, and that they might never know what the point of the map was.

After the service, Kate, Julie, and Lucy stayed in the church. Julie asked William to stay, too, but he insisted on going to the gravesite. Kate would not have dared to bring up the symbol to him at such a sad time, but she saw Julie whispering and pointing at it before William left, escorted by Charles and John. Lucy came to sit next to her, so Kate explained what she'd found in a low whisper.

"I see you've found it."

Kate jumped at the unexpected voice, then turned to see the little man who had warned them against hunting the treasure.

Mr. Wynd, the curate, spoke. "That map will be the death of me."

A shiver of fear went up her spine. They were too vulnerable, the three young women. Why had she agreed they should stay in the church? "What do you mean?"

"Come now, Miss Hogarth. I know you've spent plenty of time with old Mr. Aga's map."

Kate checked over his body posture with care. His hands were loosely clasped in front of his surplice. She noted that his stole needed mending. He seemed upset, perhaps, but not angry.

"What does it signify?" Julie asked, nodding at the carved symbol. "The Holy Trinity?"

Mr. Wynd's expression gentled. "The church took many old symbols for their own use, but that one was used by the ancient Celts as symbolic of triad deities, including the Morrígan. The symbol is called a triquetra."

"Who is that deity?" Julie asked.

"The goddess of war, of fate. Often believed to be a combination of three older sister goddesses." The curate touched his balding pate.

"There was a pagan temple here once, correct?" Kate asked. "More than seven hundred years ago."

"Indeed." He nodded. "And still exists today."

"Oh," Kate said as her brain began to calculate. She remembered that circle of stones in the woods, and the fact that the curate had been seen coming through the wild places the day of Agnes's death. "I didn't understand you before. It seemed like you hated the vicar. You're really here to protect the original faith?"

He peered at her nearsightedly, then nodded. "My family has lived here for a very long time, as have the Agas."

"No story about the Morrígan or pagan anything has ever reached William's ears," Julie countered.

Mr. Wynd straightened his stole. "When the mothers die young, much is lost."

"What would you have wanted William to know?" Julie asked.

"I'll show you the catacomb." Mr. Wynd moved his chin vaguely in the direction of Julie's belly. "That little unborn is heir to the story, after all."

"Was my William's grandfather a custodian of the pagan faith here?" Julie asked.

"He was, though I don't think William knows even that much. Mr. Aga grew strange in his later years." His expression grew thoughtful. "There always is a strain of madness in seers."

"Seers?" Kate asked, shocked. "Like an oracle?"

The curate smiled but kept his hopeful gaze on Julie. "I'm curious to see what develops in your baby. An Aga child born of that family and an actress will be quite a character, I expect."

Julie cupped her belly protectively. Lucy stood over her, in a position of imminent threat.

Mr. Wynd chuckled. "Come now, I mean you no harm. I will show you the baby's inheritance."

"The treasure?" Kate qualified.

"If we must call it that." He stepped around the pillar and went to a wall hanging on the wall just behind it, where the church narrowed. When he lifted the wall hanging, Kate took a closer look at the image depicted on it. The threads were dark with intent or age, but she saw that the wall hanging did depict three women, two black haired and one red. Here in a church, one would interpret them as martyred saints, but now she recognized this was likely a depiction of the goddess trio, and their expressions were exalted, like they were enjoying the blood, not resigned about their sacrifice for their faith.

Behind the wall hanging, a door hid in the wall. Mr. Wynd took a key from some hidden pocket in his cassock and unlocked the door. Kate, Julie, and Lucy crowded in behind him. He lit a candle fit into a carved holder at the top of pitted stone stairs.

He went down a few steps, then lit another candle with the

first, then returned it to its starting place. "Close the door behind you, and walk carefully. The steps are old and slick."

Kate went first. As she descended, the air became thick and perfumed, the scent reminiscent of incense. She strained her ears. Was that the ghost of music in the air?

By the time they reached the stone floor below, Kate's nostrils were full of the scent of mold and decaying brickwork. As the curate lit more candles, it seemed as if wings or cloaks or vestments were brushed aside, vanishing into the surrounding dark. Tall walls of dark brick made her feel very small. Rectangular boxes stretched out in every direction, set on the flagstones.

It had been fashionable in previous centuries to bury the wealthy dead under churches, despite the health risk of mingling the living with corpses. Kate shuddered as she looked at the row of coffins.

Julie, behind her, muttered to herself as the curate lit candles. "The Honorable Elizabeth How, daughter of Viscount Bankerton, died seventeen eighty-three, aged seventeen years. The Honorable Mary How Hester, wife of Charles Hester, daughter of Viscount Bankerton, died seventeen eighty-three, aged nineteen years."

"Don't read the inscriptions," Kate implored. "It is too depressing."

"Smallpox epidemic," Mr. Wynd explained. "Five daughters of the How family died within weeks of each other. I believe they had been visiting their mother here in town."

"I hope they are not contagious still." Kate shuddered.

"Coffins are lined with lead. I expect they still look fairly lifelike in their final resting places," the curate said. "Come now, I have something to show you."

With a final look at the How coffins, Julie picked up her skirts and brushed past Kate. They walked past half a dozen nearly identical coffins until they reached the edge of the light.

Kate noted that the candles looked quite new and were no more than a third burned down.

"Does the How family still pay for prayers over the coffins?" she asked.

"No." Mr. Wynd stepped to another coffin, set far enough apart from the others in the row for people to stand around it.

It didn't have an inscription plate attached to the lid. The curate moved to the broadest part of the coffin, which was not covered in dust like the rest of it and which had a cawing crow burned into the wood. He pushed the lid aside.

Lucy let out a little bark, then steadied herself. Kate clutched her arms across her chest, watching Julie anxiously. The former actress's face had two dark spots high on her cheeks, but otherwise she seemed composed.

The curate reached into the coffin and pulled back a velvet cloth. Kate's breath caught in her throat along with the heavy taste of grave dust. Underneath the cloth was not some decomposing corpse but a dark rectangular box.

"It is not terribly well hidden," the curate explained, "but then again, it would be difficult to prowl around down here."

"The candles are a giveaway," Julie said in an even tone. "All the ones coming in this direction are fresh, while there is nothing but blackened stubs moving away."

"A budgetary problem," the curate said. He turned and lit a fresh candle set into the wall next to the head of the coffin. "Your husband's grandfather used to fund the candles, but of course, he died several weeks ago."

"What is in the box?" Kate asked.

"Ah, that is under lock and key." The curate's lips curved up. He pulled another key from under his cassock and lifted the box onto the lid of the viscount's coffin.

"Outlived his daughters rather a lot," Julie said after reviewing the inscription, which included a death year almost a decade later than his daughters' coffins.

"Old age, not smallpox," the curate agreed, inserting the key. The lock released with a click, and he pushed up the lid of the box.

Gold caught the candlelight and gleamed. Kate saw armbands and rings. A brooch in the triquetra shape looked to be of tarnished silver. No sign of Christianity showed in the dozen pieces, all carefully separated on velvet cloth.

"This is worth a pretty penny," Julie observed.

"They are venerable," the curate said. "Our treasures are used for worship at various sites around the town."

"Like at the old chimney near the standing stones?"

"Yes, the stones are a very ancient site," the curate said. "We revere it greatly."

"You should protect all of this better," Julie said. "A vault perhaps, like what my aunt uses for her jewels."

"We are too humble for such things, but I hope you will keep our secret."

"Of course," Kate, Julie, and Lucy chorused.

"Your husband won't want it known that old Mr. Aga had secretly been a pagan priest," Mr. Wynd said. "It would probably destroy what is left of Aga Academy."

"I don't know if we even own it now," Julie explained. "It might belong to Mr. Sikes."

"I think you'll find that the paperwork was not completely finalized. Too much toing and froing with London lawyers. Mr. Sikes will soon realize he owns nothing. He had not turned over any final sums to Mr. Aga."

"But the school has changed so much," Julie protested.

"That rich student?" the curate said. "I've heard a great deal of the gossip at the vicar's table. He is gone now, too."

"Goodness," Julie said. "If Mr. Sikes won't be taking over, I guess the school is done for. Between Father Aga's death and the cholera."

"Not to mention Agnes's death," Kate added.

"And Monks," Lucy chimed.

"That map of the treasure location had left our followers' control." Mr. Wynd shook dust off the hem of his cassock. "We should have secured it before old Mr. Aga's death, but his decline was dreadfully sudden."

"Do you think George Aga killed him?" Kate asked.

Mr. Wynd gave her a thoughtful glance. "It could have been poison, I suppose, but why? Ah." He stared down at his treasures. "I will move them soon. But first, take this, Mrs. Aga." He lifted a gold torque and placed it into her hands.

"What? Why?" Julie spluttered.

"It belonged to old Mr. Aga. It is not ancient, as he had it made for himself."

"I see." Julie considered the necklace. "I will keep it for the baby."

"Perhaps he or she will return it to us someday." He inclined his head. "If you'll walk out, I will extinguish the candles behind you. When you reach the door, please be careful not to exit into the church unless no one is there."

Lucy reached the top first. She pushed the door open carefully, then wider, and ducked around the wall hanging. Julie followed, then Kate. They huddled around, waiting for Mr. Wynd to reappear.

"What about the torque?" Kate asked.

"Oh." Julie tucked it down her bodice, then shrugged. "That will do for now."

One of the side doors banged open. Mr. Wynd came out right then. Kate put her fingers to her lips. He nodded and smoothed back the wall hanging just as William limped down the central aisle of the nave, Charles and John at his sides.

"We need to get William back to his father's house," Charles said. "John, run down to the inn and fetch someone with a trap." He handed John a note. "Have this put on the next mail coach to Brompton."

* * *

Charles's note had been directed to Lady Lugoson, and he was certain that Julie's aunt would send a carriage sometime the next day for their return to London, given William's condition, not to mention Julie's. A few hours later, he sat in Mr. Aga's parlor with Julie as Kate settled a room upstairs for her and Lucy. They were to stay here for the night, since Mr. Aga had been the only person in the house to be struck with cholera, and the air here seemed free of contagion. They kept his bedroom closed up, however, until it could be thoroughly cleaned.

Charles saw Kate come down the stairs with Lucy through the open door of the parlor.

Julie gestured for Kate and Lucy to sit as they came in. "Mr. Sikes has been busy."

"Is he aware that he doesn't own a share of the school?" Kate asked.

"Yes, but he wasn't happy to realize that I knew it," Julie said. "He has suggested that William go into partnership with him on the same terms, and that William and I move into the house here and run the school."

Charles saw his fiancée's look of alarm. "I don't want you to become a school drudge," Kate said.

"I'm not sure I agree," Charles said. "This is William's inheritance."

"It will be up to him," Julie pointed out. "I'll be busy with the baby. The air is better here."

"That is true," Kate said. "Maybe it is a good decision for now."

"Well, not the Mr. Sikes part," Julie said. "I haven't liked what I've heard about how the school is being run recently."

"We can take the books back to London with us tomorrow," Charles suggested. "William and I can look them over with trusted advisors and see what condition the school is in." Mr. Sikes had agreed to take charge during the period of William's convalescence, regardless of the Agas' decision.

"I rang the bell for tea, but no one came," Julie said. "Lucy, come with me." They departed in the direction of the kitchen.

"I'm a bit concerned about her state of mind," Kate said.

"I fear for the Agas' future if William doesn't recover his strength," Charles answered in a low voice. "Their future seemed as bright as ours until recently."

"I don't think William is going to be able to come to our wedding," Kate added. "He's worn out."

"No. I'll ask Tom Beard to stand up with me. I've known him longer, anyway." Charles shook his head. "Oh, I just remembered. We had a note from Mrs. Bedwin. They've taken Ollie back to his dormitory. He's recovering nicely."

"Can we see him?" Kate asked.

"I think so. The cholera danger seems to be past. It has taken its victims and moved on, with no additional cases."

"I wonder what caused it?"

"We'll probably never know for certain, though it may have originated at the farm." He stood and offered his hand to Kate.

When they entered the dormitory with John a few minutes later, they found Arthur sitting on a bed. Ollie was under the covers, still pale but smiling. The surprise was that he had other visitors.

The man had fifty or so years on his face. White whiskers had come in, and his balding pate was mostly hidden under a cap. He wore the clothing of a middle-aged clerk, in good condition, and had a look of amazement on his face. Standing close to him stood a tall, peach-cheeked young lady in a purple traveling dress.

"Who is this?" Charles asked.

"My grandfather," Ollie said tremulously. "He's come for me. I'm not to live at the school anymore."

"What?" John asked. "But you're an orphan."

The old man smiled genially at John. "My name is Twist.

This is my grandson, whom I have not seen in more than a year. I had no idea what had happened to him until a guest at our recent wedding told me where I could find him."

The purple-clad young lady blushed and took Mr. Twist's arm.

"I'm very happy to meet you," Charles said. "This is my future wife. We are to be married in a few weeks."

Mr. Twist looked Kate over as she curtsied, then nodded. "My daughter married very low and paid the price," the old man said, "but you look like you'll do."

Charles raised an eyebrow. "What are your intentions for young Ollie?"

"He ran off to mudlark before I could catch him, but I'll take responsibility now that Ollie is a respectable young student. He's seen the opportunities presented by a more genteel life."

"He is my grandfather," Ollie assured them. "And I remember Miss Rose, I mean, Grandmother Twist. She lived next door to Grandfather."

"I took her to wife when her father died," Mr. Twist said. "We do well enough, and it will be a joy to have a young face in the house with us."

"What about his education?" Charles asked.

"We'll hire tutors," Mrs. Twist said, showing more backbone than had been displayed previously on her pretty face. "He'll have a good education."

"We hope to return to London tomorrow," Kate said. "Is that where you live?"

The Twists nodded in tandem. Mr. Twist explained. "In Limehouse."

"I work for a shipyard," Mr. Twist said. "It's a good life, with healthy sea air all around."

Arthur's lips twitched. Kate went to him and wrapped her arm around him. John moved to his side.

"It will just be the two of us," John said. "But we'll be fine."

"Lucy may come here, too," Kate added. "If the Agas decide to run the school."

"What larks!" Arthur exclaimed, rejoicing. "I hope they do."

"You are all such kind friends," Ollie said, smiling wanly. "But I have been at this school for many months, and most of that without any friends or family. You have each other, but I want to go home."

"You will," Charles said. "All the mysteries here are solved, and our dead have been buried."

"It's time to focus on our wedding," Kate added. "My goodness, but it is a time of change for us all."

Acknowledgments

I want to thank you, dear reader, for picking up this fifth book in the A Dickens of a Crime series. If you haven't read the earlier books yet, I hope you take the opportunity to enjoy more Dickensian adventures through 1830s London. I am so grateful for the book reviews you wrote for all the series titles. Please keep them coming!

Thank you to my beta readers, Judy DiCanio, Eilis Flynn, Cheryl Schy, and Mary Keliikoa, on this project. I also thank my local Sisters in Crime chapter, Columbia River, for their support. Thank you to my agent, Laurie McLean, at Fuse Literary, my Kensington editor, Elizabeth May, my copyeditor, Rosemary Silva, and my communications manager, Larissa Ackerman, for your work on the series, along with many unsung heroes at Kensington.

Cholera was misunderstood in the 1830s. Some twenty years later, medical experts learned how it was transmitted. I recommend *The Ghost Map*, by Steven Johnson, if you would like to learn more.

While Charles Dickens and Kate Hogarth are real people, my plot is entirely fictitious, as is most everyone in the book. Some of the locations in the book are real, but I took liberties with the physical details as my plot required.

BOOK CLUB READING GUIDE for

A Twist of Murder

1. Charles Dickens's novel *Oliver Twist* inspired aspects of this novel. What themes do you recognize? Does reading this book make you want to read or reread Dickens's work?
2. The author has been immersed in Dickens for so long now that other popular subjects and themes from his books continue to pop up. Do you recognize any other works of Dickens in this book's inspiration?
3. Did you know anything about cholera before now? Can you draw any parallels between the cholera era and today?
4. Charles and Kate had an unusually long engagement by nineteenth-century standards. What length do you think is best?
5. How do you feel about Julie Aga after reading this book?
6. Mr. Sikes embodies utilitarian principles. What do you think about the way he was changing the school?
7. Did you predict who would die and who would survive in this book?
8. Did you think the treasure map was real?
9. What do you think the future holds for Lucy Fair and the former mudlarks?
10. Which location in the book would you like to visit?
11. Should William Aga give up his newspaper career and run the school?
12. Which character would you say has changed the most over these five titles in the series? Do you like what has happened to him or her?

Keep reading for a special excerpt.

THE PICKWICK MURDERS

Heather Redmond
A Dickens of a Crime

In this latest reimagining of Dickens as an amateur sleuth, Charles is tossed into Newgate Prison on a murder charge, and his fiancée, Kate Hogarth, must clear his name . . .

London, January 1836: Just weeks before the release of his first book, Charles is intrigued by an invitation to join the exclusive Lightning Club. But his initiation in a basement maze takes a wicked turn when he stumbles upon the corpse of Samuel Knickwick, the club's president. With the victim's blood literally on his hands, Charles is locked away in notorious Newgate Prison.

Now it's up to Kate to keep her framed fiancé from the hangman's noose. To solve this labyrinthine mystery, she is forced to puzzle her way through a fiendish series of baffling riddles sent to her in anonymous poison-pen letters. With the help of family and friends, she must keep her wits about her to corner the real killer—before time runs out and Charles Dickens meets a dead end . . .

Look for The Pickwick Murders *on sale now!*

Chapter 1

Eatanswill, somewhere in Essex, January 5, 1836

A bugle blared in Charles Dickens's ear, coming from a raggedy band of marchers passing him on the way to the hustings set up in Eatanswill's market square. Yellow-brown cockades pinned to the lapels of old-fashioned tailcoats and ladies' capes demonstrated that these were the followers of the local Brown party, allied to the Whigs. Charles tipped his hat at a particularly pretty daughter of the voters. She went pink and put her hand in front of her mouth, then dashed to her mother's side. Behind her straggled a couple of young boys, beating drums out of time.

To the right, another group marched between a coal distributer and a cloth merchant's place of business, also routed to the hustings. A streaky royal purple banner attached to a bakery's awning flapped in the bitter January wind. The cloth already shone white at the top, where a light rain had loosened the dye. This must be the Purples, allied to the Tories.

He surveyed the scene from a two-foot rock embedded next to a public house door. It gave him enough height to see across the Election Day crowd. Would the vote be for Sir Augustus Smirke, the favorite son of the Purples, or go to Vernon Cecil, the darling of the Browns? One or the other would become a member of Parliament for the first time.

Charles, parliamentary reporter for the liberal *Morning Chronicle* newspaper, hoped Cecil would carry the day. With any luck, a clear majority would offer its voice and the local sheriff could call the election instead of having to schedule a poll some few days in the future, in which case Charles would not be able to go back to London that night. He'd have to write his story and send it on the express mail coach back to the *Chronicle* offices in London.

Resounding "huzzahs" blazed into the air as another phalanx of men appeared between the buildings. He recognized William Whitaker Maitland, the new High Sheriff of Essex, leading the parliamentary candidates, who were followed by their most prominent supporters. Sir Augustus towered over Sheriff Maitland, a man well above average height, with a majestic belly to match. Mr. Cecil did not have the height, though the profusion of gray-streaked reddish curls poofing out from underneath his top hat gave him at least one measure of distinction. Charles knew him to be the son of an important local landowner, but felt unease for his prospects as age and experience were not on the Brown candidate's side.

Shouts came from the left, displaying real alarm this time, instead of pride. A small group of horsemen galloped into the square, coattails fanned out behind them. The first man had a shotgun across his arm and the other half dozen held rakes or hoes as if they were jousters of old, ready to go head to head in battle with other knights. In their work-worn attire, they looked like they belonged to the logging or hunting trades in Epping Forest, rather than professions here in town.

The horsemen pressed forward through the crowd of locals.

People jumped back or fell in their wake, moving like the wind-blown brown and purple banners that hung on posts jutting from some of the houses. A horse and rider knocked over a boy. The boy clutched at his foot and screamed. A man hurried to his side, grabbed him, and hoisted him into the air, settling him on his shoulders.

While Charles had been watching the intruders, the high sheriff and candidates climbed onto the hustings. The temporary stage had bunting in the parties' colors decorating the wooden railing. A lectern, probably borrowed from St. Mary's, a venerable medieval church on the edge of the square, was set up for speeches.

Sheriff Maitland pointed his finger at the gunman as he thundered up to the very edge of the hustings. "I see you, Wilfred Poor. You and your men are welcome to vote, but not until you hand over that shotgun."

Wilfred Poor lifted the gun and for a moment Charles stiffened, afraid he would fire at the high sheriff. Instead, Poor fired into the air. The crowd ducked instinctively, including Charles. Initially, pandemonium reigned. But just as quickly as the crowd reacted with screams, they subsided, until the only nearby sound was a dog barking in one of the houses near the church.

Poor lowered the muzzle of his gun until it was pointing into the belly of that giant, Sir Augustus. "Where is my Amy, my daughter?" he screamed.

Sir Augustus's lips curled, but he said nothing. A trio of his men pushed forward, as if to provoke a reaction, but Sir Augustus's long arms spread out, holding them back.

Poor repeated his anguished query, the tendons of his neck in high relief.

"What's wrong, Wilfred?" Sir Augustus mocked. "Can't keep control of your own womenfolk?"

One of the horsemen chuckled and glanced at the man next

to him, his expression changing at the anger in his neighbor's face.

"You aren't much of a man," Sir Augustus said in a teasing lilt.

"Come now, Sir Augustus," one of the horsemen said in a rough country drawl. "Amy's been missing these past three days."

"No one's forgotten she's your maid," added another.

The shotgun, which Charles had not taken his glance from, shook in Poor's hand. The horseman closest to the upset father patted Poor's arm.

"We know you've hidden her away," another horseman said to Sir Augustus. "Just give her back and we can get about this business of the election."

"Speech," called a brave soul in the crowd.

The horseman closest to the speaker threw his hoe in that direction. A man fell. Charles craned his neck, looking for blood spill. No one screamed this time. The high sheriff called for his men, a few local constables hovering around the edges of the bunting, to arrest the rider, but he wheeled his horse around and galloped off before they gathered their wits. One of the constables broke away for crowd control, pushing a couple of women who were attempting to climb the hustings to escape the horsemen. Another knelt next to the fallen man. The last constable raced out of the square in pursuit of the villain on the horse.

Charles whipped his head around when he heard the sheriff call out an order. Charles's brand-new hat caught in a gust, which sent it flying past the window of the public house and down the shadowy street. He leapt off the rock to chase the expensive felted beaver cut in the Regent style. He loathed having to replace it so soon, and in a crowd like this, some light-fingered thief would grab it if he took his eyes off it for even a moment.

He reached out, his fingers just touching the brim before the hat flew again. Stumbling, he put on a burst of speed in front of the open door of a tobacconist and snatched his hat before it tumbled off the pavement and into the dirt road in front of the square.

He glanced up, grinning with his success, and saw a young man, hat lowered over his brows. The lean form and rather worn clothing caught Charles's eye with a note of familiarity. The youth jerked. He straightened, then vanished around the side of the tobacconist's shop, black curls fluttering around his neck.

Charles's thoughts flew back to last summer, and a vegetable plot not far from London's Eaton Square. Curls like that had spilled out from a straw hat worn by the young farmer, Prince Moss, so enamored of the cold, beautiful, and amoral Evelina Jaggers, the foster daughter of Charles's deceased neighbor.

Charles followed the pavement to an alley passing behind the shop. He stepped in, figuring this was a small town and violent criminals were unlikely to be lurking in alleyways in daylight. The young man had vanished.

Charles surveyed the collection of barrels and rubbish. He heard the crackling of a fire, probably coming from the smithy that backed up against the alley. A couple of warehouses boxed in the smithy. The youth could have gone anywhere.

He turned away. His job was to follow the election, not chase men who had a clear right to go wherever they wanted. If it had been Prince Moss, he had reason not to greet Charles after the events of last summer. Charles and his friends had hoped that Miss Jaggers and her swain had left England entirely, but they were not wanted for any crimes.

He returned to his stone perch. Two local voters were carrying the fallen man from the crowd into one of the houses on the left side of the square, probably a doctor's office. The constables were standing next to the horsemen who had remained in the square, keeping a vigilant eye on them.

Wilfred Poor had surrendered his gun into the high sheriff's hand. He gave an anguished cry, that of a wounded animal, then swayed in his saddle, shaking.

"Why don't you go home, Wilfred?" said Sheriff Maitland, not unkindly.

"I'll stay for the vote," the broken man said. "I want to make sure that blackguard doesn't win."

"Speech!" called a man from the crowd.

"Let's get on to business!" cried another.

The high sheriff cleared his throat and introduced the Brown candidate. Charles took rapid notes in his best-in-class shorthand, but the speech was nothing out of the ordinary. Protect the working man, keep trade free, expand the franchise. All the usual sort of things, customized to the town's interests.

The less-than-enthusiastic reception made Charles concerned for Mr. Cecil's success. Then Sir Augustus was introduced as the Purple candidate. He spoke about protecting the town and the country from liberal encroachment, calling out several men in a humiliating singsong, such as a local schoolteacher he called a trumped-up peasant, and similar insults. The better dressed men in the crowd shouted "Hear! Hear!" several times and Charles had the impression of a vicar speaking to his faithful, despite the insults.

His gaze drifted to Wilfred Poor, but overall, his temperament seemed far more even than that of Sir Augustus, who, as he came to the end of his speech, was red in the face, spittle flying. He finished with his fists in the air, the crowd shouting "Protect Eatanswill!" along with him.

The mayor walked to the center of the hustings and called for a vote. The back of Charles's neck prickled as Mr. Cecil's name was called. He glanced around, feeling like he was being watched by unseen eyes, but saw no one.

As expected, Mr. Cecil only received a faint round of applause. Mr. Poor wheeled his horse around, the dark circles under his eyes deepening as he saw how limited the support was for the liberal candidate. One of the other horsemen still present took his arm. Mr. Poor stared at his shotgun, but obviously decided he'd never have it returned now. The horsemen left the square at a sedate walk while the high sheriff called Sir Augustus's name.

Charles winced in disgust as the crowd of men surrounding the platform called their support. No need for this election to move to the polls. Sir Augustus had won easily, returning a Tory to Parliament for 1836.

Charles walked into the tobacconist's shop to buy a cigar as soon as the proprietor entered from the square. He asked the man for a brief history of Wilfred Poor, and soon had an earful of his family's mistreatment by the Smirkes. Dead wife, missing daughter, hand-wringing old mother who had quite lost her senses in despair.

Not twenty minutes later, Charles walked to the coaching inn at the edge of the main road, so he could catch the stage back to London to file his report. His editors would be pleased by his article, if not by the election's outcome.

"Well done. It's so pretty, Kate," said Mary Hogarth, admiring the blond lace decorating the neckline of her sister's new evening gown the next evening. "I can't believe this silk was secondhand."

Kate spread out the skirt made of spotless, unsnagged silk. "It's lucky we visited Reuben Solomon's stall that day. I'll bet you this dress was only worn once. A wine stain down the front and havers, off it goes to the old clothes man."

"It must be pleasant to be so wealthy." Mary pinched her cheeks to bring color into them.

Kate followed suit. "Wealth comes with its own burdens. I

shall like keeping our little suite of rooms with just you to help me." Charles had agreed they would add Mary to his household after they wed, assuming Mother could spare her, which would make up a foursome then, since his brother Fred lived with him, too.

"It will be a treat," Mary agreed.

The sisters talked about their neighbors while they dressed for the party. It wasn't often they were invited to an evening at a titled lady's home. In fact, they had only become acquainted with their neighbor at Lugoson House across the orchard one year before, when they had heard screams during their Epiphany Night party.

That had been the night Kate met Charles, then a new parliamentary reporter working for John Black and her father at the *Morning* and *Evening Chronicle* respectively. Little had she realized as they stood vigil in the room of dying Christiana Lugoson that she would fall so deeply in love with him less than two months later.

Both of Kate's parents and their parents before them had travelled in distinguished literary circles, first in Edinburgh and now in London, but with someone like Charles joining the family, they had acquired new status and important friends. Charles had a brilliant future ahead of him and Kate could scarcely believe she was the wife he had chosen. He had promised they would wed in the spring. In a few weeks, they would ask for the banns to be called at St. Luke's down the street. Soon, she would be his and he, hers.

The door rattled, then opened. Georgina, eight years old and bursting with self-importance, announced, "Charles is downstairs and everyone is ready to leave." They followed Georgina out of the room the sisters shared, excepting little Helen, and went down to the dining room where the family always gathered.

When Kate walked into the dining room and saw the thick dark locks, bright hazel eyes, and full lips of her fiancé, her face went so hot that her cheeks reddened of their own accord. She drank in the sight of him.

He spotted her and sketched a bow. She curtsied with a laugh, and then he touched her hand. A tremor went through her at the press of his flesh to hers. She could scarcely wait for spring.

Her mother sorted the older from the younger children with a no-nonsense air, then her father led the way to the front door and down to the street. Kate held Charles's arm on the pavement, even though she was in no danger of slipping. The rain had held off, though the air was bitter cold. Conveyances rolled by on the street, out of sight, holding other revelers.

Mary, on the other hand, stayed close to her mother. Kate knew her sister feared giving Fred, a year younger, too much attention. Fred had tender feelings for her, but Mary considered the young man a child, even though he had a position at a law firm now.

A liveried footman had the door of the renovated Elizabethan mansion open when they came up the steps, as another party was ahead of them. Kate recognized Lord and Lady Holland, quite the grandest personages she had had occasion to know.

The Hogarth and Dickens party passed through the doors behind the Hollands. The old-fashioned front hallway still had wood paneling, though Lady Lugoson was slowly modernizing the premises now that she'd committed to staying in England. Any visitor's eye went immediately to a double staircase directly ahead of them, but Lady Lugoson did much of her entertaining in the long drawing room that looked out over her formal garden.

After they left cloaks behind and the ladies changed shoes,

the footman took them to the room's entrance and Panch, the venerable butler, announced each party in turn. Few paid attention as the room held quite a crush of people.

Still, Lord Lugoson, just sixteen and home from school, dashed up to greet them, and seemed happy to meet Fred Dickens for the first time. He took the lad off to meet other youths.

Kate spotted Charles's fellow reporter, William Aga, standing next to the closer of the two fireplaces heating the room. Charles tilted his head at Kate and they disengaged from her family to greet the Agas.

Kate's father did not like Julie Aga, William's wife, who had once trod the boards and tended to create complications. But Kate and Julie were often thrown into each other's company and had come to terms.

"Excellent reporting," William exclaimed, thumping Charles on the back as soon as he was close. William, tall and athletic, had a ready smile that everyone responded to. His reporting focused on crime for the *Chronicle*. Julie, red-haired and lovely, scarcely showing her pregnancy yet, took Kate's hand and squeezed, her eyes dancing merrily as she took in the new gown.

"Part of your trousseau?"

"No," Kate said, blushing. "But I am working on that."

Lady Lugoson, an ethereal blonde, approached them on the arm of her baronet fiancé, the coroner Sir Silas Laurie. Her gown was cut much lower on the bosom than Kate's, and had few decorations. The beauty lay in the perfection of the best black silk, with a white silk and lace underskirt. Kate saw Charles's gaze dart over the gown, then he inclined his head.

"I read your latest article, Charles," Sir Silas said. "Very dynamic. I wonder that your Mr. Poor did not assassinate Sir Augustus right at the hustings, given the fervor of your descriptions."

"Sir Augustus is dreadful," Lady Lugoson interjected with a

toss of her head. She had been a political hostess while her first husband had been alive. "How unfortunate it is that he won the election."

"Do you know him well?" Charles asked. "He is a conservative."

"Sadly, he was a friend of my late husband." Lady Lugoson's soft mouth turned down. "They were at school together and remained close."

Kate winced. Everyone knew the late Lord Lugoson had been an evil seducer, with just enough charisma to charm the families of his victims. The future sounded bleak for that Mr. Poor's daughter. The shotgun-wielding assailant might be correct in his assumption that Sir Augustus had taken her. "Such dangers you find yourself in," she murmured to Charles.

"Have done," Charles said with a chuckle. "There were hundreds of men in the square, and not a few women and children. I was nowhere near the gun."

As her father came alongside Kate, William said, "I should report on the missing girl for the newspaper. Maybe I can find her."

Her father cleared his throat. "We couldnae print the story. We may be a liberal paper, but that is reaching too far, even for us."

Julie frowned. "What can be done to help the unfortunate girl?"

"Nothing until she is located," Kate rejoined. "I wonder if Sir Augustus will bring her to London?"

Charles's head felt a bit dim the next morning, the possible consequence of too much cigar smoke and rum punch at the Epiphany party. It had been a jolly night however, and unlike the previous year, no one had died.

He arrived at the *Morning Chronicle* newsroom at 332 Strand almost on time the next morning. After greeting his fellow reporters, he found a messy pile of correspondence on his desk. The letters included an offer of work at an inferior newspaper, a letter from a member of Parliament thanking Charles for quoting his speech properly, and a note from William Harrison Ainsworth, inviting him around for dinner that night.

He ignored the rest of the pile and dipped his pen into his ink pot to scrawl a note at the bottom of the note, expressing his regret that he could not attend dinner with the popular novelist. He suggested he reschedule for some time next week. That night, he and Kate were promised to a member of Parliament's dinner party.

Charles blotted the note and sealed it up, then set it aside for one of the office boys to send. Tom Beard, who had helped him procure this job two autumns ago, winked at Charles as he passed by. Charles watched his friend until he was half turned around.

"Hate mail," William Aga remarked, tossing down a letter and pushing his chair backward until it bumped against Charles's chair.

"From who?" Charles asked, extricating his legs from the position they'd become tangled in.

"Newgate Prison," William said with a shake of his head. "You would think a prisoner would better spend his money on lawyers than complaining to members of the press."

"I have nothing so exciting," Charles said, reorienting his chair before flipping through the rest of his pile. He spotted a very fine piece of linen notepaper, addressed to Charles Dickens, Esq. The seal was so large it might have covered a gold guinea, as some people did to send funds to relatives. "I may have spoken too quickly."

William leaned over the letter, exposing Charles's olfactory senses to the pomade separating his friend's tawny curls. He poked his ink-stained finger on an emblem centered on the seal. "This is from the Lightning Club."

Charles sat back, then bent forward again. He didn't know what to do with his hands. His fingers danced nervously on his thighs. "The Lightning Club? You don't think I'm being offered a membership, do you?"